ELLEN GLASGOW wrote nineteen novels, many of them best-sellers, between 1897 and 1941. Besides *Virginia*, her most widely recognized books were *Barren Ground*, 1925; *The Battle-Ground*, 1902; *The Romance of a Plain Man*, 1909; and the Queenborough novels (*The Romantic Comedians*, 1926; *They Stooped to Folly*, 1929; and *The Sheltered Life*, 1932). Her autobiography, *The Woman Within*, was published posthumously, as was her short late novel, *Beyond Defeat: An Epilogue to an Era*. Born in Virginia in 1873, Glasgow negotiated the sometimes repressive atmosphere of Southern paternalism and lived a life of accomplishment any woman could envy. She died in 1945, the recipient of many accolades and honors for her work.

LINDA WAGNER-MARTIN (formerly Wagner) was born in St. Marys, Ohio, and educated at Bowling Green State University. She has taught there, as well as at Wayne State University and Michigan State University, and is now Hanes Professor of English at University of North Carolina, Chapel Hill. Her most recent books are on Sylvia Plath (a biography in 1987; critical essays in 1984 and 1988), Anne Sexton, and modern American fiction. She has also written on Hemingway, Faulkner, Dos Passos, Levertov, Williams, Glasgow, and many other American writers.

VIRGINIA

ELLEN GLASGOW

With an Introduction by
Linda Wagner-Martin

PENGUIN BOOKS

PENGUIN BOOKS
Published by the Penguin Group
Viking Penguin, a division of Penguin Books USA Inc.,
40 West 23rd Street, New York, New York 10010, U.S.A.
Penguin Books Ltd, 27 Wrights Lane, London W8 5TZ, England
Penguin Books Australia Ltd, Ringwood, Victoria, Australia
Penguin Books Canada Ltd, 2801 John Street, Markham, Ontario, Canada L3R 1B4
Penguin Books (N.Z.) Ltd, 182–190 Wairau Road, Auckland 10, New Zealand

Penguin Books Ltd, Registered Offices:
Harmondsworth, Middlesex, England

First published in the United States of America by
Doubleday, Page and Company 1913
This edition with an introduction by Linda Wagner-Martin
published in Penguin Books 1989

1   3   5   7   9   10   8   6   4   2

LIBRARY OF CONGRESS CATALOGING IN PUBLICATION DATA

Glasgow, Ellen Anderson Gholson, 1873–1945.
Virginia / Ellen Glasgow ; with an introduction by Linda Wagner-Martin.
p. cm.—(Penguin classics)
ISBN 0 14 03.9072 3
I. Title.   II. Series.
PS3513.L34V5   1989
813'.52–dc20   89–3884

Printed in the United States of America
Set in Century Expanded

TO THE RADIANT SPIRIT
WHO WAS MY SISTER

CARY GLASGOW McCORMACK

CONTENTS

BOOK THIRD

THE ADJUSTMENT

INTRODUCTION

Ellen Glasgow's *Virginia*, one of her best novels, was published in 1913—but to much less acclaim than many of her other books had received. Glasgow was accustomed to writing "best sellers."* Of her nineteen novels, which appeared from 1897 to 1941, nearly all were popular favorites, and two—*The Romantic Comedians* and *They Stooped to Folly*—were book-club selections. *Virginia*, however, although it was the best-written novel Glasgow had produced to that time, was about the wrong kind of character: Virginia Pendleton, the book's protagonist, was a passive, submissive woman, completely dedicated to the betterment of her thoroughly Christian home and children.

It was, after all, 1913. Feminism was in the air. Glasgow herself had already marched in a suffrage parade or two (in London, with May Sinclair; in New York and Richmond, with Mary Johnston). In 1909 she had joined the Virginia League for Women Suffrage, partly because her friends were active in its formation. Later, she wrote short essays about "feminism" and in 1912 published her poem "The Call" in the July 27 issue of *Collier's Magazine*. That poem, with its refrain of "Woman calls to woman to awaken!/Woman calls to woman to arise!" tells the real story of Glasgow's feminism, which was consistently less political than it was humanistic.

Glasgow's interest in the suffrage movement stemmed from her firm belief in the importance of women's friendships, in

* Beginning with Glasgow's 1900 *The Voice of the People*, most of her fiction was high on best-seller lists. *Deliverance* (1904) held second place on the year's best-seller list; *The Wheel of Life* (1906) was tenth; and *Life and Gabriella*, the book that followed *Virginia* in 1916, was fifth. In 1932 Glasgow's *The Sheltered Life* was again fifth on the best-seller list, and in 1935 *Vein of Iron* was second. In 1942 Glasgow won the Pulitzer Prize for Fiction, for *In This Our Life*, 1941.

their capacity to support each other in times of misfortune. Before all else, Glasgow was a pragmatist, trained during her teenage years on the writing of John Stuart Mill, Mary Wollstonecraft, and Charles Darwin. As she wrote in "The Call,"

> *Queen or slave or bond or free, we battled,*
> *Bartered not our faith for love or gold;*
> *Man we served, but in the hour of anguish*
> *Woman called to woman as of old.*

With very *un*feminist leanings, Glasgow continued the poem by drawing a picture of women in bondage, women submitting to the ages-old role of passive martyr:

> *Hidden at the heart of earth we waited,*
> *Watchful, patient, silent, secret, true;*
> *All the terrors of the chains that bound us*
> *Man has seen, but only woman knew!*

> *Woman knew! Yes, still and woman knoweth! . . .*

The poet's concluding "call," "Onward to the light where Freedom lies," hardly saves the poem from its earlier expression of genuine, and continuing, anguish. For what Glasgow knew about women's lives—as she had seen them lived in her own family and among her friends—would not allow her to accept the promises of the suffrage movement as anything other than promises. Glasgow knew too well what women's lives were like.

The irony of Glasgow's writing *Virginia* when she did—in 1912 and 1913, as the eleventh of her novels—is that she had devoted the first fifteen years of her writing career to creating women who were prototypes of the "new woman," characters as unlike Virginia Pendleton as possible. The independent painter Rachel Gavin, from Glasgow's first novel, *The Descendant*; Mariana Musin, the singer from the second, *Phases of an Inferior Planet*; the three tough Southern women Glasgow wrote about from 1900 to 1904—Eugenia Battle, Betty Ambler, and Maria Fletcher—all these were nontraditional women, defiant of both family and cultural mores. Glasgow balanced these

strong women with male characters who were sometimes
equally interesting to her turn-of-the-century readers (and her
titles and heavily philosophical dialogue suggested that she was
indeed patterning this early fiction after that of male authors
like Harold Frederic), but her own fascination with these atyp-
ical women characters was recurring and compelling. In fact,
it may be because Glasgow had drawn such indomitable women
in her earlier novels that she was intrigued with the challenge
which the character of Virginia held for her. As she wrote in
the later preface to the novel,

> Although, in the beginning, I had intended to deal iron-
> ically with both the Southern lady and the Victorian tra-
> dition, I discovered, as I went on, that my irony grew
> fainter, while it yielded at last to sympathetic compassion.
> By the time I approached the end, the simple goodness
> of Virginia's nature had turned a comedy of manners into
> a tragedy of human fate . . . she was as close to me, and
> as real, as my heart or nerves. (*A Certain Measure*, pp.
> 79–80)

As the "plot" of *Virginia* suggests, there is not much to the
novel but the character of Virginia and the life of "simple goodness" she attempts to lead. But as Glasgow says in her comment, Virginia becomes a compelling character, one that
involves today's reader, almost despite the life that surrounds
her. Daughter of an Episcopalian clergyman and his incredibly
self-effacing wife, Virginia Pendleton, of Dinwiddie, Virginia,
was educated to be precisely what she became—a wife and
mother. All the standard Victorian terms apply to her: dutiful,
pure, idealistic, self-abnegating, unimaginative. From the keen
pitch of romantic love that leads to her marriage to the
stranger-in-town, Oliver Treadwell, the artistic black-sheep
nephew of the wealthy Cyrus Treadwell family, through her
wearying years of caring for her three children, Virginia fades
from the glorious brunette, the woman "cut out for happiness,"
to a dowdy, frail shadow of a person. Oliver manages to become
a popular playwright, and spends much of his time in New
York City. Both her beloved parents die, within six months of
each other. One daughter, Lucy, marries. The other two chil-

dren—Jenny and the best-loved Harry—are in college. And Oliver finally leaves her for the actress who stars in his plays.

In some ways, *Virginia* is a classic "domestic" novel, our attention riveted throughout on the woman and the home and family she cares about. But it is also a poignant *Bildungsroman*, for the first forty percent of the book deals with Virginia as she grows up: her "formal" education, her intimacy with the modern and forceful Susan Treadwell, her restricted life as daughter of the downright naive Pendleton family in the small Virginia community. What she "becomes" as a result of all this instruction is clear only after she marries. Marriage and the change of location that act mandates serves as Virginia's journey to the inimical city, as well as her crucial sexual experience—both ingredients of the traditional male novel of development.

The last third of *Virginia* becomes something still different, however, a striking portrayal of a woman's disillusion with the life of nurturing she has been trained to lead. Much more introspective than the earlier parts of the book, this concluding section impresses the reader with Glasgow's ability to shift narrative methods for intended effects. And throughout, *Virginia* is a novel of manners, as it is often described, with much attention given to community interaction, to the many minor characters that people conventional historical fiction, and to the customs of, particularly, women and issues of concern to women.

These are some of the reasons why *Virginia*, despite its comparatively uncomplicated story line, is one of Glasgow's longest novels. Another is that Glasgow uses a succession of narrative methods to achieve the complex portrayal that Virginia as character came to demand.

Glasgow's primary method—in this book as in her other great fiction, *Barren Ground* (1925) and *The Sheltered Life* (1932)—is to involve us in the character of the woman portrayed. She does this through countless well-developed scenes more often than through heavily introspective passages. We - see Virginia with her parents, her friend Susan, her husband, her children, and even with her rivals for Oliver's love—Abby Goode and Margaret Oldcastle: Glasgow provides so much information that we can rely on our own intuition about Virginia as character. And there are also the epistolary scenes, when Virginia (living away from her parents after her marriage) writes in wrenching detail about her life as wife and mother. Glasgow also uses well-paced and essential monologues, particularly toward the end of the book when Virginia is virtually alone. The method, then, underscores the tragedy of her vacant life. And the few introspective scenes are used for almost inexpressible effect, when Virginia is so distraught she cannot come to words—when she reels with the shock of Oliver's asking for a separation, or when she bargains with God for Harry's life during his diphtheria. Glasgow was able to create our involvement with Virginia not only because of her skill as writer, but because of her personal experience with emotional and physical loss* as well as because in creating Virginia, she was re-creating the two women she had loved most in her life, her mother and her sister Cary.** As she explained later, Virginia "was the evocation of an ideal and is always associated with my mother and the women of her period. I describe Virginia in the beginning exactly as I was told my mother looked when she was a girl" (*Letters*, p. 131).

Literary history is filled with novels that deal with real-life characters. What made Glasgow's *Virginia* work was less the models she had at her disposal than the artistic confidence she had developed by the time she began the novel.

In 1912, Glasgow had been earning her living from her fiction for over a decade. She was eventually to become the only living

---

* Glasgow's life before 1913, when she was only forty herself, had been studded with major bereavements. Two of her brothers died in 1875 and 1876; her mother's death in 1893 was followed the next year by the suicide of her beloved brother-in-law Walter McCormack (Cary's husband of two years); 1905 saw the end of her romance with "Gerald B.," whether through his death or the end of the love; 1909 marked her brother Frank's suicide, and 1911, the death of Cary. Around 1883, her mother had experienced a nervous breakdown when she had learned of her husband's continuing affair with a mulatto (Anne Jane Gholson had by that time borne her husband ten children herself); and that period of great upset remained vivid in Glasgow's memory (see *Woman Within*, Glasgow's autobiography).

** Cary's life was nearly as bleak as that of her mother. Although Glasgow dedicates *Virginia* to "the radiant spirit who was my sister," one assumes Cary's radiance was willed. Reared to be a loving wife, Cary was married but a few years before her husband's suicide. She then lived with her family until her own death of breast cancer, in 1911. She spent her days reading the works McCormack had loved so she would be a suitable companion for him once they were reunited.

American author to have her work published in matched editions by two different publishers (The Old Dominion Edition, 8 volumes, by Doubleday, Doran and Co., from 1929 to 1933, and The Virginia Edition, 12 volumes, by Charles Scribner's Sons, 1938). Her consistent popularity was coupled with receiving the prestigious Howells Medal for Fiction, a special *Saturday Review* award, membership in the American Academy of Arts and Letters, and several honorary doctorates. Few women writers would achieve such success, both commercially and aesthetically.

Yet Glasgow, born in 1873, was the daughter of a protective Virginia family and as such, felt pressure to become a woman very much like Virginia Pendleton. Cautiously defiant, she had managed to write and publish (though with hardly any formal education and little family support), to travel, to make friends outside the approved family circle—but the ostensibly "free" life she led was not without guilt and personal conflict. One has only to contrast her life—from the mysterious affair with a married man through friendships with Thomas Hardy, Hugh Walpole, and other literary lions to her last engagement to a Southern lawyer—with her vivid description of the normal condition of Southern womanhood:

> The Victorian era, above all, was one of waiting, as hell is an eternity of waiting.
> Women waiting for the first word of love from their lovers. Women waiting with all the inherited belief in the omnipotence of love, for the birth of their sons. Women waiting, during the civil war, for news of their sons and husbands. Women waiting beside the beds of the sick and dying—waiting—waiting—.
> As a result I think it is almost impossible to overestimate the part that religion, in one form or another, has played in the lives of southern women. Nothing else could have made them accept with meekness the wing of the chicken and the double standard of morals. (University of Virginia Glasgow Papers)

Glasgow often refers to a "strange sense of exile" that she experienced because her life as a woman was so different from the lives of other women she knew and loved. She seemed to recognize, too, that her conflict between having to be aggressive in order to write, and passive in order to exist, was intensified by living in the South. As she recalled in *The Woman Within*, "Only on the surface of things have I ever trod the beaten path. So long as I could keep from hurting anyone else, I have lived, as completely as it was possible, the life of my choice. I have been free . . ." (p. 296).

In 1912, however, Glasgow had little of this confidence. Her beloved Cary had died, and she herself had left home (her father was to live until 1916, so by leaving home she was also escaping his authority). For the first time in her life, she was comparatively free of the need to pretend. She was free to allow her ambivalence toward the traditional Southern woman to show. Virginia is the result of that freedom, and her character lives because of Glasgow's ability to capture the nuances of her own ambivalence.

The character of Cyrus Treadwell, for example, shows Glasgow working through her own personal angers. Cyrus is a clear prototype of Francis Glasgow, the staunchly religious patriarch who lived his double-standard life with little regard for his wife (Glasgow never forgave him his mulatto mistress, nor her mother's breakdown in the early 1880s); given his use of the power of the church to keep his family submissive, Ellen's refusing to attend services becomes the great act of defiance she saw it as. And in *Virginia*, Treadwell's worst behavior is toward his abused wife; but his act of outright evil comes when his mulatto lover asks him to save their son's life, and he refuses.

Structurally in the novel, Glasgow links Cyrus Treadwell's denial of his son with Oliver Treadwell's leaving Virginia for another woman. Both men are patriarchs of families; both are powerful and respected. Society does not judge them for their personal acts, only for their financial and public roles. Both—easily, unconscionably—abandon the families they have created. Whether the issue is racial or sexual, their morality is a sham.

Glasgow does not give the two plots equal time, but she ties them closely together. The subplot of Cyrus not acknowledging his illegitimate son is only briefly developed, but the issue becomes central because Gabriel Pendleton, Virginia's father, is called to investigate trouble in the black community and is killed for his involvement. Cyrus, who had reason to become involved, would not; Gabriel, by virtue of his beliefs about human beings in the abstract, loses his life. The effects of Gabriel's death on both Virginia and her mother dominate that section of the novel, and so the reader remains conscious of both Cyrus's failures as well as Gabriel's death.

Oliver's infidelity—at least his leanings toward it—suffuses the novel. First he is suspected of an affair with Abby Goode, and at this stage in her life, early in their marriage, Virginia rallies for a fight. The illness of their child prevents her from taking decisive action, however, and she makes the implicit choice between husband and son in a moving deathbed scene. Later, Oliver's growing attraction to Margaret Oldcastle runs as the antagonistic theme through the second half of the novel, with many opportunities for Glasgow as author to discourse on responsibility and self-indulgence. What saves the book from a fairly typical domestic crisis plot, with husband a blackguard off wooing another woman, is that Glasgow keeps the focus of the book, even during this time, on society's view of Virginia as the woman at fault. The whole structure of the novel becomes ironic. No one ever says that Oliver is out woman-chasing; the rhetoric instead keeps giving the reader explanations for Virginia's unattractiveness. Of course she was to blame, the society acknowledges: she never bought new clothes, she had become worn and gray, she was no longer interesting. "She had made the way too easy for others; she had never exacted of them," Glasgow says. "She had laid her youth down on the altar of her love." And, in one of her most incisive passages, Glasgow describes Virginia:

> The woman's power of sinking her ambition and even her identity into the activities of the man was deeply inter-woven with all that was essential and permanent in her soul. Her keenest joys, as well as her sharpest sorrows, had never belonged to herself, but to others. It was doubt-ful, indeed, if, since the day of her marriage, she had been profoundly moved by any feeling which was centered merely in a personal desire. She had wanted things for

Oliver and for the children, but for herself there had been no separate existence apart from them.

Glasgow is at her best showing the reader these qualities, rather than lecturing about them. The scene in New York when Virginia overhears a gossip talking about Oliver's affair with Margaret Oldcastle illustrates well the social code she has to cope with. Delighted to be in New York with Oliver for an opening, Virginia is devastated by the remark ("Have you seen the dowdy, middle-aged woman he is married to? It's a pity that all great men marry young. . . ."). Yet she does not confront Oliver with her knowledge; instead she grows quiet. The breakfast scene is typical. Virginia, distraught with anguish, is so calm Oliver knows nothing of the way she feels (not that he has been even reasonably sensitive to her feelings in the twenty-five years they have been married):

Having drunk his coffee, Oliver passed his cup to her, and laid down his paper.

"You look tired, Virginia. I hope it hasn't been too much for you?"

"Oh, no. Have you quite got over your headache?"

"Pretty much, but those lights last night were rather trying. Don't put any cream in this time. I want the stimulant."

"Perhaps it has got cold. Shall I ring for fresh?"

"It doesn't matter. This will do quite as well. Have you any shopping that you would like to do this morning?"

Shopping! When her whole world had crumbled around her! For an instant the lump in her throat made speech impossible; then summoning that mild yet indestructible spirit, which was as the spirit of all those generations of women who lived in her blood, she answered gently:

"Yes, I had intended to buy some presents for the girls."

"Then you'd better take a taxicab for the morning. I suppose you know the names of the shops you want to go to?" . . .

The way this scene, and the countless others like it, works on the reader, of course, is through involvement. Virginia may

not be angry, but the reader is. And our anger goes two ways—
toward Oliver for his selfish life-style, and toward Virginia for
the passivity, the immolation, she is willing to experience.

In this scene, as in the scene when Oliver asks for his freedom, Virginia cannot become angry. Glasgow has shown her
behaving with some sense of her own rights soon after she is
married, when she goes fox hunting with Abby and Oliver, and
when she stops to buy the blue material for a new dress and
is thereby late for dinner. Oliver's being upset with her tar-
diness is a wonderfully accurate touch on Glasgow's part. But
once her physical beauty begins to go, or she is given the
impression that she is less attractive, that she has little "right"
to Oliver, whatever spirit she had also disappears. And without anger, without channels for expression of such deep pain,
Virginia comes near insanity. Glasgow's having Virginia withdraw so completely from society that she is almost incarcer-
ated in her house is psychologically accurate. Never a fighter,
Virginia cannot confront Oliver or his lover; but she is also too
proud to admit she has lost her husband (a false pride, one
bred of the social codes she has never questioned). The only
recourse she has, aside from death, is to deny the reality of
her present life.

In her depiction of Virginia, alone, coming to terms with
Oliver's abandonment, Glasgow comes to write a somewhat
different kind of novel, a novel that questions many of the
precepts her readers lived by. The story of *Virginia*, for 1913,
was amazingly critical of the very readers who frequently
bought Miss Glasgow's fiction. In this novel she was hitting
primary issues—of both gender and race—and she was hitting
them hard.

The issue which opens the novel is that of education for
women, and the amorphous line between "women's" education
and that suitable for men. Susan Treadwell wants to go to
college; Virginia wants only to get married. Both graduated
from Miss Priscilla Batte's Dinwiddie Academy for Young Ladies, where the prime objective is to keep women from "knowledge of any sort." To be taught by Miss Batte, who "was
capable of dying for an idea, but not of conceiving one," posed
little threat to the status quo. As Glasgow says of Virginia,

The chief object of her upbringing, which differed in no essential particular from that of every other well-born and well-bred Southern woman of her day, was to paralyze her reasoning faculties so completely that all danger of mental "unsettling" or even movement was eliminated from her future.

Questions of education permeate *Virginia*, usually as integral to more apparent themes. One of Virginia's concerns about her children, the girls as well as Harry, is that they go to college. Part of her closeness with money is to save enough to pay those expenses (until he became a playwright, Oliver made a scant living working for his uncle). Much of the latter part of the novel dwells on Lucy's and Harry's experiences as they are away from home being educated. Susan Treadwell's running battle with her obdurate father about going to college merges with her plans for her own children; it is clear that Susan was a generation ahead of the times, at least in Virginia. But the most poignant reflection of a lack of education occurs during Virginia's courtship—and continues throughout her marriage. Because she feels so ignorant and insecure around Oliver, Virginia can say literally nothing. During their marriage, she moved from speechlessness to a pseudo-speech, adopting the "toneless sweetness" of her mother's incessant prattle. Rather than try to talk about things that might interest Oliver, Virginia instead abandons all attempt to communicate: the very manner of her speech suggests that she does not expect to be listened to.

Of all the women in the novel, only Susan Treadwell (who has, unfortunately, never made it to college) manages to shape her discourse to her needs. Glasgow shows again and again that Susan speaks directly to those needs, whether she is talking with her fierce father or with Virginia. She is able to express anger, bewilderment, pain, and love—all with a minimum of self-effacement or posturing. Susan is, at least in language, Glasgow's "new" woman.

Closely aligned with education, buttressing it with its unquestionable dogma, is the church. Glasgow's most severe condemnation falls on its patriarchal conventions, on its crippling attitudes toward women. She writes about Virginia that she was never a "weak" or ineffectual woman: "on the contrary, she was a woman whose vital energy had been deflected, by precept and example, into a single emotional centre. She was . . . the logical result of an inordinate sense of duty, the crowning achievement of the code of beautiful behaviour and of the Episcopal Church" (*A Certain Measure*, p. 83). By having Virginia's father be a minister, and her mother dutifully tied to her role as helpmeet and good Christian wife, Glasgow is able to criticize the tenets of the church without directly attacking it. When Mrs. Pendleton answers Virginia's question "Love is the only thing that really matters, isn't it, mother?" with "A pure and noble love, darling. It is a woman's life. God meant it so," Glasgow's indictment is plain.

Glasgow's criticism of the church, especially in regard to its treatment of women, came to its fullest statement not in *Virginia*, but in the novel that preceded it. In her 1911 *The Miller of Old Church*, she creates an influential young minister, who uses his own physical appeal to control his female parishioners. The text of a typical sermon appears in that novel, and is quoted in part here:

Woman . . . was created to look after the ways of her household in order that man might go out into the world and make a career. No womanly woman cared to make a career. What the womanly woman desired was to remain an Incentive, an Ideal, an Inspiration. If the womanly woman possessed a talent, she did not use it—for this would unsex her—she sacrificed it in herself in order that she might return it to the race through her sons. Self-sacrifice . . . was the breath of the nostrils of the womanly woman. It was for her power of self-sacrifice that men loved her and made an Ideal of her. . . . The home was founded on sacrifice, and woman was the pillar and the ornament of the home. There was her sphere, her purpose, her mission. All things outside of that sphere belonged to man, except the privilege of ministering to the sick and the afflicted in other households. (p. 130)

Virginia is, in fact, an answer to all these assumptions—a bleak answer, at that. Living this kind of prescribed life, the good Christian woman could expect great happiness, all earthly rewards. Instead, Virginia is left alone, literally bereft, laden with the shame and guilt of failure. Because Glasgow so neatly turns all Oliver's guilt to Virginia's—or so her ironic stance in the novel works—Virginia is robbed of even anger toward her betraying husband. The womanly woman of the sermon has given up countless rights—freedom, movement outside her home, the equality of her children (for her gifts are to be dispersed among the sons), ambition, talents—supposedly for the great reward of being cared for and loved. Question the rate of exchange as we might, Virginia never received the payment expected. As Glasgow points out in the novel, "She was satisfied with the crumbs of life, and yet they were denied her."

The somewhat strained ending of the novel may be explained in the context of readers' expectations. Having Harry return from college to be with Virginia smacks of the contrived "happy ending" that Glasgow consistently tried to avoid for her novels. She prided herself on writing more realistically than most popular novelists. And while the exchange of son for husband is hardly credible, and Harry's return only temporary, still the reader is faced with a character who is unquestionably distraught in her loneliness. (Glasgow had early described Virginia as a woman "who feared loneliness as if it were the smallpox.") To have Virginia "punished" in so cruel a way—losing Oliver and her position in society, losing her identity as it were—with no amelioration, no "sweetening" of any sort, may have alienated those readers who expected just rewards for good living. Glasgow saw herself as an outsider, and knew her readership well enough to know what they could accept, and where they would draw the line. The reversal from tragedy to some middling sense of rescue in the last paragraph might well have been expeditious.

Throughout the novel, Virginia has been taught to be dependent on men. The attitude of the church relegates women to chattel and supports the patriarchal notion of wife-as-property. "Value," then, can be determined chiefly by owners and buyers, so virginity—the whole phalanx of sexual accommodation—can remain a key factor in choosing a bride. Glasgow's choice of the title for this novel underscores the interrelatedness of the attributes of "Virginia"—as both well-bred daughter of the beloved state and as virgin, mental and physical. McDowell points out how thoroughly erotic Oliver and Virginia's attraction is (indeed, their fascination with each other has little else to support it), and yet how covert all such mating practices remain in the conventional society Dinwiddie represents.

Glasgow also scrutinizes the mother-daughter bond, and finds it wanting. The guidance Susan Treadwell gets from her tyrannized mother can hardly equip her for decision-making in life, just as the model Virginia finds in her self-sacrificing mother can hardly turn her into anything other than another devoted woman. Glasgow's portrait of Lucy Pendleton is scarifying. So weak from hunger she can scarcely walk, the woman trusts to the parishioners for their food, never complaining, never urging her studious husband into any household work, never allowing Virginia any skills or freedoms. Virginia and her mother are truly "perfect products" of the system. As Adrienne Rich has more recently reminded us, "The most important thing one woman can do for another is to illuminate and expand her sense of actual possibilities. . . . *To refuse to be a victim.* . . . As daughters we need mothers who want their freedom and ours" (*Of Woman Born*, p. 246).

It is particularly interesting that in this novel Glasgow writes about the well-born Virginia classes. In other of her works she had chosen the lower and often uneducated social strata, taking from them an exemplary character or two: the-rise-of plot and denouement. *Virginia* is one of the first of Glasgow's books in which she deals with characters like people she had known and grown up with. Again, her choice bespeaks her own feelings of freedom from restraint, and part of the authenticity of these characters surely springs from her familiarity with her context. That there was risk in writing about the well-born, especially with the themes of miscegenation and betrayal, no reader could deny.

Glasgow also saw *Virginia* as a wider canvas, a broad social document, with the character of Virginia at its center, but the product of countless forces. "Every person in Dinwiddie, from the greater to the least, was linked, in some obscure fashion, with her tragedy, and with the larger tyranny of tradition" (*A Certain Measure*, p. 82). The early chapters, accordingly, introduce many characters and many social patterns, and even though Virginia figures in the action, her role even then is as repository of advice and eventually as product. Many critics have pointed out Glasgow's accuracy in depicting the materialism, the reliance on religion and custom, and the numerous portraits of coping women; but her skill in drawing these parts of *Virginia* is even more impressive when one considers how integral they all become to the full characterization of her protagonist. Alfred Kazin has *Virginia* in mind when he assesses Glasgow as novelist:

> She began as the most girlish of Southern romantics and later proved the most biting critic of Southern romanticism; she was at once the most traditional in loyalty to Virginia and its most powerful satirist.
>
> (*On Native Grounds*, p. 258)

Much of the criticism of Glasgow's writing, even when it has praised her work, has tended to relegate her to the position of "Southern" writer, "Virginia" chronicler, local colorist. She has been often thought of as a writer of the old school, one more interested in description than character (however a reader makes those finite distinctions). Even positive comment can sometimes undermine the real strength of a writer's work, as in this statement by Louis D. Rubin, Jr.:

> Miss Glasgow generally depicted life through the eyes of a highly feminine, subjective percipient, one who had suffered as a woman and whose work was written in large measure out of that suffering and took much of its character from it.
>
> (*No Place*, p. 12)

Rubin's emphasis tends to give second-class citizenship to those feminine observers of life, and to look askance at their subjectivity. What needs to be pointed out, for balance, is that Glasgow knew the lives of women, found them important, and did splendid work re-creating them so that her readers—male and female alike—might come to both understand and question conventions, behaviors, life-styles, and attitudes that they previously had only accepted. As the important work of Elaine Showalter, Gilbert and Gubar, and many other feminist critics has suggested, women writers have had to push through many barriers—psychological as well as physical—before they can begin to write. Their feelings of inadequacy, of guilt, have led them to revise the genres male writers accepted so easily, and because the stories they had to tell were different, women writers could not simply copy the forms that worked to tell male stories. Yet because of their guilt and anxiety, women writers turned to evasion, disguise. It is rare that a woman writer will tell a woman's story plainly, in identifiable terms (*Madwoman*, pp. 73–74).

Historically, then, Glasgow's *Virginia* holds interest because it is so clearly a woman's story told without subterfuge, given complexity and dimension because of the author's own ambivalence and her ability to use irony and scene for such a complete effect. But reading *Virginia* in the 1980s and 1990s is more than a glimpse into history. It is an involving experience, though it is also a somewhat unpleasant one, for we know clearly—and for most of the book—where Virginia's life is heading. Like the pervasive tragic mood of *King Lear*, the tone of *Virginia* instructs us as we read: pretty scenes are set against sordid; happy moments are countered with sad ones. And Glasgow's didactic comments, whether made by her spokeswoman Susan Treadwell or by the author herself, give us little choice but to understand the tragedy of Virginia's life. Once born and well instructed, Virginia could come only to a predictable ending. As Glasgow wrote to Allen Tate in 1933, "Virginia is the incarnation of an ideal, and the irony is directed not at her, but at human nature which creates an ideal only to abandon it when that ideal comes to flower" (*Letters*, p. 134).

But Glasgow has done many things in this novel besides write an admonitory tale, a *Pilgrim's Progress* of feminine survival (although she has also done that). She has told a parallel story of an achieving, surviving, and still "womanly" woman, Susan Treadwell, a believable example of the emancipated woman of the late nineteenth century. She has portrayed vividly and with little approbation the life of Virginia's mother, and she has managed to use Lucy Pendleton and Belinda Treadwell as contemporaries (one who married luckily and was only moderately unhappy; the other, married and miserable) in a subplot that reinforces Glasgow's point that Virginia was a woman out of time, rather than a woman at fault. Society's expectations had changed between Lucy Pendleton's generation and Virginia's, so the younger woman's dilemma was even less avoidable than one might have hoped. (Glasgow draws the reader's attention to this dichotomy repeatedly in the later parts of the novel, when Virginia's daughters malign their mother for her old-fashionedness.)

Another theme that is sometimes overlooked in *Virginia* is that of the health of most of the women characters. Mrs. Peachey, Miss Batte, Miss Willy, Susan, Lucy and Jenny Pendleton, and many other minor women characters are leading productive and generally happy lives. In a Glasgow novel, there is no set formula for women's fulfillment: marry or don't marry, have children or don't have children, have a career or become a homemaker—what is most important is the way that life suits the individual woman. And what is most tragic, according to Glasgow, is the way society insists on judging people and their choices. When Glasgow shows Mrs. Pendleton lecturing Virginia about the evils of divorce, we know that that is her real failure as a parent, her susceptibility to uninformed opinion.

Oh, Jinny, a scandal, even where one is innocent, is so terrible. A woman—a true woman—would endure death rather than be talked about. I remember your cousin Jane Pendleton made an unhappy marriage, and her husband used to get drunk and beat her and even carry on dreadfully with the coloured servants—but she said that was better than the disgrace of a separation.

Readers today will find this kind of maternal "wisdom" sheer travesty.

By 1913, Ellen Glasgow had become a firm believer in relative standards, in individual moralities, and because of her beliefs, *Virginia* is very much a book of its time. The problems of being overly dependent on male authority are shown to be as debilitating as the problems of being frustrated by overprotection. Although Glasgow was to deal more directly with the issues of women's health and sanity in both *Barren Ground* and *The Sheltered Life*, she here shows great understanding of Virginia's inability to meet her coming divorce rationally. Both Virginia's eight-month withdrawal from life and her aberrant and futile trip to New York reflect Glasgow's knowledge of the issues Charlotte Perkins Gilman had expressed so forthrightly twenty years earlier in *The Yellow Wallpaper*. The choices Virginia is left with, however, seem generations behind those facing Edna Pontellier in Kate Chopin's *The Awakening* (1899). Edna saw some glimpses of personal development, some sense of fruition; but for Virginia, life without a husband was meaningless.

Virginia is also a pair novel to Edith Wharton's 1905 *The House of Mirth*, with greater emphasis placed on the postscript to a woman's attaining her great goal in life, finding a suitable (and wealthy) husband. Lily Bart's ambivalence about that goal suggests Susan Treadwell's attitudes toward marriage, but Susan is fortunate in that she is protected economically from the stark choices Lily is forced to make.

A glance at publishing history for the year 1913 shows how fruitful that prewar period was: Glasgow's *Virginia* appeared just two years after her 1911 best seller, *The Miller of Old Church*, a novel which—despite its title—was about a maverick Southern woman of illegitimate birth. The novel, like *Virginia*, included many instances of women's friendships and male-female power struggles. Willa Cather's *O Pioneers!* gave the reading world the first of her strong women characters. Edith Wharton's scathing *The Custom of the Country* followed closely her 1912 *The Reef*, a powerful double-standard novel, and the 1911 *Ethan Frome*, which may be more the story of the tragedy of a woman's choice than it is that of the title character.

From *The Custom of the Country* in 1913 it is but a short step to Wharton's Pulitzer Prize–winning *The Age of Innocence* (1920), where all male betrayals are carefully catalogued and the only heroic character succeeds in escaping American patriarchal tortures by moving to France. And 1913 also saw the publication of Mary Johnston's *Hagar*, the most important "new woman" novel of the decade. The flip side of *Virginia*, *Hagar* is about a self-possessed woman who makes a great deal of her life, but without giving up her family and personal values. Involved in settlement work and feminist public speaking, Hagar has traveled widely. She knows the world enough to realize when, relatively late in life, she has found a man to love.

Mary Johnston, like Glasgow, was disappointed in the reception her 1913 novel received. Her earlier Civil War romances had been extraordinarily popular, and she could not understand why readers found the book she admired most less readable. Charlotte Perkins Gilman wrote to Johnston about that dilemma, saying that she admired Hagar, "that strong growing woman . . . who pushed on through things. That wasn't 'pleasant' to read either, but it was a piece of life. I feel as if, having established your high reputation in historical novels, you are now doing far better and bigger work. People won't like it as well, of course—but keep on" (quoted in Jones, p. 188).

As this exchange shows, for most woman writers, no matter how well established they were or how profitable their fiction was, the act of writing honestly about women characters and women's issues was dangerous. Sandra M. Gilbert and Susan Gubar discuss what they call "the anxiety of authorship" that women writers are privy to, and the course of many women writers' careers, Glasgow's included, proves the generalization beyond doubt (*Madwoman*, p. 73).

In Glasgow's case, her capacity to write well about women characters paralleled her own sense of independence and worth as a person. That she was forty and had written ten successful novels before she could attempt a book about a woman protagonist, with the theme of woman's fulfillment, or lack of it, suggests the deeply anxious quality of her undertaking. But that she was able to go on from *Virginia*, to explore more and more completely the issues of choice and fulfillment, and to create the gallery of memorable women protagonists to come— Dorinda Oakley, Gabriella Carr, Corinna Page, Eva Birdsong, Jenny Blair Archbald, and Ada Fincastle, among others— makes what she attempted, and achieved, in *Virginia* all the more important.

—*Linda Wagner-Martin*

SUGGESTIONS FOR FURTHER READING

Abel, Elizabeth, Marianne Hirsch, and Elizabeth Langland, eds. *The Voyage In: Fictions of Female Development* (Hanover, N.H.: University Press of New England, 1983).

Glasgow, Ellen. *Barren Ground* (New York: Grosset and Dunlap, 1925).

    A Certain Measure (New York: Harcourt, Brace and Co., 1943).

    "Feminism," *New York Times Review of Books*, November 30, 1913, pp. 656–57.

    "No Valid Reason against Giving Votes to Women," *New York Times*, March 23, 1913, sec. 6, p. 11.

    The Woman Within, An Autobiography (New York: Harcourt, Brace and Co., 1954).

Godbold, E. Stanly, Jr. *Ellen Glasgow and the Woman Within* (Baton Rouge: Louisiana State University Press, 1972).

Holman, C. Hugh. *Three Modes of Southern Fiction* (Athens: University of Georgia Press, 1966).

Inge, M. Thomas, ed. *Ellen Glasgow: Centennial Essays* (Charlottesville: University Press of Virginia, 1976).

Jones, Anne Goodwyn. *Tomorrow Is Another Day: The Woman Writer in the South, 1859–1936* (Baton Rouge: Louisiana State University Press, 1981).

MacDonald, Edgar E., and Tonette Bond Inge, *Ellen Glasgow: A Reference Guide* (Boston: G. K. Hall, 1986).

McDowell, Frederick P. W. *Ellen Glasgow and the Ironic Art of Fiction* (Madison: University of Wisconsin Press, 1963).

Parent Frazee, Monique. *Ellen Glasgow: Romancière* (Paris: A. B. Nizet, 1962).

Pratt, Annis V. *Archetypal Patterns in Women's Fiction* (Bloomington: Indiana University Press, 1981).

Raper, Julius Rowan. *From the Sunken Garden: The Fiction of Ellen Glasgow, 1916–1945* (Baton Rouge: Louisiana State University Press, 1980); *Without Shelter: The Early Career of Ellen Glasgow* (ibid., 1971); and ed., *Ellen Glasgow's Reasonable Doubts: A Collection of Her Writings* (ibid., 1988).

Rouse, Blair. *Ellen Glasgow* (New York: Twayne, 1962); and ed., *Letters of Ellen Glasgow* (New York: Harcourt, Brace and World, 1958).

Rubin, Louis D., Jr. *No Place on Earth: Ellen Glasgow, James Branch Cabell, and Richmond in Virginia* (Austin: University of Texas Press, 1959).

Scura, Dorothy McInnis. "The Southern Lady in the Early Novels of Ellen Glasgow," *Mississippi Quarterly* 31, no. 1 (Winter 1977–78): 17–31.

Steele, Oliver. "Ellen Glasgow's *Virginia*: Preliminary Notes," *Studies in Bibliography* 27 (1974): 265–89.

Thiébaux, Marcelle. *Ellen Glasgow* (New York: F. Ungar, 1982).

Wagner, Linda W. *Ellen Glasgow: Beyond Convention* (Austin: University of Texas Press, 1982).

VIRGINIA

BOOK FIRST

THE DREAM

CHAPTER I

THE SYSTEM

Toward the close of a May afternoon in the year 1884, Miss Priscilla Batte, having learned by heart the lesson in physical geography she would teach her senior class on the morrow, stood feeding her canary on the little square porch of the Dinwiddie Academy for Young Ladies. The day had been hot, and the fitful wind, which had risen in the direction of the river, was just beginning to blow in soft gusts under the old mulberry-trees in the street, and to scatter the loosened petals of syringa blossoms in a flowery snow over the grass. For a moment Miss Priscilla turned her flushed face to the scented air, while her eyes rested lovingly on the narrow walk, edged with pointed bricks and bordered by cowslips and wall-flowers, which led through the short garden to the three stone steps and the tall iron gate. She was a shapeless yet majestic woman of some fifty years, with a large mottled face in which a steadfast expression of gentle obstinacy appeared to underly the more evanescent ripples of thought or of emotion. Her severe black silk gown, to which she had just changed from her morning dress of alpaca, was softened under her full double chin by a knot of lace and a cameo brooch bearing the helmeted profile of Pallas Athene. On her head she wore a three-cornered cap trimmed with a ruching of organdie, and beneath it her thin grey hair still showed a gleam of faded yellow in the sunlight. She had never been handsome, but her prodigious size had endowed her with an impressiveness which had passed in her youth, and among an indulgent people, for beauty. Only in the last few years had her fleshiness, due to rich food which she could not resist and to lack of exercise for which she had an instinctive aversion, begun seriously to inconvenience her.

3

Beyond the wire cage, in which the canary spent his involuntarily celibate life, an ancient microphylla rose-bush, with a single imperfect bud blooming ahead of summer amid its glossy foliage, clambered over a green lattice to the gabled pediment of the porch, while the delicate shadows of the leaves rippled like lace-work on the gravel below. In the miniature garden, where the small spring blossoms strayed from the prim beds into the long feathery grasses, there were syringa bushes, a little overblown; crape-myrtles not yet in bud; a holly-tree veiled in bright green near the iron fence; a flowering almond shrub in late bloom against the shaded side of the house; and where a west wing put out on the left, a bower of red and white roses was steeped now in the faint sunshine. At the foot of the three steps ran the sunken moss-edged bricks of High Street, and across High Street there floated, like wind-blown flowers, the figures of Susan Treadwell and Virginia Pendleton.

Opening the rusty gate, the two girls tripped with carefully held flounces up the stone steps and between the cowslips and wallflowers that bordered the walk. Their white lawn dresses were made with the close-fitting sleeves and the narrow waists of the period, and their elaborately draped overskirts were looped on the left with graduated bows of light blue ottoman ribbon. They wore no hats, and Virginia, who was the shorter of the two, had fastened a Jacqueminot rose in the thick dark braid which was wound in a wreath about her head. Above her arched black eyebrows, which lent an expression of surprise and animation to her vivid oval face, her hair was parted, after an earlier fashion, under its plaited crown, and allowed to break in a mist of little curls over her temples. Even in repose there was a joyousness in her look which seemed less the effect of an inward gaiety of mind than of some happy outward accident of form and colour. Her eyes, very far apart and set in black lashes, were of a deep soft blue—the blue of wild hyacinths after rain. By her eyes, and by an old-world charm of personality which she exhaled like a perfume, it was easy to discern that she embodied the feminine ideal of the ages. To look at her was to think inevitably of love. For that end, obedient to the powers of Life, the centuries had formed and coloured her, as they had formed and coloured the wild rose with its whorl of delicate petals. The air of a spoiled beauty which rested not ungracefully upon her was sweetened by her expression of natural simplicity and goodness.

For an instant she stood listening in silence to the querulous pipes of the bird and the earnest exhortations of the teacher on the joys of cage life for both bird and lady. Then plucking the solitary early bud from the microphylla rose-bush, she tossed it over the railing of the porch on the large and placid bosom of Miss Priscilla.

"Do leave Dicky alone for a minute!" she called in a winning soprano voice.

At the sound, Miss Priscilla dropped the bit of cake she held, and turned to lean delightedly over the walk, while her face beamed like a beneficent moon through the shining cloud of rose-leaves.

"Why, Jinny, I hadn't any idea that you and Susan were there!"

Her smile included Virginia's companion, a tall, rather heavy girl, with intelligent grey eyes and fair hair cut in a straight fringe across her forehead. She was the daughter of Cyrus Treadwell, the wealthiest and therefore the most prominent citizen of the town, and she was also as intellectual as the early eighties and the twenty-one thousand inhabitants of Dinwiddie permitted a woman to be. Her friendship for Virginia had been one of those swift and absorbing emotions which come to women in their school-days. The stronger of the two, she dominated the other, as she dominated every person or situation in life, not by charm, but by the force of an energetic and capable mind. Though her dress matched Virginia's in every detail, from the soft folds of tulle at the neck to the fancy striped stockings under the *bouffant* draperies, the different shapes of the wearers gave to the one gown an air of decorous composure and to the other a quaint and appealing grace. Flushed, ardent, expectant, both girls stood now at the beginning of womanhood. Life was theirs; it belonged to them, this veiled, radiant thing that was approaching. Nothing wonderful had come as yet—but to-morrow, the day after, or next year, the miracle would happen, and everything would be different! Experience floated in a luminous mystery before them. The unknown, had borrowed the sweetness and the colour of their illusions, possessed them like a secret ecstasy and shone, in spite of their shyness, in their startled and joyous look.

" Father asked me to take a message over to General Goode," explained Virginia, with a little laugh as gay as the song of a bird, " but I couldn't go by without thanking you for the cherry-bounce. I made mother drink some of it before dinner, and it almost gave her an appetite."

" I knew it was what she needed," answered Miss Priscilla, showing her pleasure by an increasing beam. " It was made right here in the house, and there's nothing better in the world, my poor mother used to say, to keep you from running down in the spring. But why can't you and Susan come in and sit a while ? "

" We'll be straight back in a minute," replied Susan before Virginia could answer. " I've got a piece of news I want to tell you before anyone else does. Oliver came home last night."

" Oliver ? " repeated Miss Priscilla, a little perplexed. " You don't mean the son of your uncle Henry, who went out to Australia ? I thought your father had washed his hands of him because he had started play-acting or something ? " Curiosity, that devouring passion of the middle-aged, worked in her breast, and her placid face grew almost intense in expression.

" Yes, that's the one," replied Susan. " They went to Australia when Oliver was ten years old, and he's now twenty-two. He lost both his parents about three years ago," she added.

" I know. His mother was my cousin," returned Miss Priscilla. " I lost sight of her after she left Dinwiddie, but somebody was telling me the other day that Henry's invest-ments all turned out badly and they came down to real poverty. Sarah Jane was a pretty girl, and I was always very fond of her, but she was one of the improvident sort that couldn't make two ends meet without tying them into a bow-knot."

" Then Oliver must be just like her. After his mother's death he went to Germany to study, and he gave away the little money he had to some student he found starving there in a garret."

"That was generous," commented Miss Priscilla thoughtfully, "but I should hardly call it sensible. I hope some day, Jinny, that your father will tell us in a sermon whether there is Biblical sanction for immoderate generosity or not."

"But what does he say?" asked Virginia softly, meaning not the rector, but the immoderate young man.

"Oh, Oliver says that there wasn't enough for both and that the other student is worth more to the world than he is," answered Susan. "Then, of course, when he got so poor that he had to pawn his clothes or starve, he wrote father an almost condescending letter and said as much as he hated business, he supposed he'd have to come back and go to work. 'Only,' he added, 'for God's sake, don't make it tobacco!' Wasn't that dreadful?"

"It was extremely impertinent," replied Miss Priscilla sternly, "and to Cyrus of all persons! I am surprised that he allowed him to come into the house."

"Oh, father doesn't take any of his talk seriously. He calls it 'starvation foolishness,' and says that Oliver will get over it as soon as he has a nice little bank account. Perhaps he will—he is only twenty-two, you know—but just now his head is full of all kinds of new ideas he picked up somewhere abroad. He's as clever as he can be, there's no doubt of that, and he'd be really good-looking, too, if he didn't have the crooked nose of the Treadwells. Virginia has seen him only once in the street, but she's more than half in love with him already."

"Do come, Susan!" remonstrated Virginia, blushing as red as the rose in her hair. "It's past six o'clock and the General will have gone if we don't hurry." And turning away from the porch, she ran between the flowering syringa bushes down the path to the gate.

Having lost his bit of cake, the bird began to pipe shrilly, while Miss Priscilla drew a straight wicker chair (she never used rockers) beside the cage, and, stretching out her feet in their large cloth shoes with elastic sides, counted the stitches in an afghan she was knitting in narrow blue and orange strips. In front of her, the street trailed between cool, dim houses

which were filled with quiet, and from the hall at her back
there came a whispering sound as the breeze moved like a
ghostly footstep through an alcove window. With that
strange power of reflecting the variable moods of humanity
which one sometimes finds in inanimate objects, the face of
the old house had borrowed from the face of its mistress the
look of cheerful fortitude with which her generation had survived the agony of defeat and the humiliation of reconstruction. After nineteen years, the Academy still bore the scars
of war on its battered front. Once it had watched the spectre
of famine stalk over the grass-grown pavement, and had heard
the rattle of musketry and the roar of cannon borne on the
southern breeze that now wafted the sounds of the saw and
the hammer from an adjacent street. Once it had seen the
flight of refugees, the overflow of the wounded from hospitals
and churches, the panic of liberated slaves, the steady conquering march of the army of invasion. And though it would
never have occurred to Miss Priscilla that either she or her
house had borne any relation to history (which she regarded
strictly as a branch of study and visualized as a list of dates
or as a king wearing his crown), she had, in fact, played a
modest yet effective part in the rapidly changing civilization
of her age. But events were powerless against the genial
heroism in which she was armoured, and it was characteristic
of her, as well as of her race, that, while she sat now in the
midst of encircling battlefields, with her eyes on the walk over
which she had seen the blood of the wounded drip when they
were lifted into her door, she should be brooding not over the
tremendous tragedies through which she had passed, but over
the lesson in physical geography she must teach in the
morning. Her lips moved gently, and a listener, had there
been one, might have heard her murmur : " The four great
alluvial plains of Asia—those of China and of the Amoo Daria
in temperate regions ; of the Euphrates and Tigris in the
warm temperate ; of the Indus and Ganges under the Tropic—
with the Nile valley in Africa, were the theatres of the most
ancient civilizations known to history or tradition——"

As she ended, a sigh escaped her, for the instruction of the
young was for her a matter not of choice, but of necessity.
With the majority of maiden ladies left destitute in Dinwiddie

after the war, she had turned naturally to teaching as the only nice and respectable occupation which required neither preparation of mind nor considerable outlay of money. The fact that she was the single surviving child of a gallant Confederate General, who, having distinguished himself and his descendants, fell at last in the Battle of Gettysburg, was sufficient recommendation of her abilities in the eyes of her fellow citizens. Had she chosen to paint portraits or to write poems, they would have rallied quite as loyally to her support. Few, indeed, were the girls born in Dinwiddie since the war who had not learned reading, penmanship ("up to the right, down to the left, my dear"), geography, history, arithmetic, deportment, and the fine arts, in the Academy for Young Ladies. The brilliant military record of the General still shed a legendary lustre upon the school, and it was earnestly believed that no girl, after leaving there with a diploma for good conduct, could possibly go wrong or become eccentric in her later years. To be sure, she might remain a trifle weak in her spelling (Miss Priscilla having, as she confessed, a poor head for that branch of study), but, after all, as the rector had once remarked, good spelling was by no means a necessary accomplishment for a lady; and, for the rest, it was certain that the moral education of a pupil of the Academy would be firmly rooted in such fundamental verities as the superiority of man and the aristocratic supremacy of the Episcopal Church. From charming Sally Goode, now married to Tom Peachey, known familiarly as "honest Tom," the editor of the Dinwiddie *Bee*, to lovely Virginia Pendleton, the mark of Miss Priscilla was ineffaceably impressed upon the daughters of the leading families.

Remembering this now, as she was disposed to do whenever she was knitting without company, Miss Priscilla dropped her long wooden needles in her lap, and leaning forward in her chair, gazed out upon the town with an expression of childlike confidence, of touching innocence. This innocence, which belonged to the very essence of her soul, had survived both the fugitive joys and the brutal disillusionments of life. Experience could not shatter it, for it was the product of a courage that feared nothing except opinions. Just as the town had battled for a principle without understanding it, so she was

capable of dying for an idea, but not of conceiving one. She
had suffered everything from the war except the necessity of
thinking independently about it, and, though in later years
memory had become so sacred to her that she rarely indulged
in it, she still clung passionately to the habits of her ancestors
under the impression that she was clinging to their ideals.
Little things filled her days—the trivial details of the classroom
and of the market, the small domestic disturbances of her
neighbours, the moral or mental delinquencies of her two
coloured servants—and even her religious veneration for the
Episcopal Church had crystallized at last into a worship of
customs.

To-day, at the beginning of the industrial awakening of the
South, she (who was but the embodied spirit of her race)
stood firmly rooted in all that was static, in all that was
obsolete and outgrown in the Virginia of the eighties. Though
she felt as yet merely the vague uneasiness with which her
mind recoiled from the first stirrings of change, she was beginning dimly to realize that the car of progress would move
through the quiet streets before the decade was over. The
smoke of factories was already succeeding the smoke of the
battlefields, and out of the ashes of a vanquished idealism the
spirit of commercial materialism was born. What was left
of the old was fighting valiantly, but hopelessly, against what
had come of the new. The two forces filled the streets of
Dinwiddie. They were embodied in classes, in individuals,
in articles of faith, in ideals of manners. The symbol of the
one spirit was the memorial wreaths on the battlefields; of
the other it was the prophetic smoke of the factories. From
where she stood in High Street, she could see this incense to
Mammon rising above the spires of the churches, above the
houses and the hovels, above the charm and the provincialism
which made the Dinwiddie of the eighties. And this charm,
as well as this provincialism, appeared to her to be so inalienable a part of the old order, with its intrepid faith in itself,
with its militant enthusiasm, with its courageous battle against
industrial evolution, with its strength, its narrowness, its
nobility, its blindness, that, looking ahead, she could discern
only the arid stretch of a civilization from which the last
remnant of beauty was banished for ever. Already she felt

the breaking of those bonds of sympathy which had held the twenty-one thousand inhabitants of Dinwiddie, as they had held the entire South, solidly knit together in a passive yet effectual resistance to the spirit of change. Of the world beyond the borders of Virginia, Dinwiddians knew merely that it was either Yankee or foreign, and therefore to be pitied or condemned according to the Evangelical or the Calvinistic convictions of the observer. Philosophy, they regarded with the distrust of a people whose notable achievements have not been in the direction of the contemplative virtues ; and having lived comfortably and created a civilization without the aid of science, they could afford not unreasonably to despise it. It was a quarter of a century since "The Origin of Species" had changed the course of the world's thought, yet it had never reached them. To be sure, there was an old gentleman in Tabb Street whose title, "the professor," had been conferred in public recognition of peaceful pursuits ; but since he never went to church, his learning was chiefly effective when used to point a moral from the pulpit. There was, also, a tradition that General Goode had been seen reading Plato before the Battle of Seven Pines ; and this picturesque incident had contributed the distinction of the scholar to the more effulgent glory of the soldier. But for purely abstract thought—for the thought that did not construct an heroic attitude or a concrete image—there was as little room in the newer industrial system as there had been in the aristocratic society which preceded it. The world still clung to the belief that the business of humanity was confined to the preservation of the institutions which existed in the present moment of history—and Dinwiddie was only a quiet backwater into which opinions, like fashions, were borne on the current of some tributary stream of thought. Human nature in this town of twenty-one thousand inhabitants differed from human nature in London or in the Desert of Sahara mainly in the things that it ate and the manner in which it carried its clothes. The same passions stirred its heart, the same instincts moved its body, the same contentment with things as they are, and the same terror of things as they might be, warped its mind.

The canary fluted on, and from beyond the mulberry-trees

there floated the droning voice of an aged negress, in tatters and a red bandanna turban, who persuasively offered strawberries to the silent houses.

"I'se got sw-e-et straw-ber'-ies! I'se got swe-e-t str-aw-ber'-ies! Yes'm, I'se got sw-e-et straw-ber'ies des f'om de coun-try!"

Then, suddenly, out of nothing, it seemed to Miss Priscilla, a miracle occurred! The immemorial calm of High Street was broken by the sound of rapidly moving wheels (not the jingling rattle of market waggons nor the comfortable roll of doctors' buggies), and a strange new vehicle, belonging to the Dinwiddie Livery Stables, and containing a young man with longish hair and a flowing tie, turned the corner by Saint James's Church, and passed over the earthen roadbed in front of the green lattice. As the young man went by, he looked up quickly, smiled with the engaging frankness of a genial nature, and lifting his hat with a charming bow, revealed to Miss Priscilla's eyes the fact that his hair was thick and dark as well as long and wavy. While he looked at her, she noticed, also, that he had a thin, high-coloured face, lighted by a pair of eager dark eyes which lent a glow of impetuous energy to his features. The Treadwell nose, she recognized, but beneath the Treadwell nose there was a clean-shaven, boyish mouth which belied the Treadwell nature in every sensitive curve and outline.

"I'd have known him anywhere from Susan's description," she thought, and added suspiciously, "I wonder why he peered so long around that corner? It wouldn't surprise me a bit if those girls were coming back that way."

Impelled by her mounting excitement, she leaned forward until the ball of orange-coloured yarn rolled from her short lap and over the polished floor of the porch. Before she could stoop to pick it up, she was arrested by the reappearance of the two girls at the corner beyond which Oliver had gazed so intently. Then, as they drew nearer, she saw that Virginia's face was pink and her eyes starry under their lowered lashes. An inward radiance shone in the girl's look, and appeared to shape her soul and body to its secret influence. Miss Priscilla, who had known her since the first day she came to school (with her lunch, from which she refused to be parted, tightly tied up in a red and white napkin), felt suddenly that she was a stranger. A quality which she had never realized her pupil possessed had risen supreme in an instant over the familiar attributes of her character. So quickly does emotion separate the individual from the inherent soul of the race.

Susan, who was a little in advance, came rapidly up the walk, and the older woman greeted her with the words :

" My dear, I have seen him !"

" Yes, he just passed us at the corner, and I wondered if you were looking. Do tell us what you think of him."

She sat down in a low chair by the teacher's side, while Virginia went over to the cage and stood gazing thoughtfully at the singing bird.

"Well, I don't think his nose spoils him," replied Miss Priscilla after a minute, " but there's something foreign looking about him, and I hope Cyrus isn't thinking seriously about putting him into the bank."

"That was the first thing that occurred to father," answered Susan; "but Oliver told me last night while we were unpacking his books—he has a quantity of books and he kept them even when he had to sell his clothes—that he didn't see to save his life how he was going to stand it."

"Stand what ?" inquired Miss Priscilla, a trifle tartly, for after the vicissitudes of her life it was but natural that she should hesitate to regard so stable an institution as the Dinwiddie Bank as something to be " stood." " Why, I thought a young man couldn't do better than get a place in the bank. Jinny's father was telling me in the market last Saturday that he wanted his nephew John Henry to start right in there if they could find room for him."

" Oh, of course, it's just what John Henry would like," said Virginia, speaking for the first time.

"Then if it's good enough for John Henry, it's good enough for Oliver, I reckon," rejoined Miss Priscilla. " Anybody who has mixed with beggars oughtn't to turn up his nose at a respectable bank."

" But he says it's because the bank is so respectable that he doesn't think he could stand it," answered Susan.

Virginia, who had been looking with her rapt gaze down the deserted street, quivered at the words as if they had stabbed her.

"But he wants to be a writer, Susan," she protested. "A great many very nice people are writers."

"Then why doesn't he go about it in a proper way, if he isn't ashamed of it?" asked the teacher; and she added reflectively after a pause, "I wish he'd write a good history of the war—one that doesn't deal so much with the North. I've almost had to stop teaching United States history because there is hardly one written now that I would let come inside my doors."

"He doesn't want to write histories," replied Susan. "Father suggested to him at supper last night that if he would try his hand at a history of Virginia, and be careful not to put in anything that might offend anybody, he could get it taught in every private school in the State. But he said he'd be shot first."

"Perhaps he's a genius," said Virginia in a startled voice. "Geniuses are always different from other people, aren't they?"

"I don't know," answered Susan doubtfully. "He talks of things I never heard of before, and he seems to think that they are the most important things in the world."

"What things?" asked Virginia breathlessly.

"Oh, I can't tell you because they are so new, but he seems on fire when he talks of them. He talks for hours about art and its service to humanity, and about going down to the people and uplifting the masses."

"I hope he doesn't mean the negroes," commented Miss Priscilla suspiciously.

"He means the whole world, I believe," responded Susan. "He quotes all the time from writers I've never heard of, and he laughs at every book he sees in the house. Yesterday he picked up one of Mrs. Southworth's novels on mother's bureau and asked her how she could allow such immoral stuff in her room. She had got it out of the bookcase to lend to Miss Willy Whitlow, who was there making my dress, but he scolded her so about it that at last Miss Willy went off with Mill's 'Essay on Liberty,' and mother burned all of Mrs. Southworth's that she had in the house. Oliver had been so nice to mother that I believe she would make a bonfire of her furniture if he asked her to do it."

"Is he really trying to unsettle Miss Willy's mind?" questioned the teacher anxiously. "How on earth could she go out sewing by the day if she didn't have her religious convictions?"

"That's just what I asked him," returned Susan, who, besides being dangerously clever, had a remarkably level head to keep her balanced. "But he answered that until people got unsettled they would never move, and when I wanted to find out where he thought poor little Miss Willy could possibly move to, he only got impatient and said that I was trying to bury the principle under the facts. We very nearly quarrelled over Miss Willy, but of course she took the book to please Oliver and couldn't worry through a line of it to save her soul."

"Did he say anything about his work? what he wants to do, I mean?" asked Virginia, and her voice was so charged with feeling that it gave an emotional quality to the question.

"He wants to write," replied Susan. "His whole heart is in it, and when he isn't talking about reaching the people, he talks about what he calls ' technique.' "

"Are you sure it isn't poetry?" inquired Miss Priscilla, humming back like a bee to the tempting sweets of conjecture. "I've always heard that poetry was the ruination of Poe."

"No, it isn't poetry—not exactly at least—it's plays," answered Susan. "He talked to me till twelve o'clock last night while we were arranging his books, and he told me that he meant to write really great dramas, but that America wasn't ready for them yet and that was why he had had to sell his clothes. He looked positively starved; but he says he doesn't mind starving a while if he can only live up to his ideal."

"Well, I wonder what his ideal is," remarked Miss Priscilla grimly.

"It has something to do with his belief that art can grow only out of sacrifice," said Susan. "I never heard anybody—not even Jinny's father in church—talk so much about sacrifice."

"But the rector doesn't talk about sacrifice for the theatre," retorted the teacher, and she added with crushing finality, " I don't believe there is a particle of sense in it. If he is going to

write, why on earth doesn't he sit straight down and do it ?
Why, when little Miss Amanda Sheppard was left at sixty
without a roof over her head, she began at once, without
saying a word to anybody, to write historical novels."

"It does seem funny until you talk with him," admitted
Susan. "But he is so much in earnest that when you listen
to him, you can't help believing in him. He is so full of convictions that he convinces you in spite of yourself."

"Convictions about what ?" demanded Miss Priscilla. "I
don't see how a young man who refuses to be confirmed can
have any convictions."

"Well, he has, and he feels just as strongly about them as
we do about ours."

"But how can he possibly feel as strongly about a wrong
conviction as we do about a right one ?" insisted the older
woman stubbornly, for she realized vaguely that they were
approaching dangerous ground and set out to check their
advance in true Dinwiddie fashion, which was strictly pro-
hibitive.

"I like a man who has opinions of his own and isn't ashamed
to stand up for them," said Virginia with a resolution that
made her appear suddenly taller.

"Not *false* opinions, Jinny !" rejoined Miss Priscilla, and
her manner carried them with a bound back to the schoolroom,
for her mental vision saw in a flash the beribboned diploma
for good conduct which her favourite pupil had borne away
from the Academy on Commencement Day two years ago, and
a shudder seized her lest she should have left a single unpro-
tected breach in the girl's mind through which an unauthorized
idea might enter. Had she trusted too confidently to the
fact that Virginia's father was a clergyman, and therefore
spiritually armed for the defence and guidance of his daughter ?
Virginia, in spite of her gaiety, had been what Miss Priscilla
called "a docile pupil," meaning one who deferentially sub-
mitted her opinions to her superiors, and to go through life
perpetually submitting her opinions was, in the eyes of her
parents and her teacher, the divinely appointed task of woman.
Her education was founded upon the simple theory that the
less a girl knew about life, the better prepared she would be to
contend with it. Knowledge of any sort (except the rudi-

ments of reading and writing, the geography of countries she would never visit, and the dates of battles she would never mention) was kept from her as rigorously as if it contained the germs of a contagious disease. And this ignorance of anything that could possibly be useful to her was supposed in some mysterious way to add to her value as a woman and to make her a more desirable companion to a man who, either by experience or by instinct, was expected "to know his world." Unlike Susan (who, in a community which offered few opportunities to women outside of the nursery or the kitchen, had been born with the inquiring spirit and would ask questions), Virginia had until to-day accepted with humility the doctrine that a natural curiosity about the universe is the beginning of infidelity. The chief object of her upbringing, which differed in no essential particular from that of every other well-born and well-bred Southern woman of her day, was to paralyze her reasoning faculties so completely that all danger of mental "unsettling" or even movement was eliminated from her future. To solidify the forces of mind into the inherited mould of fixed beliefs was, in the opinion of the age, to achieve the definite end of all education. When the child ceased to wonder before the veil of appearances, the battle of orthodoxy with speculation was over, and Miss Priscilla felt that she could rest on her victory. With Susan she had failed, because the daughter of Cyrus Treadwell was one of those inexplicable variations from ancestral stock over which the naturalists were still waging their merry war; but Virginia, with a line of earnest theologians and of saintly self-effacing women at her back, offered as little resistance as some exquisite plastic material in the teacher's hands.

Now, as if the same lightning flash which had illuminated the beribboned diploma in Miss Priscilla's mind had passed to Virginia also, the girl bit back a retort that was trembling on her lips. "I wonder if she can be getting to know things?" thought the older woman as she watched her, and she added half resentfully, "I've sometimes suspected that Gabriel Pendleton was almost too mild and easy going for a clergyman. If the Lord hadn't made him a saint, Heaven knows what would have become of him!"

"Don't try to put notions into Jinny's head, Susan," she

said after a thoughtful pause. "If Oliver were the right kind of young man, he'd give up this nonsense and settle down to some sober work. The first time I get a chance I'm going to tell him so."

"I don't believe it will be any use," responded Susan. "Father tried to reason with him last night, and they almost quarrelled."

"Quarrelled with Cyrus!" gasped the teacher.

"At one time I thought he'd walk out of the house and never come back," pursued Susan. "He told father that his sordid commercialism would end by destroying all that was charming in Dinwiddie. Afterward he apologized for his rudeness, but when he did so, he said, 'I meant every word of it.'"

"Well, I never!" was Miss Priscilla's feeble rejoinder. "The idea of his daring to talk that way when Cyrus had to pay his fare down from New York."

"Of course father brought it on," returned Susan judicially. "You know he doesn't like anybody to disagree with him, and when Oliver began to argue about its being unscrupulous to write history the way people wanted it, he lost his temper and said some angry things about the theatre and actors."

"I suppose a great man like your father may expect his family to bow to his opinions," replied the teacher, for so obscure was her mental connection between the construction of the future and the destruction of the past, that she could honestly admire Cyrus Treadwell for possessing the qualities her soul abhorred. The simple awe of financial success, which occupies in the American mind the vacant space of the monarchical cult, had begun already to generate the myth of greatness around Cyrus, and, like all other myths, this owed its origin less to the wilful conspiracy of the few than it did to the confiding superstition of the many.

"I hope Oliver won't do anything rash," said Susan, ignoring Miss Priscilla's tribute. "He is so impulsive and headstrong that I don't see how he can get on with father."

At this Virginia broke her quivering silence. "Can't you make him careful, Susan?" she asked, and without waiting for an answer, bent over and kissed Miss Priscilla on the cheek. "I must be going now or mother will worry," she added before she tripped ahead of Susan down the steps and along the palely shining path to the gate.

Rising from her chair, Miss Priscilla leaned over the railing of the porch, and gazed wistfully after the girls' vanishing figures.

" If there was ever a girl who looked as if she were cut out for happiness, it is Jinny Pendleton," she said aloud after a minute. A tear welled in her eye, and rolling over her cheek, dropped on her bosom. From some obscure corner of her memory, undevastated by war or by ruin, her own youth appeared to take the place of Virginia's. She saw herself, as she had seen the other an instant before, standing flushed and expectant before the untrodden road of the future. She heard again the wings of happiness rustling unseen about her, and she felt again the great hope which is the challenge that youth flings to destiny. Life rose before her, not as she had found it, but as she had once believed it to be. The days when little things had not filled her thoughts returned in the fugitive glow of her memory—for she, also, middle-aged, obese, cumbered with trivial cares, had had her dream of a love that would change and glorify the reality. The heritage of woman was hers as well as Virginia's. And for the first time, standing there, she grew dimly conscious of the portion of suffering which Nature had allotted to them both from the beginning. Was it all waiting—waiting, as it had been while battles were fought and armies were marching ? Did the future hold this for Virginia also ? Would life yield nothing more to that radiant girl than it had yielded to her or to the other women whom she had known ? Strange how the terrible innocence of youth had moved her placid middle-age as if it were sadness !

CHAPTER II

HER INHERITANCE

A BLOCK away, near the head of High Street, stood the old
church of Saint James, and at its back, separated by a white
paling fence from the squat pinkish tower and the solitary
grave in the churchyard (which was that of a Southern soldier
who had fallen in the Battle of Dinwiddie), was the oblong
wooden rectory in which Gabriel Pendleton had lived since he
had exchanged his sword for a prayer-book and his worn
Confederate uniform for a surplice. The church, which was
redeemed from architectural damnation by its sacred cruciform
and its low ivied buttresses, where innumerable sparrows
nested, cast its shadow, on clear days, over the beds of bleeding
hearts and lilies-of-the-valley in the neglected garden, to the
quaint old house, with its spreading wings, its outside chimneys,
and its sloping shingled roof, from which five dormer-windows
stared in a row over the slender columns of the porch. The
garden had been planned in the days when it was easy to put
a dozen slaves to uprooting weeds or trimming flower-beds,
and had passed in later years to the breathless ministrations
of negro infants, whose experience varied from the doubtful
innocence of the crawling age to the complete sophistication
of six or seven years. Dandelion and wire-grass rioted, in
spite of their earnest efforts, over the crooked path from the
porch, and periwinkle, once an intruder from the churchyard,
spread now in rank disorder down the terraced hill-side on the
left, where a steep flight of steps fell clear to the narrow cross-
street descending gradually into the crowded quarters of the
town. Directly in front of the porch on either side of the
path grew two giant paulownia-trees, royal at this season in a
mantle of violet blossoms, and it was under their arching
boughs that the girls stopped when they had entered the

20

garden. Ever since Virginia could remember, she had heard threats of cutting down the paulownias because of the litter the falling petals made in the spring, and ever since she could lisp at all she had begged her father to spare them for the sake of the enormous roots, into which she had loved to cuddle and hide.

"If I were ever to go away, I believe they would cut down these trees," she said now a little wistfully, but she was not thinking of the paulownias.

"Why should they when they give such splendid shade? And, besides, they wouldn't do anything you didn't like for worlds."

"Oh, of course they wouldn't, but as soon as I was out of sight they might persuade themselves that I liked it," answered Virginia, with a tender laugh. Though she was not by nature discerning, there were moments when she surprised Susan by her penetrating insight into the character of her parents, and this insight, which was emotional rather than intellectual, had enabled her to dominate them almost from infancy.

Silence fell between them, while they gazed through the veil of twilight at the marble shaft above the grave of the Confederate soldier. Then suddenly Susan spoke in a constrained voice, without turning her head.

"Jinny, Oliver isn't one bit of a hero—not the kind of here we used to talk about." It was with difficulty, urged by a vigorous and uncompromising conscience, that she had uttered the words.

"And besides," retorted Virginia merrily, "he is in love with Abby Goode."

"I don't believe that. They stayed in the same boarding-house once, and you know how Abby is about men."

"Yes, I know, and it's just the way men are about Abby."

"Well, Oliver isn't, I'm sure. I don't believe he's ever given her more than a thought, and he told me last night that he couldn't abide a bouncing woman."

"Does Abby bounce?"

"You know she does—dreadfully. But it wasn't because of Abby that I said what I did."

Something quivered softly between them, and a petal from

the Jacqueminot rose in Virginia's hair fluttered like a crimson moth out into the twilight. " Was it because of him, then ?" she asked in a whisper.

For a moment Susan did not answer. Her gaze was on the flight of steps, and drawing Virginia with her, she began to walk slowly toward the terraced side of the garden. An old lamp-lighter, carrying his ladder to a lamp-post at the corner, smiled up at them with his sunken toothless mouth as he went by.

" Partly, darling," said Susan. " He is so—I don't know how to make you understand—so unsettled. No, that isn't exactly what I mean."

Her fine, serious face showed clear and pale in the twilight. From the high forehead, under the girlish fringe of fair hair, to the thin, firm lips, which were too straight and colourless for beauty, it was the face of a woman who could feel strongly, but whose affections would never blur the definite forms or outlines of life. She looked out upon the world with level, dispassionate eyes in which there was none of Virginia's un-critical, emotional softness. Temperamentally she was un-compromisingly honest in her attitude toward the universe, which appeared to her, not as it did to Virginia, in mere form-less masses of colour out of which people and objects emerged like figures painted on air, but as distinct, impersonal, and final as a geometrical problem. She was one of those women who are called " sensible " by their acquaintances—meaning that they are born already disciplined and confirmed in the quieter and more orderly processes of life. Her natural in-telligence having overcome the defects of her education, she thought not vaguely, but with clearness and precision, and something of this clearness and precision was revealed in her manner and in her appearance, as if she had escaped at twenty years from the impulsive judgments and the troublous solici-tudes of youth. At forty, she would probably begin to grow young again, and at fifty, it is not unlikely that she would turn her back upon old age for ever. Just now she was too tre-mendously earnest about life, which she treated quite in the large manner, to take a serious interest in living.

" Promise me, Jinny, that you'll never let anybody take my place," she said, turning when they had reached the head of the steps.

" You silly Susan ! Why, of course, they shan't," replied Virginia, and they kissed ecstatically.

" Nobody will ever love you as I do."

" And I you, darling."

With arms interlaced they stood gazing down into the street, where the shadow of the old lamplighter glided like a ghost under the row of pale flickering lights. From a honeysuckle-trellis on the other side of the porch, a penetrating sweetness came in breaths, now rising, now dying away. In Virginia's heart, Love stirred suddenly, and blind, wingless, imprisoned, struggled for freedom.

" It is late, I must be going," said Susan. " I wish we lived nearer each other."

" Isn't it too dark for you to go alone ? John Henry will stop on his way from work, and he'll take you—if you really won't stay to supper."

" No, I don't mind in the least going by myself. It isn't night, anyway, and people are sitting out on their porches."

A minute afterwards they parted, Susan going swiftly down High Street, while Virginia went back along the path to the porch, and passing under the paulownias, stopped beside the honeysuckle-trellis, which extended to the ruined kitchen garden at the rear of the house. Once vegetables were grown here, but except for a square bed of mint which spread hardily beneath the back windows of the dining-room, the place was left now a prey to such barbarian invaders as burdock and moth mullein. On the brow of the hill, where the garden ended, there was a gnarled and twisted ailanthus-tree, and from its roots the ground fell sharply to a distant view of rear enclosures and grim smoking factories. Some clothes fluttered on a line that stretched from a bough of the tree, and turning away as if they offended her, Virginia closed her eyes and breathed in the sweetness of the honeysuckle, which mingled deliciously with the strange new sense of approaching happiness in her heart. The awakening of her imagination—an event more tumultuous in its effects than the mere awakening of emotion—had changed not only her inner life, but the ordinary details of the world in which she lived. Because a young man, who differed in no appreciable manner from dozens of other young men, had gazed into her eyes for an instant, the whole universe was altered. What had been until to-day a vague, wind-driven longing for happiness, the reaching out of the dream toward the reality, had assumed suddenly a fixed and definite purpose. Her bright girlish visions had wrapped themselves in a garment of flesh. A miracle more wonderful than any she had read of had occurred in the streets of Dinwiddie—in the very spot where she had walked, with blind eyes and deaf ears, every day since she could remember. Her soul blossomed in the twilight, as a flower blossoms, and shed its virginal sweetness. For the first time in her twenty years she felt that an unexplored region of happiness surrounded her. Life appeared so beautiful that she wanted to grasp and hold each fugitive sensation before it escaped her. "This is different from anything I've ever known. I never imagined it would be like this," she thought, and the next minute: "I wonder why no one has ever told me that it would happen? I wonder if it has ever really happened before, just like this, since the world began? Of all the ways I've dreamed of his coming, I never thought of this way—no, not for an instant. That I should see him first in the street like any stranger—that he should be Susan's cousin—that we should not have spoken a word before I knew it was he!" Everything about him, his smile, his clothes, the way he held his head and brushed his hair straight back from his forehead, his manner of reclining with a slight slouch on the seat of the cart, the picturesque blue dotted tie he wore, his hands, his way of bowing, the red-brown of his face, and above all the eager, impetuous look in his dark eyes—these things possessed a glowing quality of interest which irradiated a delicious excitement over the bare round of living. It was enough merely to be alive and conscious that some day—to-morrow, next week, or the next hour, perhaps—she might meet again the look that had caused this mixture of ecstasy and terror in her heart. The knowledge that he was in the same town with her, watching the same lights, thinking the same thoughts, breathing the same fragrance of honeysuckle—this knowledge was a fact of such tremendous importance that it dwarfed to insignificance all the proud historic past of Dinwiddie. Her imagination, seizing upon this bit of actuality, spun around it the iridescent gossamer web of her fancy. She felt that it was sufficient happiness just to stand motionless for hours and let this thought take possession of her. Nothing else mattered as long as this one thing was blissfully true.

Lights came out softly like stars in the houses beyond the church tower, and in the parlour of the rectory a lamp flared up and then burned dimly under a red shade. Looking through the low window, she could see the prim set of mahogany and horsehair furniture, with its deep, heavily carved sofa midway of the opposite wall and the twelve chairs which custom demanded arranged stiffly at equal distances on the faded Axminster carpet.

For a moment her gaze rested on the claw-footed mahogany table, bearing a family Bible and a photograph album bound in morocco ; on the engraving of the " Burial of Latane " between the long windows at the back of the room ; on the cloudy, gilt-framed mirror above the mantel, with the two standing candelabra reflected in its surface—and all these familiar objects appeared to her as vividly as if she had not lived with them from her infancy. A new light had fallen over them, and it seemed to her that this light released an inner meaning, a hidden soul, even in the claw-footed table and the threadbare Axminster carpet. Then the door into the hall opened and her mother entered, wearing the patched black silk dress which she had bought before the war and had turned and darned ever since with untiring fingers. Shrinking back into the dusk, Virginia watched the thin, slightly stooping figure as it stood arrested there in the subdued glow of the lamplight. She saw the pale oval face, so transparent that it was like the face of a ghost, the fine brown hair parted smoothly under the small net cap, the soft faded eyes in their hollowed and faintly bluish sockets, and the sweet, patient lips, with their expression of anxious sympathy, as of one who had lived not in her own joys and sorrows, but in those of others. Vaguely, the girl realized that her mother had had what is called " a hard life," but this knowledge brought no tremor of apprehension for herself, no shadow of disbelief in her own unquestionable right to happiness. A glorious certainty possessed her that her own life would be different from anything that had ever been in the past.

The front door opened and shut ; there was a step on the

soft grass under the honeysuckle-trellis, and her father came toward her, with his long black coat flapping about him. He always wore clothes several sizes too large for him under the impression that it was a point of economy and that they would last longer if there was no " strain" put upon them. He was a small, wiry man, with an amazing amount of strength for his build, and a keen, humorous face, ornamented by a pointed chin beard which he called his " goatee." His eyes were light grey with a twinkle which rarely left them except at the altar, and the skin of his cheeks had never lost the drawn and parchment-like look acquired during the last years of the war. One of the many martial Christians of the Confederacy, he had laid aside his surplice at the first call for troops to defend the borders, and had resumed it immediately after the surrender at Appomattox. It was still an open question in Dinwiddie whether Gabriel Pendleton, who was admitted to have been born a saint, had achieved greater distinction as a fighter or a clergyman ; though he himself had accepted the opposite vocations with equal humility. Only in the dead of sweltering summer nights did he sometimes arouse his wife with a groan and the halting words, " Lucy, I can't sleep for thinking of those men I killed in the war." But with the earliest breeze of dawn, his remorse usually left him, and he would rise and go about his parochial duties with the serene and childlike trust in Providence that had once carried him into battle. A militant idealism had ennobled his fighting as it now exalted his preaching. He had never in his life seen things as they are because he had seen them always by the white flame of a soul on fire with righteousness. To reach his mind, impressions of persons or objects had first to pass through a refining atmosphere in which all baser substances were eliminated, and no fact had ever penetrated this medium except in the flattering disguise of a sentiment. Having married at twenty an idealist only less ignorant of the world than himself, he had, inspired by her example, immediately directed his energies toward the whitewashing of the actuality. Both cherished the naïve conviction that to acknowledge an evil is in a manner to countenance its existence, and both clung fervently to the belief that a pretty sham has a more intimate relation to morality than has an ugly truth. Yet so unconscious were they of weaving this elaborate tissue of illusion around the world they inhabited that they called the mental process by which they distorted the reality "taking a true view of life." To "take a true view" was to believe what was pleasant against what was painful in spite of evidence: to grant honesty to all men (with the possible exception of the Yankee army and a few local scalawags known as Readjusters); to deny virtue to no woman, not even to the New England Abolitionist; to regard the period before the war in Virginia as attained perfection, and the present as falling short of that perfection only inasmuch as it had occurred since the surrender. As life in a small place, among a simple and guileless class of gentlefolk, all passionately cherishing the same opinions, had never shaken these illusions, it was but natural that they should have done their best to hand them down as sacred heirlooms to their only child. Even Gabriel's four years of hard fighting and scant rations were enkindled by so much of the disinterested idealism that had sent his State into the Confederacy, that he had emerged from them with an impoverished body, but an enriched spirit. Combined with his inherent inability to face the facts of life, there was an almost superhuman capacity for cheerful recovery from the shocks of adversity. Since he had married by accident the one woman who was made for him, he had managed to preserve untarnished his innocent assumption that marriages were arranged in Heaven—for the domestic infelicities of many of his parishioners were powerless to affect a belief that was founded upon a solitary personal experience. Unhappy marriages, like all other misfortunes of society, he was inclined to regard as entirely modern and due mainly to the decay of antebellum institutions. "I don't remember that I ever heard of a discontented servant or an unhappy marriage in my boyhood," he would say when he was forced against his will to consider either of these disturbing problems. Not progress, but a return to the "ideals of our ancestors," was his sole hope for the future; and in Virginia's childhood she had grown to regard this phrase as second in reverence only to that other familiar invocation: "If it be the will of God."

As he stood now in the square of lamplight that streamed

from the drawing-room window, she looked into his thin, humorous face, so spiritualized by poverty and self-sacrifice that it had become merely the veil for his soul, and the thought came to her that she had never really seen him as he was until to-day.

"You're out late, daughter. Isn't it time for supper?" he asked, putting his arm about her. Beneath the simple words she felt the profound affection which he rarely expressed, but of which she was conscious whenever he looked at her or spoke to her. Two days ago this affection, of which she never thought because it belonged to her by right like the air she breathed, had been sufficient to fill her life to overflowing; and now, in less than a moment, the simplest accident had pushed it into the background. In the place where it had been there was a restless longing which seemed at one instant a part of the universal stirring of the spring, and became the next an importunate desire for the coming of the lover to whom she had been taught to look as to the fulfilment of her womanhood. At times this lover appeared to have no connection with Oliver Treadwell, then the memory of his eager and searching look would flush the world with a magic enchantment. "He might pass here at any minute," she thought, and immediately every simple detail of her life was illuminated as if a quivering rosy light had fallen aslant it. His drive down High Street in the afternoon had left a trail of glory over the earthen roadbed.

"Yes, I was just going in," she replied to the rector's question, and added: "How sweet the honeysuckle smells! I never knew it to be so fragrant."

"The end of the trellis needs propping up. I noticed it this morning," he returned, keeping his arm around her as they passed over the short grassy walk and up the steps to the porch. Then the door of the rectory opened, and the silhouette of Mrs. Pendleton, in her threadbare black silk dress with her cameo-like profile softened by the dark bands of her hair, showed motionless against the lighted space of the hall.

"We're here, Lucy," said the rector, kissing her; and a minute later they entered the dining-room, which was on the right of the staircase. The old mahogany table, scarred by a century of service, was laid with a simple supper of bread, tea, and sliced ham on a willow dish. At one end there was a bowl of freshly gathered strawberries, with the dew still on them, and Mrs. Pendleton hastened to explain that they were a present from Tom Peachey, who had driven out into the country in order to get them. "Well, I hope his wife has some, also," commented the rector. "Tom's a good fellow, but he could never keep a closed fist, there's no use denying it."

Mrs. Pendleton, who had never denied anything in her life, except the Biblical sanction for the Thirteenth Amendment to the Constitution, shook her head gently and began to talk in the inattentive and anxious manner she had acquired at scantily furnished tables. Ever since the war, with the exception of the Reconstruction period, when she had lived practically on charity, she had managed to exist with serenity, and numerous negro dependents, on the rector's salary of a thousand dollars a year. Simple and wholesome food she had supplied to her family and her followers, and for their desserts, as she called the sweet things of life, she had relied with touching confidence upon her neighbours. What they would be for the day she did not know, but since poverty, not prosperity, breeds the generous heart, she was perfectly assured that when Miss Priscilla was putting up raspberries, or Mrs. Goode was making lemon pie, she should not be forgotten. During the terrible war years, it had become the custom of Dinwiddie housekeepers to remember the wife of the rector who had plucked off his surplice for the Confederacy, and among the older generation the habit still persisted, like all other links that bound them to a past which they cherished the more passionately because it guarded a defeated cause. Like the soft, apologetic murmur of Mrs. Pendleton's voice, which was meant to distract attention rather than to impart information, this impassioned memory of the thing that was dead sweetened the less romantic fact of the things that were living. The young were ignorant of it, but the old *knew*. Mrs. Pendleton, who was born a great lady, remained one when the props and the background of a great lady had crumbled around her; and though the part she filled was a narrow part—a mere niche in the world's history—she filled it superbly. From the dignity of possessions she had passed to the finer dignity of a poverty that can do without. All the intellect in her (for she was not clever) had been transmuted into character by this fiery passage from romance into reality, and though life had done its worst with her, some fine invincible blade in the depths of her being she had never surrendered. She would have gone to the stake for a principle as cheerfully as she had descended from her aristocratic niche into unceasing poverty and self-denial, but she would have gone wearing garlands on her head and with her faint, grave smile, in which there was almost every quality except that of humour, touching her lips. Her hands, which were once lovely, were now knotted and worn ; for she had toiled when it was necessary, though she had toiled always with the manner of a lady. Even to-day it was a part of her triumph that this dignity was so vital a factor in her life that there was none of her husband's laughter at circumstances to lighten her burden. To her the daily struggle of keeping an open house on starvation fare was not a pathetic comedy, as with Gabriel, but a desperately smiling tragedy. What to Gabriel had been merely the discomfort of being poor when everybody you respected was poor with you, had been to his wife the slow agony of crucifixion. It was she, not he, who had lain awake to wonder where to-morrow's dinner could be got without begging ; it was she, also, who had feared to doze at dawn lest she should oversleep herself and not be downstairs in time to scrub the floors and the furniture before the neighbours were stirring. Uncle Isam, whose knees were crippled with rheumatism, and Docia, who had a " stitch " in her side whenever she stooped, were the only servants that remained with her, and the nursing of these was usually added to the pitiless drudgery of her winter. But the bitter edge to all her suffering was the feeling which her husband spoke of in the pulpit as "false pride "— the feeling she prayed over fervently yet without avail in church every Sunday—and this was the ignoble terror of being seen on her knees in her old black calico dress before she had gone upstairs again, washed her hands with cornmeal, powdered her face with her pink flannel starchbag, and descended in her breakfast gown of black cashmere or lawn, with a net scarf tied daintily around her thin throat, and a pair of exquisitely darned lace ruffles hiding her wrists.

As she sat now, smiling and calm, at the head of her table,

there was no hint in her face of the gnawing anxiety behind the delicate blue-veined hollows in her forehead. " I thought John Henry would come to supper," she observed, while her hands worked lovingly among the old white and gold teacups which had belonged to her mother, " so I gathered a few flowers."

In the centre of the table there was a handful of garden flowers arranged, with a generous disregard of colour, in a cut-glass bowl, as though all blossoms were intended by their Creator to go peaceably together. Only on formal occasions was such a decoration used on the table of the rectory, since the happiest adornment for a meal was supposed to be a bountiful supply of visible viands ; but the hopelessly mended mats had pierced Mrs. Pendleton's heart, and the cut-glass bowl, like her endless prattle, was but a pitiful subterfuge.

" Oh, I like them !" Virginia had started to answer, when a hearty voice called, " May I come in ?" from the darkness, and a large, carelessly dressed young man, with an amiable and rather heavy countenance, entered the hall and passed on into the dining-room. In reply to Mrs. Pendleton's offer of tea, he answered that he had stopped at the Treadwells' on his way up from work. " I could hardly break away from Oliver," he added ; " but I remembered that I'd promised Aunt Lucy to take her down to Tin Pot Alley after supper, so I made a bolt while he was convincing me that it's better to be poor with an idea, as he calls it, than rich without one." Then turning to Virginia, he asked suddenly : " What's the matter, little cousin ? Been about too much in the sun ?"

" Oh, it's only the rose in my hair," responded Virginia, and she felt that there was a fierce joy in blushing like this even while she told herself that she would give everything she possessed if she could only stop it.

" If you aren't well, you'd better not go with us, Jinny," said Mrs. Pendleton. " It was so sweet of John Henry to remember that I'd promised to take Aunt Ailsey some of the bitters we used to make before the war." Everything was " so sweet " to her, the weather, her husband's sermons, the little trays that came continually from her neighbours, and she lived in a perpetual state of thankfulness for favours so insignificant that a less impressionable soul would have

accepted them as undeserving of more than the barest acknow-
ledgment.

" I am perfectly well," insisted Virginia, a little angry with
John Henry because he had been the first to notice her blushes.

Rising hurriedly from the table, she went to the door and
stood looking out into the spangled dusk under the paulownias,
while her mother wrapped the bottle in a piece of white tissue
paper and remarked with an animation which served to hide
her fatigue from the unobservant eyes of her husband, that a
walk would do her good on such a " perfectly lovely night."

Gabriel, who loved her as much as a man can love a wife
who has sacrificed herself to him wisely and unwisely for
nearly thirty years, had grown so used to seeing her suffer
with a smile that he had drifted at last into the belief that it
was the only form of activity she really enjoyed. From the
day of his marriage he had never been able to deny her anything she had set her heart upon—not even the privilege of
working herself to death for his sake when the opportunity
offered.

" Well, well, if you feel like it, of course you must go, my
dear," he replied. " I'll step over and sit a minute with Miss
Priscilla while you are away. Never could bear the house
without you, Lucy."

While this protest was still on his lips, he followed her from
the house, and turned with Virginia and John Henry in the
direction of the Young Ladies' Academy. From the darkness
beyond the iron gate there came the soothing flow of Miss
Priscilla's voice entertaining an evening caller, and when the
rector left them, as if irresistibly drawn toward the honeyed
sound of gossip, Virginia walked on in silence between John
Henry and her mother. At each corner a flickering street
lamp burned with a thin yellow flame, and in the midst of the
narrow orbit of its light, several shining moths circled swiftly
like white moons revolving about a sun. In the centre of the
blocks, where the darkness was broken only by small flower-
like flakes of light that fell in clusters through boughs of
mulberry or linden trees, there was the sound of whispering
voices and of rustling palm-leaf fans on the crowded porches
behind screens of roses or honeysuckle. Mrs. Pendleton,
whose instinct prompted her to efface herself whenever she

made a third at the meeting of maid and man (even though the man was only her nephew John Henry), began to talk at last after waiting modestly for her daughter to begin the conversation. The story of Aunt Ailsey, of her great age, and her dictatorial temper, which made living with other servants impossible to her, started valiantly on its familiar road, and tripped but little when the poor lady realized that neither John Henry nor Virginia was listening. She was so used to talking for the sake of the sound she made, rather than the impression she produced, that her silvery ripple had become almost as lacking in self-consciousness as the song of a canary.

But Virginia, walking so quietly at her side, was inhabiting at the moment a separate universe—a universe smelling of honeysuckle and filled with starry pathways to happiness. In this universe, Aunt Ailsey and her peculiarities, her mother's innocent prattle, and the solid body of John Henry touching her arm, were all as remote and trivial as the night moths circling around the lamps. Looking at John Henry from under her lowered lashes, she felt a sudden pity for him because he was so far—so very far indeed from being the right man. She saw him too clearly as he was—he stood before her in all the hard brightness of the reality, and first love, like beauty, depends less upon the truth of an outline than it does upon the softening quality of an atmosphere. There was no mystery for her in the simple fact of his being. There was nothing left to discover about his great stature, his excellent heart, and his safe, slow mind that had been compelled to forgo even the sort of education she had derived from Miss Priscilla. She knew that he had left school at the age of eight in order to become the support of a widowed mother, and she was pitifully aware of the tireless efforts he had made after reaching manhood to remedy his ignorance of the elementary studies he had missed. Never had she heard a complaint from him, never a regret for the sacrifice, never so much as an idle wonder why it should have been necessary. If the texture of his soul was not finely wrought, the proportions of it were heroic. In him the Pendleton idealism had left the skies and been transmuted into the common substance of clay. He was of a practical bent of mind and had developed a talent for his branch of business, which, to the bitter humiliation of his mother, was that of hardware, with a successful speciality in bath-tubs. Until to-day, Virginia had always believed that John Henry interested her, but now she wondered how she had ever spent so many hours listening to his talk about business. And with the thought her whole existence appeared to her as dull and commonplace as those hours. A single instant of experience seemed longer to her than all the years she had lived, and this instant had drained the colour and the sweetness from the rest of life. The shape of her universe had trembled suddenly and altered. Dimly she was beginning to realize that sensation, not time, is the true measure of life. Nothing and everything had happened to her since yesterday.

As they turned into Short Market Street, Mrs. Pendleton's voice trailed off at last into silence, and she did not speak again while they passed hurriedly between the crumbling houses and the dilapidated shops which rose darkly on either side of the narrow cinder-strewn walks. The scent of honeysuckle did not reach here, and when they stopped presently at the beginning of Tin Pot Alley, there floated out to them the sharp acrid odour of huddled negroes. In these squalid alleys, where the lamps burned at longer distances, the more primitive forms of life appeared to swarm like distorted images under the transparent civilization of the town. The sound of banjo strumming came faintly from the dimness beyond, while at their feet the Problem of the South sprawled innocently amid tomato cans and rotting cabbage leaves.

"Wait here just a minute and I'll run up and speak to Aunt Ailsey," remarked Mrs. Pendleton with the dignity of a soul that is superior to smells; and without noticing her daughter's reproachful nod of acquiescence, she entered the alley and disappeared through the doorway of the nearest hovel. A minute later her serene face looked down at them over a patchwork quilt which hung airing at half-length from the window above. "But this is not life—it has nothing to do with life," thought Virginia, while the Pendleton blood in her rose in a fierce rebellion against all that was ugly and sordid in existence. Then her mother's tread was heard descending the short flight of steps, and the sensation vanished as quickly and as inexplicably as it had come.

"I tried not to keep you waiting, dear," said Mrs. Pendleton, hastening toward them while she fanned herself rapidly with the small black fan she carried. Her face looked tired and worn, and before moving on, she paused a moment and held her hand to her thin fluttering breast, while deep bluish circles appeared to start out under the expression of pathetic cheerfulness in her eyes. This pathetic cheerfulness, so characteristic of the women of her generation, was the first thing, perhaps, that a stranger would have noticed about her face; yet it was a trait which neither her husband nor her child had ever observed. There was a fine moisture on her forehead, and this added so greatly to the natural transparency of her features that, standing there in the wan light, she might have been mistaken for the phantom of her daughter's vivid flesh and blood beauty. "I wonder if you would mind going on to Bolingbroke Street, so I may speak to Belinda Treadwell a minute?" she asked, as soon as she had recovered her breath. "I want to find out if she has engaged Miss Willy Whitlow for the whole week, or if there is any use my sending a message to her over in Botetourt. If she doesn't begin at once, Jinny, you won't have a dress to wear to Abby Goode's party."

Virginia's heart gave a single bound of joy and lay quiet. Not for worlds would she have asked to go to the Treadwells', yet ever since they had started, she had longed unceasingly to have her mother suggest it. The very stars, she felt, had worked together to bring about her desire.

"But aren't you tired, mother? It really doesn't matter about my dress," she murmured; for it was not in vain that she had wrested a diploma for deportment from Miss Priscilla.

"Why can't I take the message for you, Aunt Lucy? You look tired to death," urged John Henry.

"Oh, I shan't mind the walk as soon as we get out into the breeze," replied Mrs. Pendleton. "It's a lovely night, only a little close in this alley." And as she spoke she looked gently down on the Problem of the South as the Southern women had looked down on it for generations, and would continue to look down on it for generations still to come—without seeing that it was a problem.

"Well, it's good to get a breath of air, anyway!" exclaimed John Henry with fervour, when they had passed out of the alley into the lighted street. Around them the town seemed to beat with a single heart, as if it waited, like Virginia, in breathless suspense for some secret that must come out of the darkness. Sometimes the sidewalks over which they passed were of flagstones, sometimes they were of gravel or of strewn cinders. Now and then an old stone house, which had once sheltered crinoline and lace ruffles, or had served as a trading station with the Indians before Dinwiddie had become a city, would loom between two small shops where the owners, coatless and covered with sweat, were selling flat beer to jaded and miserable customers. Up Bolingbroke Street a faint breeze blew, lifting the moist satin-like hair on Mrs. Pendleton's forehead. Already its ancient dignity had deserted the quarter in which the Treadwells lived, and it had begun to wear a forsaken and injured look, as though it resented the degradation of commerce into which it had descended.

"I can't understand why Cyrus Treadwell doesn't move over to Sycamore Street," remarked John Henry after a moment of reflection in which he had appeared to weigh this simple sentence with scrupulous exactness. "He's rich enough, I suppose, to buy anything he wants."

"I've heard Susan say that it was her mother's old home and she didn't care to leave it," said Mrs. Pendleton.

"I don't believe it's that a bit," broke in Virginia with characteristic impulsiveness. "The only reason is that Mr. Treadwell is stingy. With all his money, I know Mrs. Treadwell and Susan hardly ever have a dollar they can spend on themselves."

Though she spoke with her accustomed energy, she was conscious all the time that the words she uttered were not the ones in her thoughts. What did Cyrus Treadwell's stinginess matter when his only relation to life consisted in his being the uncle of Oliver ? It was as if a single shape moved alive through a universe peopled with shadows. Only a borrowed radiance attached itself now to the persons and objects that had illumined the world for her yesterday. Yet she approached the crisis of her life so silently that those around her did not recognize it beneath the cover of ordinary circumstances. Like most great moments, it had come unheralded ; and though the rustling of its wings filled her soul, neither her mother nor John Henry heard a stir in the quiet air that surrounded them. Walking between the two who loved her, she felt that she was separated from them both by an eternity of experience.

There were several blocks of Bolingbroke Street to walk before the Treadwells' house was reached, and as they sauntered slowly past decayed dwellings, Virginia's imagination ran joyously ahead of her to the meeting. Would it happen this time as it had happened before when he looked at her that something would pass between them which would make her feel that she belonged to him ? So little resistance did she offer to the purpose of Life that she seemed to have existed from the beginning merely as an exquisite medium for a single emotion. It was as if the dreams of all the dead women of her race, who had lived only in loving, were concentrated into a single shining centre of bliss—for the accumulated vibrations of centuries were in her soul when she trembled for the first time beneath the eyes of a lover. And yet all this blissful violence was powerless to change the most insignificant external fact in the universe. Though it was the greatest thing that could ever happen to her, it was nothing to the other twenty-one thousand human beings among whom she lived ; it left no mark upon that procession of unimportant details which they called life.

They were in sight of the small old-fashioned brick house of the Treadwells, with its narrow windows set discreetly between outside shutters, and she saw that the little marble porch was deserted except for the two pink oleander-trees, which stood in green tubs on either side of the curved iron railings. A minute later John Henry's imperative ring brought a young coloured maid to the door, and Virginia, who had lingered on the pavement, heard almost immediately an effusive duet from her mother and Mrs. Treadwell.

" Oh, do come in, Lucy, just for a minute !"

" I can't possibly, my dear ; I only wanted to ask you if you have engaged Miss Willy Whitlow for the entire week or if you could let me have her for Friday and Saturday ? inny hasn't a rag to wear to Abby Goode's lawn party, and I don't know anybody who does quite so well for her as poor Miss Willy. Oh, that's so sweet of you ! I can't thank you enough! And you'll tell her without my sending all the way over to Botetourt!"

By this time Susan had joined Virginia on the sidewalk, and the liquid honey of Mrs. Pendleton's voice dropped softly into indistinctness.

"Oh, Jinny, if I'd only known you were coming!" said Susan. "Oliver wanted me to take him to see you, and when I couldn't, he went over to call on Abby."

So this was the end of her walk winged with expectancy! A disappointment as sharp as her joy had been pierced her through as she stood there smiling into Susan's discomfited face. With the tragic power of youth to create its own torment, she told herself that life could never be the same after this first taste of its bitterness.

CHAPTER III

FIRST LOVE

THE next morning, so indestructible is the happiness of youth, she awoke with her hope as fresh as if it had not been blighted the evening before. As she lay in bed, with her loosened hair making a cloud over the pillows, and her eyes shining like blue flowers in the band of sunlight that fell through the dormer-window, she quivered to the early sweetness of honeysuckle as though it were the charmed sweetness of love of which she had dreamed in the night. She was only one of the many millions of women who were awaking at the same hour to the same miracle of Nature, yet she might have been the first woman seeking the first man through the vastness and the mystery of an uninhabited earth. Impossible to believe that an experience so wonderful was as common as the bursting of the spring buds or the humming of the thirsty bees around the honeysuckle arbour !

Slipping out of bed, she threw her dressing-gown over her shoulders, and kneeling beside the window, drank in the flower-scented air of the May morning. During the night, the paulownia-trees had shed a rain of violet blossoms over the wet grass, where little wings of sunshine, like golden moths, hovered above them. Beyond the border of lilies-of-the-valley she saw the squat pinkish tower of the church, and beneath it, in the narrow churchyard, rose the gleaming shaft above the grave of the Confederate soldier. On her right, in the centre of the crooked path, three negro infants were prodding earnestly at roots of wire-grass and dandelion ; and brushing carelessly their huddled figures, her gaze descended the twelve steps of the almost obliterated terrace, and followed the steep street down which a mulatto vegetable vendor was urging his slow-footed mule.

A wave of joy rose in her breast, and she felt that her heart melted in gratitude for the Divine beauty of life. The world showed to her as a place filled with shining vistas of happiness, and at the end of each of these vistas there awaited the unknown enchanting thing which she called in her thoughts "the future." The fact that it was the same world in which Miss Priscilla and her mother lived their narrow and prosaic lives did not alter by a breath her unshakable conviction that she herself was predestined for something more wonderful than they had ever dreamed of. "He may come this evening!" she thought, and immediately the light of magic suffused the room, the street outside, and every scarred roof in Dinwiddie.

At the head of her bed, wedged in between the candle-stand and the window, there was a cheap little bookcase of walnut which contained the only volumes she had ever been permitted to own—the poems of Mrs. Hemans and of Adelaide Anne Procter, a carefully expurgated edition of Shakespeare, with an inscription in the rector's handwriting on the flyleaf ; Miss Strickland's "Lives of the Queens of England" ; and several works of fiction belonging to the class which Mrs. Pendleton vaguely characterized as "sweet stories." Among the more prominent of these were "Thaddeus of Warsaw," a complete set of Miss Yonge's novels, with a conspicuously tear-stained volume of "The Heir of Redclyffe," and a romance or two by obscure but innocuous authors. That any book, which told, however mildly, the truth about life should have entered their daughter's bedroom would have seemed little short of profanation to both the rector and Mrs. Pendleton. The sacred shelves of that bookcase (which had been ceremoniously presented to her on her fourteenth birthday) had never suffered the contaminating presence of realism. The solitary purpose of art was, in Mrs. Pendleton's eyes, to be "sweet," and she scrupulously judged all literature by its success or failure in this particular quality. It seemed to her as wholesome to feed her daughter's growing fancy on an imaginary line of pious heroes, as it appeared to her moral to screen her from all suspicion of the existence of immorality. She did not honestly believe that any living man resembled the Heir of Redclyffe, any more than she believed that the path of self-sacrifice leads inevitably to happiness; but there was no doubt in her mind that she advanced the cause of righteousness when she taught these sanctified fallacies to Virginia.

As she rose from her knees, Virginia glanced at her white dress, which was too crumpled for her to wear again before it was smoothed, and thought regretfully of Aunt Docia's heart, which invariably gave warning whenever there was extra work to be done. "I shall have to wear either my blue lawn or my green organdie this evening," she thought. "I wish I could have the sleeves changed. I wonder if mother could run a tuck in them?"

It did not occur to her that she might smooth the dress herself, because she knew that the iron would be wrested from her by her mother's hands, which were so knotted and worn that tears came to Virginia's eyes when she looked at them. She let her mother slave over her because she had been born into a world where the slaving of mothers was a part of the natural order, and she had not as yet become independent enough to question the morality of the commonplace. At any minute she would gladly have worked, too, but the phrase "Spare Virginia" had been uttered so often in her hearing that it had acquired at last almost a religious significance. To have been forced to train her daughter in any profitable occupation which might have lifted her out of the class of unskilled labour in which indigent gentlewomen by right belonged, would have been the final dregs of humiliation in Mrs. Pendleton's cup. On one of Aunt Docia's bad days, when Jinny had begged to be allowed to do part of the washing, she had met an almost passionate refusal from her mother. "It will be time enough to spoil your hands after you are married, darling!" And again, "Don't do that rough sewing, Jinny. Give it to me." From the cradle she had borne her part in this racial custom of the sacrifice of generation to generation—of the perpetual immolation of age on the flowery altars of youth. Like most customs in which we are nurtured, it had seemed natural and pleasant enough until she had watched the hollows deepen in her mother's temples and the tireless knotted hands stumble at their work. Then a pang had seized her and she had pleaded earnestly to be permitted to help.

"If you only knew how unhappy it makes me to see you ruining your pretty fingers, Jinny. My child, the one comfort I have is the thought that I am sparing you."

Sparing her! Always that from the first! Even Gabriel chimed in when it became a matter of Jinny. "Let me wash the dishes, Lucy," he would implore. "What? Will you trust me with other people's souls, but not with your china?"

"It's not a man's work, Mr. Pendleton. What would the neighbours think?"

"They would think, I hope, my dear, that I was doing my duty."

"But it would not be dignified for a clergyman. No, I cannot bear the sight of you with a dishcloth."

In the end she invariably had her way with them, for she was the strongest. Jinny must be spared, and Gabriel must do nothing undignified. About herself it made no difference unless the neighbours were looking; she had not thought of herself, except in the indomitable failing of her "false pride," since her marriage, which had taken place in her twentieth year. A clergyman's wife might do menial tasks in secret, and nobody minded, but they were not for a clergyman.

For a minute, while she was dressing, Virginia thought of these things—of how hard life had been to her mother, of how pretty she must have been in her youth. What she did not think of was that her mother, like herself, was but one of the endless procession of women who pass perpetually from the sphere of pleasure into the sphere of service. It was as impossible for her to picture her mother as a girl of twenty as it was for her to imagine herself ever becoming a woman of fifty.

When she had finished dressing she closed the door softly after her as if she were afraid of disturbing the silence, and ran downstairs to the dining-room, where the rector and Mrs. Pendleton greeted her with subdued murmurs of joy.

"I was afraid I'd miss you, daughter," from the rector, as he drew her chair nearer.

"I was just going to carry up your tray, Jinny," from her mother. "I kept a nice breast of chicken for you which one of the neighbours sent me."

"I'd so much rather you'd eat it, mother," protested Jinny, on the point of tears.

"But I couldn't, darling, I really couldn't manage it. A cup of coffee and a bit of toast is all I can possibly stand in the morning. I was up early, for Docia was threatened with one of her heart attacks, and it always gives me a little headache to miss my morning nap."

"Then you can't go to market, Lucy; it is out of the question," insisted the rector. "After thirty years you might as well make up your mind to trust me, my dear."

"But the last time you went you gave away our shoulder of lamb to a beggar," replied his wife, and she hastened to add tenderly, lest he should accept the remark as a reproof, "it's sweet of you, dearest, but a little walk will be good for my head if I am careful to keep on the shady side of the street. I can easily find a boy to bring home the things, and I am sure it won't hurt me a bit."

"Why can't I go, mother?" implored Virginia. "Susan always markets for Mrs. Treadwell." And she felt that even the task of marketing was irradiated by this inner glow which had changed the common aspect of life.

"Oh, Jinny, you know how you hate to feel the chickens, and one can never tell how plump they are by the feathers."

"Well, I'll feel them, mother, if you'll let me try."

"No, darling, but you may go with me and carry my sunshade. I'm so sorry Docia can't smooth your dress. Was it much crumpled?"

"Oh, dreadfully! And I did so want to wear it this evening. Do you think Aunt Docia could show me how to iron?"

Docia, who stood like an ebony image of Bellona behind her mistress's chair, waving a variegated tissue-paper fy-screen over the coffee-urn, was heard to think aloud that "dish yer stitch ain' helt up er blessed minute sence befo' daylight." Not unnaturally, perhaps, since she was the most prominent figure in her own vision of the universe, she had come at last to regard her recurrent "stitch" as an event of greater consequence than Virginia's appearance in immaculate white muslin. An uncertain heart combined with a certain temper had elevated her from a servile position to one of absolute autocracy in the household. Everybody feared her, so nobody had ever dared ask her to leave. As she had rebelled long ago against the badge of a cap and an apron, she appeared in the dining-room clad in garments of various hues, and her dress on this particular morning was a purple calico crowned majestically by a pink cotton turban. There was a tradition still afloat that Docia had been an excellent servant before the war; but this amiable superstition had, perhaps, as much reason to support it as had Gabriel's innocent conviction that there were no faithless husbands when there were no divorces.

"I'm afraid Docia can't do it," sighed Mrs. Pendleton, for her ears had caught the faint thunder of the war goddess behind her chair, and her soul, which feared neither armies nor adversities, trembled before her former slaves. "But it won't take me a minute if you'll have it ready right after dinner."

"Oh, mother, of course I couldn't let you for anything. I only thought Aunt Docia might be able to teach me how to iron."

At this Docia muttered audibly that she "ain' got no time ter be sho'in' nobody nuttin'."

"There, now, Docia, you mustn't lose your temper," observed Gabriel as he rose from his chair. It was at such moments that the remembered joys of slavery left a bitter after-taste on his lips. Clearly it was impossible to turn into the streets a servant who had once belonged to you!

When they were in the hall together, Mrs. Pendleton whispered nervously to her husband that it must be "poor Docia's heart that made her so disagreeable and that she would feel better to-morrow."

"Wouldn't it be possible, my dear?" inquired the rector in his pulpit manner, to which his wife's only answer was a startled "Sh-sh-ush."

An hour later the door of Gabriel's study opened softly, and Mrs. Pendleton entered with the humble and apologetic manner in which she always intruded upon her husband's pursuits. There was an accepted theory in the family, shared even by Uncle Isam and Aunt Docia, that whenever Gabriel was left alone for an instant, his thoughts naturally deflected into spiritual paths. In the early days of his marriage he had tried honestly to live up to this exalted idea of his character; then finding the effort beyond him, and being a man with an innate detestation of hypocrisy, he had earnestly endeavoured to disabuse his wife's imagination of the mistaken belief in his divinity. But a notion once firmly fixed in Mrs. Pendleton's mind might as well have been embedded in rock. By virtue of that gentle obstinacy which enabled her to believe in an illusion the more intensely because it had vanished, she had triumphed not only over circumstances, but over truth itself. By virtue of this quality, she had created the world in which she moved, and had wrought beauty out of chaos.

"Are you busy with your sermon, dear?" she asked, pausing in the doorway, and gazing reverently at her husband over the small black silk bag she carried. Like the other women of Dinwiddie who had lost relatives by the war, she had never laid aside her mourning since the surrender; and the frame of crape to her face gave her the pensive look of one who has stepped out of the pageant of life into the sacred shadows of memory.

"No, no, Lucy, I'm ready to start out with you," replied the rector apologetically, putting a box of fishing tackle he had been sorting back into the drawer of his desk. He was as fond as a child of a day's sport, and never quite so happy as when he set out with his rod and an old tomato can filled with worms, which he had dug out of the back garden, in his hands; but owing to the many calls upon him and his wife's conception of his clerical dignity, he was seldom able to gratify his natural tastes.

"Oh, father, please hurry!" called Virginia from the porch, and, rising obediently, he followed Mrs. Pendleton through the hall and out into the May sunshine, where the little negroes stopped an excited chase of a black-and-orange butterfly to return doggedly to their weeding.

"Are you sure you wouldn't rather I'd go to market, Lucy?"

"Quite sure, dear," replied his wife, sniffing the scent of lilies-of-the-valley with her delicate, slightly pinched nostrils. "I thought you were going to see Mr. Treadwell about putting John Henry into the bank," she added. "It is such a pity to keep the poor boy selling bath-tubs. His mother felt it so terribly."

"Ah, so I was—so I was," reflected Gabriel, who, though both of them would have been indignant at the suggestion, was

as putty in the hands of his wife. " Well, I'll look into the
bank on Cyrus after I've paid my sick calls."

With that they parted, Gabriel going on to visit a bed-
ridden widow in the Old Ladies' Home, while Mrs. Pendleton
and Virginia turned down a cross street that led toward the
market. At every corner, it seemed to Virginia, middle-aged
ladies, stout or thin, wearing crape veils and holding small
black silk bags in their hands, sprang out of the shadows of
mulberry - trees, and barred their leisurely progress. And
though nothing had happened in Dinwiddie since the war, and
Mrs. Pendleton had seen many of these ladies the day before,
she stopped for a sympathetic chat with each one of them,
while Virginia, standing a little apart, patiently prodded the
cinders of the walk with the end of her sunshade. All her life
the girl had been taught to regard time as the thing of least
importance in the universe ; but occasionally, while she
listened in silence to the liquid murmur of her mother's voice,
she wondered vaguely how the day's work was ever finished
in Dinwiddie. The story of Docia's impertinence was told
and retold a dozen times before they reached the market.
" And you really mean that you can't get rid of her ?   Why,
my dear Lucy, I wouldn't stand it a day !   Now, there was
my Mandy.   Such an excellent servant until she got her head
turned——"   This from Mrs. Tom Peachey, an energetic
little woman, with a rosy face and a straight grey " bang " cut
short over her eyebrows.   " But, Lucy, my child, are you
doing right to submit to impertinence ?   In the old days, I
remember, before the war——"   This from Mrs. William
Goode, who had been Sally Peterson, the beauty of Dinwiddie,
and who was still superbly handsome in a tragic fashion, with
a haunted look in her eyes and masses of snow-white hair under
her mourning bonnet.   Years ago Virginia had imagined her
as dwelling perpetually with the memory of her young husband,
who had fallen in his twenty-fifth year in the Battle of Cold
Harbour, but she knew now that the haunted eyes, like all
things human, were under the despotism of trifles.   To the
girl, who saw in this universal acquiescence in littleness
merely the pitiful surrender of feeble souls, there was a
passionate triumph in the thought that her own dreams
were larger than the actuality that surrounded her.   Youth's

scorn of the narrow details of life left no room in her mind for
an understanding of the compromise which middle-age makes
with necessity. The pathos of resignation—of that inevitable
submission to the petty powers which the years bring—was
lost upon the wistful ignorance of inexperience. While she
waited dutifully, with her absent gaze fixed on the old mulberry-trees, which whitened as the wind blew over them and
then slowly darkened again, she wondered if servants and
gossip were the only things that Oliver had heard of in his
travels ? Then she remembered that even in Dinwiddie men
were less interested in such matters than they were in the
industries of peanuts and tobacco. Was it only women, after
all, who were in subjection to particulars ?

When they turned into Old Street, John Henry hailed
them from the doorway of a shop, where he stood flanked by
a row of spotless bath-tubs. He wore a loose pongee coat,
which sagged at the shoulders, his straight flaxen hair had
been freshly cut, and his crimson necktie had got a stain on it
at breakfast; but to Virginia's astonishment, he appeared
sublimely unconscious both of his bath-tubs and his appearance.
He was doubtless under the delusion that a pongee coat, being
worn for comfort, was entirely successful when it achieved that
end ; and as for his business, it was beyond his comprehension
that a Pendleton could have reason to blush for a bath-tub
or for any other object that afforded him an honest livelihood.

He called to them at sight, and Mrs. Pendleton, following
her instinct of fitness, left the conversation to youth.

" John Henry, father is going to see Mr. Treadwell about the
place in the bank. Won't it be lovely if he gives it to you !"

" He won't," replied John Henry. " I'll bet you anything
he's keeping it for his nephew."

Virginia's blush came quickly, and turning her head away,
she gazed earnestly down the street to the octagonal market,
which stood on the spot where slaves were offered for sale
when she was born.

" Mr. Treadwell is crossing the street now," she said, after
a minute. " I wonder why he keeps his mouth shut so tight
when he is alone ?"

A covered cart, which had been passing slowly, moved up
the hill, and from beyond it there appeared the tall spare

figure of a man with iron-grey hair, curling a little on the temples, a sallow skin, splotched with red over the nose, and narrow colourless lips that looked as if they were cut out of steel. As he walked quickly up the street, every person whom he passed turned to glance after him.

"I wonder if it is true that he hasn't made his money honestly?" asked Virginia.

"Oh, I hope not!" exclaimed Mrs. Pendleton, who in her natural desire to believe only good about people was occasionally led into believing the truth.

"Well, I don't care," retorted Virginia, "he's mean. I know just by the way his wife dresses."

"Oh, Jinny!" gasped Mrs. Pendleton, and glanced in embarrassment at her nephew, whose face, to her surprise, was beaming with enjoyment. The truth was that John Henry, who would have condemned so unreasonable an accusation had it been uttered by a full-grown male, was enraptured by the piquancy of hearing it on the lovely lips of his cousin. To demand that a pretty woman should possess the mental responsibility of a human being would have seemed an affront to his inherited ideas of gallantry. His slow wit was enslaved by Jinny's audacity as completely as his kind, ox-like eyes were enthralled by the young red and white of her beauty.

"But he's a great man. You can't deny that," he said with the playful manner in which he might have prodded a kitten in order to make it claw.

"A great man! Just because he has made money!"

"Well, he couldn't have got rich, you know, if he hadn't had the sense to see how to do it," replied the young man with enthusiasm. Like most Southerners who had been forced without preparation into the hard school of industry, he had found that his standards followed inevitably the changing measure of his circumstances. From his altered point of view, the part of owning property appeared so easy, and the part of winning it so difficult, that his respect for culture had yielded almost unconsciously to his admiration for commerce. When the South came again to the front, he felt instinctively that it would come, shorn of its traditional plumage, a victor from the hard-fought industrial battlefields of the century; and because Cyrus Treadwell led the way toward this triumph, he was ready to follow him. Of the whole town, this grim, half-legendary figure (passionately revered and as passionately hated) appeared to him to stand alone not for the decaying past, but for the growing future. The stories of the too rapid development of the Treadwell fortune he cast scornfully aside as the malicious slanders of failure. What did all this tittle-tattle about a great man prove anyhow except his greatness ? Suppose he *had* used his railroad to make a fortune—well, but for him where would the Dinwiddle and Central be to-day if not in the junk shop ? Where would the lumber market be ? the cotton market ? the tobacco market ? For around Cyrus, standing alone and solitary on his height, there had gathered the great illusion that makes theft honest and falsehood truth—the illusion of Success ; and simple John Henry Pendleton, who, after nineteen years of poverty and memory, was bereft alike of classical pedantry and of physical comforts, had grown a little weary of the endless lip-worship of a single moment in history. Granted even that it was the greatest moment the world had seen, still why couldn't one be satisfied to have it take its place beside the wars of the Spartans and of the ancient Britons ? Perpetual mourning was well enough for ladies in crape veils and heroic gentlemen on crutches ; but when your bread and meat depended not upon the graves you had decorated, but upon the bath-tubs you had sold, surely something could be said for the Treadwell point of view.

As Virginia could find no answer to this remark, the three stood in silence, gazing dreamily, with three pairs of Pendleton eyes, down toward the site of the old slave market. Directly in their line of vision, an overladen mule with a sore shoulder was straining painfully under the lash, but none of them saw it, because each of them was morally incapable of looking an unpleasant fact in the face if there was any honourable manner of avoiding it. What they beheld, indeed, was the most interesting street in the world, filled with the most interesting people, who drove happy animals that enjoyed their servitude and needed the sound of the lash to add cheer and liveliness to their labours. Never had the Pendleton idealism achieved a more absolute triumph over the actuality.

" Well, we must go on," murmured Mrs. Pendleton, withdrawing her visionary gaze from the hot street littered with fruit rinds and blood-stained papers from a neighbouring butcher shop. "It was lovely to have this glimpse of you, John Henry. What nice bath-tubs you have!" Smiling her still lovely smile into the young man's eyes, she proceeded on her leisurely way, while Virginia raised the black silk sunshade over her head. In front of them they could see long rows of fish carts and vegetable stalls around which hovered an army of eager housekeepers. The social hours in Dinwiddie at that period were the early morning ones in the old market, and Virginia knew that she should hear Docia's story repeated again for the benefit of the curious or sympathetic listeners that would soon gather about her mother. Mrs. Pendleton's marketing, unlike the hurried and irresponsible sort of to-day, was an affair of time and ceremony. Among the greetings and the condolences from other marketers there would ensue lengthy conversations with the vendors of poultry, of fish, or of vegetables. Every vegetable must be carefully selected by her own hands and laid aside into her special basket, which was in the anxious charge of a small coloured urchin. While she felt the plump breasts of Mrs. Dewlap's chickens, she would inquire with flattering condescension after the members of Mr. Dewlap's family. Not only did she remember each one of them by name, but she never forgot either the dates of their birthdays or the number of turkeys Mrs. Dewlap had raised in a season. If marketing is ever to be elevated from an occupation to an art, it will be by a return to Mrs. Pendleton's method.

"Mother, please buy some strawberries," begged Virginia.

"Darling, you know we never buy fruit, or desserts. Somebody will certainly send us something. I saw Mrs. Carrington whipping syllabub on her back porch as we passed."

"But they're only five cents a basket."

"Well, put a basket with my marketing, Mr. Dewlap. Yes, I'll take that white pullet if you're sure that she is plumper than the red one."

She moved on a step or two, while the white pullet was handed over by its feet to the small coloured urchin and to destruction. If Mrs. Pendleton had ever reflected on the tragic fate of pullets, she would probably have concluded that it was " best " for them to be fried and eaten, or Providence, whose merciful wisdom she never questioned, would not have permitted it. So, in the old days, she had known where the slave market stood, without realizing in the least that men and women were sold there. " Poor things, it does seem dreadful, but I suppose it is better for them to have a change sometimes," she would doubtless have reasoned had the horror of the custom ever occurred to her—for her heart was so sensitive to pain that she could exist at all only by inventing a world of exquisite fiction around her.

" Aren't you nearly through, mother ?" pleaded Virginia at last. " The sun will be so hot going home that it will make your head worse."

Mrs. Pendleton, who was splitting a pea-shell with her thumb in order to ascertain the size and quality of the peas, murmured soothingly, " Just a minute, dear " ; and the girl, finding it impossible to share her mother's enthusiasm for slaughtered animals, fell back again into the narrow shade of the stalls. She revolted with a feeling of outrage against the side of life that confronted her—against the dirty floor, strewn with withered vegetables, above which flies swarmed incessantly, and against the pathos of the small bleeding forms which seemed related neither to the lamb in the fields nor to the Sunday roast on the table. That Divine gift of evasion, which enabled Mrs. Pendleton to see only the thing she wanted to see in every occurrence, was but partially developed as yet in Virginia ; and while she stood there in the midst of her unromantic surroundings, the girl shuddered lest Oliver Treadwell should know that she had ever waited, hot, perspiring, with a draggled skirt, and a bag of tomatoes grasped in her hands, while her mother wandered from stall to stall in a tireless search for peas a few cents cheaper than those of Mr. Dewlap. Youth, with its ingenuous belief that love dwells in external circumstances, was protesting against the bland assumption of age that love creates its own peculiar circumstances out of itself. It was absurd, she knew, to imagine that her father's affection for her mother would alter because she haggled over the price of peas ; yet the emotion with which she endowed Oliver Treadwell was so delicate and elusive that she felt that the sight of a soiled skirt and a

perspiring face would blast it for ever. It appeared imperative that he should see her in white muslin, and she resolved
that if it cost Docia her life she would have the flounces of her
dress smoothed before evening. She, who was by nature
almost morbidly sensitive to suffering, became, in the hands
of this new and implacable power, as ruthless at Fate.

"Now I'm ready, Jinny dear. Are you tired waiting?"
asked Mrs. Pendleton, coming toward her with the coloured
urchin in her train. "Why, there's Susan Treadwell. Have
you spoken to her?"

The next instant, before the startled girl could turn, a voice
cried out triumphantly: "O Jinny!" and in front of her,
looking over Susan's shoulder, she saw the eager eyes and the
thin, high-coloured face of Oliver Treadwell. For a moment
she told herself that he had read her thoughts with his penetrating gaze, which seemed to pierce through her; and she
blushed pink while her eyes burned under her trembling
lashes. Then the paper bag, containing the tomatoes, burst
in her hands, and its contents rolled, one by one, over the
littered floor to his feet. Both stooped at once to recover it,
and while their hands touched amid welted cabbage-leaves,
the girl felt that love had taken gilded wings and departed
for ever!

"Put them in the basket, dear," Mrs. Pendleton could be
heard saying calmly in the midst of her daughter's agony—
for, having lived through the brief illumination of romance,
she had come at last into that steady glow which encompasses
the commonplace.

"This is my cousin Oliver, Virginia," remarked Susan as
casually as if the meeting of the two had not been planned
from all eternity by the beneficent Powers.

"I'm afraid I've spoiled your nice red tomatoes," said a
voice that filled Virginia's whirling mind with a kind of ecstatic
dizziness. As the owner of the voice held out his hand, she
saw that it was long and thin like the rest of him, with blue
veins crossing the back, and slender, slightly crooked fingers
that hurt hers with the strength of their pressure. "To
confess the truth," he added gaily after an instant, "my
breath was quite taken away because, somehow, this was the
last place on earth in which I expected to find you. It's a

dreadful spot—don't you think so? If we've got to be cannibals, why in Heaven's name make a show and a parade of it?"

"What an extraordinary young man!" said Mrs. Pendleton's eyes; and Virginia found herself blushing again because she felt that her mother had not understood him. A delicious embarrassment—something different and more vivid than any sensation she had ever known—held her speechless while he looked at her. Had her life depended on it, she could not have uttered a sentence—could hardly even have lifted her lashes, which seemed suddenly to have become so heavy that she felt the burden of them weighing over her eyes. All the picturesque phrases she had planned to speak at their first meeting had taken wings with perfidious romance, yet she would have given her dearest possession to have been able to say something really clever. "He thinks me a simpleton, of course," she thought—perfectly unconscious that Oliver was not thinking of her wits at all, but of the wonderful rose-pink of her flesh. At one and the same instant, she felt that this silence was the most marvellous thing that had ever happened to her and longed to break it with some speech so brilliant that he would never forget it. Little thrills of joy, like tiny flames, ran over her, and the light in her eyes shone on him through the quivering dusk of her lashes. Even when she looked away from him, she could still see his expression of tender gaiety, as though he were trying in vain to laugh himself free from an impulse that was fast growing too strong for him. What she did not know was that the spring was calling to him through her youth and sex as it was calling through the scented winds and the young buds on the trees. She was as ignorant that she offered herself to him through her velvet softness, through the glow in her eyes, through her quivering lips, as the flower is that it allures the bee by its perfume. So subtly did Life use her for its end that the illusion of choice in first love remained unimpaired. Though she was young desire incarnate, he saw in her only the unique and solitary woman of his dreams.

"Do you come here every day?" he asked, and immediately the blue sky and the octagonal market spun round at his voice.

As nothing but commonplace words would come to her, she was obliged at last to utter them. " Oh, no, not every day."

" I've always had a tremendous sympathy for women because they have to market and housekeep. I wonder if they won't revolt some time ?"

This was so heretical a point of view that she tried earnestly to comprehend it ; but all the time her heart was busy telling her how different he was from every other man—how much more interesting ! how immeasurably superior ! Her attention, in spite of her efforts at serious thought, would not wander from the charm of his voice, from the peculiar whimsical trick of his smile, which lifted his mouth at one corner and made odd little wrinkles come and go about his eyes. His manner was full of sudden nervous gestures which surprised and enchanted her. All other men were not merely as clay beside him—they were as straw ! Seeing that he was waiting for a response, she made a violent endeavour to think of one, and uttered almost inaudibly : " But don't they like it ?"

" Ah, that's just it," he answered as seriously as if she hadn't known that her speech bordered on imbecility. " Do they really like it ? or have they been throwing dust in our eyes through the centuries ?" And he gazed at her as eagerly as if he were hanging upon her answer. Oh, if she could only say something clever ! If she could only say the sort of thing that would shock Miss Priscilla ! But nothing came of her wish, and she was reduced at last to the pathetic rejoinder, " I don't know. I'm afraid I've never thought about it."

For a moment he stared at her as though he were enraptured by her reply. With such eyes and such hair, she might have been as simple as she appeared and he would never have known it. " Of course you haven't, or you wouldn't be you !" he responded ; and by the time she came to her senses, she was following her mother and the negro urchin out of the market. Though she was in reality walking over cinders, she felt that her feet were treading on golden air.

CHAPTER IV

THE TREADWELLS

ABOVE the Dinwiddie of Virginia's girlhood, rising sharply out of the smoothly blended level of personalities, there towered, as far back as she could remember, the grim and yet strangely living figure of Cyrus Treadwell. From the intimate social life of the town he had remained immovably detached ; but from the beginning it had been impossible for that life to ignore him. Among a people knit by a common pulse, yet separated by a multitude of individual differences, he stood aloof and indispensable, like one of the gaunt iron bridges of his great railroad. He was at once the destroyer and the builder—the inexorable foe of the old feudal order and the beneficent source of the new industrialism. Though half of Dinwiddie hated him, the other half (hating him, perhaps none the less) ate its bread from his hands. The town, which had lived, fought, lost, and suffered not as a group of individuals, but as a psychological unit, had surrendered at last, less to the idea of readjustment than to the indomitable purpose of a single mind.

And yet nobody in Dinwiddie, not even Miss Willy Whitlow, who sewed out by the day, and knew the intimate structure of every skeleton in every closet of the town—nobody could tell the precise instant at which Cyrus had ceased to be an ordinary man and become a great one. A phrase, which had started as usual, " The Mr. Treadwell, you know, who married poor Belinda Bolingbroke—" swerved suddenly to " Cyrus Treadwell told me that, and you must admit that *he* knows what he is talking about "—and a reputation was made ! His marriage to " poor Belinda," which had at first appeared to be the most conspicuous fact in his career, dwindled to insignificance beside the rebuilding of the tobacco industry and his immediate elevation to the vacant presidency of one of the Machlin railroads.

It was true that in the meantime he had fought irreproachably, but without renown, through a number of battles ; and returning to a vanquished and ruined city, had found himself still young enough to go to school again in matters of finance. Whether he had learned from Antrum, the despised carpetbagger for Machlin and Company, or had taken his instructions at first hand from the great Machlin himself, was in the eighties an open question in Dinwiddie. The choice was probably given him to learn or starve ; and aided by the keen understanding and the acute sense of property he had inherited from his Scotch-Irish parentage, he had doubtless decided that to learn was, after all, the easier way. Saving he had always been, and yet with such strange and sudden starts of generosity that he had been known to seek out distant obscure maiden relatives and redeem the mortgaged roof over their heads. His strongest instinct, which was merely an attenuated shoot from his supreme feeling for possessions, was that of race, though he had estranged both his son and his daughter by his stubborn conviction that he was not doing his duty by them except when he was making their lives a burden. For, as with most men who have suffered in their youth under oppression, his ambition was not so much to relieve the oppressed as to become in his turn the oppressor. Owing, perhaps, to his fine Scotch-Irish blood, which ran a little muddy in his veins, he had never lost a certain primitive feeling of superstition, like the decaying root of a religious instinct ; and he was as strict in his attendance upon church as he was loose in applying the principles of Christianity to his daily life. Sunday was vaguely associated in his mind with such popular fetiches as a frock-coat and a roast of beef ; and if the roast had been absent from dinner, he would have felt precisely the same indefinite disquietude that troubled him when the sermon was left out of the service. So completely did his outward life shape itself around the inner structure of his thought, that, except for the two days of the week which he spent with unfailing regularity in Wall Street, he might have been said to live only in his office. Once when his doctor had prescribed exercise for a slight dyspepsia, he had added a few additional blocks to his morning and evening walk, and it was while he was performing this self-inflicted penance that he came upon Gabriel, who was hastening toward him in behalf of John Henry.

For an instant a gleam of light shone on Cyrus's features, and they stood out, palely illuminated, like the features of a bronze statue above which a torch suddenly flares. His shoulders, which stooped until his coat had curved in the back, straightened themselves with a jerk, while he held out his hand, on which an old sabre cut was still visible. This faded scar had always seemed to Gabriel the solitary proof that the great man was created of flesh and blood.

" I've come about a little matter of business," began the rector in an apologetic tone, for in Cyrus's presence he was never without an uneasy feeling that the problems of the spirit were secondary to the problems of finance.

" Well, I'm just going into the office. Come in and sit down. I'm glad to see you. You bring back the four happiest years of my life, Gabriel."

" And of mine, too. It's queer, isn't it, how the savage seems to sleep in the most peaceable of men ? We were half starved in those days, half naked, and without the certainty that we'd live until sunset—but, dreadful as it sounds, I was happier then—God help me !—than I've ever been before or since."

Passing through an outer office, where a number of young men were bending over ledgers, they entered Cyrus's private room, and sat down in two plain pine chairs under the coloured lithograph of an engine which ornamented the largest space on the wall. The room was bare of the most ordinary comforts, as though its owner begrudged the few dollars he must spend to improve his surroundings.

" Well, those days are over, and you say it's business that you've come about ?" retorted Cyrus, not rudely, but with the manner of a man who seldom wastes words and whose every expenditure either of time or of money must achieve some definite result.

" Yes, it's business." The rector's tone had chilled a little, and he added in spite of his judgment, " I'm afraid it's a favour. Everybody comes begging to you, I suppose ?"

" Then it's the Sunday-school picnic, I reckon. I haven't forgotten it. Smithson !" An alert young man appeared at the door. " Make a note that Mr. Pendleton wants coaches for the Saint James's Church picnic on the twenty-ninth. You said twenty-ninth, didn't you, Gabriel ?"

" If the weather's good," replied Gabriel meekly, and then as Smithson withdrew, he glanced nervously at the lithograph of the engine. " But it wasn't about the picnic that I came," he said. " The fact is, I wanted to ask you to use your influence in the matter of getting John Henry a place in the bank. He has done very well at the night-school, and I believe that you would find him entirely satisfactory."

At the first mention of the bank, a look of distrust crept into Cyrus's face—a look cautious, alert, suspicious, such as he wore at directors' meetings when there was a chance that something might be got out of him if for a minute he were to go off his guard.

" I feel a great responsibility for him," resumed Gabriel almost sternly, though he was painfully aware that his assurance had deserted him.

" Why don't you go to James ? James is the one to see about such a matter."

If the rector had spoken the thought in his mind, he would have answered, " Because James reminds me of a fish and I can't abide him " ; but instead, he replied simply, " I know James so slightly that I don't feel in a position to ask a favour of him."

The expression of suspicion left Cyrus's face, and he relaxed from the strained attitude in which he had sat ever since the Sunday-school picnic had been dismissed from the conversation. Leaning back in his chair, he drew two cigars from the pocket of his coat, and after glancing a little reluctantly at them both, offered one to the rector. " I believe he really wanted me to refuse it !" flashed through Gabriel's mind like an arrow—though the other's hesitation had been, in fact, only an unconscious trick of manner which he had acquired during the long lean years when he had fattened chiefly by not giving away. The gift of a cigar could mean nothing to a man who willingly contributed to every charity in town, but the trivial gestures that accompany one's early habits occasionally outlast the peculiar circumstances from which they spring.

For a few minutes they smoked in silence. Then Cyrus remarked in his precise voice : " James is a clever fellow—a clever fellow."

" I've heard that he is as good as right hand to you. That's a fine thing to say of a son."

" Yes, I don't know what I should do without James. He's a saving hand, and, I tell you, there are more fortunes made by saving than by gambling."

" Well, I don't think James need ever give you any concern on that account," replied Gabriel, not without gentle satire, for he recalled several unpleasant encounters with the younger Treadwell on the subject of charity. " But I've heard different tales of that nephew of yours who has just come back from God knows what country."

" He's Henry's son," replied Cyrus with a frown. " You haven't forgotten Henry ?"

" Yes, I remember. Henry and George both went out to Austrialia to open the tobacco market, and Henry died poor while George lived and got rich, I believe ?"

" George kept free of women and attended to his affairs," returned Cyrus, who was as frank about his family as he was secretive about his business.

" But what about Henry's son ? He's a promising chap, isn't he ?"

" It depends upon what you call promising, I reckon. Before he came I thought of putting him into the bank, but since I've seen him, I can't, for the life of me, think of anything to do with him. Unless, of course, you could see your way toward taking him into the ministry," he concluded with sardonic humour.

" His views on theology would prevent that, I fear," replied the rector, while all the kindly little wrinkles leaped out around his eyes.

" Views ? What do anybody's views matter who can't make a living ? But to tell the truth, there's something about him that I don't trust. He isn't like Henry, so he must take after that pretty fool Henry married. Now, if he had James's temper, I could make something out of him, but he's different—he's fly-up-the-creek—he's as flighty as a woman."

Gabriel, who had been a little cheered to learn that the young man, with all his faults, did not resemble James, hastened to assure Cyrus that there might be some good in the boy, after all—that he was only twenty-two, and that, in any case, it was too soon to pass judgment.

"I can't stand his talk," returned the other grimly. "I've never heard anybody but a preacher—I beg your pardon, Gabriel, nothing personal!—who could keep going so long when nobody was listening. A mere wind-bag, that's what he is, with a lot of nonsensical ideas about his own importance. If there wasn't a girl in the house, it would be no great matter, but that Susan of mine is so headstrong that I'm half afraid she'll get crazy and imagine she's fallen in love with him."

This proof of parental anxiety touched Gabriel in his tenderest spot. After all, though Cyrus had a harsh surface, there was much good at the bottom of him. "I can enter into your feelings about that," he answered sympathetically, "though my Jinny, I am sure, would never allow herself to think seriously about a man without first asking my opinion of him."

"Then you're fortunate," commented Cyrus dryly, "for I don't believe Susan would give a red cent for what I'd think if she once took a fancy. She'd as soon elope with that wild-eyed scamp as eat her dinner, if it once entered her head."

A knock came at the door, and Smithson entered and conferred with his employer over a telegram, while Gabriel rose to his feet.

"By the way," said Cyrus, turning abruptly from his secretary and stopping the rector as he was about to pass out of the door, "I was just wondering if you remembered the morning after Lee's surrender, when we started home on the road together?"

"Why, yes." There was a note of surprise in Gabriel's answer, for he remembered, also, that he had sold his watch a little later in the day to a Union soldier, and had divided the eighty dollars with Cyrus. For an instant, he almost believed that the other was going to allude for the first time to that incident.

"Well, I've never forgotten that green persimmon-tree by the roadside," pursued the great man, "and the way you stopped under it and said, 'O Lord, wilt Thou not work a miracle and make persimmons ripen in the spring?'"

"No, I'd forgotten it," rejoined Gabriel coolly, for he was hurt by the piece of flippancy, and was thinking the worst of Cyrus again.

"You'd forgotten it? Well, I've a long memory, and I never forget. That's one thing you may count on me for," he added, "a good memory. As for John Henry—I'll see James about it. I'll see what James has to say."

When Gabriel had gone, accompanied as far as the outer door by the secretary, Cyrus turned back to the window, and stood gazing out over a steep street or two, and past the gabled roof of an old stone house, to where in the distance the walls of the new building of the Treadwell Tobacco Company were rising. Around the skeleton structure he could see the workmen moving like ants, while in a widening circle of air the smoke of other factories floated slowly upward under a brazen sky. "There are too many of them," he thought bitterly. "It's competition that kills. There are too many of them."

So rapt was his look while he stood there, that there came into his face an expression of yearning sentiment that made it almost human. Then his gaze wandered to the gleaming tracks of the two great railroads which ran out of Dinwiddie toward the north, uncoiling their length like serpents between the broad fields sprinkled with the tender green of young crops. Beside them trailed the ashen country roads over which farmers were crawling with their covered waggons; but, while Cyrus watched from his height, there was as little thought in his mind for the men who drove those waggons through the parching dust as for the beasts that drew them. It is possible even that he did not see them, for just as Mrs. Pendleton's vision eliminated the sight of suffering because her heart was too tender to bear it, so he overlooked all facts except those which were a part of the dominant motive of his life. Nearer still, within the narrow board fences which surrounded the backyards of negro hovels, under the moving shadows of broad-leaved mulberry or sycamore - trees, he gazed down on the swarms of mulatto children; though to his mind that problem, like the problem of labour, loomed vague, detached, and unreal—a thing that existed merely in the air, not in the concrete images that he could understand.

"Well, it's a pity Gabriel never made more of himself," he thought kindly," "Yes, it's a pity. I'll see what I can do for him."

At six o'clock that evening, when the end of his business day had come, he joined James at the door for his walk back to Bolingbroke Street.

"Have you done anything about Jones's place in the bank?" was the first question he asked after his abrupt nod of greeting.

"No, sir. I thought you were waiting to find out about Oliver."

"Then you thought wrong. The fellow's a fool. Look up that nephew of Gabriel Pendleton, and see if he is fit for the job. I am sorry Jones is dead," he added with a touch of feeling. "I remember I got him that place the year after the war, and I never knew him to be ten minutes late during all the time that I worked with him."

"But what are we to do with Oliver?" inquired James after a pause. "Of course he wouldn't be much good in the bank, but——"

And without finishing his sentence, he glanced up in a tentative, non-committal manner into Cyrus's face. He was a smaller and somewhat imperfect copy of his father, naturally timid, and possessed of a superstitious feeling that he should die in an accident. His thin anæmic features lacked the strength of the Treadwells, though in his cautious and taciturn way he was very far indeed from being the fool people generally thought him. Since he had never loved anything with passion except money, he was regarded by his neighbours as a man of unimpeachable morality.

At the end of the block, while the long pointed shadows of their feet kept even pace on the stone crossing, Cyrus answered abruptly: "Put him anywhere out of my sight. I can't bear the look of him."

"How would you like to give him something to do on the

road ? Put him under Borrows, for instance, and let him learn a bit about freight ?"

" Well, I don't care. Only don't let me see him—he turns my stomach."

" Then as long as we've got to support him, I'll tell him he may try his hand at the job of assistant freight agent, if he wants to earn his keep."

" He'll never do that—just as well put him down under ' waste,' and have done with him," replied Cyrus, chuckling.

A little girl, rolling a hoop, tripped and fell at his feet, and he nodded at her kindly, for he had a strong physical liking for children, though he had never stopped to think about them in a human or personal way. He had, indeed, never stopped to think about anything except the absorbing problem of how to make something out of nothing. Everything else, even his marriage, had made merely a superficial impression upon him. What people called his " luck " was only the relentless pursuit of an idea ; and in this pursuit all other sides of his nature had been sapped of energy. From the days when he had humbly accepted small commissions from the firm of Machlin and Company, to the last few years, when he had come to be regarded almost superstitiously as the saviour of sinking properties, he had moved quietly, cautiously, and unswervingly in one direction. The blighting panic of ten years before had hardly touched him, so softly had he ventured, and so easy was it for him to return to his little deals and his diet of crumbs. They were bad times, those years, alike for rich and poor, for Northerner and Southerner ; but in the midst of crashing firms and noiseless factories, he had cut down his household expenses to a pittance and had gone on as secretively as ever—waiting, watching, hoping, until the worst was over and Machlin and Company had found their man. Then, a little later, with the invasion of the cigarette, there went up the new Treadwell factory which the subtle-minded still attributed to the genius of Cyrus. Even before George and Henry had sailed for Australia, the success of the house in Dinwiddie was assured. There was hardly a drug store in America in those days that did not offer as its favourite, James's crowning triumph, the Magnolia cigarette. A few years later, competition came like a whirlwind, but in the beginning the Treadwell brand held the market alone, and in those few years Cyrus's fortune was made.

"Heard from George lately?" he inquired, when they had traversed, accompanied by their long and narrow shadows, another couple of blocks. The tobacco trade had always been for him merely a single pawn in the splendid game he, was playing, but he had suspected recently that James felt something approaching a sentiment for the Magnolia cigarette, and true to the Treadwell scorn of romance, he was for ever trying to trick him into an admission of guilt.

"Not since that letter I showed you a month ago," answered James. "Too much competition, that's the story everywhere. They are flooding the market with cigarettes, and if it wasn't for the way the Magnolia holds on, we'd be swamped in little or no time."

"Well, I reckon the Claypole would pull us through," commented Cyrus. The Claypole was an old brand of plug tobacco with which the first Treadwell factory had started. "But you're right about competition. It's got to stop or we'll be driven clean out of the business."

He drew out his latchkey as he spoke, for they had reached the corner of Bolingbroke Street, and the small dingy house in which they lived was only a few doors away. As they passed between the two blossoming oleanders in green tubs on the sidewalk, James glanced up at the flat square roof, and observed doubtfully, "You'll be getting out of this old place before long now, I reckon."

"Oh, some day, some day," answered Cyrus. "There'll be time enough when the market settles and we can see where the money is coming from."

Once every year, in the spring, James asked his father this question, and once every year he received exactly the same answer. In his mind, Cyrus was always putting off the day when he should move into a larger house, for though he got richer every week, he never seemed to get quite rich enough to commit himself to any definite change in his circumstances. Of course, in the nature of things, he knew that he ought to have left Bolingbroke Street long ago; there was hardly a family still living there with whom his daughter associated, and she complained daily of having to pass saloons and barber shops whenever she went out of doors. But the truth was that, in spite of his answer to James's annual question, neither of them wanted to move away from the old home, and each hoped in his heart that he should never be forced into doing so. Cyrus had become wedded to the house as a man becomes wedded to a habit, and since the clinging to a habit was the only form of sentiment of which he was capable, he shrank more and more from what he felt to be the almost unbearable wrench of moving. A certain fidelity of purpose, the quality which had lifted him above the petty provincialism that crippled James, made the display of wealth as obnoxious to him as the possession of it was agreeable. As long as he was conscious that he controlled the industrial future of Dinwiddie, it was a matter of indifference to him whether people supposed him to be a millionaire or a pauper. In time he would probably have to change his way of living and put an end to his lifelong practice of saving; but, meanwhile, he was quite content to go on year after year mending the roof and the chimneys of the old house into which he had moved the week after his marriage.

Entering the hall, he hung his hat on the walnut hat-rack in the dark corner behind the door, and followed the worn strip of blue and red oilcloth which ran up the narrow staircase to the floor above. Where the staircase bent sharply in the middle, the old-fashioned mahogany balustrade shone richly in the light of a gas-jet which jutted out on a brass stem from the wall. Although a window on the upper floor was opened wide to the sunset, the interior of the house had a close, musty smell, as if it had been shut up, uninhabited, for months. Cyrus had never noticed the smell, for his senses, which were never acute, had been rendered even duller than usual by custom.

At the top of the stairs, a coloured washerwoman, accompanied by a bright mulatto boy, who carried an empty clothes-basket on his head, waited humbly in the shadow for the two men to pass. She was a dark, glistening creature, with ox-like eyes, and the remains of a handsome figure, now running to fat.

"Howdy, Marster?" she murmured under her breath as Cyrus reached her, to which he responded brusquely, "Howdy,

Mandy ?'' while he glanced with unseeing eyes at the mulatto boy at her side. Then, as he walked rapidly down the hall with James at his heels, the woman turned back for a minute and gazed after him with an expression of animal submission and acquiescence. So little personal to Cyrus and so free from individual consciousness was this look, that it seemed less the casual glance from a servant to a master than the intimate aspect of a primitive racial attitude toward life.

At the end of the hall, beyond the open door of the bedroom (which he still occupied with his wife from an ineradicable conviction that all respectable married persons slept together no matter how uncomfortable they might be), Cyrus discerned the untidy figure of Mrs. Treadwell reflected in a mirror, before which she stood brushing her back hair straight up from her neck to a small round knot on the top of her head. She was a slender, flat-chested woman, whose clothes, following some natural bent of mind, appeared never to be put on quite straight or properly hooked and buttoned. It was as if she perpetually dressed in a panic, forgetting to fasten her placket, to put on her collar, or to mend the frayed edges of her skirt. When she went out, she still made some spasmodic attempts at neatness; but Susan's untiring efforts and remonstrances had never convinced her that it mattered how one looked in the house—except indeed when a formal caller arrived, for whom she hastily tied a scarf at the neck of her dirty basque and flung a purple wool shawl over her shoulders. Her spirit had been too long broken for her to rebel consciously against her daughter's authority; but her mind was so constituted that the sense of order was missing, and the pretty coquetry of youth, which had masqueraded once as the more enduring quality of self-respect, was extinguished in the five-and-thirty penitential years of her marriage. She had a small, vacant face, where the pink and white had run into muddiness, a mouth that sagged at the corners like the mouth of a frightened child, and eyes of a sickly purple, which had been compared by Cyrus to '' sweet violets,'' in the only compliment he ever paid her. Thirty-five years ago, in one of those attacks of indiscretion which overtake the most careful man in the spring, Cyrus had proposed to her; and when she declined him, he had immediately repeated his offer, animated less by any active desire to possess her, than by the dogged male determination to override all obstacles, whether feminine or financial. And pretty Belinda Bolingbroke, being alone and unsupported by other suitors at the instant, had entwined herself instinctively around the nearest male prop that offered. It had been one of those marriages of opposites which people (ignoring the salient fact that love has about as much part in it as it has in the pursuit of a spring chicken by a hawk) speak of with sentiment as " a triumph of love over differences." Even in the first days of their engagement there could be found no better reason for their marriage than the meeting of Cyrus's stubborn propensity to have his way with the terror of imaginary spinsterhood which had seized Belinda in a temporary lapse of suitors. Having married, they immediately proceeded, as if by mutual consent, to make the worst of it. She, poor, fluttering, dove-like creature, had lost hope at the first rebuff, and had let go all the harmless little sentiments that had sweetened her life ; while he, having married a dove by choice and because of her doveliness, had never forgiven her that she did not develop into a brisk, cackling hen of the barnyard. As usually happens in the cases where " love triumphs over differences," he had come at last to hate her for the very qualities which had first caught his fancy. His ideal woman (though he was perfectly unconscious that she existed) was a managing thrifty soul, in a starched calico dress, with a natural capacity for driving a bargain ; and Life, with grim humour, had rewarded this respectable preference by bestowing upon him feeble and insipid Belinda, who spend sleepless nights trying to add three and five together, but who could never, to save her soul, remember to put down the household expenses in the petty cash book. It was a case, he sometimes told himself, of a man, who had resisted temptation all his life, being punished for one instant's folly more harshly than if he were a practised libertine. No libertine, indeed, could have got himself into such a scrape, for none would have surrendered so completely to a single manifestation of the primal force. To play the fool once, he reflected bitterly, when his brief intoxication was over, is after all more costly than to play it habitually. Had he pursued a different pair of violet eyes every evening, he would never have ended by embracing the phantom that was Belinda.

But it was more than thirty years since Cyrus had taken the trouble to turn his unhappiness into philosophy—for, aided by time, he had become reconciled to his wife as a man becomes reconciled to a physical infirmity. Except for that one eventful hour in April, women had stood for so little in his existence, that he had never stopped to wonder if his domestic relations might have been pleasanter had he gone about the business of selection as carefully as he picked and chose the tobacco for his factory. Even the streak of sensuality in his nature did not run warm as in the body of an ordinary mortal, and his vices, like his virtues, had become so rarefied in the frozen air of his intelligence that they were no longer recognizable as belonging to the common frailties of men.

"Ain't you dressed yet?" he inquired without looking at his wife as he entered—for having long ago lost his pride of possession in her, he had ceased to regard her as of sufficient importance to merit the ordinary civilities.

"I was helping Miss Willy whip one of Susan's flounces," she answered, turning from the mirror, with the hairbrush held out like a peace-offering before her. "We wanted to get through to-day," she added nervously, "so Miss Willy can start on Jinny Pendleton's dress the first thing in the morning."

If Cyrus had ever permitted himself the consolation of doubtful language, he would probably have exclaimed with earnestness, "Confound Miss Willy!" but he came of a stock which condemned an oath, or even an expletive, on its face value, so this natural outlet for his irritation was denied him. Instead, therefore, of replying in words, he merely glanced sourly at the half-open door, through which issued the whirring noise of the little dressmaker at her sewing. Now and then, in the intervals when her feet left the pedal, she could be heard humming softly to herself with her mouth full of pins.

"Isn't she going?" asked Cyrus presently, while he washed his hands at the washstand in one corner and dried them on a towel which Belinda had elaborately embroidered in red. Peering through the crack of the door as he put the question, he saw Miss Willy hurriedly pulling basting threads out of a muslin skirt, and the fluttering, bird-like motions of her hands increased the singular feeling of repulsion with which she inspired him. Though he was aware that she was an entirely harmless person, and, moreover, that her " days " supplied the only companionship his wife really enjoyed, he resented angrily the weeks of work and gossip which the little seam-stress spent under his roof. Put two gabbling women like that together and you could never tell what stories would be set going about you before evening ! A suspicion, unfortu-nately too well founded, that his wife had whimpered out her heart to the whirring accompaniment of Miss Willy's machine, had caused him once or twice to rise in his authority and forbid the dressmaker the house ; but, in doing so, he had reckoned without the strength which may lie in an unscrupulous weakness. Belinda, who had never fought for anything else in her life, refused absolutely to give up her dressmaker. " If I can't see her here, I'll go to her house," she had said, and Cyrus had yielded at last as the bully always yields before the frenzied violence of his victim.

After a hasty touch to the four round flat curls on her fore-head, Mrs. Treadwell turned from the bureau with her habitu-ally hopeless air, and slipped her thin arms into the tight sleeves of a black silk basque which she took up from the bed.

" Did you see Oliver when you came in ?" she asked. " He was in here looking for you a few minutes ago."

" No, I didn't see him, but I'm going to. He's got to give up this highfalutin nonsense of his if he expects me to support him. There's one thing the fellow's got to understand, and that is that he can choose between his precious stuff and his bread and meat. Before I give him a job, he'll have to let me see that he is done with all this business of play-writing."

A frightened look came into his wife's face, and indifferently glancing at her as he finished, he was arrested by something enigmatical and yet familiar in her features. A dim vision of the way she had looked at him in the early days of their marriage floated an instant before him.

" Do you think he wants to do that ?" she asked, with a little sound as if she had drawn her breath so sharply that it whistled. What in thunder was the matter with the woman ? he wondered irritably. Of course she was a fool about the scamp—all the women, even Susan, lost their heads over him —but, after all, why should it make any difference to her whether he wrote plays or took freight orders, as long as he managed to feed himself?

"Well, I don't reckon it has come to a question of what he wants," he rejoined shortly.

"But the boy's heart is bound up in his ambition," urged Belinda, with an energy he had witnessed in her only once before in her life, and that was on the occasion of her historic defence of the seamstress.

For a moment Cyrus stared at her with attention, almost with curiosity. Then he opened his lips for a crushing rejoinder, but thinking better of his impulse, merely repeated dryly, "His heart?" before he turned toward the door. On the threshold he looked back and added, "The next time you see him, tell him I'd like a word with him."

Left alone in her room, Mrs. Treadwell sat down in a rocking-chair by the window, and clasped her hands tightly in her lap with a nervous gesture which she had acquired in long periods of silent waiting on destiny. Her mental attitude, which was one of secret, and usually passive, antagonism to her husband, had stamped its likeness so indelibly upon her features, that, sitting there in the wan light, she resembled a woman who suffers from the effects of some slow yet deadly sickness. Lacking the courage to put her revolt into words, she had allowed it to turn inward and embitter the hidden sources of her being. In the beginning she had asked so little of life that the denial of that little by Fate had appeared niggardly rather than tragic. A man—any man who would have lent himself gracefully as an object of worship—would have been sufficient material for the building of her happiness. Marriage, indeed, had always appeared to her so desirable as an end in itself, entirely apart from the personal peculiarities or possibilities of a husband, that she had awakened almost with surprise one morning to the knowledge that she was miserable. It was not so much that her romance had met with open disaster as that it had simply faded away. This gradual fading away of sentiment, which she had accepted at the time as only one of the inevitable stages in the slow process of emotional adjustment, would perhaps have made but a passing impression on a soul to whom every other outlet into the world had not been closed by either temperament or tradition. But love had been the one window through which light could enter her house of Life ; and when this darkened, her whole nature had sickened and grown morbid. Then at last all the corroding bitterness in her heart had gathered to a canker which ached ceaselessly, like a physical sore, in her breast.

"He saw I'd taken to Oliver—that's why he's anxious to spite him," she thought resentfully as she stared with unseeing eyes out into the grey twilight. "It's all just to worry me, that's why he's doing it. He knows I couldn't be any fonder of the boy if he had come of my own blood." And she who had been a Bolingbroke set her thin lips together with the only consciousness of superiority to her husband that she had ever known—the secret consciousness that she was better born. Out of the wreck of her entire life, this was the floating spar to which she still clung with a sense of security, and her imagination, by long concentration upon the support that it offered, had exaggerated its importance out of all proportion to the other props among which it had its place. Like its imposing symbol, the Saint Memin portrait of the great Archibald Bolingbroke, which lent distinction, by its very inappropriateness, to the wall on which it hung, this hidden triumph imparted a certain pathetic dignity to her manner.

"That's all on earth it is," she repeated with a kind of smothered fierceness. But, even while the words were on her lips, her face changed and softened, for in the adjoining room a voice, full of charm, could be heard saying : " Sewing still, Miss Willy ? Don't you know that you are guilty of an immoral act when you work overtime ?"

"I'm just this minute through, Mr. Oliver," answered the seamstress in fluttering tones. "As soon as I fold this skirt, I'm going to quit and put on my bonnet."

A few more words followed, and then the door opened wider and Oliver entered—with his ardent eyes, his irresolute mouth, and his physical charm which brought an air of vital well-being into the depressing sultriness of the room.

"I missed you downstairs, Aunt Belinda. You haven't a headache, I hope," he said, and there was the same caressing kindness in his tone which he had used to the dressmaker. It was as if his sympathy, like his charm, which cost him so little because it was the gift of Nature, overflowed in every casual expression of his temperament.

"No, I haven't a headache, dear," replied Mrs. Treadwell, putting up her hand to his cheek as he leaned over her. "Your uncle is waiting for you in the library, so you'd better go down at once," she added, catching her breath as she had done when Cyrus first spoke to her about Oliver.

"Have you any idea what it means? Did he tell you?"

"Yes, he wants to talk to you about business."

"The deuce he does! Well, if that's it, I'd be precious glad to get out of it. You don't suppose I could cut it, do you? Susan is going to take me to the Pendletons after supper, and I'd like to run upstairs now and make a change."

"No, you'd better go down to him. He doesn't like to be kept waiting."

"All right, then—since you say so."

Meeting the dressmaker on the threshold, he forgot to answer her deprecating bow in his eagerness to have the conversation with Cyrus over and done with.

"I declare, he does startle a body when you ain't used to him," observed Miss Willy, with a bashful giggle. She was a diminutive, sparrow-like creature, with a natural taste for sick-rooms and death-beds, and an inexhaustible fund of gossip. As Mrs. Treadwell, for once, did not respond to her unspoken invitation to chat, she tied her bonnet strings under her sharp little chin, and taking up her satchel went out again, after repeating several times that she would be "back the very minute Mrs. Pendleton was through with her." A few minutes later, Belinda, still seated by the window, saw the shrunken figure ascend the area steps and cross the dusty street with a rapid and buoyant step, as though she, also, plain, overworked, and penniless, was feeling the delicious restlessness of the spring in her blood. "I wonder what on earth she's got to make her skip like that," thought Belinda, not without bitterness. "I reckon she thinks she's just as important as anybody," she added after an instant, touching, though she was unaware of it, the profoundest truth of philosophy. "She's got nothing in the world but herself, yet I reckon to her that is everything, even if it doesn't make a particle of difference to anybody else whether she is living or dead."

Her eyes were still on Miss Willy, who stepped on briskly, swinging her bag joyously before her, when the sound of Cyrus's voice, raised high in anger, came up to her from the library. A short silence followed ; then a door opened and shut quickly, and rapid footsteps passed up the staircase and along the hall outside of her room. While she waited, overcome by the nervous indecision which attacked her like palsy whenever she was forced to take a definite action, Susan ran up the stairs and called her name in a startled and shaking voice.

"Oh, mother, father has quarrelled dreadfully with Oliver and ordered him out of the house !"

CHAPTER V

OLIVER, THE ROMANTIC

An hour later Oliver stood before the book-shelves in his room, wrapping each separate volume in newspapers. Downstairs in the basement, he knew, the family were at supper, but he had vowed, in his splendid scorn of material things, that he would never eat another morsel under Cyrus's roof. Even when his aunt, trembling in every limb, had brought him secretly from the kitchen a cup of coffee and a plate of waffles, he had refused to unlock his door and permit her to enter. "I'll come out when I am ready to leave," he had replied to her whispered entreaties.

It was a small room, furnished chiefly by book-shelves, which were still unfinished, and with a depressing view from a single window of red tin roofs and blackened chimneys. Above the chimneys a narrow band of sky, spangled with a few stars, was visible from where Oliver stood, and now and then he stopped in his work and gazed up at it with an exalted and resolute look. Sometimes a thin shred of smoke floated in from the kitchen chimney, and hung, as if drawn and held there by some magnetic attraction, around the kerosene lamp on a corner of the washstand. The sultriness of the night, which was oppressive even in the street, was almost stifling in the little room with its scant western exposure.

But the flame burning in Oliver's breast had purged away such petty considerations as those for material comforts. He had risen above the heat, above the emptiness of his pockets, above the demands of his stomach. It was a matter of complete indifference to him whether he slept in a house or out of doors, whether he ate or went hungry. His exaltation was so magnificent that while it lasted he felt that he had conquered the physical universe. He was strong ! He was free !

74

And it was characteristic of his sanguine intellect that the
future should appear to him at the instant as something
which existed not beyond him, but actually within his grasp.
Anger had liberated his spirit as even art had not done ; and
he felt that all the blood in his body had rushed to his brain
and given him the mastery over circumstances. He forgot
yesterday as easily as he evaded to-day and subjugated to-
morrow. The past, with its starved ambitions, its tragic
failures, its blighting despondencies, melted away from him
into obscurity ; and he remembered only the brief alternating
hours of ecstasy and of accomplishment. With his wind-
blown, flame-like temperament, oscillating in the heat of
youth between the inclinations he miscalled convictions, he
was still, though Cyrus had disowned him, only a romantic
variation from the Treadwell stock. Somewhere, in the
depths of his being, the essential Treadwell persisted. He
hated Cyrus as a man hates his own weakness ; he revolted
from materialism as only a materialist in youth revolts.

A knock came at his door, and pausing, with a volume of
Heine still unwrapped in his hand, he waited in silence until
his visitor should retire down the stairs. But instead of
Mrs. Treadwell's trembling tones, he heard, after a moment,
the firm and energetic voice of Susan.

" Oliver, I must speak to you. If you won't unlock your
door, I'll sit down on the steps and wait until you come out."

" I'm packing my books. I wish you'd go away, Susan."

" I haven't the slightest intention of going away until I've
talked with you——" and, then, being one of those persons
who are born with the natural gift of their own way, she laid
her hand on the door-knob while Oliver impatiently turned
the key in the lock.

" Since you are here, you might as well come in and help,"
he remarked none too graciously, as he made way for her to
enter.

" Of course I'll help you ; but, oh, Oliver, what in the world
are you going to do ?"

"I haven't thought. I'm too busy, but I'll manage somehow."

" Father was terrible. I heard him all the way upstairs in
my room. But," she looked at him a little doubtfully, " don't
you think he will get over it ?"

"He may, but I shan't. I'd rather starve than live under a petty tyranny like that."

"I know," she nodded, and he saw that she understood him. It was wonderful how perfectly, from the very fist instant, she had understood him. She grasped things, too, by intelligence, not by intuition, and he found this refreshing in an age when the purely feminine was in fashion. Never had he seen a finer example of young, buoyant, conquering womanhood—of womanhood freed from the consciousness and the disabilities of sex. "She's not the sort of girl a man would lose his head over," he reflected; "there's too little of the female about her—she's as free from coquetry as she is from the folderol of sentimentality. She's a free spirit, and God knows how she ever came out of the Treadwells." Her beauty even wasn't the kind that usually goes by the name. He didn't suppose there were ten men in Dinwiddie who would turn to look back at her—but, by Jove! if she hadn't beauty, she had the character that lends an even greater distinction. She looked as if she could ride Life like a horse—could master it and tame it and break it to the bridle.

"It's amazing how you know things, Susan," he said, "and you've never been outside of Dinwiddie."

"But I've wanted to, and I sometimes think the wanting teaches one more than the going."

He thought over this for an instant, and then, as if the inner flame which consumed him had leaped suddenly to the surface, he burst out joyously: "I've come to the greatest decision of my life in this last hour, Susan."

Her eyes shone. "You mean you've decided not to do what father asks no matter what happens?"

"I've decided not to accept his conditions—no matter what happens," he answered.

"He was in earnest, then, about wanting you to give up writing?"

"So much in earnest that he would give me a job only on those terms."

"And you declined absolutely?"

"Of course I declined absolutely."

"But how will you live, Oliver?"

"Oh, I can easily make thirty dollars a month by reviewing

German books for New York papers, and I dare say I can manage to pull through on that. I'll have to stay in Dinwiddie, of course, because I couldn't live anywhere else on nearly so little, and, besides, I shouldn't be able to buy a ticket away."

"That will be twenty dollars for your board," said the practical Susan, "and you will have to make ten dollars a month cover all your other expenses. Do you think you can do it?"

"I've got to. Better men have done worse things, haven't they? Better men have done worse things and written great plays while they were about them."

"I believe Mrs. Peachey would let you have a back room and board for that," pursued Susan. "But it will cost you something to get your books moved and the shelves put up there."

"As soon as I get through this I'll go over and see her. Oh, I'm free, Susan; I'm happy! Did you ever see an absolutely happy man before? I feel as if a weight had rolled off my shoulders. I'm tired—dog-tired of compromise and commercialism and all the rest of it. I've got something to say to the world, and I'll go out and make my bed in the gutter before I'll forfeit the opportunity of saying it. Do you know what that means, Susan? Do you know what it is to be willing to give your life if only you can speak out the thing that is inside of you?" The colour in his face mounted to his forehead, while his eyes grew black with emotion. In the smoky little room, Youth, with its fierce revolts, its impassioned egoism, its inextinguishable faith in itself, delivered its ultimatum to Life. "I've got to be true to myself, Susan! A man who won't starve for his ambition isn't worth his salt, is he? And, besides, the best work is all done not in plenty, but in poverty—the most perfect art has grown from the poorest soil. If I were to accept Uncle Cyrus's offer, I'd grow soft to the core in a month and be of no more use than a rotten apple."

His conviction lent a golden ring to his voice, and so winning to Susan was the impetuous flow of his words, that she felt herself swept away from all the basic common sense of her character. She saw his ambition as clearly as he saw it:

she weighed his purpose, as he weighed it, in the imaginary scales of his judgment ; she accepted his estimate of his powers as passionately as he accepted it.

"Of course you mustn't give up, Oliver ; you couldn't," she said.

"You're right, I couldn't."

"If you can get steady reviewing, I believe you can manage," she resumed. "Living in Dinwiddie costs really so very little." Her voice thrilled suddenly. "It must be beautiful to have something that you feel about like this. Oh, I wish I were you, Oliver ! I wish a thousand times I were you !"

Withdrawing his eyes from the sky at which he had been gazing, he turned to look at her as if her words had arrested him. "You're a dear girl," he answered kindly, "and I think all the world of you." As he spoke he thought again what a fine thing it would be for the man who could fall in love with her. "It would be the best thing that could happen to any man to marry a woman like that," he reflected ; "she'd keep him up to the mark and never let him grow soft. Yes, it would be all right if only one could manage to fall in love with her—but I couldn't. She might as well be a rose-bush for all the passion she'd ever arouse in me." Then his charming egoism asserted itself, and he said caressingly : "I don't believe I could stand Dinwiddie but for you, Susan."

She smiled back at him, but there was a limpid clearness in her look which made him feel that she had seen through him while he was thinking. This clearness, with its utter freedom from affectation or sentimentality, embarrassed him by its unlikeness to all the attributes he mentally classified as feminine. To look straight seemed to him almost as un-womanly as to throw straight, and Susan would, doubtless, be quite capable of performing either of these difficult feats. He liked her fine brow under the short fringe, which he hated, and he liked the arched bridge of her nose and the generous curve of her mouth. Yet had he stopped to analyze her, he would probably have said that the woman spirit in her was expressed through character rather than through emotion—a mani-festation disconcerting to one whose vision of her sex was chiefly as the irresponsible creature of drama. The old shackles—even the shackles of that drama whose mistress and slave woman had been—were out of place on the spirit which was incarnated in Susan. Amid the cramping customs of the period, she moved large, free, and simple, as though she walked already in the purer and more bracing air of the future.

" I wish I could help you," she said, stooping to pick up a newspaper from a pile on the floor. " Here, let me wrap that Spinoza. I'm afraid the back will come off if you aren't careful."

" Of course, a man has to work out his own career," he replied, as he handed over the volume. " I doubt, when it comes to that, if anybody can be of much help to another where his life's work is concerned. The main thing, after all, is not to get in one's way, not to cripple one's energy. I've got to be free—that's all there is about it. I've got to belong to myself every instant."

" And you know already just what you are going to do ? About your writing, I mean ?"

" Absolutely. I've ideas enough to fill fifty ordinary life-times. I'm simply seething with them. Why, that box over there in the corner is full of plays that would start a national drama if the fool public had sense enough to see what they are about. The trouble is that they don't want life on the stage ; they want a kind of theatrical wedding-cake. And, by Jove ! they get it. Any dramatist who tries to force people to eat bread and meat when they are crying for sugar plums may as well prepare to starve until the public begins to suffer from acute indigestion. Then, if he isn't dead—or, perhaps, if he is—his hour will come, and he will get his reward either here or in heaven."

" So you'll go on just the same and wait until they're ready for you ?" asked Susan, laughing from sheer pride in him. " You'll never, never cheapen yourself, Oliver ?" For the first time in her life she was face to face with an intellectual passion, and she felt almost as if she herself were inspired.

" Never. I've made my choice. I'll wait half a century if need be, but I'll wait. I know, too, what I am talking about, for I could do the other thing as easily as I could eat my dinner. I've got the trick of it. I could make a fortune to-morrow if I were to lose my intellectual honesty and go in simply for the making of money. Why I am a Treadwell, after all, just as you are, my dear cousin, and I could commercialize the stage, I haven't a doubt, as successfully as your father has commercialized the railroad. It's in the blood—the instinct, you know—and the only thing that has kept it down in me is that I sincerely—yes, I sincerely and enthusiastically believe that I am a genius. If I didn't, do you think I'd stick at this starvation business another fortnight ? That's the whole story, every blessed word of it, and I'm telling you because I feel expansive to-night—I'm such a tremendous egoist, you know, and because—well, because you are Susan."

"I think I understand a little bit how you feel," replied Susan. "Of course, I'm not a genius, but I've thought sometimes that I should almost be willing to starve if only I might go to college."

Checking the words on his lips, he looked at her with sympathy. "It's a shame you can't, but I suppose Uncle Cyrus won't hear of it."

"I haven't asked him, but I am going to do it. I am so afraid of a refusal—and, of course, he'll refuse—that I've lacked the courage to speak of it."

"Good God ! Why is one generation left so absolutely at the mercy of the other ?" he demanded, turning back to the strip of sky over the roof. "It makes a man rage to think of the lives that are spoiled for a whim. Money, money—curse it !—it all comes to that in the end. Money makes us and destroys us."

"Do you remember what father said to you the other night—that you would come at last to what you called the property idea and be exactly like James and himself ?"

"If I thought that, I'd go out and hang myself. I can understand a man selling his soul for drink, though I rarely touch a drop, or for women, though I've never bothered about them, but never, not even in the last extremity, for money."

A door creaked somewhere on the second floor, and a minute afterwards the slow and hesitating feet of Mrs. Treadwell were heard ascending the stairs.

"Let her come in just a moment, Oliver," begged Susan, and her tone was full of the impatient, slightly arrogant affection with which she regarded her mother. There was little sympathy and less understanding between them, but on Susan's side there was a feeling of protective tenderness which was almost maternal. This tenderness was all her own, while the touch of arrogance in her manner belonged to the universal inability of youth to make allowances for age.

"Oh, well," said Oliver indifferently; and going to the door, he opened it and stood waiting for Mrs. Treadwell to enter.

"I came up to ask if you wouldn't eat something, dear?" she asked. "But I suppose Susan has brought you your supper?"

"He won't touch a morsel, mother; it is useless to ask him. He is going away just as soon as we have finished packing."

"But where is he going? I didn't know that he had any place to go to."

"Oh, a man can always find a place somewhere."

"How can you take it so lightly, Susan?" protested Mrs. Treadwell, beginning to cry.

"That's the only sensible way to take it, isn't it, Oliver?" asked Susan, gaily.

"Don't get into a fidget about me, Aunt Belinda," said Oliver, pushing the pile of newspapers out of her way, while she sat down nervously on the end of a packing-case and wiped her eyes on the fringe of her purple shawl. The impulsive kindness with which he had spoken to her a few hours before had vanished from his tone, and left in its place an accent of irritation. His sympathy, which was never assumed, resulted so entirely from his mood that it was pratically independent of the person or situation which appeared to inspire it. There were moments when, because of a sensation of mental or physical well-being, he overflowed with a feeling of tenderness for the beggar at the crossing; and there were longer periods, following a sudden despondency, when the suffering of his closest friend aroused in him merely a sense of personal outrage. So complete, indeed, was his absorption in himself, that even his philosophy was founded less upon an intellectual conception of the universe than it was upon an intense preoccupation with his own personality.

"But you don't mean that you are going for good?—that you'll never come back to see Susan and me again?" whimpered his aunt, while her sagging mouth trembled.

"You can't expect me to come back after the things Uncle Cyrus has said to me."

A look so bitter that it was almost venomous crept into Mrs. Treadwell's face. "He just did it to worry me, Oliver. He has done everything he could think of to worry me ever since he persuaded me to marry him. I sometimes believe," she added, gloating over the idea like a decayed remnant of the aristocratic spirit, "that he has always been jealous of me because I was born a Bolingbroke."

To Oliver, who had not like Susan grown accustomed through constant repetition to Mrs. Treadwell's delusion, this appeared so fresh a view of Cyrus's character, that it caught his interest even in the midst of his own absorbing perplexities. Until he saw Susan's head shake ominously over her mother's shoulder, it did not occur to him that his aunt, whom he supposed to be without imagination, had created this consoling belief out of her own mental vacancy.

"Oh, he wanted to worry me all right, there's no doubt about that," he replied.

"He hasn't spoken to me when he could help it for twenty years," pursued his aunt, who was so possessed by the idea of her own relation to her husband that she was incapable of dwelling upon any other.

"I wouldn't talk about it, mother, if I were you," said Susan with resolute cheerfulness.

"I don't know why I shouldn't talk about it. It's all I've got to talk about," returned Mrs. Treadwell peevishly ; and she added with smothered resentment, "even my children haven't been any comfort to me since they were little. They've both turned against me because of the way their father treats me. James hardly ever has so much as a word to say to me."

"But I do, mother. How can you say such an unkind thing to me ?"

"You never do the things that I want you to. You know I'd like you to go out and enjoy yourself and have attention as other girls do."

"You are disappointed because I'm not a belle like Abby Goode or Jinny Pendleton," said Susan with the patience that is born of a basic sense of humour. "But I couldn't help that, could I ?"

"Any girl in my day would have felt badly if she wasn't admired," pursued Mrs. Treadwell with the venom of the embittered weak ; "but I don't believe you'd care a particle if a man never looked at you twice."

"If one never looked at me once, I don't see why you should want me to be miserable about it," was Susan's smiling rejoinder ; "and if the girls in your day couldn't be happy without admiration, they must have been silly creatures. I've a life of my own to live, and I'm not going to let my happiness depend on how many times a man looks at me." In the clear light of her ridicule, the spectre of spinsterhood, which was still an object of dread in the Dinwiddie of the eighties, dissolved into a shadow.

"Well, we've about finished, I believe," remarked Oliver, closing the case over which he was stooping, and devoutly thanking whatever beneficent Powers had not created him a woman. "I'll send for these some time to-morrow, Aunt Belinda."

"You'd just as well spend the night," urged Mrs. Treadwell stubbornly. "He need never know of it."

"But I'd know of it—that's the great thing—and I'd never forget it."

Rising unsteadily from the box, she stood with the ends of her purple shawl clutched tightly over her flat bosom. "Then you'll wait just a minute. I've got something downstairs I'd like to give you," she said.

"Why, of course, but won't you let me fetch it ?"

"You'd never find it," she answered mysteriously, and hurried out while he held the door open to light her down the dark staircase.

When her tread was heard at last on the landing below, Susan glanced at the books that were still left on the shelves. "I'll pack the rest for you to-morrow, Oliver, and your clothes too. Have you any money ?"

"A little left from selling my watch in New York. My clothes don't amount to much. I've got them all in that bag ; but I'll leave my books in your charge until I can find a place for them."

"I'll take good care of them. Oh, Oliver!" her face grew disturbed. "I forgot all about my promise to Virginia that I'd bring you to see her to-night."

"Well, I've no time to meet girls now, of course, but that doesn't mean that I'm not awfully knocked up about it."

"I hate so to disappoint her!"

"She won't think of it twice, the beauty!"

"But she will. I'm sure she will. Hush! Mother is coming."

As he turned to the door, it opened slowly to admit the figure of his aunt, who was panting heavily from her hurried ascent of the stairs. Her ill-humour towards Susan had entirely disappeared, for the only resentment she had ever harboured for more than a few minutes was the lifelong one which she had borne her husband.

"It was not in the place where I had put it, so I thought one of the servants had taken it," she explained. "Mandy was alone in my room to-day while I was at dinner."

In her hand she held a small pasteboard box bearing a jeweller's imprint, and opening this, she took out a roll of money and counted out fifty dollars on the top of a packing-case. "I've saved this up for six months," she said. "It came from selling some silver forks that belonged to the Bolingbrokes, and I always felt easier to think that I had a little laid away that he had nothing to do with. From the very day that I married him, he was always close about money," she added.

The sordid tragedy—not of poverty, but of meanness—was in the gesture with which she gathered up the notes and pressed them into his shrinking hands. And yet Cyrus Treadwell was a rich man—the richest man living in Dinwiddie! Oliver understood now why she was crushed—why she had become the hopeless victim of the little troubles of life. "From the very day of our marriage, he was always close about money."

"I had three dozen forks and spoons in the beginning," she resumed as if there were no piercing significance in the fact she stated so simply, "but I've sold them all now, one or two at a time, when I needed a little money of my own. He has always paid the bills, but he never gave me a cent in my life to do as I pleased with."

"I can't take it from you, Aunt Belinda. It would burn my fingers."

"It's mine. I've got a right to do as I choose with it," she persisted almost passionately, "and I'd rather give it to you than buy anything in the world." Something in her face—the look of one who has risen to a generous impulse and finds happiness in the sacrifice—checked the hand with which he was thrusting the money away from him. He was deeply touched by her act; it was useless for him to pretend either to her or to himself that she had not touched him. The youth in him, unfettered, strong, triumphant, pitied her because she was no longer young; the artist in him pitied her because she was no longer beautiful. Without these two things, or at least one of these two, what was life worth to a woman?

"I'll take it on condition that you'll let me pay it back as soon as I get out of debt to Uncle Cyrus," he said in obedience to Susan's imploring nod.

To this she agreed after an ineffectual protest. "You needn't think about paying it back to me," she insisted; "I haven't anything to spend money on now, so it doesn't make much difference whether I have any or not. I can help you a little more after a while," she finished with enthusiasm. "I'm raising a few squabs out in the backyard, and Meadows is going to buy them as soon as they are big enough to eat."

An embarrassment out of all proportion to the act which produced it held him speechless while he gazed at her. He felt at first merely a sense of physical revolt from the brutality of her self-revelation—from the nakedness to which she had stripped the horror of her marriage under the eyes of her daughter. Nothing, not even the natural impulse to screen one's soul from the gaze of the people with whom one lived, had prevented the appalling indignity of this exposure. The delusion that it is possible for a woman by mere virtue of being a woman to suffer in sweetness and silence, evaporated as he looked at her. He had believed her to be a nonentity, and she was revealing an inner life as intense, as real, as acutely personal as his own. A few words of casual kindness and he had made a slave of her. He regretted it. He was embarrassed. He was sorry. He wished to Heaven she hadn't brought him the money—and yet in spite of his regret and his embarrassment, he was profoundly moved. It occurred to him as he took it from her how easy it would have been for Cyrus to have subjugated and satisfied her in the beginning. All it needed was a little kindness, the cheapest virtue, and the tragedy of her ruined soul might have been averted. To make allowances! Ah, that was the philosophy of human relations in a word! If men and women would only stop judging each other and make allowances!

"Well, I shan't starve just yet, thanks to you, Aunt Belinda," he said cheerfully enough as he thrust the notes into his pocket. It was a small thing, after all, to make her happy by the sacrifice of his pride. Pride was not, he remembered, included among the Christian virtues, and, besides, as he told himself the next instant, trifling as the sum was, it would at least tide him over financially until he received the next payment for his reviewing. "I'd better go, it's getting late," he said with a return of his old gaiety, while he bent over to kiss her. He was half ashamed of the kiss—not because he was self-conscious about kissing; he had long since lost that mark of provincialism—but because of the look of passionate gratitude which glowed in her face. Gratitude always made him uncomfortable. It was one of the things he was for ever evading and yet for ever receiving. He hated it; he had never in his life done anything to deserve it, but he could never escape it.

"Good-bye, Susan." His lips touched hers, and though he was moving only a few streets away, the caress contained all the solemnity of a last parting. Words wouldn't come when he searched for them, and the bracing sense of power he had felt half an hour ago was curiously mingled now with an enervating tenderness. He was still confident of himself, but he became suddenly conscious that these women were necessary to his happiness and his success, that his nature demanded the constant daily tonic of their love and service. He understood now the primal necessity of woman, not as an individual, but as an incentive and an appendage to the dominant personality of man.

"Send for me if you need me," said Susan, resting her loving eyes upon him; "and, Oliver, please promise me to be very careful about money."

"I'll be careful, never fear!" he replied with a laugh, as he took up his bag and opened the door. A few minutes later, when he was leaving the house, he reflected that the fifty dollars in his pocket would keep life in him for a considerable time in Dinwiddie.

CHAPTER VI

A TREADWELL IN REVOLT

York Street, in which Mrs. Peachey lived and supplied the necessaries of life to a dozen boarders, ran like a frayed seam of gentility between the prosperous and the impoverished quarters of Dinwiddie ; and in order to reach it, Oliver was obliged to pass the rectory, where, though he did not see her, Virginia sat in stiffly starched muslin on the old horsehair sofa. The fragrance of honeysuckle floated to his nostrils from the dim garden, but so absorbed was he in the engrossing problems of the moment, that only after he had passed the tower of the church did he remember that the house behind him sheltered the girl who reminded him of one of the adorable young virgins of Perugino. For an instant, he permitted himself to dwell longingly on the expression of gentle goodness that looked from her face ; but this memory proved so disturbing, that he put it obdurately away from him while he returned to the prudent consideration of the fifty dollars in his pocket. The appeal of first love had been almost as urgent to him as to Virginia ; but the emotion which had visited both alike had affected each differently, and this difference was due to the fundamental distinction between woman, for whom love is the supreme preoccupation of being, and man, to whom it is at best a partial manifestation of energy. To the woman nothing else really mattered ; to the man at least a dozen other pursuits mattered very nearly as much.

The sultriness of the weather dampened his body, but not his spirits, and as he walked on, carrying his heavy bag along York Street, his consciousness of the tremendous importance to the world of his decision exhilarated him like a tonic. He had freed himself from Cyrus and from commercialism at a single blow, and it had all been as easy as talking ! The joke

about starvation he had of course indulged in merely
for the exquisite pleasure of arousing Susan. He wasn't
going to starve ; nobody was going to starve in Dinwiddie on
thirty dollars a month, and there was no doubt in the world
of his ability to make that much by his reviewing. It was
all simple enough. What he intended to do was to write the
national drama and to practise economy.

He had, indeed, provided for everything in his future, he
was to discover a little later, except for the affable condescension of Mrs. Peachey toward the profession of letters. Cyrus's
antagonism he had attributed to the crass stupidity of the
commercial mind ; but it was a blow to him to encounter the
same misconception, more discreetly veiled, in a woman of
the charm and the character of Mrs. Peachey. Bland, plump,
and pretty, she received the modest avowal of his occupation
with the smiling scepticism peculiar to a race whose genius has
been chiefly military.

" I understand—it is very interesting," she observed
sweetly. " But what do you do besides—what do you do,
I mean, for a living ?"

Here it was again, this fatuous intolerance ! this incomprehensible provincialism ! And the terrible part of it was, that
he had suddenly the sensation of being overwhelmed by the
weight of it, of being smothered under a mountain of prejudice. The flame of his anger against Cyrus went out abruptly,
leaving him cold. It was the world now against which he
rebelled. He felt that the whole world was provincial.

" I shall write reviews for a New York paper," he answered,
trying in vain to impress her by a touch of literary hauteur.
At the moment it seemed to him that he could cheerfully bear
anything if they would only at least pretend to take him seriously. What appalled him was not the opposition, but the
utter absence of comprehension. And he could never hope
to convince them ! Even if he were to write great plays,
they would still hold as obstinately by their assumption that the
writing of plays did not matter—that what really mattered was
to create and then to satisfy an inordinate appetite for tobacco.
This was authentic success, and by no illegitimate triumph
of genius could he persuade an industrial country that he was
as great a man as his uncle. The smiling incredulity in Mrs.

Peachey's face ceased to be individual and became a part of the American attitude toward the native-born artist. This attitude, he admitted, was not confined to Dinwiddie, since it was national. He had encountered it in New York, but never had the destructive force of it impressed him as it did on the ripe and charming lips of the woman before him. In that illuminating instant he understood why the American consciousness in literature was still unawakened, why the creative artist turned manufacturer, why the original thinker bent his knee in the end to the tin gods of convention.

Her eyes—beautiful as the eyes of all happy women are beautiful—dwelt on him kindly while he struggled to explain his mission. All the dread of the unusual, all the inherited belief in the sanctity of fixed opinions, all the passionate distrust of ideas that have not stood the test of centuries—these things which make for the safety and the permanence of the racial life, were in the look of motherly indulgence with which she regarded him. She had just risen from a rocking-chair on the long porch, where honest Tom sat relating ponderous war anecdotes to an attentive group of borders ; and beyond her in the dimly lighted hall he could see the wide old staircase climbing leisurely into the mysterious silence of the upper storeys.

" I have a small room at the back that I might rent to you," she said hesitatingly after a pause. " I am afraid you will find it warm in summer, as it is just under the roof and has a western exposure, but I hardly think I could do better for you at the price you are able to pay. I understood that you intended to live with your uncle," she added in a burst of enthusiasm. " My husband has always been one of his greatest admirers."

The mention of Cyrus was like a spur to Oliver's ambition, and he realized with gratitude that it was merely his sensibility, not his resolution, which had been shaken.

" I'll take the room," he returned, ignoring what she had said as well as what she had implied about Cyrus. Then as she tripped ahead of him, he entered the dismantled hall, filled with broken pieces of fine old furniture, and ascended the stairs as far as the third storey. When she turned a loosened door-knob and passed before him into the little room at the back, he saw first of all the narrow window, with its torn green shade, beyond which clustered a blur of silvery foliage in the midst of red roofs and huddled chimneys. From this hill-top he could look down unseen on that bit of the universal life which was Dinwiddie. He could watch the town at work and at play ; he could see those twenty-one thousand souls either moved as a unit by the secret forces which ignore individuality, or separated and enclosed by that impenetrable wall of personality which surrounded each atom among them. He could follow the divisions of class and the still deeper divisions of race as they were symbolized in the old brick walls, overgrown with young grasses, which girdled the ancient gardens in High Street. From the dazzling glimpses of white muslin under honeysuckle arbours, to the dusky forms that swarmed like spawn in the alleys, the life of Dinwiddie loved, hated, enjoyed, and suffered beneath him. And over this love and this hatred, this enjoyment and this suffering, there presided—an outward and visible sign of the triumph of industrialism—the imposing brick walls of the new Treadwell tobacco factory.

A soft voice spoke in his ear, and turning, he looked into the face of Mrs. Peachey, whom he had almost forgotten.

" You will find the sun warm in the afternoon, I am afraid," she murmured, still with her manner of pleasantly humouring him which he found later to be an unconscious expression of her half-maternal, wholly feminine attitude toward his sex.

' Oh, I dare say it will be all right," he responded. " I shall work so hard that I shan't have time to bother about the weather."

Leaving the window, he gazed around the little room with an impulse of curiosity. Who had lived here before him ? A clerk ? A travelling salesman ? Perhaps one of the numerous indigent gentlewomen that formed so large and so important a part of the population of Dinwiddie ? The walls were smeared with a sickly blue wash, and in several places there were the marks left from the pictures of the preceding lodger. An old mahogany bureau, black with age and ill usage, stood crosswise in the corner behind the door, and reflected in the dim mirror he saw his own face looking back at him. A film of dust lay over everything in the room, over

the muddy blue of the walls, over the strip of discoloured
matting on the floor, over the few fine old pieces of furniture,
fallen now into abject degradation. The handsome French
bed, placed conveniently between door and window, stood
naked to the eyes, with its cheap husk mattress rolled half
back, and its bare slats, of which the two middle ones were
tied together with rope, revealing conspicuously its descent
from elegance into squalor. As he saw it, the room was the
epitome of tragedy, yet in the centre of it, on one of the
battered and broken-legged Heppelwhite chairs, sat Mrs.
Peachey, rosy, plump, and pretty, regarding him with her
slightly quizzical smile. "Yes, life, of course, is sad if you
stop to think about it," her smile seemed to assure him;
"but the main thing, after all, is to be happy in spite of it."

"Do you wish to stay here to-night?" she asked, seeing
that he had put down his bag.

"If you will let me. But I am afraid it will be inconvenient."

She shook her head. "Not if you don't mind the dust.
The room has been shut up for weeks, and the dust is so
dreadful in the spring. The servants have gone out," she
added, "but I'll bring you some sheets for your bed, and you
can fill your pitcher from the spout at the end of the hall.
Only be careful not to stumble over the step there. It is
hard to see when the gas is not lit."

"You won't object to my putting shelves around the
walls?" he asked, while she pushed the mattress into place
with the light and condescending touch of one who preserves
the aristocratic manner not only in tragedy, but even in toil.
It was, indeed, her peculiar distinction, he came to know
afterward, that she worked as gracefully as other women
played.

"Couldn't you find room enough without them?" she
inquired while her gaze left the mattress and travelled dubi-
ously to the mantelpiece. "It seems a pity for you to go to
any expense about shelves, doesn't it?"

"Oh, they won't cost much. I'll do the work myself, and
I'll do it in the mornings when it won't disturb anybody. I
dare say I'll have to push that bed around a bit in order to
make space."

Something in his vibrant voice—so full of the richness and the buoyant energy of youth—made her look at him as she might have looked at one of her children, or at that overgrown child whom she had married. And just as she had managed Tom all his life by pretending to let him have his way, so she proceeded now by instinct to manage Oliver. " You dear boy ! Of course you may turn things upside down if you want to. Only wait a few days until you are settled and have seen how you like it."

Then she tripped out with her springy step, which had kept its elasticity through war and famine, while Oliver, gazing after her, wondered whether it was philosophy or merely a love of pleasure that sustained her ? Was it thought or the absence of thought that produced her wonderful courage ?

He heard her tread on the stairs ; then the sound passed to the front hall ; and a minute later there floated up the laughter with which the assembled boarders received her. Closing the door, which she had left open, he turned back to the window and stared from his hill-top down on the red roofs of Dinwiddie. White as milk, the moonlight lay on the brick wall at the foot of the garden, and down the gradual hill rows of chimneys were outlined against the faintly dappled sky in the west. In the next yard a hollow tree looked as if it were cut out of silver, and beneath its boughs, which drooped into the alley, he could see the huddled figure of an aged negress who had fallen asleep on a flagstone. So still was the night that the very smoke appeared to hang suspended above the tops of the chimneys, as though it were too heavy to rise and yet too light to float downward toward the motionless trees. Under the pale beams the town lost its look of solidity and grew spectral. Nothing seemed to hold it to the earth except the stillness which held the fallen flowers of the syringa there also. Even the church towers showed like spires of thistledown, and the winding streets, which ran beside clear walls and dark shining gardens, trailed off from the ground into the silvery air. Only the black bulk of the Treadwell factory beside the river defied the magic of the moon's rays and remained a solid reminder of the brevity of all enchantment.

Gradually, while Oliver waited for Mrs. Peachey's return,

he ceased to think of the furniture in his room ; he ceased to think even of the way in which he should manage to do his work, and allowed his mind to dwell, almost with a feeling of ecstasy, on the memory of Virginia.   He saw the mist of little curls on her temples, her blue eyes, with their good and gentle expression, and the look of radiant happiness which played like light over her features.   The beauty of the night acted as a spur to his senses. He wanted companionship. He wanted the smile and the touch of a woman. He wanted to fall in love with a girl who had blue eyes and a mouth like a flower !

" It wouldn't take me ten minutes to become a fool about her," he thought.   " Confound this moonlight, anyhow.   It's making an idiot of me."

Like many persons of artistic sensibility, he had at times the feeling that his imagination controlled his conduct, and under the sharp pressure of it now, he began to picture what the end would be if he were to fling himself headlong in the direction where his desires were leading him.   If he could only let himself go !   If he could only defy the future !   If he could only forget in a single crisis that he was a Treadwell !

" If I were the right sort, I suppose I'd rush in and make her fall in love with me, and then marry her and let her starve," he thought.   " But somehow I can't. I'm either not enough of a genius or not enough of a Treadwell. When it comes to starving a woman in cold blood, my conscience begins to balk.   There's only one thing it would balk at more violently, and that is starving my work.   That's what Uncle Cyrus would like—nothing better.   By Jove ! the way he looked when he had the nerve to make that proposition ! And I honestly believe he thought I was going to agree to it. I honestly believe he was surprised when I stood out against him.   He's a downright idiot, that's what is the matter with him.   Why, it would be a crime, nothing less than a crime, for me to give up and go hunting after freight orders.   Any ninny can do that.   James can do that—but he couldn't see, he positively couldn't see, that I'd be wasted at it."

The vision of Cyrus had banished the vision of Virginia, and leaving the window, Oliver began walking rapidly back and forth between the washstand and the bare bedstead.   The fire of his ambition, which opposition had fanned into a blaze, had never burned more brightly in his heart than it did at that instant. He felt capable not only of renouncing Virginia, but of reforming the world. While he walked there, he dedicated himself to art as exclusively as Cyrus had ever dedicated himself to money—since Nature, who had made the individual, had been powerless to eradicate this basic quality of the type. A Treadwell had always stood for success, and success meant merely seeing but one thing at a time and seeing that thing at every instant. It meant to Cyrus and to James the thought of money as absolutely as it meant to Oliver the thought of art. The way to it was the same, only the ideas that pointed the way were different. To Cyrus and to James, indeed, as to all Treadwells everywhere, the idea was hardly an idea at all, since it had been crystallized by long usage into a fact. The word " success " (and what was success except another name for the universal Treadwell spirit ?) invariably assumed the image of the dollar in the mind of Cyrus, while to Oliver, since his thinking was less carefully co-ordinated, it was without shape or symbol. Pacing the dusty floor, with the pale moonlight brooding like a flock of white birds over the garden, the young man would have defined the word as embracing all the lofty aspirations in the human soul. It was the hour when youth scaled the heights and wrested the Divine fire from the heavens. At the moment he was less an individual than the embodied age of two-and-twenty. He was intellect in adolescence—intellect finding its strength—intellect in revolt against the tyranny of industrialism.

The staircase creaked softly, and following a knock at the door, Mrs. Peachey entered with her arms full of bedclothes.

"I am so sorry I kept you waiting, Mr. Treadwell, but I was obliged to stop to speak to a caller. Oh, thank you. Do you really know how to make up a bed ? How very clever of you ! I'm sure Mr. Peachey couldn't do such a thing if his life depended upon it. Men are so helpless that it surprises me —it really does—when they know how to do anything. Oh, of course, you have lived about the world so much that you have had to learn how to manage. And you've been abroad ? How very interesting ! Some day when I have the time you must tell me about it. Not that I should ever care to go myself, but I love to hear other people talk about their travels. Professor Trimble—he lived over there a great many years—gave a talk before the Ladies' Aid Society of our church, and everybody said it was quite as instructive as going oneself. And then, too, one escaped all the misery of seasickness."

All the time she was busily spreading his bed, while he assisted her with what she described to her husband afterward as the "most charming manner, just as if he enjoyed it." This charming manner, which was the outward expression of an inborn kindliness, won her entirely to his side before the bed-making was over. That anyone so frank and pleasant, with such nice boyish eyes, and so rich a colour, should prove untrustworthy, was unbelievable to that part of her which ruled her judgment. And since this ruling part was not reason, but instinct, she possessed, perhaps, as infallible a guide to opinions as ever falls to the lot of erring humanity. "I know he's all right. Don't ask me *how* I know it, Mr. Peachey," she observed, while she brushed her hair for the night; "I don't know how I know it, but I do know it."

Oliver, meanwhile, had thrown off his coat, and settled down to work under the flickering gas, at the end of the mantelpiece. Inspiration had seized him while he helped Mrs. Peachey make his bed, and his "charming manner," which had at first been natural enough, had become at last something of an effort. He was writing the second act of a play in which he meant to supplant the pretty shams of the stage by the aspect of sober reality. The play dealt with woman—with the new woman who has grown so old in the last twenty years—with the woman whose past is a cross upon which she crucifies both herself and the public. Like most men of twenty-two, he was convinced that he understood all about women, and like most men of any age, he was under the impression that women acted, thought, and felt, not as individuals, but as a sex. The classic phrases, "women are like that," and "women think so queerly about things," were on his lips as constantly as if he were an average male and not an earnest-minded student of human nature. But while the average male applies general principles loosely and almost unconsciously, with Oliver the habit was the result of a distinctly formulated policy. He had, as he would probably have put it, a feeling for reality, and the stage appeared to him, on the whole, to be the most effective vehicle for revealing the universe to itself. If he was not a genius, he possessed the unconquerable individualism of genius ; and he possessed, also, a cleverness which could assume the manner of genius without apparent effort. His ability, which no one but Cyrus had ever questioned, may not have been of the highest order, but at least it was better stuff than had ever gone into the making of American plays. In the early eighties profound darkness still hung over the stage, for the intellect of a democracy, which first seeks an outlet in statesmanship, secondly in commerce, and lastly in art and literature, had hardly begun to express itself, with the immaturity of youth, in several of these latter fields. It was Oliver's distinction as well as his misfortune that he lived before his country was ready for him. Coming a quarter of a century later, he might have made part of a national emancipation of intellect. Coming when he did, he stood merely for one of the spasmodic reactions against the dominant spirit. Unwritten history is full of such reactions, since it is by the accumulated energy of their revolts that the world moves on its way.

But at the age of twenty-two, though he was assured that he understood both woman and the universe in which she belonged, he was pathetically ignorant of his own place in the extravagance of Nature. With the rest of us, he would have been astounded at the suggestion that he might have been born to be wasted. Other things were wasted, he knew, since those who called Nature an economist had grossly flattered her. Types and races and revolutions were squandered with royal prodigality—but that he himself should be so was clearly unthinkable. Deep down in him there was the obstinate belief that his existence was a vital matter to the awful Power that ruled the universe ; and while he worked that May evening at the second act of his great play, with the sweat raining from his brow in the sweltering heat, it was as impossible for him to conceive of ultimate failure as it was for him to realize that he should ever cease to exist. The air was stagnant, the light was bad, his stomach was empty, and he was tormented by the stinging of the gnats that circled around the flame—but he was gloriously happy with the happiness of a man who has given himself to an idea.

CHAPTER VII

THE ARTIST IN PHILISTIA

At dawn, after a sleepless night, Oliver dressed himself and made a cup of coffee on the spirit lamp he carried in his bag. While he drank, a sense of power passed over him like warmth. He was cheered, he was even exhilarated. A single cup of this miraculous fluid, and his depression was vanquished as no argument could have vanquished it. Without sermonizing, without logic even, the demon of pessimism, which has its home in an empty stomach, was expelled into spiritual darkness. He remembered that he had eaten nothing for almost twenty-four hours (having missed yesterday's dinner) and this thought carried him downstairs, where he begged a roll from a yawning negro cook in the kitchen. Coming up to his room again, he poured out a second cup of coffee, added a dash of cream, which he had brought with him in a handleless pitcher, and leaning comfortably back in the worn horsehair-covered chair by the window, relapsed into a positive orgy of enjoyment. His whole attitude toward the universe had been altered by a bubbling potful of brown liquid, and the tremendous result—so grotesquely out of proportion to its cause—appeared to him at the minute entirely right and proper. Everything was entirely right and proper, and he felt able to approve with a clear conscience the Divine arrangement of existence.

Outside, the sunrise, which he could not see, was flooding the roofs of Dinwiddie with a dull golden light. The heat had given way before the soft wind which smelt of flowers, and scattered tiny shreds of mist, like white rose-leaves, over the moist gardens. The look of unreality, which had been a fiction of the moonlight, faded gradually as the day broke, and left the harsh outlines and blackened chimneys of the town

unsoftened by any shadow of illusion. Presently, as the sunlight fell aslant the winding streets, there was a faint stir in
the house; but since the day was Sunday, and Dinwiddie
observed the Sabbath by sleeping late, this stir was slow and
drowsy, like the movement of people but half awake. First,
a dilapidated milk waggon rumbled through the alleys to the
back gates, where dishevelled negro maids ran out with earthen-
ware pitchers, which went back foaming around the brims.
Then the doors of the houses opened slowly; the green outside
shutters were flung wide; and an army of coloured servants
bearing brooms appeared on the porches, and made expressive gestures to one another over the railings. Occasionally,
when one lifted a doormat in order to beat the dust out of
it, she would forget to put it down again while she stared
after the milk-cart. Nobody—not even the servants—seemed
to regard the wasted hours as of any importance. It struck
Oliver that the only use Dinwiddie made of time was to kill it.

He fell to work with enthusiasm, and he was still working
when the reverberations of the breakfast bell thundered in
his ears. Going downstairs to the dining-room, he found
several thin and pinched-looking young women, with their
hats on and Sunday-school lessons beside their plates. Mrs.
Peachey, still smiling her quizzical smile, sat at the head of
the table, pouring coffee out of an old silver coffee-pot, which
was battered in on one side as if it had seen active service in
the war. When, after a few hurried mouthfuls, he asked
permission to return to his work, she received his excuses with
the same cheerful acquiescence with which she accepted the
decrees of Providence. It is doubtful, indeed, if her serenity,
which was rooted in an heroic hopelessness, could have been
shaken either by the apologies of a boarder or by the appearance of an earthquake. Her happiness was of that invulner-
able sort which builds its nest not in the luxuriant gardens
of the emotions, but in the bare, rockbound places of the
spirit. Courage, humour, an adherence to conviction which
is wedded to an utter inability to respect any opinion except
one's own; loyalty which had sprung from a principle into a
passion; a fortifying trust, less in the Power that rules the
universe than in the peculiar virtues of the Episcopal prayer-
book when bound in black; a capacity for self-sacrifice which

had made the South a nation of political martyrs; complacency, exaltation, narrowness of vision, and uncompromising devotion to an ideal—these were the qualities which had passed from the race in to the individual and through the individual again back into the very blood and the fibre of the race.

"Do you work on Sunday?" she inquired sweetly, yet with the faintest tinge of disapproval in her tor e.

He nodded. "Once in a while."

"Saint James's Church is only a few minutes' walk from here; but I suppose you are a Presbyterian, like your uncle?"

His respectability he saw hung in the balance—for to have avowed himself a freethinker would have dyed him socially only one shade less black than to have declared himself a Republican—so, escaping without a further confession of faith he ascended to his room and applied himself anew to the regeneration of the American drama. The dull gold light, which slept on the brick walls, began presently to slant in long beams over the roofs, which mounted like steps up the hill-side, while as the morning advanced, the mellow sound of chimes floated out on the stillness, calling Dinwiddians to worship, as it had called their fathers and grandfathers and great-grandfathers before them. The Sabbath calm, so heavy that an axe could hardly have dispelled it, filled the curving streets and the square gardens like an invisible fog—a fog that dulled the brain and weighed down the eyelids and made the grim walls of the Treadwell tobacco factory look as if they were rising out of a dream. Into this dream, under the thick boughs of mulberry-trees, there passed presently a thin file of people, walking alone or in pairs. The men were mostly old; but the women were of every age, and all except the very young were clad in mourning and wore hanging veils on their bonnets. Though Oliver did not know it, he was, in reality, watching a procession of those who, having once embraced a cause and lost it, were content to go on quietly in a hush of memory for the rest of life. Passion had once inflamed them, but they moved now in the inviolable peace which comes only to those who have nothing left that they may lose. At the end of the line, in the middle of the earthen roadbed, walked an old horse, with an earnest face and a dump-cart hitched to him, and in the cart were the boxes of books which Susan had helped Oliver to pack the evening before. "Who'd have thought she'd get them here so soon?" he said to himself. "By George, she is a wonder! And Sunday too!"

The old horse, having reached the hill-top, disappeared behind the next house, and ten minutes later Mrs. Peachey escorted the smallest of his boxes into his bedroom.

"Your cousin is downstairs, but I didn't know whether you wanted me to bring her up here or not?" she said.

"Of course you do, don't you, Oliver?" asked Susan's voice, and entering the room she coolly presented her cheek to him. This coolness, which impressed him almost as much as her extraordinary capability, made him feel sometimes as if she had built a stone wall between them. Years afterwards he asked himself if this was why his admiration for her had never warmed into love.

"Well, you're a good one!" he exclaimed, as she drew back from the casual embrace.

"I knew you were here," she answered, "because John Henry Pendleton" (was it imagination, or did the faintest blush tinge her face?) "saw Major Peachey last night and told me on his way home."

"You can't help me straighten up, I suppose? The room looks a sight."

"Not now—I'm on my way to church and I'll be late if I don't hurry." She wore a grey cashmere dress, made with a draped polonaise which accentuated her rather full hips, and a hat with a steeple crown that did not suit the Treadwell arch of her nose. He thought she looked plain, but he did not realize that in another dress and hat she might have been almost beautiful—that she was, indeed, one of those large-minded, passionately honest women who, in their scorn of pretence or affectation, rarely condescend to make the best of their appearances. To have consciously selected a becoming hat would have seemed to her a species of coquetry, and coquetry, even the most innocent, she held in abhorrence. Her sincerity was not only intellectual; it was of that rarer sort which has its root in a physical instinct.

After she had gone, he worked steadily for a couple of hours, and then opened one of the boxes Susan had brought and arranged a few of his books in a row on the mantelpiece. It was while he stood still undecided whether to place "The Origin of Species" or "The Critique of Pure Reason" on the end nearest his bed, that a knock came at his door, and the figure of Miss Priscilla Batte, attired in a black silk dolman with bugle trimmings, stood revealed on the threshold.

"Sally Peachey just told me that you were here," she said, enfolding him in the embrace which seemed common to Dinwiddie, "so I thought I would speak to you on my way back from church. I don't suppose you've ever heard of me, but I am your cousin Priscilla Batte."

Though he was entirely unaware of it, the moment was a momentous one in his experience. The visit of Miss Priscilla may have appeared an insignificant matter to those who have not learned that the insignificant is merely the significant seen from another angle—but the truth was that it marked a decisive milestone in his emotional history. Even Mrs. Peachey, who had walked back from church with her, and who harboured the common delusion that Life selects only slim bodies for its secret agents, did not dream as she watched that enormous figure toil up the staircase that she was gazing upon the movement of destiny. Had Oliver been questioned as to the dominant influence in shaping his career, he would probably have answered blindly, but sincerely, "The Critique of Pure Reason"—so far was he from suspecting that his philosophy had less control over his future than had the accident that his mother was the third cousin of Priscilla Batte.

He pushed a chair into the widest space he could find, and she seated herself as modestly as if she were not the vehicle of the invisible Powers. The stiff grosgrain strings of her bonnet stood out like small wings under her double chin, and on her massive bosom he saw the cameo brooch bearing the war-like profile of Athene. As she sat there, beaming complacently upon him, with her prayer-book and hymnal held at a decent angle in front of her, she seemed to Oliver to dominate the situation simply by the solid weight of her physical presence. In her single person she managed to produce the effect of a majority. As a mere mass of humanity she carried conviction.

" I was sorry not to see you at church," she said, " but I suppose you went with Cyrus ?" As he shook his head silently, she added hastily, " I hope there's nothing wrong between you and him."

" Nothing except that I have decided not to go into the tobacco business."

" But what in the world are you going to do ? How are you going to live if he doesn't provide for you ?"

" Oh, I'll manage somehow. You needn't worry, Cousin Priscilla." He smiled at her across the unfinished page of his play, and this smile won her as it had won Mrs. Peachey. Like most spinsters, she had remained a creature of sentiment, and the appeal of the young and masculine she found difficult to resist. After all, he was a charming boy, her heart told her. What he needed was merely some good girl to take care of him and convert him to the Episcopal Church. And immediately, as is the way with women, she became as anxious to sacrifice Virginia to this possible redemption of the male as she had been alarmed by the suspicion that such a desire existed in Susan. Though it would have shocked her to hear that she held any opinion in common with Mohammed (who appeared in the universal history she taught only in a brief list of " false prophets "), there existed deep down in her the feeling that a man's soul was of greater consequence than a woman's in the eyes of God.

" I hope you haven't been foolish, Oliver," she said in a tone which conveyed an emotional sympathy as well as a moral protest.

" That depends upon what you mean by foolishness," he returned, still smiling.

" Well, I don't think you ought to quarrel with Cyrus. He may not be perfect. I am not saying that he mightn't have been a better husband, for instance—though I always hold the woman to blame when a marriage turns out a failure —but when all's said and done, he is a great man, Oliver."

He shook his head impatiently. " I've heard that until I'm sick of it—forgive me, Cousin Priscilla."

" Everybody admires him—that is, everybody except Belinda."

" I should say she'd had excellent opportunities for form-

ing an opinion. What's he ever done, anyhow, that's great,"
he asked almost angrily, " except accumulate money ? It
seems to me that you've gone mad over money in Dinwiddie.
I suppose it's the reaction from having to do without it so
long."

Miss Priscilla, whose native serenity drew strength from
another's loss of temper, beamed into his flushed face as if she
enjoyed the spectacle of his heightened colour.

" You oughtn't to talk like that, Oliver," she said. " How
on earth are you going to fall in love and marry, if you haven't
any money to keep a wife ? What you need is a good girl to
look after you. I never married, myself, but I am sometimes
tempted to believe that even an unhappy marriage is better
than none at all. At least, it gives you something to think
about."

" I have enough to think about already. I have my work."

" But work isn't a wife."

" I know it isn't, but I happen to like it better."

Her matchmaking instinct had received a check, but the
placid determination which was the basis of her character was
merely reinforced thereby to further efforts. It was for his
good to marry (had not her mother and her grandmother
instilled into her the doctrine that an early marriage was the
single masculine safeguard, since, once married, a man's
morality became not his own business, but his wife's ?), and
marry him she was resolved to do, either with his cheerful
co-operation, or, if necessary, without it. He had certainly
looked at Virginia as if he admired her, and surely a girl like
that—lovely, loving, unselfish to a fault, and trained from
her infancy to excel in all the feminine virtues—surely, this
perfect flower of sex specialization could have been designed
by Providence only for the delight and the sanctification of
man.

" Then, if that is the way your mind is made up, I hope
you will be careful not to trifle with the feelings of a girl like
Jinny Pendleton," she retorted severely.

By a single stroke of genius, inspired by the diplomacy
inherent in a sex whose chief concern has been the making of
matches, she transfixed his imagination as skilfully as she
might have impaled a butterfly on a bodkin. While he stared

at her she could almost see the iridescent wings of his fancy whirling madly around the idea by which she had arrested their flight. Trifle with Virginia! Trifle with that radiant vision of girlhood! All the chivalry of youth revolted from the suggestion, and he thought again of the wistful adoration in the eyes of a Perugino virgin. Was it possible that she could ever look at him with that angelic expression of weakness and surrender? The fire of first love, which had smouldered under the weight of his reason, burst suddenly into flame. His thoughts, which had been as clear as a geometrical figure, became suddenly blurred by the mystery upon which passion lives. He was seized by a consuming wonder about Virginia, and this wonder was heightened when he remembered the appealing sweetness in her face as she smiled up at him. Did she already love him? Had he conquered by a look the exquisite modesty of her soul? With this thought the memory of her virginal shyness stung his senses as if it were the challenge of sex. Chivalry, love, vanity, curiosity—all these circled helplessly around the invisible axis of Miss Priscilla's idea.

"What do you mean? Surely you don't suppose—she hasn't said anything——"

"You don't imagine that Jinny is the kind of girl who would say anything, do you?" inquired Miss Priscilla.

"But there must be some reason why you should have——"

"If there is, my dear boy, I'm not going to tell it," she answered with a calmness which he felt, in his excited state, to be positively infernal. "All I meant was to warn you not to trifle with any girl as innocent of life as Jinny Pendleton is. I don't want her to get her heart broken before she has the chance to make some man happy."

"Do you honestly mean to imply that I could break her heart if I tried to?"

"I don't mean to imply anything. I am only telling you that she is just the kind of girl a man would want to marry. She is her mother all over again, and I don't believe Lucy has ever thought of herself a minute since she married."

"She looks like an angel," he said, "but——"

"And she isn't a bit the kind of girl that Susan is, though they are so devoted. Now, I can understand a man not wanting to marry Susan, because she is so full of ideas, and has a mind of her own about things. But Jinny is different."

Then, seeing that she had " unsettled " his mind sufficiently for her purpose, she rose and looked around the room with the inordinate curiosity about details which kept her still young in spite of her sixty years.

" You don't mean to tell me you brought all those books with you, Oliver ?" she asked. " Why on earth don't you get rid of some of them ?"

" I can't spare any of them. I never know which one I may want next."

" What are those you're putting on the mantelpiece ? Isn't Darwin the name of the man who said we were all descended from monkeys ?"

As he made no answer to this except to press her hand and thank her for coming, she left the mantelpiece and wandered to the window, where her gaze rested, with a look of maternal satisfaction, on the roofs of Dinwiddie.

" It's a jolly view of the town, isn't it ?" he said. " There's nothing like looking down from a hill top to give one a sense of superiority."

" You can see straight into Mrs. Goode's backyard," she replied, " and I never knew before that she left her clothes hanging on the line on Sunday. That comes, I suppose, from not looking after her servants and gadding about on all sorts of charities. She told me the other day that she belonged to every charitable organization in Dinwiddie."

" Is she Abby's mother ?"

" Yes, but you'd never imagine they were any relation. Abby gave me more trouble than any girl I ever taught. She never would learn the multiplication table, and I don't believe to this day she knows it. There isn't any harm in her except that she is a scatterbrain, and will make eyes or burst. I sometimes think it isn't her fault—that she was just born man-crazy."

" She's awfully good fun," he laughed.

" Are you going to her garden-party on Wednesday ?"

" I accepted before I quarrelled with Uncle Cyrus, but I'll have to get out of it now."

" Oh, I wouldn't. All the pretty girls in town will be there."

" Are there any plain ones ?   And what becomes of them ?''

" The Lord only knows !   Old Judge Bassett used to say that there wouldn't be any preserves and pickles in the world if all women were born good-looking.   I declare I never realized how small the tower of Saint James's Church is !''

For a moment he hesitated, and when he spoke his voice had taken a deeper tone.   " Will Virginia Pendleton be at the party ?'' he asked.

" She wouldn't miss it for anything in the world.   Miss Willy Whitlow was sewing there yesterday on a white organdie dress for her to wear.   Have you ever seen Jinny in white organdie ?   I always tell Lucy the child looks sweet enough to eat when she puts it on.''

He laughed again, but not as he had laughed at her description of Abby.   " Ask her, please, to put blue bows on her flounces and a red rose in her hair,'' he said.

" Then you are going ?''

" Not if I can possibly keep away.   Oh, Cousin Priscilla, why didn't I inherit my soul from your side of the family ?''

" Well, for my part I don't believe in all this talk about inheritance.   Nobody ever heard of inheriting anything but money when I was a girl.   You've got the kind of soul the good Lord wanted to put into you, and that's all there is about it.''

When he returned from assisting her in her panting and difficult descent of the stairs, he sat down again before the unfinished act of his play, but his eyes wandered from the manuscript to the town, which lay as bright and still in the sunlight as if it were imprisoned in crystal.   The wonder aroused in his mind by Miss Priscilla's allusion to Virginia persisted as a disturbing element in the background of his thoughts.   What had she meant ?   Was it possible that there was truth in the wildest imaginings of his vanity ?   Virginia's face, framed in her wreath of hair, floated beneath the tower of Saint James's Church, at which he was gazing, and the radiant goodness in her look mounted like a draught of strong wine to his brain.   Passion, which he had discounted in his plans for the future, appeared suddenly to shake the very foundations of his life.   Never before had the spirit and the flesh united in the appeal of a woman to his imagination.

Never before had the Divine virgin of his dreams assumed the living red and white of young girlhood. He thought how soft her hair must be to the touch, and how warm her mouth would glow from his kisses. With a kind of wonder he realized that this was first love—that it was first love he had felt when he met her eyes under the dappled sunlight in High Street. The memory of her beauty was like a net which enmeshed his thoughts when he tried to escape it. Look where he would, he saw always a cloud of dark hair and two deep blue eyes that shone as softly as wild hyacinths after a shower. Think as he would, he met always the haunting doubt—"What did she mean? Can it be true that she already loves me?" So small an incident as Miss Priscilla's Sunday call had not only upset his work for the morning, but had changed in an instant the even course of his future. He decided suddenly that he must see Virginia again—that he would go to Abby Goode's party, and though the party was only three days off, it seemed to him that the waiting would be almost unbearable. Only after he had once seen her would it be possible, he felt, to stop thinking of her and to return comfortably to his work.

CHAPTER VIII

WHITE MAGIC

In the centre of her bedroom, with her back turned to that bookcase which was filled with sugared falsehoods about life, Virginia was standing very straight while Miss Willy Whitlow knelt at her feet and sewed pale blue bows on her overskirt of white organdie. Occasionally, the door opened softly, and the rector or one of the servants looked in to see " Jinny," or " Miss Jinny dressed for the party," and when such interruptions occurred, Mrs. Pendleton, who sat on an ottoman at the dressmaker's right hand and held a spool of thread and a pair of scissors in her lap, would say sternly : " Don't move, Jinny ; stand straight, or Miss Willy won't get the bows right." At these warning words, Virginia's thin shoulders would spring back and the filmy ruffles stir gently over her girlish breast.

Through the open window, beyond the drooping boughs of the paulownia-trees, a few wistful stars shone softly through the web of purple twilight. The night smelt of a thousand flowers—all the mingled sweetness of old gardens floated in on the warm wind and caressed the faded figure of Miss Willy as lovingly as it did the young and radiant vision of Virginia. Once or twice the kneeling seamstress had glanced up at the girl and thought : " I wonder how it feels to be as lovely as that ?" Then she sighed as one who had missed her heritage, for she had been always plain, and went on patiently sewing the bows on Virginia's overskirt. " You can't have everything in this world, and I ought to be thankful that I've kept out of the poorhouse," she added a minute later, when a little stab of envy went through her at hearing the girl laugh from sheer happiness.

" Am I all right, mother ? Tell me how I look."

"Lovely, darling. There won't be anyone there sweeter than you are."

The maternal passion lit Mrs. Pendleton's eyes with splendour, and her worn face was illuminated as if a lamp had been held suddenly close to it. All day, in spite of a neuralgic pain in her temples, she had worked hard hemming the flounces for Virginia's dress, and into every stitch had gone something of the Divine ecstasy of martyrdom. Her life centred so entirely in her affections that apart from love she could be hardly said to exist at all. In spite of her trials she was probably the happiest woman in Dinwiddie, for she had found her happiness in the only way it is ever won—by turning her back on it. Never once had she thought of it as an end to be pursued, never even as a flower to be plucked from the wayside. It is doubtful if she had ever stopped once in the thirty years of her marriage to ask herself the questions : " Is this what I want to do ?" or " Does this make me happy ?" Love meant to her not grasping, but giving, and in serving others she had served herself unawares. Even her besetting sin of " false pride " she indulged not on her own account, but because she, who could be humble enough for herself, could not bear to associate the virtue of humility with either her husband or her daughter.

The last blue bow was attached to the left side of the over-skirt, and while Miss Willy rose from her knees, Virginia crossed to the window and gazed up at the pale stars over the tops of the paulownias. A joy so vibrant that it was like living music swelled in her breast. She was young ! She was beautiful ! She was to be loved ! This preternatural certainty of happiness was so complete that the chilling disappointments of the last few days had melted before it like frost in the sunlight. It was founded upon an instinct so much deeper, so much more primitive than reason, that it resisted the logic of facts with something of the exalted obstinacy with which faith has resisted the arguments of philosophy. Like all young and inexperienced creatures, she was possessed by the feeling that there exists a magnetic current of attraction between desire and the object which it desires. "Something told " her that she was meant for happiness, and the voice of this " something " was more con-

vincing than the chaotic march of phenomena. Sorrow, decay,
death—these appeared to her as things which must happen
inevitably to other people, but from which she should be for
ever shielded by some beneficent Providence. She thought
of them as vaguely as she did of the remote tragedies of
history. They bore no closer relation to her own life than
did the French Revolution or the beheading of Charles I.
It was natural, if sad, that Miss Willy Whitlow should fade
and suffer. The world, she knew, was full of old people, of
weary people, of blighted people ; but she cherished passionately the belief that these people were all miserable
because, somehow, they had not chosen to be happy. There
appeared something positively reprehensible in a person who
could go sighing upon so kind and beautiful a planet. All
things, even joy, seemed to her a mere matter of willing. It
was impossible that any hostile powers should withstand the
radiant energy of her desire.

Leaning there from the window, with her face lifted to the
stars, and her mother's worshipping gaze on her back, she
thought of the " happiness " which would be hers in the
future : and this " happiness " meant to her only the solitary
experience of love. Like all the women of her race, she had
played gallantly and staked her world upon a single chance.
Whereas a man might have missed love and still have retained
life, with a woman love and life were interchangeable terms.
That one emotion represented not only her sole opportunity
of joy, it constituted as well her single field of activity. The
chasm between marriage and spinsterhood was as wide as
the one between children and pickles. Yet so secret was this
intense absorption in the thought of romance, that Mrs.
Pendleton, forgetting her own girlhood, would have been
startled had she penetrated that lovely head and discovered
the ecstatic dreams that flocked through her daughter's brain.
Though love was the one window through which a woman
might look on a larger world, she was fatuously supposed
neither to think of it nor to desire it until it had offered itself
unsolicited. Every girl born into the world was destined for
a heritage of love or of barrenness—yet she was forbidden to
exert herself either to invite the one or to avoid the other.
For, in spite of the fiery splendour of Southern womanhood

during the war years, to be feminine, in the eyes of the period, was to be morally passive.

"Your father has come to see your dress, dear," said her mother in the voice of a woman from whom sentiment overflowed in every tone, in every look, in every gesture.

Turning quickly, Virginia met the smiling eyes of the rector —those young and visionary eyes, which Nature, with a wistful irony, had placed beneath beetling brows in the creased and wrinkled face of an old man. The eyes were those of a prophet—of one who had lived his life in the light of a transcendent inspiration rather than by the prosaic rule of practical reason ; but the face belonged to a man who had aged before his time under the accumulated stress of physical burdens.

"How do I look, father ? Am I pretty ?" asked Virginia, stretching her thin young arms out on either side of her, and waiting with parted lips to drink in his praise.

"Almost as beautiful as your mother, and she grows lovelier every day that she lives, doesn't she ?"

His adoring gaze, which held the spirit of beauty as a crystal holds the spirit of light, passed from the glowing features of Virginia to the lined and pallid face of his wife. In that gaze there had been no shadow of alteration for thirty years. It is doubtful even if he had seen any change in her since he had first looked upon her face, and thought it almost unearthly in its angelic fairness. From the physical union they had entered into that deeper union of souls in which the body dissolves, as the shadow dissolves into the substance, and he saw her always as she had appeared to him on that first morning, as if the pool of sunlight in which she had stood had never darkened around her. Yet to Virginia his words brought a startled realization that her mother—her own mother, with her faded face and her soft, anxious eyes—had once been as young and radiant as she. The love of her parents for each other had always seemed to her as natural and as far removed from the cloudless zone of romance as her own love for them—for, like most young creatures, she regarded love as belonging, with bright eyes and rosy cheeks, to the blissful period of youth.

"I hear John Henry's ring, darling. Are you ready ?" asked Mrs. Pendleton.

"In a minute. Is the rose right in my hair?" replied
Virginia, turning her profile towards her mother, while she
flung a misty white scarf over her shoulders.

"Quite right, dear. I hope you will have a lovely time. I
shall sit up for you, so you needn't bother to take a key."

"But you'll be so tired. Can't you make her go to bed,
father?"

"I couldn't close my eyes till I knew you were safely
home, and heard how you'd enjoyed yourself," answered Mrs.
Pendleton, as they slowly descended the staircase, Virginia
leading the way, and the rest following in a procession behind
her. Turning at the gate, with her arm in John Henry's, the
girl saw them standing in the lighted doorway, with their
tender gaze following her, and the faces of the little seamstress
and the two coloured servants staring over their shoulders.
Trivial as the incident was, it was one of the moments which
stood out afterwards in Virginia's memory as though a white
light had fallen across it. Of such simple and expressive
things life is woven, though the years had not taught her this
on that May evening.

On the Goodes' lawn lanterns bloomed, like yellow flowers
among the branches of poplar-trees, and beneath them Mrs.
Goode and Abby—a loud, handsome girl, with a coarsened
complexion and a " sporting " manner—received their guests
and waved them on to a dancing platform which had been
raised between a rose-crowned summer-house and the old
brick wall at the foot of the garden. Ropes were stretched
over the platform, from the roof of the summer-house to a
cherry-tree at the end of the walk, and on these more lanterns
of red, blue, and yellow paper were hanging. The air was
scented with honeysuckle, and from an obscure corner behind
a trellis the sound of a waltz floated. As music, it was not
of a classic order, but this did not matter, since nobody was
aware of it ; and Dinwiddie, which developed quite a taste
for Wagner at the beginning of the next century, could listen
in the eighties with what was perhaps a sincerer pleasure to
stringed instruments, a little rough, but played with fervour
by mulatto musicians. As Virginia drifted off in John Henry's
arms for the first dance, which she had promised him, she
thought : " I wonder if he will not come, after all?" and a

pang shot through her heart where the daring joy had been only a moment before. Then the music grew suddenly heavy while she felt her feet drag in the waltz. The smell of honeysuckle made her sad as if it brought back to her senses an unhappy association which she could not remember, and it seemed to her that her soul and body trembled, like a bent flame, into an attitude of expectancy.

"Let me stop a minute. I want to watch the others," she said, drawing back into the scented dusk under a rose arbour.

"But don't you want to fill your card ? If the men once catch sight of you, you won't have a dance left."

"No—no, I want to watch a while," she said, with so strange an accent of irritation that he stared at her in surprise. The suspense in her heart hurt her like a drawn cord in throbbing flesh, and she felt angry with John Henry because he was so dull that he could not see how she suffered. In the distance, under the waving gilded leaves of the poplars, she saw Abby laughing up into a man's face, and she thought : "Can he possibly be in love with Abby ? Some men are mad about her, but I know he isn't. He could never like a loud woman, and, besides, he couldn't have looked at me that way if he hadn't cared." Then it seemed to her that something of the aching suspense in her own heart stole into Abby's laughing face while she watched it, and from Abby it passed onward into the faces of all the girls who were dancing on the raised platform. Suspense ! Was that a woman's life, after all ? Never to be able to go out and fight for what one wanted ! Always to sit at home and wait, without moving a foot or lifting a hand toward happiness ! Never to dare gallantly ! Never even to suffer openly ! Always to will in secret, always to hope in secret, always to triumph or to fail in secret. Never to be one's self—never to let one's soul or body relax from the attitude of expectancy into the attitude of achievement. For the first time, born of the mutinous longing in her heart, there came to her the tragic vision of life. The faces of the girls, whirling in white muslin to the music of the waltz, became merged into one, and this was the face of all womanhood. Love, sorrow, hope, regret, wonder, all the sharp longing and the slow waiting of the centuries—

above all, the slow waiting—these things were in her brief
vision of that single face that looked back at her out of the
whirling dance. Then the music stopped, the one face dissolved into many faces, and from among them Susan passed
under the swinging lanterns and came towards her.

" Oh, Jinny, where have you been hiding ? I promised
Oliver I would find you for him. He says he came only to
look at you."

The music began joyously again ; the young leaves, gilded
by the yellow lantern-light, danced in the warm wind as if
they were seized by the spirit of melody ; and from the dusk
of the trellis the ravished sweetness of honeysuckle flooded
the garden with fragrance. With the vanished sadness in her
heart there fled the sadness in the waltz and in the faces of
the girls who danced to the music. Waiting no longer seemed
pain to her, for it was enriched now by the burning sweetness
of fulfilment.

Suddenly, for she had not seen him approach, she was conscious that he was at her side, looking down at her beneath
a lantern which was beginning to flicker. A sense of deep
peace—of perfect contentment with the world as God planned
it—took possession of her. Even the minutes of suspense
seemed good, because they had brought at last this swift rush
of happiness. Every line of his face—of that face which had
captured her imagination as though it had been the face of
her dreams—was illumined by the quivering light that gilded
the poplars. His eyes were so close to hers that she saw little
flecks of gold on the brown,. and she grew dizzy while she
looked into them, as if she stood on a height and feared to
turn lest she should lose her balance and fall. A delicious
stillness, which began in her brain and passed to her throbbing
pulses, enveloped her like a perfume. While she stood there
she was incapable of thought—except the one joyous thought
that this was the moment for which she had waited since the
hour of her birth. Never could she be the same afterwards !
Never could she be unhappy again in the future ! For, like
other mortals in other ecstatic instants, she surrendered herself to the intoxicating illusion of their immortality.

After that silence, so charged with emotion for them both,
it seemed that when he spoke it must be to utter words that

would enkindle the world to beauty; but he said merely:
"Is this dance free? I came only to speak to you."

His look added, "I came because my longing had grown
unbearable"; and though she replied only to his words, it
was his look that made the honeysuckle-trellis, the yellow
lanterns, and the sky, with its few soft stars, go round like
coloured balls before her eyes. The world melted away from
her, and the distance between her and the whirling figures in
white muslin seemed greater than the distance between star
and star. She had the sense of spiritual remoteness, of shining
isolation, which ecstasy brings to the heart of youth, as though
she had escaped from the control of ordinary phenomena and
stood in a blissful pause beyond time and space. It was the
supreme moment of love; and to her, whose soul acknowledged
no other supremacy than that of love, it was, also, the supreme
moment of life.

His face, as he gazed down at her under the swinging leaves,
seemed to her as different from all other faces as the exquisite
violence in her soul was different from all other emotions she
had ever known. She knew nothing more of him than that
she could not be happy away from him. She needed no more
infallible proof of his perfection than the look in his eyes when
he smiled at her. So convincing was the argument of his
smile that it was not only impregnable against any assault of
facts, but rendered futile even the underlying principle of
reason. Had Aristotle himself risen from his grave to prove
to her that blind craving, when multiplied by blind possession,
does not equal happiness, his logic would have been powerless
before that unconquerable instinct which denied its truth.
And around them little white moths, fragile as rose-leaves,
circled deliriously in the lantern-light, for they, also, obeyed
an unconquerable instinct which told them that happiness
dwelt in the flame above which they were whirling.

"I am glad you wore blue ribbons," he said suddenly.

Her lashes trembled and fell, but they could not hide the
glow that shone in her eyes and in the faint smile which
trembled, like an edge of light, on her lips.

"Will you come into the summer-house and sit out this
dance?" he asked, when she did not speak, and she followed
him under the hanging clusters of early roses to a bench in

the dusk beside a little rustic table. Here, after a moment's silence, he spoke again recklessly, yet with a certain constraint of manner.

"I suppose I oughtn't to have come here to-night."

"Why not?" Their glances, bright as swords, crossed suddenly, and it seemed to her that the music grew louder. Had it been of any use, she would have prayed Life to dole the minutes out, one by one, like a miser. And all the time she was thinking : "This is the moment I've waited for ever since I was born. It has come. I am in the midst of it. How can I keep it for ever?"

"Well, I haven't any business thinking about anything but my work," he answered. "I've broken with my uncle, you know. I'm as poor as a church mouse, and I'll never be better off until I get a play on the stage. For the next few years I've got to cut out everything but hard work."

"Yes." Her tongue was paralyzed ; she couldn't say what she felt, and everything else seemed to her horribly purposeless and ineffectual. She wondered passionately if he thought her a fool, for she could not look into his mind and discover how adorable he found her monosyllabic responses. The richness of her beauty combined with the poverty of her speech made an irresistible appeal to the strongest part of him, which was not his heart, but his imagination. He wondered what she would say if she were really to let herself go, and this wonder began gradually to enslave him.

"That's the reason I hadn't any business coming here," he added, "but the truth is I've wanted to see you again ever since that first afternoon. I got to wondering whether,"—he laughed in an embarrassed way, and added with an attempt at levity, "whether you would wear a red rose in your hair."

At his change of tone, she reached up suddenly, plucked the rose from her hair, and flung it out on the grass. Her action, which belied her girlish beauty so strangely that only her mother would have recognized it as characteristic of the hidden force of the woman, held him for an instant speechless under her laughing eyes. Then, turning away, he picked up the rose and put it into his pocket.

"I suppose you will never tell me why you did that?" he asked.

She shook her head. " I can't tell. I don't know. Something took me."

" Did you think I came just for the rose ?"

" I didn't think."

" If I came for the rose, I ought to go. I wish I could. Do you suppose I'll be able to work again now that I've seen you ? I've told myself for three days that if I could only see you again I'd be able to stop thinking about you."

She was not looking at him, but in every line of her figure, in every quiver of her lashes, in every breath that she drew, he read the effect of his words. It was as if her whole palpitating loveliness had become the vehicle of an exquisite entreaty. Her soul seemed to him to possess the purity, not of snow, but of flame, and this flame, in whose light nothing evil could live, curved towards him as if blown by a wind. He felt suddenly that he was swept onward by some outside power which was stronger than his will. An enchantment had fallen over him, and at one and the same instant he longed to break the power of the spell and knew that life would cease to be worth living if he were ever to do so. He saw her eyes, like blue flowers in the soft dusk, and the mist of curls on her temples stirred gently in the scented breeze that blew over the garden. All the sweetness of the world was gathered into the little space that she filled. Every impulse of joy he had ever felt—memories of autumn roads, of starlit mountains, of summer fields where bees drifted in golden clouds—all these were packed like honey into that single minute of love. And with the awakening of passion there came the exaltation, the consciousness of illimitable possibilities which passion brings to the young. Never before had he realized the power that was in him ! Never until this instant had he seen his own soul in the making ! All the unquenchable faith of youth burned at white heat in the flame which his desire had kindled. He felt himself divided between an invincible brutality and an invincible tenderness. He would have fought with beasts for the sake of the gentle and passive creature beside him, yet he would have died rather than sully the look of angelic goodness with which she regarded him. To have her always gentle, always passive, never reaching out her hand, never descending to his level, but sitting for ever aloof and colourless, waiting eternally, patient, beautiful and unwearied, to crown the victory—this was what the conquering male in him demanded.

"I ought to go," he said, so ineffectual was speech to convey the tumult within his brain. "I am keeping you from the others."

She had shrunk back into the dimness beyond the circle of lanterns, and he saw her face like a pale moon under the clustering rose-leaves. Her very breath seemed suspended, and there was a velvet softness in her look and in the gesture of timid protest with which she responded to his halting words. She was putting forth all her woman's power as innocently as the honeysuckle puts forth its fragrance. The white moths whirling in their brief passion over the lantern flame were not more helpless before the movement of those inscrutable forces which we call Life. A strange stillness surrounded her—as though she were separated by a circle of silence from the dancers beyond the rose-crowned walls of the summer-house—and into this stillness there passed, like an invisible current, the very essence of womanhood. The longing of all the dead women of her race flowed through her into the softness of the spring evening. Things were there which she could know only through her blood—all the mute patience, all the joy that is half fear, all the age-long dissatisfaction with the merely physical end of love—these were in that voiceless entreaty for happiness; and mingled with them, there were the inherited ideals of self-surrender, of service, pity, loyalty, and sacrifice.

"I wish I could help you," she said, and her voice thrilled with the craving to squander herself magnificently in his service.

"You are an angel, and I'm a selfish beast to bring you my troubles."

"I don't think you are selfish—of course, you have to think of your work—a man's work means so much to him."

"It's wonderful of you to feel that," he replied; and, indeed, at the instant while he searched her eyes in the dusk, the words seemed to him to embody all the sympathetic understanding with which his imagination endowed her. How perfectly her face expressed the goodness and gentleness of her soul! What a companion she would make to a man! What a lover! What a wife! Always soft, exquisite, tender, womanly to the innermost fibre of her being, and perfect in unselfishness as all womanly women are. How easy it would be to work if she were somewhere within call, ready to fly to him at a word! How glorious to go out into the world if he knew that she sat at home waiting—always waiting, with those eyes like wells of happiness, until he should return to her! A new meaning had entered swiftly into life. A feeling that was like a religious conversion had changed not only his spiritual vision, but the material aspect of nature. Whatever happened, he felt that he could never be the same man again.

"I shall see you soon?" he said, and the words fell like snow on the inner flame of his senses.

"Oh, soon!" she answered, bending a little towards him, while a sudden glory illumined her features. Her voice, which was vibrant as a harp, had captured the wistful magic of the spring—the softness of the winds, the sweetness of flowers, the mellow murmuring of the poplars.

She rose from the bench, moving softly as if she were under an enchantment which she feared to break by a gesture. An ecstasy as inarticulate as grief kept him silent, and it was into this silence that the voice of Abby floated, high, shrill, and dominant.

"Oh, Virginia, I've looked everywhere for you!" she cried. "Mr. Carrington is simply dying to dance with you!"

She bounced, as only the solid actuality can bounce, into the dream, precipitating the unwelcome presence of Mr. Carrington—a young man with a golden beard and the manner of a commercial minor prophet—there also. A few minutes later, as Virginia drifted away in his arms to the music of the waltz, she saw, over the heads of the dancers, Oliver and Abby walking slowly in the direction of the gate. A feeling of unreality seized her, as though she were looking through an azure veil at the world. The dancers among whom she whirled, the anxious mothers sitting uneasily on chairs under the poplars, the flowering shrubs, the rose-crowned summer-house, the yellow lanterns with the clouds of white moths circling around them—all these things had turned suddenly to shadows ; and through a phantom garden the one living figure moved beside an empty shape, which was Abby. Her feet had wings. She flew rather than danced in the arms of a shadow through this blue veil which enveloped her. Life burned within her like a flame in a porcelain vase, and this inner fire separated her, as genius separates its possessor, from the ordinary mortals among whom she moved.

Walking home with John Henry after the party was over, it seemed to her that she was lifted up and cradled in all the wonderful freshness of the spring. The sweet moist air fanned her face ; the morning stars shone softly on her through the pearly mist ; and the pale fingers of dawn were spread like a beneficent hand above the eastern horizon. "To-morrow !" cried her heart, overflowing with joy ; and something of this joy passed into the saddest hour of day and brightened it to radiance.

At the gate she parted from John Henry, and running eagerly along the path, opened the front-door, which was unlocked, and burst into the dining-room, where her mother, wearied of her long watch, had fallen asleep beside the lamp, which was beginning to flicker.

"To-morrow !" still sang her heart, and the wild, sweet music of it filled the world. "To-morrow !"

CHAPTER IX

THE GREAT MAN MOVES

SEVERAL weeks later, at the close of a June afternoon, Cyrus Treadwell sat alone on the back porch of his house in Bolingbroke Street. He was smoking, and, between the measured whiffs of his pipe, he leaned over the railing and spat into a bed of miniature sunflowers which grew along the stone ledge of the area. For thirty years these flowers had sprung up valiantly every spring in that bleak strip of earth, and for thirty years Cyrus had spat among them while he smoked alone on the back porch on June afternoons.

While he sat there a great peace enfolded and possessed him. The street beyond the sagging wooden gate was still; the house behind him was still; the kitchen, in which showed the ebony silhouette of a massive cook kneading dough, was still with the uncompromising stillness of the Sabbath. In the midst of this stillness, his thoughts, which were usually as angular as lean birds on a bough, lost their sharpness of outline and melted into a vague and feathery mass. At the moment it was impossible to know of what he was thinking, but he was happy with the happiness which visits men of small parts and of sterile imagination. By virtue of these limitations and this sterility he had risen out of obscurity— for the spiritual law which decrees that to gain the world one must give up one's soul, was exemplified in him as in all his class. Success, the shibboleth of his kind, had controlled his thoughts and even his impulses so completely for years, that he had come at last to resemble an animal less than he resembled a machine; and Nature (who has a certain large and careless manner of dispensing justice) had punished him in the end by depriving him of the ordinary animal capacity for pleasure. The present state of vacuous contentment was, perhaps, as near the condition of enjoyment as he would ever approach.

Half an hour before he had had an encounter with Susan on the subject of her going to college, but even his victory, which had been sharp and swift, was robbed of all poignant satisfaction by his native inability to imagine what his refusal must have meant to her. The girl had stood straight and tall, with her commanding air, midway between the railing and the weather-stained door of the house.

"Father, I want to go to college," she had said quite simply, for she was one who used words very much as Cyrus used money, with a temperamental avoidance of all extravagance.

Her demand was a direct challenge to the male in Cyrus, and, though this creature could not be said to be either primitive or predatory, he was still active enough to defend himself from the unprovoked assault of an offspring.

"Tut-tut," he responded. "If you want something to occupy you, you'd better start about helping your mother with her preserving."

"I put up seventy-five jars of strawberries."

"Well, the blackberries are coming along. I was always partial to blackberries."

He sat there, bald, shrunken, yellow, as soulless as a steam-engine, and yet to Susan he represented a pitiless manifestation of destiny—of those deaf, implacable forces by which the lives of men and women are wrecked. He had the power to ruin her life, and yet he would never see it, because he had been born blind. That in his very blindness had lain his strength was a fact which, naturally enough, escaped her for the moment. The one thought of which she was conscious was a fierce resentment against life, because such men possessed such power over others.

"If you will lend me the money, I will pay it back to you as soon as I can take a position," she said, almost passionately.

Something that was like the ghost of a twinkle appeared in his eyes, and he let fall presently one of his rare pieces of humour.

"If you'd like a chance to repay me for your education,"

he said, "there's your schooling at Miss Priscilla's still owing, and I'll take it out in help about the housekeeping."

Then Susan went, because going in silence was the only way that she could save the shreds of dignity which remained to her, and bending forward, with a contented chuckle, Cyrus spat benevolently down upon the miniature sunflowers.

In the half-hour that followed he did not think of his daughter. From long discipline his mind had fallen out of the habit of thinking of people except in their relation to the single vital interest of his life, and this interest was not father-hood. Susan was an incident—a less annoying incident, it is true, than Belinda—but still an incident. An inherent con-tempt for women, due partly to qualities of temperament and partly to the accident of a disillusioning marriage, made him address them always as if he were speaking from a platform. And, as is often the case with men of cold-blooded sensuality, women, from Belinda downward. had taken their revenge upon him.

The front-door bell jangled suddenly, and a little later he heard a springy step passing along the hall. Then the green lattice door of the porch opened, and the face of Mrs. Peachey, wearing the look of unnatural pleasantness which becomes fixed on the features of persons who spend their lives making the best of things, appeared in the spot where Susan had been half an hour before. She had trained her lips to smile so persistently and so unreasonably, that when, as now, she would have preferred to present a serious countenance to an observer, she found it impossible to relax the muscles of her mouth from their expression of perpetual cheerfulness. Cyrus, who had once remarked of her that he didn't believe she could keep a straight face at her own funeral, wondered, while he rose and offered her a chair, whether the periodical sprees of honest Tom were the cause or the result of the look of set felicity she wore. For an instant he was tempted to show his annoyance at the intrusion. Then, because she was a pretty woman and did not belong to him, he grew almost playful, with the playfulness of an uncertain tempered ram that is offered salt.

"It is not often that I am honoured by a visit from you," he said.

"The honour is mine, Mr. Treadwell," she replied, and she really felt it. "I was on my way upstairs to see Belinda and it just crossed my mind, as I saw you sitting out here, that I'd better stop and speak to you about your nephew. I wonder Belinda doesn't plant a few rose-bushes along that back wall," she added.

"I'd pay you fifty dollars, ma'am, if you'd get Belinda to plant anything"—which was not delicately put, perhaps, but was, after all, spoken in the only language that Cyrus knew.

"I thought she was so fond of flowers. She used to be, as a girl."

"Humph!" was Cyrus's rejoinder, and then : "Well, what about my nephew, madam?" Clasping his bony hands over his knee, he leaned forward and waited, not without curiosity, for her answer. He did not admire Oliver—he even despised him—but when all was said, the boy had succeeded in riveting his attention. However poorly he might think of him, the fact remained that think of him he did. The young man was in the air as inescapably as if he were the measles.

"I'm worrying about him, Mr. Treadwell; I can't help myself. You know he boards with me."

"Yes'm, I know," replied Cyrus—for he had heard the fact from Miss Priscilla on his way home from church one Sunday.

"And he's not well. There's something the matter with him. He's so nervous and irritable that he's almost crazy. He doesn't eat a morsel, and I can hear him pacing up and down his room until daybreak. Once I got up and went upstairs to ask him if he was sick, but he said that he was perfectly well, and was walking about for exercise. I am sure I don't know what it can be, but if it keeps up, he'll land in an asylum before the summer is over."

The look of satisfaction which her first words had brought to Cyrus's face deepened gradually as her story unfolded. "He's wanting money, I reckon," he commented, his imagination seizing upon the only medium in which it could work. As a philosopher may discern in all life different manifestations of the Deity, so he saw in all affliction only the wanting of money under varied aspects. Sorrows in which the lack of money did not bear a part always seemed to him to be unnecessary, and generally self-inflicted by the sufferers. Of such people he would say impatiently that they took a morbid view of their troubles and were "nursing grief."

"I don't think it's that," said Mrs. Peachey. "He always pays his bills promptly on the first day of the month, and I know that he gets cheques from New York for the writing he does. I'm sometimes tempted to believe that he has fallen in love."

"Love? Pshaw!" said Cyrus, and dismissed the passion.

"But it goes hard with some people, and he's one of that kind," rejoined the little lady with spirit, for in spite of her wholesome awe of Cyrus, she could not bear to hear the sentiment derided. "We aren't all as sensible as you are, Mr. Treadwell.

"Well, if he is in love, as you say, whom is he in love with?" demanded Cyrus.

"It's all guesswork," answered Mrs. Peachey. "He isn't paying attention to any girl that I know of—but, I suppose, if it's anybody, it must be Virginia Pendleton. All the young men are crazy about her."

She had been prepared for opposition—she had been prepared, being a lady, for anything, as she told Tom afterwards, short of an oath—but to her amazement the unexpected, which so rarely happened in the case of Cyrus, happened at that minute. Human nature, which she had treated almost as a science, proved suddenly that it was not even an art. One of those glaring inconsistencies which confute every theory and overturn all psychology was manifested before her.

"That's the daughter of old Gabriel, ain't it?" asked Cyrus, and unconsciously to himself his voice softened.

"Yes, she's Gabriel's daughter, and one of the sweetest girls that ever lived."

"Gabriel's a good man," said Cyrus. "I always liked Gabriel. We fought through the war together."

"A better man never lived, nor a better woman than Lucy. If she's got a fault on earth, it's that she's too unselfish."

"Well, if this girl takes after them, the young fool has shown more sense than I gave him credit for."

"I don't think he's a fool," returned Mrs. Peachey, reflecting how wonderfully she had "managed" the great man, "but, of course, he's queer—all writers are queer, aren't they?"

"He's kept it up longer than I thought, but I reckon he's about ready to give in," pursued Cyrus, ignoring her question, as he did all excursions into the region of abstract wonder. "If he'll start in to earn his living now, I'll let him have a job on the railroad out in Matoaca City. I meant to teach him a lesson, but I shouldn't like Henry's son to starve. I've nothing against Henry except that he was too soft. He was a good brother, as brothers go, and I haven't forgotten it."

"Perhaps, if you'd talk to Oliver," suggested Mrs. Peachey. "I'm afraid I couldn't induce him to come to you, but——"

"Oh, I ain't proud—I don't need to be," interrupted Cyrus with a chuckle. "Only fools and the poor have any use for pride. I'll look in upon him sometime along after supper, and see if he's come to his wits since I last talked to him."

"Then, I'm glad I came to you. Tom would be horrified almost to death if he knew of it; but I've always said that when an idea crosses my mind just like that,"—she snapped her thumb and forefinger—"there's something in it."

As she rose from her seat, she looked up at him with the coquetry which was so inalienable an attribute of her soul that, had the Deity assumed masculine shape before her, she would instinctively have used this weapon to soften the severity of His judgment. "It was so kind of you not to send me away, Mr. Treadwell," she said in honeyed accents.

"It is a pleasure to meet such a sensible woman," replied Cyrus with awkward gallantry. Her flattery had warmed him pleasantly, and in the midst of the dried husks of his nature, he was conscious suddenly that a single blade of living green still survived. He had ceased to feel old—he felt almost young again—and this rejuvenation had set in merely because a middle-aged woman, whom he had known since childhood, had shown an innocent pleasure in his society. Mrs. Peachey's traditional belief in the power of sex had proved its own justification.

When she had left him, Cyrus sat down again and took up his pipe from the railing where he had placed it. "I'll go round and have some words with the young scamp," he thought. "There's no use waiting until after supper. I'll go round now, while it is light."

Then, as if the softening impulse were a part of the Sabbath stillness, he leaned over the bed of sunflowers, and fixed his eyes on the pinkish tower of Saint James's Church, which he could see palely enkindled against the afterglow. A single white cloud floated like a dove in the west, and beneath it a rain of light fell on the shadowy roofs of the town. The air was so languorous that it was as if the day were being slowly smothered in honeysuckle, the heavy scent of which drifted to him from the next garden. A vast melancholy—so vast that it seemed less the effect of a Southern summer than of a universal force residing in nature—was liberated, with the first cooling breath of the evening, from man and beast, from tree and shrub, from stock and stone. The very bricks, sunbaked and scarred, spoke of the weariness of heat, of the parching thirst of the interminable summers.

But to Cyrus the languor and the intense sweetness of the air suggested only that the end of a hot day had come. "It's likely to be a drought," he was thinking, while his upward gaze rested on the illuminated tower of the church. "A drought will go hard with the tobacco."

Having emptied his pipe, he was about to take down his straw hat from a nail on the wall, when the sound of the opening gate arrested him, and he waited with his eyes fixed on the winding brick walk, where the negro washerwoman appeared presently with a basket of clean clothes on her head. Beneath her burden he saw that there were some primitive attempts at Sunday adornment. She wore a green muslin dress, a little discoloured by perspiration, but with many compensating flounces; a bit of yellow ribbon floated from her throat, and in her hand she carried the festive hat which would decorate her head after the removal of the basket. Her figure, which had once been graceful, had grown heavy; and her face, of a light gingerbread colour, with broad, not unpleasant features, wore a humble, inquiring look—the look of some trustful wild animal that man has tamed and only partly domesticated. Approaching the steps, she brought down the basket from her head, and came on, holding it with a deprecating swinging movement in front of her.

"Howdy, Marster ?" she said, as if uncertain whether to stop or to pass on into the doorway.

"Howdy, Mandy ?" responded Cyrus. "There's a hot spell coming, I reckon."

Lowering the basket to the floor of the porch, the woman drew a red bandanna handkerchief from her bosom and began slowly to wipe the drops of sweat from her face and neck. The acrid odour of her flesh reached Cyrus, but he made no movement to draw away from her.

"I'se been laid up wid er stitch in my side, Marster, so I'se jes got dese yer close done dis mawnin'. Dar wan' noner de chillen at home ter tote um down yer, so I low I 'uz gwine ter drap by wid um on my way ter church."

As he did not reply, she hesitated an instant, and over her features, which looked as if they had been flattened by a blow, there came an expression which was half scornful, half inviting, yet so little personal that it might have been worn by one of her tree-top ancestors while he looked down from his sheltering boughs on a superior species of the jungle. The chance effect of light and shadow on a grey rock was hardly less human or more primitive.

"I'se gittin' moughty well along, Marster," she said ; "I reckon I'se gittin' on toward a hunnard."

"Nonsense, Mandy, you ain't a day over thirty-five. There's a plenty of life left in you yet."

"Go way f'om yer, Marster ; you knows I'se a heap older 'n dat. How long ago was hit I done fust come yer ter you all ?"

He thought a moment. A question of calculation always interested him, and he prided himself on his fine memory for dates.

"You came the year our son Henry died, didn't you ? That was in '66—eighteen years ago. Why, you couldn't have been over fifteen that summer."

For the first time a look of cunning—of the pathetic cunning of a child pitted against a man—awoke in her face.

"En Miss Lindy sent me off befo' de year was up, Marster.

My boy Jubal was born de mont' atter she done tu'n me out."
She hesitated a minute, and then added, with a kind of savage
coquetry, " I 'uz a moughty likely gal, Marster. You ain't
done furgit dat, is you ?"

Her words touched Cyrus like the flick of a whip on a
sore, and he drew back quickly while his thin lips grew
tight.

"You'd better take that basket into the house," he said
sharply.

In the negress's face an expression of surprise wavered for
a second, and then disappeared. Her features resumed their
usual passive and humble look—a look which said, if Cyrus
could have read human nature as easily as he read finance,
"I don't understand, but I submit without understanding.
Am I not what you have made me ? Have I not been what
you wanted ? And yet you despise me for being the thing
you made."

"I didn't mean nuttin', Marster. I didn't mean nuttin',"
she protested aloud.

"Then get into the house," retorted Cyrus harshly, " and
don't stand gaping there. Any more of your insolence, and
I'll never let you set foot in this yard again."

"'Fo' de Lawd, I didn't mean nuttin' ! Gawd a'moughty,
I didn't mean nuttin' ! I jes lowed as you mought be willin'
ter gun me fo' dollars a mont' fur de washin'. My boy
Jubal——"

"I'll not give you a red cent more. If you don't want it,
you can leave it. Get out of here !"

All the primitive antagonism of race—that instinct older
than civilization—was in the voice with which he ordered her
out of his sight. "It was downright blackmail. The fool
was trying to blackmail me," he thought. "If I'd yielded
an inch I'd have been at her mercy. It's a pretty pass things
have come to when men have to protect themselves from
negro women." The more he reflected on her impudence,
the stronger grew his conviction that he had acted remarkably well. "Nipped it in the root. If I hadn't——" he
thought.

And behind him in the doorway the washerwoman continued to regard him, over the lowered clothes-basket, with

her humble and deprecating look, which said, like the
look of a beaten animal: "I don't understand, but I
submit without understanding, because you are stronger
than I."

Taking down his hat, Cyrus turned away from her, and
descended the steps. "I'll look up Henry's son before
supper," he was thinking. "Even if the boy's a fool, I'm
not one to let those of my own blood come to want."

CHAPTER X

OLIVER SURRENDERS

WHEN Cyrus's knock came at his door, Oliver crossed the room to let in his visitor, and then fell back, startled, at the sight of his uncle. " I wonder what has brought him here ?" he thought inhospitably. But even if he had put the question, it is doubtful if Cyrus could have enlightened him—for the great man was so seldom visited by an impulse that when, as now, one actually took possession of him, he obeyed the pressure almost unconsciously. Like most men who pride themselves upon acting solely from reason, he was the abject slave of the few instincts which had managed to take root and thrive in the stony ground of his nature. The feeling for family, which was so closely entwined with his supreme feeling for property that the two had become inseparable, moved him to-day as it had done on the historic occasion when he had redeemed the mortgaged roof over the heads of his spinster relations. Perhaps, too, some of the vague softness of June had risen in him, and made him gentler in his judgments of youth.

"I didn't expect you, or I'd have straightened up a bit," said Oliver, not over graciously, while he hastily pushed his supper of bread and tea to one end of the table. He resented what he called in his mind " the intrusion," and he had no particular objection to his uncle's observing his resentment. His temper, never of the most perfect equilibrium, had been entirely upset by the effects of a June Sunday in Dinwiddie, and the affront of Cyrus's visit had become an indignity because of his unfortunate selection of the supper - hour. Some hidden obliquity in the Treadwell soul, which kept it always at cross-purposes with life, prevented any lessening of the deep antagonism between the old and the young of the race. And so incurable was this obliquity in the soul of Cyrus that it forced him now to take a tone which he had resolutely set his mind against from the moment of Mrs. Peachey's visit. He wanted to be pleasant, but something deep down within him—some inherited tendency to bully—was stronger than his will.

"I looked in to see if you hadn't about come to your senses," he began.

"If you mean come to your way of looking at things—then I haven't," replied Oliver; and added in a more courteous tone : "Won't you sit down ?"

"No, sir, I can stand long enough to say what I came to say," retorted the other, and it seemed to him that the pleasanter he tried to make his voice, the harsher grew the sound of it in his ears. What was it about the rascal that rubbed him the wrong way only to look at him ?

"As you please," replied Oliver quietly. "What in thunder has he got to say to me ?" he thought. "And why can't he say it and have it over ?" While Cyrus merely despised him, he detested Cyrus with all the fiery intolerance of his age. "Standing there like an old turkey gobbler, ugh !" he said contemptuously to himself.

"So you ain't hungry yet ?" asked the old man, and felt that the words were forced out of him by that obstinate cross-grain in his nature over which he had no control.

"I've just had tea."

"You haven't changed your mind since you last spoke to me, eh ?"

"No, I haven't changed my mind. Why should I ?"

"Getting along pretty well, then ?"

"As well as I expected to."

"That's good," said Cyrus mildly. "That's good. I just dropped in to make sure that you were getting along, that's all."

"Thank you," responded Oliver, and tried from the bottom of his soul to make the words sincere.

"If the time ever comes when you feel that you have changed your mind, I'll find a place out at Matoaca City for you. I just wanted you to understand that I'd do as much for Henry's son then as now. If you weren't Henry's son, I shouldn't think twice about you."

"You mean that you'll still give me the job if I stop writing plays ?"

"Oh, I won't make a point of that as long as it doesn't interfere with your work. You may write in off hours as much as you want to. I won't make a point of that."

"You mean to be generous, I can see; but I don't think it likely that I shall ever make up my mind to take a regular job. I'm not built for it."

"You're not thinking about getting married, then, I reckon ?"

A dark flush rose to Oliver's forehead, and turning away, he stared with unseeing eyes out of the window.

"No; I haven't any intention of that," he responded.

A certain craftiness appeared in Cyrus's face.

"Well, well, you're young yet, and you may be in want of a wife before you're many years older."

"I'm not the kind to marry. I'm too fond of my freedom."

"Most of us have felt like that at one time or another, but when the thought of a woman takes you by the throat, you'll begin to see things differently. And if you ever do, a good steady job at twelve hundred a year will be what you'll look out for."

"I suppose a man could marry on that down here," said Oliver, half unconscious that he was speaking aloud.

"I married on less, and I've known plenty of others that have done so. A good saving wife puts more into a man's pocket than she takes out of it."

As he paused, Oliver's attention, which had wandered off into a vague mist of feeling, became suddenly riveted to the appalling spectacle of his uncle's marriage. He saw the house in Bolingbroke Street, with the worn drab oilcloth in the hall, and he smelt the smell of stale cooking which floated through the green lattice door at the back. All the sweetness of life, all the beauty, all the decency, even, seemed strangled in that smell as if in some malarial air. And in the midst of it, the unkempt, slack figure of Belinda, with her bitter eyes and her sagging skirt, passed perpetually under the flickering gas-jet up and down the dimly lighted staircase. This was how one marriage had ended—one marriage among many which had started out with passion and courage and the belief in happiness. Knowing but little of the April brevity of his uncle's mating impulse, he had mentally embroidered the bare instinct with some of the idealism in which his own emotion was clothed. His imagination pictured Cyrus and Belinda starting as light-hearted adventurers to sail the chartless seas of romance. What remained of their gallant ship to-day except a stark and battered hulk wrecked on the pitiless rocks of the actuality ? A month ago that marriage had seemed merely ridiculous to him. Standing now beside the little window, where the wan face of evening, languid and fainting sweet, looked in from the purple twilight, he was visited by one of those rare flashes of insight which come to men of artistic sensibility after long periods of spiritual warfare. Pity stabbed him as sharply as ridicule had done a moment before, and with the first sense of human kinship he had ever felt to Cyrus he understood suddenly the tragedy that underlies all comic things. Could there be a deeper pathos, after all, than simply being funny ? This absurd old man, with his lean, crooked figure, his mottled skin, and his piercing, bloodshot eyes, like the eyes of an overgorged bird of prey, appeared now as an object that moved one to tears, not to laughter. And yet because of this very quality which made him pitiable —this vulture-like instinct to seize and devour the smaller— he stood to-day the most conspicuously envied figure in Dinwiddie.

" I'm not the kind of man to marry," he repeated, but his tone had changed.

" Well, perhaps you're wise," said Cyrus, " but if you should ever want to——" The confidence which had gone out of Oliver had passed into him. With his strange power of reading human nature—masculine human nature, for the silliest woman could fool him hopelessly—he saw that his nephew was already beginning to struggle against the temptation to yield. And he was wise enough to know that this temptation would become stronger as soon as Oliver felt that the outside pressure was removed. The young man's passion was putting forward a subtler argument than Cryus could offer.

When his visitor had gone, Oliver turned back to the window, and, resting his arms on the sill, leaned out into the velvet softness of the twilight. His wide vision had deserted him. It was as if his gaze had narrowed down to a few roofs and the single street without a turning — but beyond them the thought of Virginia lay always like an enclosed garden of sweetness and bloom. To think of her was to pass from the scorching heat of the day to the freshness of dew-washed flowers under the starlight.

"It is impossible," he said aloud, and immediately, as if in answer to a challenge, a thousand proofs came to him that other men were doing the impossible every day. How many writers—great writers, too—would have jumped at a job on a railroad to insure them against starvation ? How many had married young and faced the future on less than twelve hundred dollars a year ? How many had let love lead them where it would without butting their brains for ever against the damned wall of expediency ?

"It's impossible," he said again, and, turning from the window, made himself ready to go out. While he brushed his hair and pulled the end of his necktie through the loop, his gaze wandered back over the roofs to where a solitary mimosa-tree drooped against the lemon-coloured afterglow. The dust lay like gauze over the distance. Not a breath stirred. Not a leaf fell. Not a figure moved in the town— except the crouching figure of a stray cat that crawled, in search of food, along the brick wall under the dead tree.

"God ! What a life !" he cried suddenly. And beyond this parching desert of the present he saw again that enclosed garden of sweetness and bloom, which was Virginia. His resolution, weakened by the long hot afternoon, seemed to faint under the pressure of his longing. All the burden of the day—the heat, the languor, the scorching thirst of the fields, the brazen blue of the sky, the stillness as of a suspended breath which wrapt the town—all these things had passed into the intolerableness of his desire. He felt it like a hot wind blowing over him, and it seemed to him that he was as helpless as a leaf in the current of this wind which was sweeping him onward. Something older than his will was driving him ; and this something had come to him from out the twilight, where the mimosa-trees dropped like a veil against the afterglow.

Taking up his hat, he left the room and descended the stairs to the wide hall where Tom Peachey sat, gasping for breath, midway of two open doors.

" I'll be darned if I can make a draught," muttered the old soldier irascibly, while he picked up his alpaca coat from the balustrade, and slipped into it before going out upon the front porch into the possible presence of ladies. His usually cheerful face was clouded, for his habitual apathy had deserted him, and he had reached the painful decision that when you looked things squarely in the face there was precious little that was worth living for—a conclusion to which he had been brought by the simple accident of an overdose of Kentucky rye in his mint julep after church. The overdose had sent him to sleep too soon after his Sunday dinner, and when he had awakened from his heavy and by no means quiet slumber, he had found himself confronting a world of gloom.

" I'm damned tired making the best of things, if you want to know what is the matter with me," he had remarked crossly to his wife.

" The idea, Mr. Peachey ! You ought to be ashamed of yourself !" that sprightly lady had responded while she prepared herself for her victory over Cyrus.

" Well, I ain't," honest Tom had retorted. " I've gone on pretending for fifty years, and I'm going to stop it. What good has it done, anyway ? It hasn't put a roof on, has it ?"

" I told you you oughtn't to go to sleep right on top of your dinner," she had replied soothingly. " I declare you're perfectly purple. I never saw you so upset. Here, take this palm-leaf fan, and go and see if you can't find a draught. You know it's downright sinful to talk that way after the Lord has been so good to you."

But Philosophy, though she is unassailable when she clings to her safeguard of the universal, meets her match whenever she descends to an open engagement with the particular.

" W-what's He done for me ?" demanded not Tom, but the whisky inside of him.

Driven against that bleak rock of fact upon which so many shining generalizations have come to wreck, Mrs. Peachey had cast about helplessly for some floating spar of logic which might bear her to the firm ground of established optimism. " I declare, Tom, I believe you are out of your head !" she exclaimed, adding immediately, " You ought to be ashamed of yourself to be so ungrateful when the good Lord has kept you out of the poorhouse. If you weren't tipsy, I'd give you a hard shaking. Now, you take that palm-leaf fan, and go right straight downstairs."

So Tom had gone, for his wife, who lacked the gift of argument, possessed the energy of character which renders such minor attributes unnecessary ; and Oliver, passing through the hall a couple of hours later, found him still helplessly seeking the draught towards which she had directed him.

" Any chance of a breeze springing up ?" inquired the young man as they moved together to the porch.

The force which was driving him out of the house into the suffocating streets was in his voice when he spoke, but honest Tom did not hear it. After the four war years in which he had been almost sublime, the old soldier had gradually ceased even to be human, and that vegetable calm which envelops persons who have fallen into the habit of sitting still had endowed him at last with the perfect serenity of a cabbage. The only active principle which ever moved in him was the borrowed principle of alcohol—for when that artificial energy subsided, he sank back, as he was beginning to do now, into the spiritual inertia which sustains those who have outlived their capacity for the heroic.

" I ain't felt a breath," he replied, peering southward, where the stars were coming out in a cloudless sky. " I don't reckon we'll get it till on about eleven."

" Looks as if we were in for a scorching summer, doesn't it ?"

" You never can tell. There's always a spell in June." And he who had been a hero, sat down in his cane-bottomed chair and waved the palm-leaf fan feebly in front of him. He had had his day ; he had fought his fight ; he had helped to make the history of battles—and now what remained to him ? The stainless memory of the four years when he was a hero ; a smouldering ember still left from that flaming glory which was his soul !

In the street the dust lay thick and still, and the wilted

foliage of the mulberry-trees hung motionless from the great arching boughs. Only an aspen at the corner seemed alive and tremulous, while sensitive little shivers ran through the silvery leaves, which looked as if they were cut out of velvet. As Oliver left the house, the town awoke slowly from its lethargy, and the sound of laughter floated to him from the porches behind their screens of honeysuckle or roses. But even this laughter seemed to him to contain the burden of weariness which oppressed and disenchanted his spirit. The pall of melancholy spread from the winding yellow river at the foot of the hill to the procession of cedars which stood pitch-black against the few dim stars on the eastern horizon.

"What is the use ?" he asked himself suddenly, uttering aloud that grim question which lies always beneath the vivid, richly clustering impressions in the imaginative mind. Of his struggle, his sacrifice—of his art even—what was the use ? A bitter despondency—the crushing despondency of youth which age does not feel and has forgotten—weighed upon him like a physical burden. And because he was young and not without a certain pride in the intensity of his suffering, he increased his misery by doggedly refusing to trace it back to its natural origin in an empty stomach.

But the laws that govern the variable mind of man are as inscrutable as the secret of light. Turning into a cross-street he came upon the tower of Saint James's Church, and he grew suddenly cheerful. The quickening of his pulses changed the aspect of the town as completely as if an invigorating shower had fallen upon it. The supreme, haunting interest of life revived.

He had meant merely to pass the rectory without stopping, but as he turned into the slanting street at the foot of the twelve stone steps, he saw a glimmer of white on the terrace, and the face of Virginia looked down at him over the palings of the gate. Immediately it seemed to him that he had known from the beginning that he should meet her. A sense of recognition so piercingly sweet that it stirred his pulses like wine was in his heart as he moved towards her. The whole universe appeared to him to have been planned and perfected for this instant. The languorous June evening, the fainting sweetness of flowers, the strange lemon-coloured afterglow, and her face, shining there like a star in the twilight—these had waited for him, he felt, since the beginning of earth. That fatalistic reliance upon an outside Power, which assumed for him the radiant guise of first love, and for Susan the stark certainties of Presbyterianism, dominated him as completely as if he were the predestined vehicle of its expression. Ardent, yet passive, Virginia leaned above him on the dim terrace. So still she seemed, that her breath left her parted lips as softly as the perfume detached itself from the opening rose-leaves. She made no gesture, she said no word—but suddenly he became aware that her stillness was stronger to draw him than any speech. All her woman's mystery was brooding there about her in the June twilight; and in this strange strength of quietness Nature had placed, for once, an invincible weapon in the weaker hands. Her appeal had become a part of the terrible and beneficent powers of Life.

Crossing the street, he went up the steps to where she leaned on the gate.

"It has been so long," he said, and the words seemed to him hideously empty. "I have not seen you but three times since the party."

She did not answer, and as he looked at her closer, he saw that her eyes were full of tears.

"Virginia!" he cried out sharply, and the next instant, at her first movement away from him, his arms were around her and his lips seeking hers.

The world stopped suddenly while a starry eternity enveloped them. All youth was packed into that minute, all the troubled sweetness of desire, all the fugitive ecstasy of fulfilment.

"I—I thought you did not care," she murmured beneath his kisses.

He could not speak—for it was a part of his ironic destiny that he, who was prodigal of light words, should find himself stricken dumb in any crucial instant.

"You know—you know——" he stammered, holding her closer.

"Then it—it is not all a dream?" she asked.

"I adored you from the first minute—you saw that—you

knew it. I've wanted you day and night since I first looked at you."

"But you kept away. You avoided me. I couldn't understand."

"It was because I knew I couldn't be with you five minutes without kissing you. And I oughtn't to—it's madness in me—for I'm desperately poor, darling ; I've no right to marry you."

A little smile shone on her lips. "As if I cared about that, Oliver."

"Then you'll marry me ? You'll marry me, my beautiful ?"

She lifted her face from his breast, and her look was like the enkindled glory of the sunrise. "Don't you see ? Haven't you seen from the beginning ?" she asked.

"I was afraid to see, darling—but, Virginia—oh, Virginia, let it be soon !"

When he went from her a little later, it seemed to him that all of life had been pressed down into the minute when he had held her against his breast ; and as he walked through the dimly lighted streets, among the shadows of men who, like himself, were pursuing some shadowy joy, he carried with him that strange vision of a heaven on earth which has haunted mortal eyes since the beginning of love. Happiness appeared to him as a condition which he had achieved by a few words, by a kiss, in a minute of time, but which belonged to him so entirely now that he could never be defrauded of it again in the future. Whatever happened to him, he could never be separated from the bliss of that instant when he had held her.

He was going to Cyrus while his ecstasy ennobled even the prosaic fact of the railroad. And just as on that other evening, when he had rushed in anger away from the house of his uncle, so now he was exalted by the consciousness that he was following the lead of the more spiritual part of his nature —for the line of least resistance was so overgrown with exquisite impressions that he no longer recognized it. The sacrifice of art for love appeared to him to-day as splendidly romantic as the sacrifice of comfort for art had seemed to him a few months ago. His desire controlled him so absolutely that he obeyed its different promptings under the belief that he was obeying the principles whose names he borrowed. The thing he wanted was transmuted by the fire of his temperament into some artificial likeness to the thing that was good for him.

On the front steps, between the two pink oleanders, Cyrus was standing with his gaze fixed on a small grocery store across the street, and at the sight of his nephew a look of curiosity, which was as personal an emotion as he was in the habit of feeling, appeared on his lean yellow face. Behind him, the door into the hall stood open, and his stooping figure was outlined against the light of the gas-jet by the staircase.

"You see I've come," said Oliver; for Cyrus, who never spoke first unless he was sure of dominating the situation, had waited for him to begin.

"Yes, I see," replied the old man, not unkindly. "I expected you, but hardly so soon—hardly so soon."

"It's about the place on the railroad. If you are still of the same mind, I'd like you to give me a trial."

"When would you want to start?"

"The sooner the better. I'd rather get settled there before the autumn. I'm going to be married some time in the autumn —October, perhaps."

"Ah!" said Cyrus softly, and Oliver was grateful to him because he didn't attempt to crow.

"We haven't told anyone yet—but I wanted to make sure of the job. It's all right, then, isn't it?"

"Oh yes, it's all right, if you do your part. She's Gabriel Pendleton's girl, isn't she?"

"She's Virginia Pendleton. You know her, of course." He tried honestly to be natural, but in spite of himself he could not keep a note of constraint out of his voice. Merely to discuss Virginia with Cyrus seemed, in some subtle way, an affront to her. Yet he knew that the old man wanted to be kind, and the knowledge touched him.

"Oh yes, I know her. She's a good girl, and there doesn't live a better man than Gabriel."

"I don't deserve her, of course. But, then, there never lived a man who deserved an angel."

"Ain't you coming in?" asked Cyrus.

" Not this evening. I only wanted to speak to you. I suppose I'd better go down to the office to-morrow and talk to Mr. Burden, hadn't I ?"

" Come about noon, and I'll tell him to expect you. Well, if you ain't coming in, I reckon I'll close this door."

Looking up a minute later from the pavement, Oliver saw his aunt rocking slowly back and forth at the window of her room, and the remembrance of her fell like a blight over his happiness.

By the time he reached High Street a wind had risen beyond the hill near the river, and the scattered papers on the pavement fled like grey wings before him into the darkness. As the air freshened, faces appeared in the doors along the way, and the whole town seemed drinking in the cooling breeze as if it were water. On the wind sped, blowing over the slack figure of Mrs. Treadwell ; blowing over the conquering smile of Susan, who was unbinding her long hair ; blowing over the joy-brightened eyes of Virginia, who dreamed in the starlight of the life that would come to her ; blowing over the ghost-haunted face of her mother, who dreamed of the life that had gone by her ; blowing at last, beyond the river, over the tired hands of the little seamstress, who dreamed of nothing except of how she might keep her living body out of the poorhouse and her dead body out of the potter's field. And over the town, with its twenty-one thousand souls, each of whom contained within itself a separate universe of tragedy and of joy, of hope and of disappointment, the wind passed as lightly as it passed over the unquiet dust in the streets below.

BOOK SECOND

THE REALITY

CHAPTER I

VIRGINIA PREPARES FOR THE FUTURE

"MOTHER, I'm so happy! Oh! was there ever a girl so happy as I am?"

"I was, dear, once."

"When you married father? Yes, I know," said Virginia, but she said it without conviction. In her heart she did not believe that marrying her father—perfect old darling that he was!—could ever have caused any girl just the particular kind of ecstasy that she was feeling. She even doubted whether such stainless happiness had ever before visited a mortal upon this planet. It was not only wonderful, it was not only perfect, but it felt so absolutely new that she secretly cherished the belief that it had been invented by the universe especially for Oliver and herself. It was ridiculous to imagine that the many million pairs of lovers that were marrying every instant had each experienced a miracle like this, and yet left the earth pretty much as they had found it before they fell in love.

It was a week before her wedding, and she stood in the centre of the spare room in the west wing, which had been turned over to Miss Willy Whitlow. The little seamstress knelt now at her feet, pinning up the hem of a black silk polonaise, and turning her head from time to time to ask Mrs. Pendleton if she was " getting the proper length." For a quarter of a century, no girl of Virginia's class had married in Dinwiddie without the crowning benediction of a black silk gown, and ever since the announcement of Virginia's betrothal her mother had cramped her small economies in order that she might buy " grosgrain " of the best quality.

"Is that right, mother? Do you think I might curve it a little more in front?" asked the girl, holding her feet still with difficulty, because she felt that she wanted to dance.

"No, dear, I think it will stay in fashion longer if you don't shorten it. Then it will be easier to make over the more goods you leave in it."

"It looks nice on me, doesn't it?" Standing there, with the stiff silk slipping away from her thin shoulders, and the dappled sunlight falling over her neck and arms through the tawny leaves of the paulownia-tree in the garden, she was like a slim white lily unfolding softly out of its sheath.

"Lovely, darling, and it will be so useful. I got the very best quality, and it ought to wear for ever."

"I made Mrs. William Goode one ten years ago, and she's still wearing it," remarked Miss Willy, speaking with an effort through a mouthful of pins.

A machine, which had been whirring briskly by the side window, stopped suddenly, and the girl who sewed there— a sickly, sallow-faced creature of Virginia's age, who was hired by Mrs. Pendleton, partly out of charity because she supported an invalid father who had been crippled in the war, and partly because, having little strength and being an unskilled worker, her price was cheap—turned for an instant and stared wistfully at the black silk polonaise over the strip of organdie which she was hemming. All her life she had wanted a black silk dress, and though she knew that she should probably never have one, and should not have time to wear it if she ever had, she liked to linger over the thought of it, very much as Virginia lingered over the thought of her lover, or as little Miss Willy lingered over the thought of having a tombstone over her after she was dead. In the girl's face, where at first there had been only admiration; a change came gradually. A quiver, so faint that it was hardly more than a shadow, passed over her drawn features, and her gaze left the trailing yards of silk and wandered to the blue October sky over the swinging leaves of the paulownia. But instead of the radiant autumn weather at which she was looking, she still saw that black silk polonaise which she wanted as she wanted youth and pleasure, and which she knew that she should never have.

"Everything is finished but this, isn't it, Miss Willy?"

asked Virginia, and at the sound of her happy voice, that strange quiver passed again through the other girl's face.

"Everything except that organdie and a couple of night-gowns." There was no quiver in Miss Willy's face, for from constant consideration of the poorhouse and the cemetery, she had come to regard the other problems of life, if not with indifference, at least with something approaching a mild contempt. Even love, when measured by poverty or by death, seemed to lose the impressiveness of its proportions.

"And I'll have enough clothes to last me for years, shan't I, mother?"

"I hope so, darling. Your father and I have done the best that we could for you."

"You've been angels. Oh, how I shall hate to leave you!"

"If only you weren't going away, Jinny!" Then she broke down, and, dropping the tomato-shaped pincushion she had been holding, she slipped from the room, while Virginia thrust the polonaise into Miss Willy's hands and fled breath-lessly after her.

In the girl's room, with her head bowed on the top of the little bookcase, above those thin rows of fiction, Mrs. Pendleton was weeping almost wildly over the coming separation. She, who had not thought of herself for thirty years, had suddenly broken the constraint of the long habit. Yet it was characteristic of her, that even now her first feeling, when Virginia found her, should be one of shame that she had clouded for an instant the girl's happiness.

"It is nothing, darling. I have a little headache, and—oh, Jinny! Jinny!——"

"Mother, it won't be long. We are coming back to live just as soon as Oliver can get work. It isn't as if I were going for good, is it? And I'll write you every day—every single day. Mother, dearest, darling mother, I can't stay away from you——"

Then Virginia wept, too, and Mrs. Pendleton, forgetting her own sorrow at sight of the girl's tears, began to comfort her.

"Of course, you'll write and tell me everything. It will be almost as if I were with you."

"And you love Oliver, don't you, mother?"

"How could I help it, dear? Only I can't quite get used to your calling your husband by his name, Jinny. It would have horrified your grandmother, and somehow it does seem lacking in respect. However, I suppose I'm old-fashioned."

"But, mother, he laughs if I call him 'Mr. Treadwell.' He says it reminds him of his Aunt Belinda."

"Perhaps he's right, darling. Anyway, he prefers it, and I fancy your grandfather wouldn't have liked to hear his wife address him so familiarly. Times have changed since my girlhood."

"And Oliver has lived out in the world so much, mother."

"Yes," said Mrs. Pendleton, but her voice was without enthusiasm. The "world" to her was a vague and sinister shape, which looked like a bubble, and exerted a malignant influence over those persons who lived beyond the borders of Virginia. Her imagination, which seldom wandered farther afield than the possibility of the rector or of Virginia falling ill, or the dreaded likelihood that her market bills would overrun her weekly allowance, was incapable of grasping a set of standards other than the one which was accepted in Dinwiddie.

"Wherever you are, Jinny, I hope that you will never forget the ideas your father and I have tried to implant in you," she said.

"I'll always try to be worthy of you, mother."

"Your first duty now, of course, is to your husband. Remember, we have always taught you that a woman's strength lies in her gentleness. His will must be yours now, and wherever your ideas cross, it is your duty to give up, darling. It is the woman's part to sacrifice herself."

"I know, mother, I know."

"I have never forgotten this, dear, and my marriage has been very happy. Of course," she added, while her forehead wrinkled nervously, "there are not many men like your father."

"Of course not, mother, but Oliver——"

In Mrs. Pendleton's soft, anxious eyes the shadow darkened, as if for the first time she had grown suspicious of the traditional wisdom which she was imparting. But this suspicion was so new and young that it could not struggle for existence against the archaic roots of her inherited belief in the Pauline measure of her sex. It was characteristic of her—and indeed of most women of her generation—that she would have endured martyrdom in support of the consecrated doctrine of her inferiority to man.

"Even in the matter of religion you ought to yield to him, darling," she said after a moment in which she had appealed to that orthodox arbiter, her conscience. "Your father and I were talking about what church you should go to, and I said that I supposed Oliver was a Presbyterian, like all of the Treadwells."

"Oh, mother, I didn't tell you before because I hoped I could change him—but he doesn't go to any church; he says they all bore him equally. He has broken away from all the old ideas, you know. He is dreadfully—unsettled."

The anxiety, which had been until then merely a shadow in Mrs. Pendleton's eyes, deepened into a positive pain.

"Your father must have known, for he talked to him—but he wouldn't tell me," she said.

"I made father promise not to. I hoped so I could change Oliver, and maybe I can after we're married, mother."

"If he has given up the old spiritual standards, what has he in place of them?" asked Mrs. Pendleton, and she had suddenly a queer feeling as if little fine needles were pricking her skin.

"I don't know, but he seems to have a great deal, more than any of us," answered Virginia; and she added passionately, "he is good, mother."

"I never doubted it, darling, but he is young, and his character cannot be entirely formed at his age. A man must be very strong in order to be good without faith."

"But he has faith, mother—of some kind."

"I am not judging him, my child, and neither your father nor I would ever criticize your husband to you. Your happiness was set on him, and we can only pray from our hearts that he will prove worthy of your love. He is very lovable, and I am sure that he has fine, generous traits. Your father has been completely won over by him."

"He likes me to be religious, mother. He says the Church

has cultivated the loveliest type of woman the world has ever seen."

"Then by fulfilling that ideal you will please him best."

"I shall try to be just what you have been to father—just as unselfish, just as devoted."

"I have made many mistakes, Jinny; but I don't think I have ever failed in love—not in love, at least."

Then the pain passed out of her eyes, and because it was impossible for her to look on any fact in life except through the transfiguring idealism with which the ages had endowed her, she became immediately convinced that everything, even the unsettling of Oliver's opinions, had been arranged for the best. This assurance was the more solacing because it was the result, not of external evidence, but of that instinctive decision of temperament which breeds the deepest conviction of all.

"Love is the only thing that really matters, isn't it, mother?"

"A pure and noble love, darling. It is a woman's life. God meant it so."

"You are so good! If I can only be half as good as you are."

"No, Jinny, I'm not really good. I have had many temptations—for I was born with a high temper, and it has taken me a lifetime to learn really to subdue it. I had—I have still an unfortunate pride. But for your father's daily example of humility and patience, I don't know how I could have supported the trials and afflictions we have known. Pray to be better than your mother, my child, if you want to become a perfect wife. What I am that seems good to you, your father has made me——"

"And father says that he would have been a savage but for you."

A tremor passed through Mrs. Pendleton's thin bosom, and bending over, she smoothed a fine darn in the skirt of her alpaca dress.

"We have loved each other," she answered. "If you and Oliver love as much, you will be happy whatever comes to you." Then choking down the hard lump in her throat, she took up her leather key basket from the little table beside the bed, and moved slowly towards the door. " I must see about supper now, dear," she said in her usual voice of quiet cheerfulness.

Left to herself, Virginia opened the worn copy of the prayer-book, which she kept at her bedside, and read the marriage service from beginning to end, as she had done every day since her engagement to Oliver. The words seemed to her, as they seemed to her mother, to be almost divine in their nobility and beauty. She was troubled by no doubt as to the inspired propriety of the canonical vision of woman. What could be more beautiful or more sacred than to be " given " to Oliver—to belong to him as utterly as she had belonged to her father ? What could make her happier than the knowledge that she must surrender her will to his from the day of her wedding until the day of her death ? She embraced her circumscribed lot with a passion which glorified its limitations. The single gift which the ages permitted her was the only one she desired. Her soul craved no adventure beyond the permissible adventure of being sought in marriage. Love was all that she asked of a universe that was overflowing with manifold aspects of life.

Beyond the window the tawny leaves of the paulownia were swinging in the October sunshine, and so gay they seemed that it was impossible to imagine them insensible to the splendour of the Indian summer. Under the half-bared boughs, on the green grass in the yard, those that had already fallen sped on, like a flock of frightened brown birds, towards the white paling fence of the churchyard.

While she sat there, with her prayer-book in her hand, and her eyes on the purple veil of the distance, it seemed to her that her joy was so complete that there was nothing left even to hope for. All her life she had looked forward to the coming of what she thought of vaguely as " happiness," and now that it was here, she felt that it put an end to the tremulous expectancy which had filled her girlhood with such wistful dreams. Marriage appeared to her (and, indeed, to Oliver also) as a miraculous event, which would make not only herself, but every side of life, different for the future. After that there would be no vain longings, no spring restlessness, no hours of drab weariness, when the interests of living seemed to crumble from mere despondency. After that they would be always happy, always eager, always buoyantly alive.

Leaving the marriage service, her thoughts brooded in a radiant stillness on the life of love which would begin for her on the day of her wedding. A strange light—the light that quivered like a golden wing over the autumn fields—shone, also, into the secret chambers of her soul, and illumined the things which had appeared merely dull and commonplace until to-day. Those innumerable little cares which fill the lives of most women were steeped in the magic glow of this miraculous charm. She thought of the daily excitement of marketing, of the perpetual romance of mending his clothes, of the glorified monotony of pouring his coffee, as an adventurer on sunrise seas might dream of the rosy islands of hidden treasure. And then, so perfectly did she conform in spirit to the classic ideal of her sex, her imagination ecstatically pictured her in the immemorial attitude of women. She saw herself waiting—waiting happily—but always waiting. She imagined the thrilling expectancy of the morning waiting for him to come home to his dinner; the hushed expectancy of the evening waiting for him to come home to his supper; the blissful expectancy of hoping that he might be early; the painful expectancy of fearing that he might be late. And it seemed to her divinely right and beautiful that, while he should have a hundred other absorbing interests in his life, her whole existence should perpetually circle around this single centre of thought. One by one, she lived in anticipation all the exquisite details of their life together, and in imagining them, she overlooked all possible changes that the years might bring, as entirely as she ignored the subtle variations of temperament which produce in each individual that fluid quantity we call character. She thought of Oliver, as she thought of herself, as though the fact of marriage would crystallize him into a shape from which he would never alter or dissolve in the future. And with a reticence peculiar to her type, she never once permitted her mind to stray to her crowning beatitude—the hope of a child; for, with that sacred inconsistency possible only to fixed beliefs, though motherhood was supposed to comprise every desire, adventure, and activity in the life of woman, it was considered indelicate for her to dwell upon the thought of it until the condition had become too obvious for refinement to deny.

The shadow of the church tower lengthened on the grass, and at the end of the cross-street she saw Susan appear and stop for a minute to speak to Miss Priscilla, who was driving by in a small waggonette. Then the girl and the teacher parted, and ten minutes later there came Susan's imperative knock at Virginia's door.

"Miss Willy told mother that your wedding dress was finished, Jinny, and I am dying to see it!"

Going to the closet, which was built into one corner of the wall, Virginia unpinned a long white sheet scented with rose-leaves, and brought out a filmy mass of satin and lace. Her face as she looked down upon it was the face of girlhood incarnate. All her virginal dreams clustered there like doves quivering for flight. Its beauty was the beauty of fleeting things—of the wind in the apple blossoms at dawn, of the music of bees on an August afternoon.

"Mother wouldn't let me be married in anything but satin," she said with a catch in her voice. "I believe it is the first time in her life she was ever extravagant, but she felt so strongly about it that I had to give in and not have white muslin as I wanted to do."

"And it's so lovely!" said Susan. "I had no idea Miss Willy could do it. She's as proud, too, as if it were her own."

"She took a pleasure in every stitch, she told me. Oh, Susan, I sometimes feel that I haven't any right to be so happy. I seem to have everything and other women to have nothing."

For the first time Susan smiled, but it was a smile of understanding. "Perhaps they have more than you think, darling."

"But there's Miss Willy—what has she ever got out of life?"

"Well, I really believe she gets a kind of happiness out of saving up the money to pay for her tombstone. It's a funny thing, but the people who ought to be unhappy, somehow never are. It doesn't seem to be a matter of what you have, but of the way you are born. Now, according to us,

Miss Willy ought to be miserable, but the truth is that she isn't a bit so. Mother saw her once skipping for pure joy in the spring."

"But people who haven't things can't be as grateful to God as those who have. I feel that I'd like to spend every minute of my life on my knees thanking Him. I don't see how I can ever have a disappointed or a selfish thought again. I wonder if you can understand, you precious Susan, but I want to open my arms and take the whole world into them."

"Jinny," said Susan suddenly, "don't spoil Oliver."

"I couldn't—not if I tried every minute."

"I don't know, dear. He is very lovable, he has fine, generous traits, he has the making of a big man in him—but his character isn't formed yet, you must remember. So much of him is imagination that he will take longer than most men to grow up to his stature."

"Oh, Susan!" exclaimed Virginia, and turned away.

"Perhaps I oughtn't to have said it, Jinny—but, no, I ought to tell you just what I think, and I don't regret it."

"Mother said the same thing to me," responded Virginia, looking as if she were on the point of tears ; "but that is just because neither of you know him as I do."

"He is a Treadwell and so am I, and the chief character-istic of every Treadwell is that he is going to get the thing he wants most. It doesn't make any difference whether it is money or love or fame, the thing he wants most he will get sooner or later. So all I mean is that you needn't spoil Oliver by giving him the universe before he wants it."

"I can't give him the universe. I can only give him myself."

Stooping over, Susan kissed her.

"Happy, happy little Jinny !"

"There are only two things that trouble me, dear—one is going away from mother and father, and the other is that you are not so happy as I am."

"Some day I may get the thing I want like every other Treadwell."

"Do you mean going to college ?"

"No," said Susan. "I don't mean that," and into her calm grey eyes a new light shone for an instant.

A clairvoyance, deeper than knowledge, came to Virginia while she looked at her.

" You darling !" she exclaimed.   " I never suspected !"

" There's nothing to suspect, Jinny.   I was only joking."

" Why, it never crossed my mind that you would think of him for a minute."

" He hasn't thought of me for a minute yet."

" The idea !   He'd be wild about you in ten seconds if he ever thought——"

" He was wild about you ten seconds ago, dear."

" He never was.   It was just his fancy.   Why, you are made for each other."

A laugh broke from Susan, but with that large and quiet candour which was characteristic of her, she did not seek to evade or deny Virginia's suspicion.   That her friend should discover her feeling for John Henry seemed to her as natural as that she should be conscious of it herself—for they were intimate with that full and perfect intimacy which exists only between two women who trust each other.

" There goes Miss Willy," said Susan, looking through the window to where the little dressmaker tripped down the stone steps to the street.   " Mother wants to have early supper, so I must be running away."

" Good-bye, darling.   Oh, Susan, I never loved you as I do now.   It will be all right—I trust and pray that it will !   And, just think, you will walk out of church together at my wedding !"

For a minute, standing on the threshold, Susan looked back at her with an expression of tender amusement in her eyes.   " Don't imagine that I'm unhappy, dear," she said, " because I'm not—it isn't that kind—and, after all, even an unrequited affection may be simply an added interest in life, if we choose to take it that way."

When she had gone, Virginia lingered over her wedding dress, while she wondered what the wise Susan could see in the simple John Henry ?   Was it possible that John Henry was not so simple, after all ?   Or did Susan, forsaking the ancient tradition of love, care about him merely because he was good ?

For a week the hours flew by with golden wings, and at

last the most sacred day of her life dawned softly in a sunrise of rose and flame. When she looked back on it afterwards, there were three things which stood out unforgettably in her memory—the kiss that her mother gave her when she turned to leave her girlhood's room for the last time ; the sound of her father's voice as he spoke her name at the altar ; and the look in Oliver's eyes when she put her hand into his. All the rest was enveloped in a shining mist which floated, like her wedding veil, between the old life and the new.

"It has been so perfect—so perfect—if I can only be worthy of this day and of you, Oliver," she said as the carriage started from the rectory gate to the station.

" You angel !" he murmured ecstatically.

Her eyes hung blissfully on his face for an instant, and then, moved by a sudden stab of reproach, she leaned from the window and looked back at her mother and father, who stood, with clasped hands, gazing after her over the white palings of the gate.

CHAPTER II

MATOACA CITY, WEST VIRGINIA,
October 16, 1884.

DEAREST, DEAREST MOTHER,

We got here this morning after a dreadful trip—nine or ten hours late—and this is the first minute I've had when I could sit down and write to you. All the way on the train I was thinking of you and dear father, and longing for you so that I could hardly keep back the tears. I don't see how I can possibly stay away from you for a whole year. Oliver says he wants to take me home for Christmas if everything goes all right with us here and his work proves satisfactory to the manager. Oh, mother, he is the loveliest thing to me ! I don't believe he has thought of himself a single minute since I married him. He says the only wish he has on earth is to make me happy—and he is so careful about me that I'm afraid I'll be spoiled to death before you see me again. He says he loves the little grey dress of shot silk, with the bonnet that makes me look like a Quaker. I wish now I'd got my other hat the bonnet shape as you wanted me to do ; but perhaps, after all, it will be more useful and keep in fashion longer as it is. When I took out my clothes this morning, while Oliver was downstairs, and remembered how you had folded and packed everything, I just sat down on the floor in the midst of them and had a good cry. I never realized how much I loved you until I got into the carriage to come away. Then I wanted to jump out and put my arms around you and tell you that you are the best and dearest mother a girl ever had. My things were so beautifully packed that there wasn't a single crease anywhere—not even in the black silk polonaise that we

159

were so afraid would get rumpled. I don't see how on earth
you folded them so smoothly. By the way, I hardly think I
shall have any need of my wedding dress while I am here, so
you may as well put it away at home until I come back. This
place seems to be just a mining town, with very few people
of our class, and those all connected with the railroad. Of
course, I may be mistaken, but from my first impressions I
doubt if I'll ever want to have much to do with anybody that
I've seen. It doesn't make a bit of difference, of course, because I shan't be lonesome a minute with the house to look
after and Oliver's clothes to attend to ; and, besides, I don't
think a married woman ought to make many new friends.
Her husband ought to be enough for her. Mrs. Payson, the
manager's wife, was here to welcome me, but I hope I shan't
see very much of her, because she isn't just exactly what I
should call ladylike. Of course, I wouldn't breathe this to
any other living soul, but I thought her entirely too free and
easy in her manner, and she dresses in such very bright colours.
Why, she had a red feather in her hat, and she must have been
married at least fifteen years. Oliver says he doesn't believe
she's a day under forty-five. He says he likes her well enough
and thinks she's a good sort, but he is awfully glad that I'm
not that kind of woman. I feel sorry for her husband, for I'm
sure no man wants his wife to make herself conspicuous, and
they say she even makes speeches when she is in the
North. Maybe she isn't to blame, because she was brought
up that way, but I am going to see just as little of her
as I can.

And now I must tell you about our house, for I know you
are dying to hear how we are fixed. It's the tinest one you
ever imagined, with a front yard the size of a pocket handkerchief, and it is painted the most perfectly hideous shade
of yellow—the shade father always calls bilious. I can't
understand why they made it so ugly—but, then, the whole
town is just as ugly as our house is. The people here don't
seem to have the least bit of taste. All the porches have
dreadful brown ornaments along the top of them, and they
look exactly as if they were made out of gingerbread. There
are very few gardens, and nobody takes any care of these. I
suppose one reason is that it is almost impossible to get servan

for love or money. There are hardly any darkies here, they say, and the few they have are perfectly worthless. Mrs. Midden—the woman who opened my house for me—hasn't been able to get me a cook, and we'll either have to take our meals at a boarding-house across the street, or I shall have to put to practise the lessons you gave me. I am so glad you made me learn how to housekeep and to cook, because I am certain that I shall have greater need of both of these accomplishments than of either drawing or music. Oliver was simply horrified when I told him so. He said he'd rather starve than see me in the kitchen, and he urged me to get you to send us a servant from Dinwiddie ; but things are so terribly costly here—you never dreamed of such prices—that I really don't believe we can afford to have one come. Then, Mrs. Midden says that they get ruined just as soon as they are brought here. Everybody tries it at first, she told me, and it has always proved a disappointment in the end. I am perfectly sure that I shan't mind cooking at all, and as for cleaning up this little house—why it won't take me an hour. But Oliver almost weeps every time I mention it. He is afraid every instant he is away from me that I am lonesome or something has happened to me, and whenever he has ten minutes free he runs up here to see what I am doing. Do you know, he has made me promise not to go out by myself until I am used to the place. Isn't that too absurd ?

Dearest mother, I must stop now, and write some notes of thanks for my presents. The barrels of china haven't come yet, but the silver box got here almost as soon as we did. Freight takes a long time, Oliver says. It will be such fun unpacking all my presents and putting them away on the shelves. I was so excited those last few days that I hardly paid any attention to the things that came. Now I shall have time really to enjoy them, and to realize how sweet and lovely everybody has been to me. Wasn't it too dear of Miss Priscilla to give me that beautiful tea-set ? And I was so touched by poor little Miss Willy spending her hard-earned money on that vase. I wish she hadn't. It makes me feel badly to think of it ; but I don't see what I could do about it, do you ? I think I'll try to send her a cloak or something at Christmas.

I haven't said half that I want to ; but I shall keep the rest for to-morrow.

With a dozen kisses and my dearest love to father,

Your ever, ever loving and grateful daughter,

VIRGINIA.

MATOACA CITY,
December 25, 1884.

DEAREST MOTHER,

It almost broke my heart not to be able to go home for Christmas. It doesn't seem like Christmas at all away from you—though, of course, I try not to let Oliver see how I mind it. He has so much to bother him, poor dear, that I keep all of my worries, big and little, in the background. When anything goes wrong in the house I never tell him, because he has so many important things on his mind that I don't think I ought to trouble him about small ones. We have given up going to the boarding-house for our meals, because neither of us could eat a morsel of the food they had there— did you ever hear of such a thing as having pie and preserves for breakfast ?—and Oliver says it used to make him sick to see me in the midst of all of those people. They came from all over the country, and hardly anybody could speak a grammatical sentence. The man who sat next to me always said " He don't " and " I ain't feeling good to-day," and once even " I done it "—can you imagine such a thing ? Every other word was " guess," and yet they had the impertinence to laugh at me when I said " reckon," which, I am sure father told me was Shakespearian English. Well, we stood it as long as we could, and then we started having our meals here, and it is so much nicer. Oliver says the change from the boarding-house has given him a splendid appetite, and he enjoys everything that I make so much—particularly the waffles by Aunt Ailsey's recipe. Be sure to tell her. At first I had a servant, but she was so dreadful that I let her go at the end of the month, and I really get on ever so much better without her. She hadn't the faintest idea how to cook, and had never made a piece of light bread in her life. Besides, she was too untidy for anything, and actually swept the trash under the bed except once a week, when she pretended to give a thorough cleaning. The first time she changed the sheets, I found that she had simply put on one fresh one, and was going to use the bottom one on top. She said she'd never heard of doing it any other way, and I had to laugh when I thought of how your face would have looked if you could have heard her. It really is the greatest relief to get rid of her, and I'd a hundred times rather do the work myself than have another of that kind. At first Oliver hated dreadfully to have me do everything about the house, but he is beginning to get used to it now, because, of course, I never let him see if anything happens to worry me or if I am tired when he comes home. It takes every minute of my time, but, then, there is nothing else here that I care to do, and I never leave the house except to take a little walk with Oliver on Sunday afternoon. Mrs. Midden says that I make a mistake to give a spring cleaning every day, but I love to keep the house looking perfectly spick and span, and I make hot bread twice a day, because Oliver is so fond of it. He is just as sweet and dear as he can be and wants to help about everything, but I hate to see him doing housework. Somehow it doesn't seem to me to look manly. We have had our first quarrel about who is to get up and make the fires in the morning. Oliver insisted that he was to do it, but I wake so much earlier than he does, because I've got the bread on my mind, that I almost always have the wood burning before he gets up. The first few times he was really angry about it, and he didn't seem to understand why I hated so to wake him. He says he hates still worse to see my hands get rough—but I am so thankful that I am not one of those girls (like Abby Goode) who are for ever thinking of how they look. But Oliver made such a fuss about the fires that I didn't tell him that I went down to the cellar one morning and brought up a basket of coal. The boy didn't come the day before, so there wasn't any to start the kitchen fire with, and I knew that by the time Oliver got up and dressed it would be too late to have hot rolls for breakfast. By the way, could you have a bushel of cornmeal sent to me from Dinwiddie? The kind they have here isn't the least bit like the water-ground sort we have at home, and most of it is yellow. Nobody ever has batterbread here. All the food

is different from ours. I suppose that is because most of
the people are from the North and West.

I have the table all set for our Christmas dinner, and in a
few minutes I must put the turkey into the oven. I was
so glad to get the plum-pudding in the Christmas box, because
I could never have made one half so good as yours, and the
fruit cake will last me for ever—it is so big. I wrote you
about the box yesterday just as soon as it came, but after
I had sent my letter, I went back to it and found that rose
point scarf of grandmother's wrapped in tissue paper in the
bottom. Darling mother, it made me cry. You oughtn't
to have given it to me. It always looked so lovely on your
black silk, and it was almost the last thing you had left.
I don't believe I shall ever make up my mind to wear it. I
have on my little grey silk to-day, and it looks so nice. You
must tell Miss Willy that it has been very much admired.
Mrs. Payson asked me if it was made in Dinwiddie, and, you
know, she gets all of her clothes from New York. That
must have been why I thought her overdressed when I first
saw her. By the way, I've almost changed my mind about
her since I wrote you what I thought of her. I believe now
that the whole trouble with her is simply that she isn't a
Southern lady. She means well, I am sure, but she isn't
what I should call exactly refined. There's something
"horsey" about her—I can't think of any other way to
express it—something that reminds me just a little bit of
Abby—and, you remember, we always said Abby got that
from being educated in the North. Tell dearest Susan I
really think it is fortunate that she did not go to one of their
colleges. Mrs. Payson is a college woman, and it seems to
me that she is always trying to appear as clever as a man.
She talks in a way sometimes that sounds as if she believed
in women's rights and all that sort of thing. I told Oliver
about it, and he laughed and said that men hated talk like
that. He says all a man admires in a woman is her power
of loving, and that when she begins to ape a man she loses
her charm for him. I can't understand why Mr. Payson
married his wife. He said such nice things to me the other
day about my being so domestic and such a home lover, that
I really felt sorry for him. When I told him that I was so

fond of staying indoors that I would never cross my threshold
if Oliver didn't make me, he laughed and said that he wished
I'd convert his wife to my way of thinking. Yet he seems
to have the greatest admiration for her, and, do you know,
I believe he even admires that red feather, though he doesn't
approve of it. He never turns his eyes away from her when
they are together, which isn't very much, as she goes about
just as she pleases without him. Can you understand how
a person can both admire and disapprove of a thing ? Oliver
says he knows how it is, but I must say that I don't. I hope
and pray that our marriage will always be different from
theirs. Oliver and I are never apart for a single minute
except when he is at work in the office. He hasn't written
a line since we came here, but he is going to begin as soon as
we get settled, and then he says that I may sit in the room
and sew if I want to. I can't believe that people really love
each other unless they want to be together every instant,
no matter what they are doing. Why, if Oliver went out
to men's dinners without me as Mr. Payson does (though
she doesn't seem to mind it) I should just sit at home by
myself and cry my eyes out. I think love, if it is love, ought
to be all in all. I am perfectly sure that if I live to be a
hundred I shall never want any society but Oliver's. He is
the whole world to me, and when he is not here I spend my
time, unless I am at work, just sitting and thinking about him.
My one idea is to make him as happy as I can, and when a
woman does this for a man I don't think she has time to run
around by herself as Mrs. Payson does. Tell dearest father
that I so often think of his sermons and the beautiful things
he said about women. The rector here doesn't compare with
him as a preacher.

This is such a long letter it will take two stamps. I've
just let myself run on without thinking what I was writing,
so if I have made any mistakes in grammar or in spelling,
please don't let father see them, but read my letter aloud
to him. I can shut my eyes and see you sitting at dinner,
with Docia bringing in the plum-pudding, and I know you
will talk of me while you help to it. Write me who comes
to dinner with you. I wonder if Miss Priscilla and John
Henry are there as usual. Do you know whether John Henry

ever goes to the Treadwells' or not ? I wish you would ask
him to take Susan to see his old mammy in Pink Alley. Now
that I am not there to go to see her occasionally, I am afraid
she will get lonesome.

Good-bye, dearest mother. I will write to you before
New Year. I am so busy that I don't have time to write
every day, but you will understand and so will father.

With my heart's fondest love to you both,

Your
VIRGINIA.

MATOACA CITY,
June 6, 1885.

DARLING MOTHER,

The little patterns were exactly what I wanted—thank
you a thousand times. I knew you would be overjoyed at
the news, and you are the only person I've breathed it to—
except, of course, dear Oliver, who is frightened to death
already. He has made me stop everything at once, and
whenever he sees me lift my hand, he begins to get nervous
and begs me not to do it. Oh, mother, he loves me so that
it is really pathetic to see his anxiety. And—can you believe
it ?—he doesn't appear to be the least bit glad about it. When
I told him, he looked amazed—as if he had never thought
of its happening—and said, " Oh, Virginia, not so soon !"
He told me afterwards that, of course, he'd always thought
we'd have children after a while, before we were middle-aged,
but that he had wanted to stay like this for at least five or
ten years. When the baby comes, he says he supposes he'll
like it, but that he can't honestly say he is glad. It's funny
how frightened he is, because I am not the least bit so. All
women must expect to have children when they marry, and
if God makes them suffer for it, it must be because it is best
that they should. Perhaps they wouldn't love their babies
so much if they got them easily. I never think of the pain
a minute. It all seems so beautiful and sacred to me that
I can't understand why Oliver isn't enraptured just as I am.
To think of a new life starting into the world from me—a life
that is half mine and half Oliver's, and one that would never
be at all except for our love. The baby will seem from the

very first minute to be our love made into flesh. I don't see how a woman who feels this could waste a thought on what she has to suffer.

I am so glad you are going to send me a nurse from Dinwiddie, because I'm afraid I could never get one here that I could trust. The servant Oliver got me is no earthly account, and I still do as much of the cooking as I can. The house doesn't look nearly so nice as it used to, but the doctor tells me that I mustn't sweep, so I only do the light dusting. I sew almost all the time, and I've already finished the little slips. To-day I'm going to cut out the petticoats. I couldn't tell from the pattern you sent whether they fasten in front or in the back. There are no places for buttonholes. Do you use safety pins to fasten them with? The embroidery is perfectly lovely, and will make the sweetest trimming. I am using pink for the basket because Oliver and I both hope the baby will be a girl. If it is, I shall name her after you, of course, and I want her to be just exactly like you. Oliver says he can't understand why anybody ever wants a boy—girls are so much nicer. But then he insists that if she isn't born with blue eyes, he will send her to the orphanage.

I am trying to do just as you tell me to, and to be as careful as I possibly can. The doctor thinks I've stayed indoors too much since I came here, so I go out for a little walk with Oliver every night. I am so afraid that somebody will see me that I really hate to go out at all, and always choose the darkest streets I can find. Last night I had a bad stumble, and Oliver says he doesn't care if the whole town discovers us, he's not going to take me down any more unlighted alleys.

It has been terribly hot all day—not a breath of air stirring —and I never felt the heat so much in my life. The doctor says it's because of my condition—and last night, after Oliver went to sleep, I got up and sat by the window until daybreak. At first I was dreadfully frightened, and thought I was going to stifle—but poor Oliver had come home so tired that I made up my mind I wasn't going to wake him if I could possibly help it. This morning I didn't tell him a word about it, and he hasn't the least idea that I didn't sleep soundly all night. I suppose that's why I feel so dragged and worn out to-day, just as if somebody had given me a

good beating. I was obliged to lie down most of the afternoon, but I am going to take a bath in a few minutes and
try to make myself look nice and fresh before Oliver comes
home. I have let out that flowered organdie—the one you
liked so much—and I wear it almost every evening. I know
I look dreadful, but Oliver says I am more beautiful than
ever. It seems to me sometimes that men are born blind
where women are concerned, but perhaps God made it that
way on purpose. Do you know Oliver really admires Mrs.
Payson, and he thinks that red feather very becoming to
her. He says she's much too good for her husband, but I
have been obliged to disagree with him about that. Even
if Mr. Payson does drink a little, I am sure it is only because
he gets lonesome when he is left by himself, and that she
could prevent it if she tried. Oliver and I never talk about
these things because he sees that I feel so strongly about them.

Oh, darling mother, I shall be so glad to see you! I hope
and pray that father will be well enough for you to come a
whole month ahead. In that case you will be here in less
than two months, won't you? If the baby comes on the
twelfth of August, she (I am perfectly sure it will be a girl)
and father will have the same birthday. I am so anxious
that she shall be born on that day.

Well, I must stop now, though I could run on for ever.
I never see a living soul from one day to another—Mrs.
Payson is out of town—so when Oliver stays late at the office,
and I am too tired to work, I get a little—just a little bit
lonesome. Mr. Payson sent me a pile of novels by Oliver
the other night—but I haven't looked into them. I always
feel that it is a waste of time to read when there are things
about the house that ought to be done. I wish everything
didn't cost so much here. Money doesn't go half as far as
it does in Dinwiddie. The price of meat is almost there times
as much as it is at home, and chickens are so expensive that
we have them only twice a week. It is hard to housekeep
on a small allowance, and now that we have to save for the
baby's coming, I have to count every penny. I have bought
a little book like yours, and I put down all that I spend during
the day, and then add it up at night before going to bed.
Oliver says I'm dreadfully frugal, but I am always so terribly

afraid of running over my allowance (which is every cent that we can afford) and not having the money to pay the doctor's bills when they are due. Nobody could be more generous with money than Oliver is—I couldn't endure being married to a stingy man like Mr. Treadwell—and the other day when one of the men in the office died, he sent the most beautiful wreath that cost ten dollars. I am trying to save enough out of the housekeeping balance to pay for it, for Oliver always runs out of his pocket money before the middle of the month. I haven't bought anything for the baby because you sent me all the materials I needed, and I have been sewing on those ever since they came. Of course, my own clothes are still as good as new, so the only expense will be the doctor and the nurse and the extra things I shall be obliged to have to eat when I am sick.

Give dear father a dozen kisses from me, and tell him to hurry and get well so he can christen his granddaughter.

Your devoted and ever grateful

VIRGINIA.

MATOACA CITY,
August 11, 1885.

DARLING MOTHER,

Just a line to say that I am so, so sorry you can't come, but that you mustn't worry a minute, because everything is going beautifully, and I am not the least bit afraid. The doctor says he never saw anyone in a better frame of mind or so little nervous. Give my dear love to father. I am so distressed that he should suffer as he does. Rheumatism must be such terrible pain, and I don't wonder that you are frightened lest it should go to his heart. I shall send you a telegram as soon as the baby comes.

Your devoted daughter,

VIRGINIA.

MATOACA CITY,
August 29, 1885.

MY PRECIOUS MOTHER,

This is the first time I have sat up in bed, and I am trying to write a little note to you on a pillow instead of a desk. My hand shakes so that I'm afraid you won't be able to read it, but I felt that I wanted to send you a few words of my very own, not dictated to the nurse or to Mrs. Payson. I can't tell you how perfectly lovely Mrs. Payson has been to me. She was here all that dreadful night, and I believe I should have died without her. The doctor said I had such a hard time because I'd let myself get run down and stayed indoors too much. But I'm getting all right now—and the rest is over and doesn't matter. As soon as I am strong again I shall be perfectly happy.

Oh, mother, aren't you delighted that the baby is a girl, after all ? It was the first question I asked when I came back to consciousness the next morning, and when they told me it was, I said, " Her name is Lucy Pendleton," and that was all. I was so weak they wouldn't let me open my lips again, and Oliver was kept out of the room for almost ten days because I would talk to him. Poor fellow, it almost killed him. He is as white as a sheet still, and looks as if he had been through tortures. It must have been terrible for him, because I was really very, very ill at one time.

But it is all over now, and the baby is the sweetest thing you ever imagined. I believe she knows me already, and Mrs. Payson says she is exactly like me, though I can see the strongest resemblance to Oliver, even if she has blue eyes and he hasn't. Wasn't it lovely how everything came just as we wanted it to—a girl, born on father's birthday, with blue eyes, and named Lucy ? But, mother, darling, the most wonderful thing of all was that you seemed to be with me all through it. The whole time I was unconscious I thought you were here, and the nurse tells me that I was calling " Mother ! Mother !" all that night. Nothing ever made me feel as close to you as having a baby of my own. I never knew before what you were to me, and how dearly, dearly I love you.

The nurse is taking the pencil away from me.

Your loving
VIRGINIA.

Isn't it funny that Oliver won't take any interest in the baby at all ? He says she caused more trouble than she is worth. Was father like that ?

MATOACA CITY,
April 3, 1886.

DEAREST MOTHER,

My last letter was written an age ago, but I have been
so busy since Marthy left that I've hardly had a moment in
which to draw breath. It was a blow to me that she wouldn't
stay, for she was really an excellent nurse and the baby got
on so well with her, but there aren't any coloured people of
her kind here, and she got so homesick for Dinwiddie that
I thought she would lose her mind if she stayed. You know
how dependent they are upon company, and going out on
Sunday afternoon and all that kind of thing, and there really
wasn't any amusement for her except taking the baby out
in the morning. She got so low spirited that it was almost
a relief when she went, but, of course, I feel her loss dreadfully. I haven't let the baby out of my sight because I
wouldn't trust Daisy with her for anything in the world.
She is so terribly flighty. I have the crib brought into my
room (though Oliver hates it) and I take entire charge of her
night and day. I should love to do it if only Oliver didn't
mind it so much. He says I think more of the baby now
than I do of him. Isn't that absurd ? But, of course, she
does take every single minute of my time, and I can't dress
myself for him every evening as carefully as I used to do, and
look after all the housekeeping arrangements. Daisy is a
very poor cook, and she simply throws the things on the table,
but it seems to me that my first duty is to the baby, so I try
to put up with the discomforts as well as I can. It is hard
to eat what she cooks since everything tastes exactly alike,
but I try to swallow as much as I can because the doctor
says that if I don't keep up my strength I shall have to stop
nursing the baby. Wouldn't that be dreadful ? It almost
breaks my heart to think of it, and I am sure we'd never
get any artificial food to agree with her. She is perfectly
well now, the sweetest, fattest thing you ever saw, and a real
beauty, and she is so devoted to me that she cries whenever
I go out of her sight. I am never tired of watching her, and
even when she is asleep I sit sometimes for an hour by her
crib just thinking how pretty she looks with her eyes closed
and wishing you could see her. Oliver says I spoil her to

death, but how can a baby of seven months be spoiled? He doesn't enjoy her half as much as I do, and sometimes I almost think that he gets impatient of seeing her always in my arms. At first he absolutely refused to have her crib brought into our room, but when I cried, he gave in and was very sweet about it. I feel so ashamed sometimes of the way the house looks, but there doesn't seem to be any help for it because the doctor says if I let myself get tired it will be bad for the baby. Of course, I wouldn't put my own health before his comfort, but I am obliged to think first of the baby, am I not? Last night, for instance, the poor little thing was ill with colic, and I was up and down with her until daybreak. Then this morning she woke early, and I had to nurse her and give her her bath, and, added to everything else, Daisy's cousin died, and she sent word she couldn't come. I slipped on a wrapper before taking a bath or fixing my hair, and ran down to try and get Oliver's breakfast, but the baby began to cry and he came after me and said he wanted to make the coffee himself. Then he brought a cup upstairs to me, but I was so tired and nervous that I couldn't drink it. He didn't seem to understand why, feeling as badly as I did, I wouldn't just put the baby back into her crib and make her stay there until I got some rest, but the little thing was so wide awake that I hadn't the heart to do it. Besides, it is so important to keep regular hours with her, isn't it? I don't suppose a man ever realizes how a woman looks at these things, but you will understand, won't you, mother?

I am all alone in the house to-night because a play is in town that Oliver wanted to see and I made him go to it. He wanted to ask Mrs. Midden to sit downstairs (she has offered over and over again to do it) so that I might go too, but, of course, I wouldn't let him. I really couldn't have enjoyed it a minute for thinking of the baby, and besides I never cared for the theatre. Then, too, he doesn't know (for I never tell him) how very tired I am by the time night comes. Sometimes when Oliver comes home and we sit in the dining-room (we never use the drawing-room, because it is across the hall, and I'm afraid I shouldn't hear the baby cry), it is as much as I can do to keep my eyes open. I try not to let him notice it, but one night when he read me the first act of a play he is writing, I went to sleep, and though he didn't say anything, I could see that he was very much hurt. He worries a good deal about my health, too, and he even went out one day and engaged a nurse without saying anything to me about it. After I had talked to her though, I saw that she would never do, so I sent her away before he came home. I wish I could get really strong and feel well again, but the doctor insists I never will until I get out of doors and use my muscles. But you stay in the house all the time and so did grandmother, so I don't believe there's a word of truth in what he says. Anyway, I go out every day now with the baby.

Thank you so much for the little bands. They are just what I wanted.

With dearest love,

Your devoted
VIRGINIA.

MATOACA CITY,
June 10, 1886.

DEAREST MOTHER,

Daisy left a week ago and we couldn't find another servant until to-day. I must say that I prefer coloured servants. They are so much more dependable. I didn't know until the evening before Daisy left that she was going, and I had to send Oliver straight out to see if he could find somebody to come in and help me. There wasn't a soul to be had until to-day, however, so for a week I was obliged to make Oliver get his dinner at the boarding-house. It doesn't make any difference what I have because I haven't a particle of appetite, and I'd just as soon eat tea and toast as anything else. Of course, but for the baby, I could have managed perfectly well—but she has been so fretful of late that she doesn't let me put her down a minute. The doctor says her teeth are beginning to hurt her, and that I must expect to have trouble the first summer. She has been so well until now that he thinks it has been really remarkable. He tells me he never knew a healthier baby, but, of course, I am terribly anxious about her teething in the hot weather. If she grows much more fretful I'm afraid I shall have to take her to the country for July and August. It seems dreadful to leave Oliver all alone, but I don't see how I can help it if the doctor advises me to go. Oliver has gone to some musical comedy at the Academy to-night, and I am so tired that I am going to bed just as soon as I finish this letter. I hope and pray that the baby will have a quiet night. Don't you think that Daisy treated me very badly considering how kind I had been to her? Only a week ago, when she was taken with pains in the night, I got up and made her a mustard plaster, and sat by her bed until she felt easier. The next day I did all of her work, and yet she has so little gratitude that she could leave me this way when she knows perfectly well that I am worried to death about the baby's first summer. I'd give anything if I could go home in July as you suggest, but it is such a long trip, and the heat will probably be quite as bad in Dinwiddie as here. Of course, it would make all the difference in the world to me to be where I could have you to advise me about the baby, and I'd go to-morrow if it only wasn't so far. Mrs. Midden has told me of a boarding house in the country not more than twenty miles from here where Oliver could come down every evening, and we may decide to go there for a month or two. I can't help feeling very anxious, especially as Mrs. Scott's little boy—he is just the age of baby—was taken ill the other night, and they thought he would die before they could get a doctor.

This letter is full of my worries, but in spite of them I am the happiest woman that ever lived. Oliver is the best thing to me you can imagine, and the baby is so fascinating that I enjoy every minute I am with her. It is the greatest fun to watch her in her bath. I know you would simply go into raptures over her—and she is so bright that she already understands every word that I say. She grows more like Oliver all the time, and the other day, while I was watching her playing with her rubber doll, she looked so beautiful that it almost frightened me.

I am so glad dear father is well, and what you wrote me about John Henry's admiration for Susan interested me so much that I sat straight down and wrote to him. Why do you think that it is only friendship and that he isn't in love with her ? If he really thinks her the "finest girl in the world," I should imagine he was beginning to be pretty serious. I am delighted to hear that he is going to take her to the festival. Tell Susan from me that I shall never be satisfied until she is as happy as I am. Mr. Treadwell was right, I believe, not to let her go to college, though, of course, I want dear Susan to have whatever she sets her heart on. But, when all is said, you were wise in teaching me that nothing matters to a woman except love. More and more I am learning that if we only love unselfishly enough, everything else will work out for good to us. My little worries can't keep me from being so blissfully happy that I want to sing all the time. Work is a joy to me because I feel that I am doing it for Oliver and the baby. And with two such treasures to live for I should be the most ungrateful creature alive if I ever complained.

Your ever loving daughter,

VIRGINIA.

MATOACA CITY,
July 1, 1886.

DEAREST MOTHER,

We are leaving suddenly for the country, and I'll send our address just as soon as we get there. The doctor thinks I ought to take the baby away from town, so I am going to the boarding-house I wrote you about. Oliver will come down every evening—it's only an hour's trip.

I am so tired from packing that I can't write any more.

Lovingly,

VIRGINIA.

MATOACA CITY,
September 15, 1886.

DEAREST MOTHER,

Here we are back again in our home, and I was never so thankful in my life to get away from any place. I wrote you how dreadfully inconvenient it was, but it would take pages to tell you all of my experiences in the last few days. Such people you never saw in your life ! And the food got so uneatable that I lived on crackers for the last fortnight. Fortunately I was still nursing the baby, but the doctor has just told me that I must stop. I am so distressed about it.

Do you think it will go hard with her after the first year? She is as fat and well as she can be now, but I live in hourly terror of her getting sick. If anything should happen to her, I believe it would kill me.

Oliver sends love. He is working very hard at the office now, and he hates it.

Your loving
VIRGINIA.

I forgot to tell you that Mrs. Midden has found me such a nice servant. She is a very young coloured girl, but looks so kind and capable, and says she is perfectly devoted to children. Her name is Marthy, and I feel that she's going to be a great comfort to me.

MATOACA CITY,
October 12, 1886.

MY DARLING MOTHER,

I was overjoyed to find your letter in the hall when I came out from breakfast. Has it really been two weeks since I wrote to you? That seems dreadful, but the days go by so fast that I hardly realize how long it is between my letters.

We are all well, and Marthy has become the greatest help to me. Of course, I don't let her do anything for the baby, but she is so careful and trustworthy, that I am going to try having her take out the carriage in the morning. At first I shan't let her go off the block, so that I can have my eye on her all the time. Little Lucy took a fancy to her at once, and really enjoys playing with her. This makes it possible for me to do a little sewing, and I am working hard trying to make over one or two of my dresses. Oliver wants me to have a dressmaker do it, but we have so many extra expenses all the time that I don't feel we can afford to put out any sewing. We have spent a great deal on doctors since we were married, but, of course, with a young child we can't very well expect anything else.

And now, dearest mother, I have something to tell you, which no one knows—not even Oliver—except Doctor Marshall and myself. We are going to have another darling baby in March, if everything goes as it ought to. I have kept it a secret because Oliver has had a good many business worries, and I knew it would make him miserable. It never

seems to have entered his head that it might happen again
so soon, and for his sake I do wish we could have waited
until we got a little more money in the bank, but I suppose
I oughtn't to say this, because God would certainly not send
children into the world unless it was right for them to be born.
I try to remember what dear grandmamma said when somebody condoled with her at the time she was expecting her
tenth child—that she hoped she was too good a Christian
to dictate to the Lord as to how many souls He should send
into the world. As for me, I should be perfectly delighted
—it will be so much better for baby to have a little brother
or sister to play with when she gets bigger—but I can't help
worrying about Oliver's peculiar attitude of mind. I am
sure that father wouldn't have felt that way, and think how
poor he has always been. Perhaps it comes from dear Oliver
having lived abroad so much and away from the Christian
influences, which have been one of the greatest blessings of
my life. I have put off telling him every day just because
I dread to think of the blow it will be to him. He is the
dearest and best husband that ever lived, and I worship the
ground he walks on, but, do you know, things are always
a surprise to him when they happen ? He never looks ahead
a single minute. I am sometimes afraid that he isn't the
least bit practical, and it makes him impatient when I talk
to him about trying to cut down expenses. Of course, I
have to save as much as I can and I count every single penny,
or we'd never have enough money to get through the month.
I never buy a stitch for either the baby or myself, though
Oliver complains now and then that I don't dress as well as
I used to do. But how can I, when I've worn the same things
ever since my marriage, besides making the baby's clothes
out of my old ones ? You can understand from this how
grateful I am for the check you sent—but, dearest mother,
I know that you oughtn't to have done it, and that you
sacrificed your own comfort and father's to give it to me.

I wish Oliver could get something to do in Dinwiddie.
He will never be happy here, and we could live on so much
less money at home—in a little house near the rectory.

Your loving child,
Virginia.

CHAPTER III

THE RETURN

On a February morning five years later, Mrs. Pendleton, who was returning from her daily trip to the market, met Susan Treadwell at the corner of Old Street.

"You are coming up to welcome Jinny, aren't you, Susan?" she asked. "The train gets in at four o'clock."

"Why, of course. I couldn't sleep a wink until I'd seen her. It has been seven years, and it seems a perfect eternity."

"She hasn't changed much—at least she hadn't six months ago when I was out there at the birth of her last baby. The little thing lived only two hours, you know, and I thought at first his death would kill her."

"It was a great blow—but she has been fortunate never to have had a day's sickness with the other three. I am dying to see them—especially the eldest. That's your namesake, isn't it?"

"Yes, that's Lucy. She's six years old now, and as good as an angel, but she hasn't fulfilled her promise of beauty. Virginia says she was the prettiest baby she ever saw."

"Everybody says that Jenny, the youngest, is a perfect beauty."

"That's why her father makes so much of her, I reckon. I told him when I was out there that he oughtn't to show such a difference between them. Do you know, Susan, I wouldn't say it to anybody else, but I don't believe Oliver has a real fondness for children. He gets tired of having them always about, and that makes him impatient. Now, Virginia is a born mother, just like her grandmother and all the women of our family."

"I should think Oliver would be crazy about the boy. He was named after his father, too."

178

"Virginia felt she ought to name him Henry, but we call him Harry. No, Oliver hardly ever takes any notice of him. I don't mean, of course, that he isn't nice and kind to them —but he isn't wrapped up in them heart and soul as Virginia is. I really believe he is more absorbed in this play he has written than he is in the children."

"I am so glad to hear that two of his plays are going to be staged. That's splendid, isn't it?"

"He is coming back to Dinwiddie because of it. Now that he is assured of recognition, he says he is going to devote all his time to writing. Poor fellow, he did so hate the work out at Matoaca City, though I must say he was very faithful and persevering about it."

"You've taken that little house in Prince Street for them, where old Miss Franklin used to live, haven't you? The last time I saw you, you hadn't quite decided about it."

"I couldn't resist it because it is only three squares from the rectory. Mr. Pendleton set his heart on it from the first minute."

"Well, I'm so glad," said Susan, shifting the small basket of fruit she carried from one arm to the other, "and I'll certainly run in and see them this evening—I suppose they'll be at the rectory for supper?"

"Why, no. Jinny said she couldn't bear to be away from the children the first night, so we are all going there. I shall send Docia over to cook supper before they get here, and I've just been to market to see if I could find anything that Oliver would particularly like. He used to be so fond of sweetbreads."

"Mr. Dewlap has some very nice ones. I got one for mother. She hasn't been well for the last few days."

"I'm sorry to hear that. Give her my love and tell her I'll come down just as soon as I get Jinny settled. I've been so taken up getting the house ready that I haven't thought of another thing for three weeks."

"When will Oliver's play be put on in New York?" asked Susan, turning back after they had parted.

"In three weeks. He is going back again for the last rehearsals. I wish Jinny could go with him, but I don't

believe she would spend a night away from the children for
anything on earth."

"Isn't it beautiful that her marriage has turned out so
well ?"

"Yes; I don't believe she could be any happier if she tried,
and I must say that Oliver makes a much better husband
than I ever thought he would. I never heard them disagree
the whole time I was there. Of course, Jinny gives up to
him in everything except where the children are concerned;
but, then, a woman always expects to do that. One thing
I'm certain of—he couldn't have found a better wife if he'd
searched the world over. She never thinks of herself a
minute, and you know how fond she used to be of pretty
clothes and of fixing herself up. Now, she simply lives in
Oliver and the children, and she is the proudest thing of his
plays ! The rector says that she thinks he is Shakespeare
and Milton rolled into one."

"Nothing could be nicer," said Susan, "and it is all such a
happy surprise to me. Of course, I always thought Oliver
very attractive—everybody does—but he seemed to me to
be selfish and undisciplined, and I wasn't at all sure that
Jinny was the kind of woman to bring out the best in him."

"You'll think so when you see them together."

Then they smiled and parted, Mrs. Pendleton hurrying back
to the little house, while Susan turned down Old Street, in
the direction of her home. She walked rapidly, with an easy,
swinging pace seldom seen in the women of Dinwiddie, and
not heartily approved by the men. At twenty-seven she was
far handsomer than she had been at twenty, for her figure
had grown more shapely and her face had lost the look of
intence preoccupaton which had once marred its charm.
Strong, capable, conquering, she still appeared; but in some
subtle way she had grown softer. Mrs. Pendleton would
probably have said that she had "settled."

At the first corner she met John Henry on his way to the
bank, and turning, he walked with her to the end of the block,
where they stood a moment discussing Virginia's return.

"I've just been to attend to some bills," he explained;
"that's why I'm out at this hour. You never come into the
bank now, I notice."

"Not often. Are you going to see Jinny this evening?"

"If you'll let me bring you home. I can't imagine Virginia with three children, can you? I'm half afraid to see her again."

"You mean you think she may have changed? Mrs. Pendleton says not."

"Oh, that's Aunt Lucy all over. If Virginia had got as fat as Miss Priscilla, she'd still believe she hadn't altered a particle."

"Well, she isn't fat, anyway. She weighs less than she ever did."

Her serious eyes dwelt on him under the green sunshade she held, and it is possible that she wondered vaguely what it was about John Henry that had made her love him unsought ever since she could remember. He was certainly not handsome—though he was less stout and much better looking than he used to be : he was not particularly clever, even if he was successful with the work Cyrus had given him. She was under no delusion concerning him (being a remarkably clear-sighted young person), yet she knew that taking him just as he was, large, slow, kind, good, he aroused in her a tenderness that was almost ridiculous. She had waited patiently seven years for him to discover that he cared for her—a fact which had been perfectly evident to her long before his duller wit had perceived it.

"Do you want to be there to welcome Jinny?" he asked.

"I'd thought I'd go up about five, so I could get a glimpse of the children before they are put to bed."

"Then I'll meet you there and bring you home. I wouldn't take anything for meeting you, Susan. There's something about you that always cheers me."

She met his eyes frankly. "Well, I'm glad of that," she replied in her confident way, and held out her hand through the handle of the basket. An instant later, when she passed on into Bolingbroke Street, there was a smile on her face which made it almost pretty.

The front door was open, and as she entered the house, her mother came groping toward her out of the close-smelling dusk of the hall.

"I thought you'd never get back, Susan. I've had such a funny feeling."

"What kind of feeling, mother? It must be just nervousness. Here are some beautiful grapes I've brought you."

"I wish you wouldn't leave me alone. I don't like to be left alone."

"Well, I don't leave you any more than I'm obliged to, but if I stay shut up here I feel as if I'd smother. I've asked Miss Willy to come and sit with you this evening while I run up to welcome Virginia."

"Is she coming back? Nobody told me. Nobody tells me anything."

"But I did tell you. Why, we've been talking about it for weeks. You must have forgotten."

"I shouldn't have forgotten it. I'm sure I shouldn't have forgotten it if you had told me. But you keep everything from me. You are just like your father. You and James are both just like your father." Her voice had grown peevish, and an expression of fury distorted her usually passive features.

"Why, mother, what in the world is the matter?" asked Susan, startled by her manner. "Come upstairs and lie down. I don't believe you are well. You didn't eat a morsel of breakfast, so I'm going to fix you a nice little lunch. I got you a beautiful sweetbread from Mr. Dewlap."

Putting her arm about her, she led her up the long flight of steps to her room, where Mrs. Treadwell, pacified by the attention, began immediately to doze on the chintz-covered couch by the window.

"I don't see what on earth ever made me marry your father, Susan," she said, starting up half an hour later, when her daughter appeared with the tray. "Everybody knew the Treadwells couldn't hold a candle to my family."

"I wouldn't worry about that now, mother," replied Susan briskly, while she placed the tray on a little table at the head of the couch. "Sit up and eat these oysters."

"I'm obliged to worry over it," returned Mrs. Treadwell irritably, while she watched her daughter arrange her plate and pour out the green tea from the little Rebecca-at-the-well teapot. "I don't see what got into my head and made me do it. Why, his branch of the Treadwells had petered out until they were as common as dirt."

"Well, it's too late to mend matters, so we'd better turn in and try to make the best of them." She held out an oyster on the end of a fork, and her mother received and ate it obediently.

"If I could only once understand why I did it, I think I could rest easier, Susan."

"Perhaps you were in love with each other. I've heard of such a thing."

"Well, if I was going to fall in love, I reckon I could have found somebody better to fall in love with," retorted Mrs. Treadwell with the same strange excitement in her manner. Then she took up her knife and fork, and began to eat her luncheon with relish.

At five o'clock that afternoon, when Susan reached the house in Prince Street, Virginia, with her youngest child in her arms, was just stepping out of a dilapidated "hack," from which a grinning negro driver handed a collection of lunch baskets into the eager hands of the rector and Mrs. Pendleton, who stood on the pavement.

"Here's Susan!" called Mrs. Pendleton in her cheerful voice, rather as if she feared her daughter would overlook her friend in the excitement of homecoming.

"Oh, you darling Susan!" exclaimed Virginia, kissing her over the head of a sleeping child in her arms. "This is Jenny —poor little thing, she hasn't been able to keep her eyes open. Don't you think she is the living image of our Saint Memin portrait of great-grandmamma?"

"She's a cherub," said Susan. "Let me look at you first, Jinny. I want to see if you've changed."

"Well, you can't expect me to look exactly as I did before I had four babies!" returned Virginia with a happy laugh. She was thinner, and there were dark circles of fatigue from the long journey under her eyes, but the Madonna-like possibilities in her face were fulfilled, and it seemed to Susan that she was, if anything, lovelier than before. The loss of her girlish bloom was forgotten in the expression of love and goodness which irradicated her features. She wore a black cloth skirt, and a blouse of some ugly blue figured silk finished at the neck with the lace scarf Susan had sent her at Christmas. Her hat was a characterless black straw trimmed with a bunch of yellow daisies; and by its shape alone, Susan discerned that Virginia' had ceased to consider whether or not her clothes were becoming. But she shone with an air of calm and radiant happiness in which all trivial details were transfigured as by a flood of light.

"This is Lucy. She is six years old, and to think that she has never seen her dear Aunt Susan," said Virginia, while she pulled forward the little girl who was shyly clinging to her skirt. "And the other is Harry. Marthy, bring Harry here and let him speak to Miss Susan. He is nearly four, and so big for his age. Where is Harry, Marthy?"

"He's gone into the yard, ma'am, I couldn't keep him back," said Marthy. "As soon as he caught sight of that pile of bricks he wanted to begin building."

"Well, we'll go, too," replied Virginia. "That child is simply crazy about building. Has Oliver paid the driver, mother? And what has become of him? Susan, have you spoken to Oliver?"

No, Susan hadn't, but as they turned, he appeared on the porch and came eagerly forward. Her first impression was that he had grown handsomer than she had ever believed possible; and the next minute she asked herself how in the world he had managed to exercise his vitality in Matoaca City. He was one of those men, she saw, in whom the spirit of youth burned like a flame. Every year would pass as a blessing, not as a curse, to him, and already, because of her intenser emotions and her narrower interests, Virginia was beginning to look older than he. There was a difference, too, in their dress, for he had the carefully groomed and well-brushed appearance so rare in Dinwiddie, while Virginia's clothes might have been worn, with equal propriety, by Miss Priscilla Batte. She was still lovely, but it was a loveliness, Susan felt with a pang, that would break early.

"Why, there's Susan!" exclaimed Oliver, coming toward her with an eager pleasure in his face which made it more boyish than ever. "Well, well, it's good to see you, Susan. Are you the same old dear I left behind me?"

"The same," said Susan laughing. "And so glad about your plays, Oliver, so perfectly delighted."

"By Jove! you're the first person to speak of them," he replied. "Nobody else seems to think a play is worth mentioning as long as a baby is in sight. That's a delusion of Virginia's too. I wish you'd convince her, Susan, that a man is of some use except as a husband and a father."

"But they are such nice babies, Oliver."

"Oh, nice enough as babies go. The boy's a trump. He'd be a man already if his mother would let him. But babies ought to have their season like everything else under the sun. For God's sake, Susan, talk to me about something else!" he added in mock despair.

Virginia was already in the house, and when Oliver and Susan joined her, they found Mrs. Pendleton trying to persuade her to let Marthy carry the sleeping Jenny up to the nursery.

"Give me that child, Jinny," said Oliver, a trifle sharply. "You know the doctor told you not to carry her upstairs."

"But I'm sure it won't hurt me," she responded with an angelic sweetness of voice. "It will wake her to be changed, and the poor little thing has had such a trying day."

"Well, you aren't going to carry her, if she wakes twenty times," retorted Oliver. "Here, Marthy, if she thinks I'd drop her, suppose you try it."

"Why, bless you, sir, I can take her so she won't know it," returned Marthy reassuringly, and coming forward, she proved her ability by sliding the unconscious child from Virginia's arms into her own.

"Where is Harry?" asked Mrs. Pendleton anxiously. "Nobody has seen Harry since we got here."

"I is, ma'am," replied the cheerful Marthy over her shoulder, as she toiled up the stairs, with Virginia and little Lucy noiselessly following. "I've undressed him and I was obliged to hide his clothes to keep him from putting 'em on again. He's near daft with excitement."

"Perhaps I'd better go up and help get them to bed," said Mrs. Pendleton, turning from the rector to Oliver. "I'm afraid Jinny will be too tired to enjoy her supper. Harry is in such a gale of spirits I can hear him talking."

"You might as well, my dear," rejoined the rector mildly, as he stooped over to replace one of the baby's bottles in the basket from which it had slipped. "Don't you think we might get some of these things out of the way?" he added. "If you take that alcohol stove, Oliver, I'll follow with these caps and shawls."

"Certainly, sir," rejoined Oliver readily. He always addressed the rector as "sir," partly because it seemed to him to be appropriate, partly because he knew that the older man expected him to do so. It was one of Oliver's most engaging characteristics that he usually adapted himself with perfect ease to whatever life or other people expected of him.

While they were carrying the baskets into the passage at the back of the dining-room, Mrs. Pendleton, whose nervous longing had got at last beyond her control, deserted Susan, with an apology, and flitted up the stairs.

"Come up and tell Jinny good-night before you go, dear," she added; "I'm afraid she will not get down again to see you."

"Oh, don't worry about me," replied Susan. "I want to say a few words to Oliver, and then I'm coming up to see Harry. Harry appears to me to be a man of personality."

"He's a darling child," replied Mrs. Pendleton, a little vaguely, "and Jinny says she never saw him so headstrong before. He is usually as good as gold."

"Well, well, it's a fine family," said the rector, beaming upon his son-in-law, when they returned from the passage. "I never saw three healthier children. It's a pity you lost the other one," he added in a graver tone; "but as he lived such a short time, Virginia couldn't take it so much to heart as if he had been older. She seems to have got over the disappointment."

"Yes, I think she's got over it," said Oliver.

"It will be good for her to be back in Dinwiddie. I never felt satisfied to think of her so far away."

"Yes, I'm glad we could come back," agreed Oliver pleasantly, though he appeared to Susan's quick eye to be making an effort.

"By the way, I haven't spoken of your literary work,"

remarked the rector, with the manner of a man who is saying
something very agreeable. "I have never been to the theatre,
but I understand that it is losing a great deal of its ill odour.
I always remember when anything is said about the stage
that, after all, Shakespeare was an actor. We may be old-
fashioned in Dinwiddie," he pursued in the complacent tone
in which the admission of this failing is invariably made, "but
I don't think we can have any objection to sweet, clean plays,
with an elevating moral tone to them. They are no worse,
anyway, than novels."

Though Oliver kept his face under such admirable control,
Susan, glancing at him quickly, saw a shade of expression,
too fine for amusement, too cordial for resentment, pass
over his features. His colour, which was always high,
deepened, and raising his head, he brushed the smooth dark
hair back from his forehead. Through some intuitive strain
of sympathy, Susan understood, while she watched him, that
his plays were as vital a matter in his life as the children
were in Virginia's.

"I must run up and see Harry before he goes to sleep,"
she said, feeling instinctively that the conversation was
becoming a strain.

At the allusion to his grandson, the rector's face lost
immediately its expression of forced pleasantness and relapsed
into its look of genial charm.

"You ought to be proud of that boy, Oliver," he observed,
beaming. "There's the making of a fine man in him, but
you mustn't let Jinny spoil him. It took all my strength
and authority to keep Lucy from ruining Jinny, and I've
always said that my brother-in-law Tom Bland would have
been a first-rate fellow if it hadn't been for the way his
mother raised him. God knows, I like a woman to be wrapped
up heart and soul in her household—and I don't suppose
anybody ever accused the true Southern lady of lacking
in domesticity—but if they have a failing, which I refuse
to admit, it is that they are almost too softhearted where
their children—especially their sons—are concerned."

"I used to tell Virginia that she gave in to Harry too much
when he was a baby," said Oliver, who was evidently not
without convictions regarding the rearing of his offspring;

" but she hasn't been nearly so bad about it since Jenny came.
Jenny is the one I'm anxious about now. She is a headstrong little beggar, and she has learned already how to get
around her mother when she wants anything. It's been
worse, too," he added, " since we lost the last poor little
chap. Ever since then Virginia has been in mortal terror
for fear something would happen to the others."

" It was hard on her," said the rector. " We men can't
understand how women feel about a thing like that, though,"
he added gently. " I remember when we lost our babies—
you know we had three before Virginia came, but none of
them lived more than a few hours—that I thought Lucy
would die of grief and disappointment. You see, they have
all the burden and the anxiety of it, and I sometimes think
that a child begins to live for a woman a long time before
a man ever thinks of it as a human being."

" I suppose you're right," returned Oliver in the softened
tone which proved to Susan that he was emotionally stirred.
" I tried to be as sympathetic with Virginia as I could, but
—do you know ?—I stopped to ask myself sometimes if I
could really understand. It seemed to her so strange that
I wasn't knocked all to pieces by the thing—that I could go
on writing as if nothing had happened."

" I am not sure that it isn't beyond the imagination of
a man to enter into a woman's most sacred feeling," remarked
the rector, with a touch of the sentimentality in which he
religiously shrouded the feminine sex. So ineradicable,
indeed, was his belief in the inherent virtue of every woman,
that he had several times fallen a helpless victim in the
financial traps of conscienceless Delilahs. But since his
innocence was as temperamental a quality as was Virginia's
maternal passion, experience had taught him nothing, and
the fact that he had been deceived in the past threw no
shadow of safeguard around his steps in the present. This
endearing trait, which made him so successful as a husband,
was probably the cause of his unmitigated failure as a re-
former. In looking at a woman, it was impossible for him
to see anything except perfection.

When Susan reached the top of the staircase, Mrs. Pendleton called to her, through the half-open door of the nursery,

to come in and hear how beautifully Lucy was saying her prayers. Her voice was full of a suppressed excitement; there was a soft pink flush in her cheeks; and it seemed to Susan that the presence of her grandchildren had made her almost a girl again. She sat on the edge of a trundle-bed slipping a nightgown over the plump shoulders of little Lucy, who held herself very still and prim, for she was a serious child,. with a natural taste for propriety. Her small, plain face, with its prominent features and pale blue eyes, had a look of intense earnestness and concentration, as though the business of getting to bed absorbed all her energies ; and the only movement she made was to toss back the slender and very tight braid of brown hair from her shoulders. She said her prayer as if it were the multiplication table, and having finished, slid gently into bed, and held up her face to be kissed.

"Jenny wouldn't drink but half of her bottle, Miss Virginia," said Marthy, appearing suddenly on the threshold of Virginia's bedroom, for the youngest child slept in the room with her mother. "She dropped off to sleep so sound that I couldn't wake her."

"I hope she isn't sick, Marthy," responded Virginia in an anxious tone. "Did she seem at all feverish ?"

"Naw'm, she ain't feverish, she's jest sleepy-headed."

"Well, I'll come and look at her as soon as I can persuade Harry to finish his prayers. He stopped in the middle of them, and he refuses to bless anybody but himself."

She spoke gravely, gazing with her exhaustless patience over the impish yellow head of Harry, who knelt, in his little nightgown, on the rug at her feet. His roving blue eyes met Susan's as she came over to him, while his chubby face broke into a delicious smile.

"Don't notice him, Susan," said Virginia, in her lovely voice which was as full of tenderness and as lacking in humour as her mother's. "Harry, you shan't speak to Aunt Susan until you've been good and finished your prayers."

"Don't want to speak to Aunt Susan," retorted the monster of infant depravity, slipping his bare toes through a rent in the rug, and doubling up with delight at his insubordination.

"I never knew him to behave like this before," said Virginia, almost in tears from shame and weariness. "It must be the excitement of getting here. He is usually so good. Now, Harry, begin all over again. 'God bless dear papa, God bless dear mamma, God bless dear grandmamma, God bless dear grandpapa, God bless dear Lucy, God bless dear Jenny, God bless all our dear friends.' "

"God bless dear Harry," recited the monster.

"He has gone on like that ever since I started," said poor Virginia. "I don't know what to do about it. It seems dreadful to let him go to bed without saying his prayers properly. Now, Harry, please, please be good; poor mother is so tired, and she wants to go and kiss little Jenny good-night. 'God bless dear papa,' and I'll let you get in bed."

"God bless Harry," was the imperturbable rejoinder to this pleading.

"Don't you want your poor mother to have some supper, Harry?" inquired Susan severely.

"Harry wants supper," answered the innocent.

"I suppose I'll have to let him go," said Virginia distractedly, "but Oliver will be horrified. He says I don't reason with them enough. Harry," she concluded sternly, "don't you understand that it is naughty of you to behave this way and keep mamma away from poor little Jenny?"

"Bad Jenny," said Harry.

"If you don't say your prayers this minute, you shan't have any preserves on your bread to-morrow."

"Bad preserves," retorted Harry.

"Well, if he won't, I don't see how I can make him," said Virginia. "Come, then, get into bed, Harry, and go to sleep. You have been a bad boy and hurt poor mamma's feelings so that she is going to cry. She won't be able to eat her supper for thinking of the way you have disobeyed her."

Jumping into bed with a bound, Harry dug his head into the pillows, gurgled, and then sat up very straight.

"God bless dear papa, God bless dear mamma, God bless dear grandmamma, God bless dear grandpapa, God bless dear Lucy, God bless dear Jenny, God bless our dear friends everywhere," he repeated in a resounding voice.

"Oh, you precious lamb!" exclaimed Virginia. "He couldn't

bear to hurt poor mamma, could he ?" and she kissed him ecstatically before hastening to the slumbering Jenny in the adjoining room.

" I like the little scamp," said Susan, when she reported the scene to John Henry on the way home, " but he manages his mother perfectly. Already his sense of humour is better developed than hers."

" I can't get over seeing Virginia with children," observed John Henry, as if the fact of Virginia's motherhood had just become evident to him. " It suits her, though. She looked happier than I ever saw her—and so, for that matter, did Aunt Lucy."

" It made me wonder how Mrs. Pendleton had lived away from them for seven years. Why, you can't imagine what she is—she doesn't seem to have any life at all until you see her with Virginia's children."

" It's a wonderful thing," said John Henry slowly, " and it taught me a lot just to look at them. I don't know why, but it seemed to make me understand how much I care about you, Susan."

" Hadn't you suspected it before ?" asked Susan as calmly as he had spoken. Emotionalism, she knew, she would never find in John Henry's wooing, and, though she could not have explained the reason of it to herself, she liked the brusque directness of his courtship. It was part of that large sincerity of nature which had first attracted her to him.

" Of course, in a way I knew I cared more for you than for anybody else ; but I didn't realize that you were more to me than Virginia had ever been. I had got so in the habit of thinking I was in love with her that it came almost as a surprise to me to find that it was over."

" I knew it long ago," said Susan.

" Why didn't you make me see it ?"

" Oh, I waited for you to find it out yourself. I was sure that you would some day."

" Do you think you could ever care for me, Susan ?"

A smile quivered on Susan's lips as she looked up at him, but with the reticence which had always characterized her, she answered simply :

" I think I could, John Henry."

His hand reached down and closed over hers, and in the long look which they exchanged under the flickering street lamp, she felt suddenly that perfect security which is usually the growth of happy years. Whatever the future brought to them, she knew that she could trust John Henry's love for her.

"And we've lost seven years, dearest," he said with a catch in his voice. "We've lost seven years just because I happened to be born a fool."

"But we've got fifty ahead of us," she replied with a joyous laugh.

As she spoke, her heart cried out, "Fifty years of the thing I want!" and she looked up into the kind, serious face of John Henry as if it were the face of incarnate happiness. A tremendous belief in life surged from her brain through her body, which felt incredibly warm and young. She thought exultantly of herself as of one who did not accept destiny, but commanded it.

They walked the rest of the way in silence, but he held her hand pressed closely against his heart, and once or twice he turned in the deserted street and looked into her eyes as if he found there all the words that he needed.

"We won't waste any more time, will we, Susan?" he asked when they reached the house. "Let's be married in December."

"If mother is better by then. She hasn't been well, and I am anxious about her."

"We'll go to housekeeping at once. I'll begin looking about to-morrow. God bless you, darling, for what you are giving me."

She caressed his hand gently with her fingers, and he was about to speak again, when the door behind them opened and the head of Cyrus appeared like that of a desolate bird of prey.

"Is that you, Susan?" he inquired. "Where have you been all this time? Your mother was taken ill more than an hour ago, and the doctor says that she has been paralyzed."

Breaking away from John Henry, Susan ran up the steps and past her father into the hall, where Miss Willy stood weeping.

"I was all by myself with her. There wasn't another living

soul in the house," sobbed the little dressmaker. " She fell over just like that, with her face all twisted, while I was talking to her."

" Oh, poor mother, poor mother !" cried the girl as she ran upstairs. " Is she in her room, and who is with her ?"

" The doctor has been there for over an hour, and he says that she'll never be able to move again. Oh, Susan, how will she stand it ?"

But Susan had already outstripped her, and was entering the sick-room, where Mrs. Treadwell lay unconscious, with her distorted face turned toward the door, as though she were watching expectantly for someone who would never come. As the girl fell on her knees beside the couch, her happiness seemed to dissolve like mist before the grim facts of mortal anguish and death. It was not until dawn, when the night's watch was over and she stood alone beside her window, that she said to herself with all the courage she could summon:

" And it's over for me too. Everything is over for me too. Oh, poor, poor mother !"

Love, which had seemed to her last night the supreme spirit in the universe, had surrendered its authority to the diviner image of Duty.

CHAPTER IV

HER CHILDREN

"POOR Aunt Belinda was paralyzed last night, Oliver," said Virginia the next morning at breakfast. "Miss Willy Whitlow just brought me a message from Susan. She spent the night there and was on her way this morning to ask mother to go."

Oliver had come downstairs in one of his absent-minded moods, but by the time Virginia had repeated her news he was able to take it in, and to show a proper solicitude for his aunt.

"Are you going there ?" he asked. "I am obliged to do a little work on my play while I have the idea, but tell Susan I'll come immediately after dinner."

"I'll stop to inquire on my way back from market, but I won't be able to stay, because I've got all my unpacking to do. Can you take the children out this afternoon so Marthy can help me ?"

"I'm sorry, but I simply can't. I've got to get on with this idea while I have control of it, and if I go out with the children I shan't be able to readjust my thoughts for twenty-four hours."

"I'd like to go out with papa," said Lucy, who sat carefully drinking her cambric tea, so that she might not spill a drop on the mahogany table.

"I want to go with papa," remarked Harry obstreperously, while he began to drum with his spoon on the red tin tray which protected the table from his assaults.

"Papa can't go with you, darling, but if mamma finishes her unpacking in time, she'll come out into the park and play with you a little while. Be careful, Harry, you are spilling your milk. Let mamma take your spoon out for you."

Her coffee, which she had poured out a quarter of an hour ago, stood untasted and tepid beside her plate, but from long habit she had grown to prefer it in that condition. When the waffles were handed to her, she had absent-mindedly helped herself to one, while she watched Harry's reckless efforts to cut up his bacon, and it had grown sodden before she remembered that it ought to be buttered. She wore the black skirt and blue blouse in which she had travelled, for she had neglected to unpack her own clothes in her eagerness to get out the things that Oliver and the children might need. Her hair had been hastily coiled around her head, without so much as a glance in the mirror, but the expression of unselfish goodness in her face lent a charm even to the careless fashion in which she had put on her clothes. She was one of those women whose beauty, being essentially virginal, belongs, like the blush of the rose, to a particular season. The delicacy of her skin invited the mark of time or of anxiety, and already fine little lines were visible, in the strong light of the morning, at the corners of her eyes and mouth. Yet neither the years nor her physical neglect of herself could destroy the look of almost angelic sweetness and love which illumined her features.

"Are you obliged to go to New York next week, Oliver?" she asked, dividing her attention equally between him and Harry's knife and fork. "Can't they rehearse 'The Beaten Road' just as well without you?"

"No, I want to be there. Is there any reason why I shouldn't?"

"Of course not. I was only thinking that Harry's birthday comes on Friday, and we should miss you."

"Well, I'm awfully sorry, but he'll have to grow old without me. By the way, why can't you run on with me for the first night, Virginia? Your mother can look after the babies for a couple of days, can't she?"

But the absent-minded look of young motherhood had settled again on Virginia's face, for the voice of Jenny, raised in exasperated demand, was heard from the nursery above.

"I wonder what's the matter?" she said, half rising in her chair, while she glanced nervously at the door. "She was so fretful last night, Oliver, that I'm afraid she is going to be sick. Will you keep an eye on Harry while I run up and see ?"

Ten minutes later she came down again, and began, with a relieved manner, to stir her cold coffee.

"What were you saying, Oliver ?" she inquired so sweetly that his irritation vanished.

"I was just asking you if you couldn't let your mother look after the youngsters for a day or two and come on with me."

"Oh, I'd give anything in the world to see it, but I couldn't possibly leave the children. I'd be so terribly anxious for fear something would happen."

"Sometimes I get in a blue funk about that play," he said seriously. "I've staked so much on it that I'll be pretty well cut up, morally and financially, if it doesn't go."

"But of course it will go, Oliver. Anybody could tell that just to read it. Didn't Mr. Martin write you that he thought it one of the strongest plays ever written in America ?—and I'm sure that is a great deal for a manager to say. Nobody could read a line of it without seeing that it is a work of genius."

For an instant he appeared to draw assurance from her praise; then his face clouded, and he responded doubtfully :

"But you thought just as well of ' April Winds,' and nobody would look at that."

"Well, that was perfect too, of its kind, but, of course, they are different."

"I never thought much of that," he said, "but I honestly believe that ' The Beaten Road ' is a great play. That's my judgment, and I'll stand by it."

"Of course it's great," she returned emphatically. "No, Harry, you can't have any more syrup on your buckwheat cake. You have eaten more already than sister Lucy, and she is two years older than you are."

"Give it to the little beggar. It won't hurt him," said Oliver impatiently, as Harry began to protest.

"But he really oughtn't to have it, Oliver. Well, then, just a drop. Oh, Oliver, you've given him a great deal too much. Here, take mamma's plate, and give her yours, Harry."

But Harry made no answer to her plea, because he was busily eating the syrup as fast as he could under pressure of the fear that he might lose it all if he procrastinated.

"He'll be sick before night and you'll have yourself to blame, Oliver," said Virginia reproachfully.

Ever since the babies had come she had assumed naturally that Oliver's interest in the small details of his children's clothes or health was perpetually fresh and absorbing like her own, and her habit of not seeing what she did not want to see in life had protected her from the painful discovery that he was occasionally bored. Once he had even tried to explain to her that, although he loved the children better than either his plays or the political fate of nations, there were times when the latter questions interested him considerably more; but the humour with which he inadvertently veiled his protest had turned the point of it entirely away from her comprehension. A deeper impression was made upon her by the fact that he had refused to stop reading about the last Presidential campaign long enough to come and persuade Harry to swallow a dose of medicine. She, who seldom read a newspaper, and was innocent of any desire to exert even the most indirect influence upon the elections, had waked in the night to ask herself if it could possibly be true that Oliver loved the children less passionately than she did.

"I've got to get to work now, dear," he said, rising. "I haven't had a quiet breakfast since Harry first came to the table. Don't you think Marthy might feed him upstairs again?"

"Oh, Oliver! It would break his heart. He would think that he was in disgrace."

"Well, I'm not sure that he oughtn't to be. Now, Lucy's all right. She behaves like a lady; but if you consider Harry an appetizing table companion, I don't."

"But, dearest, he's only a baby! And boys are different from girls. You can't expect them to have as good manners."

"I can't remember that I ever made a nuisance of myself."

"Your father was very strict with you. But surely you don't think it is right to make your children afraid of you?"

The genuine distress in her voice brought a laugh from him.

"Oh, well, they are your children, darling, and you may do as you please with them."

"Bad papa!" said Harry suddenly, chasing the last drop of syrup around his plate with a bit of breadcrumb.

"Oh, no, precious; good papa! You must promise papa to be a little gentleman, or he won't let you breakfast with him any more."

It was Virginia's proud boast that Harry's smile would melt even his great-uncle, Cyrus, and she watched him with breathless rapture as he turned now in his high chair and tested the effect of this magic charm on his father. His baby mouth broadened deliciously, showing two rows of small, irregular teeth; his blue eyes shone until they seemed full of sparkles; his roguish, irresistible face became an incarnation of infant entreaty.

"I want to bekfast wid papa, an' I want more 'lasses," he remarked.

"He's a fascinating little rascal, there's no doubt of that," observed Oliver, in response to Virginia's triumphant look. Then, bending over, he kissed her on the cheek, before he picked up his newspapers and went into his study at the back of the parlour.

Some hours later, at their early dinner, she reported the result of her visit to the Treadwells.

"It is too awful, Oliver. Aunt Belinda has not spoken yet, and she can't move the lower part of her body at all. The doctor says she may live for years, but he doesn't think she will ever be able to walk again. I feel so sorry for her and for poor Susan. Do you know, Susan engaged herself to John Henry last night just before her mother was paralyzed, and they were to be married in December. But now she says she will give him up."

"John Henry!" exclaimed Oliver in amazement. "Why, what in the world does she see in John Henry?"

"I don't know; one never knows what people see in each other, but she has been in love with him all her life, I believe.

"Well, it's rough on her. Is she obliged to break off with him now?"

"She says it wouldn't be fair to him not to. Her whole time must be given to nursing her mother. There's something splendid about Susan, Oliver. I never realized it as much as I did to-day. Whatever she does, you may be sure it will be because it is right to do it. She sees everything so clearly, and her wishes never obscure her judgment."

"It's a pity. She'd make a great mother, wouldn't she? But life doesn't seem able to get along without a sacrifice of the fittest."

In the afternoon Mrs. Pendleton came over, but the two women were so busy arranging the furniture in its proper place, and laying away Oliver's and the children's things in drawers and closets, that not until the entire house had been put in order, did they find time to sit down for a few minutes in the nursery and discuss the future of Susan.

"I believe John Henry will want to marry her and go to live at the Treadwells', if Susan will let him," remarked Mrs. Pendleton.

"How on earth could he get on with Uncle Cyrus?" Ever since her marriage, Virginia had followed Oliver's habit and spoken of Cyrus as "uncle."

"Well, I don't suppose even John Henry could do that, but perhaps he thinks anything would be better than losing Susan."

"And he's right," returned Virginia loyally, while she got out her work-bag and began sorting the array of stockings that needed darning. "Do you know, mother, Oliver seems to think that I might go to New York with him."

"And leave the children, Jinny?"

"Of course, I've told him that I can't, but he's asked me two or three times to let you look after them for a day or two."

"I'd love to do it, darling; but you've never spent a night away from one of them since Lucy was born, have you?"

"No; and I'd be perfectly miserable—only I can't make Oliver understand it. Of course, they'd be just as safe with you as with me, but I'd keep imagining every minute that something had happened."

"I know exactly how you feel, dear. I never spent a night outside my home after my first child came until you grew up. I don't see how any true woman could bear to do it, unless, of course, she was called away because of a serious illness."

" If Oliver were ill, or you, or father, I'd go in a minute unless one of the children was really sick—but just to see a play is different, and I'd feel as if I were neglecting my duty. The funny part is that Oliver is so wrapped up in this play, that he doesn't seem to be able to get his mind off it, poor darling. Father was never that way about his sermons, was he ?"

" Your father never thought of himself or of his own interests enough, Jinny. If he ever had a fault, it was that. But I suppose he approaches perfection as nearly as a man ever did."

Slipping the darning gourd into the toe of one of Lucy's little white stockings, Virginia gazed attentively at a small round hole while she held her needle arrested slightly above it. So exquisitely Madonna-like was the poise of her head and the dreaming, prophetic mystery in her face, that Mrs. Pendleton waited almost breathlessly for her words.

" There's not a single thing that I would change in Oliver, if I could," she said at last.

" It is so beautiful that you feel that way, darling. I suppose all happily married women do."

A week later, across Harry's birthday cake, which stood surrounded by four candles in the centre of the rectory table, Virginia offered her cheerful explanation of Oliver's absence, in reply to a mild inquiry from the rector. " He was obliged to go to New York yesterday about the rehearsal of 'The Beaten Road,' father. We were both so sorry he couldn't be here to-day, but it was impossible for him to wait over."

" It's a pity," said the rector gently. " Harry will never be just four years old again, will you, little man ?" Even the substantial fact that Oliver's play would, it was hoped, provide a financial support for his children, did not suffice to lift it from the region of the unimportant in the mind of his father-in-law.

" But he'll have plenty of other birthdays when papa will be here," remarked Virginia brightly. Though she had been a little hurt to find that Oliver had arranged to leave home the night before, and that he had appeared perfectly blind to the importance of his presence at Harry's celebration, her native good sense had not permitted her to make a grievance out of the matter. On her wedding day she had resolved that she would not be exacting of Oliver's time or attention, and the sweetness of her disposition had smoothed away any difficulties which had intervened between her and her ideal of wifehood. From the first, love had meant to her the opportunity of giving rather than the privilege of receiving, and her failure to regard herself as of supreme consequence in any situation had protected her from the minor troubles and disillusionments of marriage.

"It is too bad to think that dear Oliver will have to be away for two whole weeks," said Mrs. Pendleton.

"Is he obliged to stay that long?" asked the rector sympathetically. Never having missed an anniversary since the war, he could look upon Oliver's absence as a fit subject for condolence.

"He can't possibly come home until the play is produced, and that won't be for two weeks yet," replied Virginia.

"But I thought it rested with the actors now. Couldn't they go on just as well without him?"

"He thinks not; and, of course, it is such a great play that he doesn't want to take any risks with it."

"Of course he doesn't," assented Mrs. Pendleton, who had believed that the stage was immoral until Virginia's husband began to write for it.

"I know he'll come back the very first minute that he can get away," said Virginia with conviction, before she stooped to comfort Harry, who was depressed by the discovery that he was not expected to eat his entire cake, but instantly hopeful when he was promised a slice of sister Lucy's in the summer.

Late in the afternoon, when the children, warmly wrapped in extra shawls by Mrs. Pendleton, were led back through the cold to the house in Prince Street, one and all of the party agreed that it was the nicest birthday that had ever been. "I like grandma's cake better than our cake," announced Harry above his white muffler. "Why can't we have cake like that, mamma?"

He was trotting sturdily, with his hand in Virginia's, behind the perambulator, which contained a much muffled Jenny, and at his words Mrs. Pendleton, who walked a little ahead, turned suddenly and hugged him tight for an instant.

"Just listen to the darling boy!" she exclaimed in a choking voice.

"Because nobody else can make such good cake as grandma's," answered Virginia, quite as pleased as her mother. "And she's going to give you one every birthday as long as you live."

"Can't I have another birthday soon, mamma?"

"Not till after sister Lucy's. You want sister Lucy to have one, don't you? and dear little Jenny?"

"But why can't I have a cake without a birthday, mamma?"

"You may, precious, and grandma will make you one," said Mrs. Pendleton, as she helped Marthy wheel the perambulator over the slippery crossing and into the front gate.

On the hall table there was a telegram from Oliver, and Virginia tore it open while her mother and Marthy unfastened the children's wraps.

"He's at the Hotel Bertram," she said joyously, "and he says the rehearsals are going splendidly."

"Did he mention Harry's birthday?" asked Mrs. Pendleton, trying to hide the instinctive dread which the sight of a telegram aroused in her.

"He must have forgotten it. Can't you come upstairs to the nursery with us, mother?"

"No, your father is all alone. I must be getting back," replied Mrs. Pendleton gently.

An hour or two later, when Virginia sat in her rocking-chair before the nursery fire, with Harry, worn out with his play and forgetful of the dignity of his four years, asleep in her lap, she opened the telegram again and re-read it hungrily while the light of love shone in her face. She knew intuitively that Oliver had sent the telegram because he had not written—and would not write, probably, until he had finished with the hardest work of his play. It was an easy thing to do—it took considerably less of his time than a letter would have done; but she had inherited from her mother the sentimental vision of life which unconsciously magnifies the meaning of trivial attentions. She looked through her emotions as through a prism on the simple fact of his telegraphing, and it became immediately transfigured. How dear it was of him to realize that she would be anxious until she heard from him ! How lonely he must be all by himself in that great city ! How much he must have wanted to be with Harry on his birthday ! Sitting there in the fire-lit nursery, her heart sent out waves of love and sympathy to him across the distance and the twilight. On the rug at her feet Lucy rocked in her little chair, crooning to her doll with the beginnings of the mother instinct already softening her voice, and in the adjoining room Jenny lay asleep in her crib while the faithful Marthy watched by her side. Beyond the window a fine icy rain had begun to fall, and down the long street she could see the lamps flickering in revolving circles of frost. In the midst of the frozen streets, that little centre of red fire-light separated her as completely from the other twenty-one thousand human beings among whom she lived as did the glow of personal joy that suffused her thoughts. From the dusk below she heard the tapping of a blind beggar's stick on the pavement, and the sound made, while it lasted, a plaintive accompaniment to the lullaby she was singing. "Two whole weeks," she thought, while her longing reached out to that unknown room in which she pictured Oliver sitting alone. "Two whole weeks ! How hard it will be for him !" In her guarded ignorance of the world she could not imagine that Oliver was suffering less from this enforced absence from all he loved than she herself would have suffered had she been in his place. Of course, men were different from women—that ancient dogma was embodied in the leading clause of her creed of life; but she had always understood that this difference vanished in some miraculous way after marriage. She knew that Oliver had to work, of course—how otherwise could he support his family ?—but the idea that his work might ever usurp the place in his heart that belonged to her and the children would have been utterly incomprehensible to her had she ever thought of it. Jealousy was an alien weed, which could not take root in the benign soil of her nature.

For a week there was no letter from Oliver, and at the end

of that time a few lines scrawled on a sheet of hotel paper explained that he spent every minute of his time at the theatre.

"Poor fellow, it's dreadfully hard on him, isn't it?" Virginia said to her mother, when she showed her the imposing picture of the hotel at the head of his letter.

There was no hint of compassion for herself in her voice. Her pity was entirely for Oliver, constrained to be away for two whole weeks from his children, who grew more interesting and delightful every day that they lived. "Harry has gone into the first reader," she added, turning from the storeroom shelves on which she was laying strips of white oilcloth. "He will be able to read his lesson to Oliver when he comes home."

"I have always understood that your father could read his Bible at the age of four," remarked Mrs. Pendleton, who passionately treasured this solitary proof of the rector's brilliancy.

"I am afraid Harry is backward. He hates his letters especially the letter A—so much that it takes me an hour sometimes to get him to say it after me. My only comfort is that Oliver says he couldn't read a line until he was over seven years old. Would you scallop this oilcloth, mother, or leave it plain?"

"I always scallop mine. Mrs. Treadwell must be better, Jinny; Susan sent me a dessert yesterday."

"Yes; but she will never be able to move herself. Do you think that poor Susan will marry John Henry now?"

"I wonder," replied Mrs. Pendleton vaguely. Then the sound of Harry's laughter floated in suddenly from the back-yard, and her eyes, following Virginia's, turned automatically to the pantry window.

"They've come home for a snack, I suppose," she said. "Shall I fix some bread and preserves for them?"

"Oh, I'll do it," responded Virginia, while she reached for the crock of blackberry jam on the shelf at her side.

Another week passed and there was no word from Oliver, until Mrs. Pendleton came in at dusk one evening, with an anxious look on her face and a folded newspaper held tightly in her hand.

"Have you seen any of the accounts of Oliver's play, Jinny?" she asked.

"No, I haven't had time to look at the papers to-day; Harry has hurt his foot."

She spoke placidly, looking up from the nursery floor, where she knelt beside a basin of warm water at Harry's feet. "Poor little fellow, he fell on a pile of bricks," she added; "but he's such a hero he never even whimpered, did he, darling?"

"But it hurt bad," said Harry eagerly.

"Of course, it hurt dreadfully, and if he hadn't been a man he would have cried."

"Sister would have cried," exulted the hero.

"Indeed, sister would have cried. Sister is a girl," responded Virginia, smothering him with kisses over the basin of water.

But Mrs. Pendleton refused to be diverted from her purpose even by the heroism of her grandson.

"John Henry found this in a New York paper and brought it to me. He thought you ought to see it, though, of course, it may not be so serious as it sounds."

"Serious?" repeated Virginia, letting the soapy washrag fall back into the basin while she stretched out her moist and reddened hand for the paper.

"It says that the play didn't go very well," pursued her mother guardedly. "They expect to take it off at once, and —and Oliver is not well—he is ill in the hotel——"

"Ill?" cried Virginia, and as she rose to her feet the basin upset and deluged Harry's shoes and the rug on which she had been kneeling. Her mind, unable to grasp the significance of a theatrical failure, had seized upon the one salient fact which concerned her. Plays might succeed or fail, and it made little difference, but illness was another matter—illness was something definite and material. Illness could neither be talked away by religion nor denied by philosophy. It had its place in her mind not with the shadow, but with the substance of things. It was the one sinister force which had always dominated her, even when it was absent, by the sheer terror it aroused in her thoughts.

"Let me see," she said chokingly. "No, I can't read it— tell me."

"It only says that the play was a failure—nobody understood it, and a great many people said it was—oh, Virginia—*immoral!* There's something about its being foreign and an attack on American ideals—and then they add that the author refused to be interviewed, and they understood that he was ill in his room at the Bertram."

The charge of immorality, which would have crushed Virginia at another time, and which, even in the intense excitement of the moment, had been an added stab to Mrs. Pendleton, was brushed aside as if it were the pestiferous attack of an insect.

"I am going to him now—at once; when does the train leave, mother?"

"But, Jinny, how can you? You have never been to New York. You wouldn't know where to go."

"But he is ill! Nothing on earth is going to keep me away from him! Will you please wipe Harry's feet while I try to get on my clothes?"

"But, Jinny, the children?"

"You and Marthy must look after the children. Of course I can't take them with me. Oh, Harry, won't you please hush and let poor mamma dress? She is almost distracted."

Something—a secret force of character which even her mother had not suspected that she possessed—had arisen in an instant and dominated the situation. She was no longer the gentle and doting mother of a minute ago, but a creature of a fixed purpose and an iron resolution. Even her face appeared to lose its soft contour and hardened until Mrs. Pendleton grew almost frightened. Never had she imagined that Virginia could look like this.

"I am sure there is some mistake about it. Don't take it so terribly to heart, Jinny," she pleaded, while she knelt down, cowed and obedient, to wipe Harry's feet.

Virginia, who had already torn off her house dress, and was hurriedly buttoning the navy blue waist in which she had travelled, looked at her calmly without pausing for an instant in her task.

"Will you bind up his foot with some arnica?" she asked. "There's an old handkerchief in my work-basket. I want you and father to come here and stay until I get back. It will be less trouble than moving all their things over to the rectory."

"Very well, darling," replied Mrs. Pendleton meekly; "we'll do everything that we can, of course." And she added timidly, "Have you money enough?"

"I have thirty dollars. I just got it out of the bank to-day to pay Marthy and my housekeeping bills. Do you think that will be as much as I'll need?"

"I should think so, dear. Of course, if you find you want more, you can telegraph your father."

"The train doesn't leave for two hours, so I'll have plenty of time to get ready. It's just half-past six now, and Oliver didn't leave the house till eight o'clock."

"Won't you take a little something to eat before you go?"

"I couldn't swallow a morsel, but I'll sit with you and the children as soon as I've put the things in my satchel. I couldn't possibly need but this one dress, could I? If Oliver isn't really ill, I hope we can start home to-morrow. That will be two nights that I'll spend away. Oh, mother, ask father to pray that he won't be ill."

Her voice broke, but she fiercely bit back the sob before it escaped her lips.

"I will, dear, I promise you. We will both think of you and pray for you every minute. Jinny, are you sure it's wise? Couldn't we send someone—John Henry would go, I know— in your place?"

A spasm of irritation contracted Virginia's features. "Please don't, mother," she begged, "it just worries me. Whatever happens, I am going." Then she sobbed outright. "He wanted me to go with him at first, and I wouldn't because I thought it was my duty to stay at home with the children. If anything should happen to him, I'd never forgive myself."

She was slipping her black cloth skirt over her head as she spoke, and her terror-stricken face disappeared under the pleats before Mrs. Pendleton could turn to look at her. When her head emerged again above the belt of her skirt, the expression of her features had grown more natural.

"You'll go down in a carriage, won't you?" inquired her mother, whose mind achieved that perfect mixture of the sentimental and the practical which is rarely found in any except Southern women.

"I suppose I'll have to. Then I can take my satchel with me, and that will save trouble. You won't forget, mother, that I give Lucy a teaspoonful of cod-liver oil after each meal, will you? She has had that hacking cough for three weeks, and I want to break it up."

"I'll remember, Jinny; but I'm so miserable about your going alone."

Turning to the closet, Virginia unearthed an old black satchel from beneath a pile of toys, and began dusting it inside with a towel. Then she took out some underclothes from a bureau drawer and a few toilet articles, which she wrapped in pieces of tissue paper. Her movements were so methodical that the nervousness in Mrs. Pendleton's mind slowly gave way to astonishment. For the first time in her life, perhaps, the mother realized that her daughter was no longer a child, but a woman, and a woman whose character was as strong and as determined as her own. Vaguely she understood, without analyzing the motives that moved Virginia, that this strength and this determination which so impressed her had arisen from those deep places in her daughter's soul where emotion and not thought had its source. Love was guiding her now as surely as it had guided her when she had refused to go with Oliver to New York, or when, but a few minutes ago, she had knelt down to wash and bandage Harry's little earth-stained feet. It was the only power to which she would ever surrender. No other principle would ever direct or control her.

Marthy, who appeared with Jenny's supper, was sent out to order the carriage and to bear a message to the rector, and Virginia took the little girl in her lap and began to crumble the bread into the bowl of milk.

"Wouldn't you like me to do that, dear?" asked Mrs. Pendleton, with a submission in her tone which she had never used before except to the rector. "Don't you want to fix your hair over?"

"Oh, no, I'll keep on my hat till I go to bed, so it doesn't matter. I'd rather you'd finish my packing if you don't mind. There's nothing more to go in except some collars and my bedroom slippers and that red wrapper hanging behind the door in the closet."

"Are you going to take any medicine ?"

"Only that bottle of camphor and some mustard plasters. Yes, you'd better put in the brandy flask and the aromatic ammonia. You can never tell when you will need them. Now, my darlings, mother is going away and you must keep well and be as good as gold until she comes back."

To the amazement of Mrs. Pendleton (who reflected that you really never knew what to expect of children), this appeal produced an immediate and extraordinary result. Lucy, who had been fidgeting about and trying to help with the packing, became suddenly solemn and dignified, while an ennobling excitement mounted to Harry's face. Never particularly obedient before, they became, as soon as the words were uttered, as amenable as angels. Even Jenny stopped feeding long enough to raise herself and pat her mother's cheek with ten caressing, milky fingers.

"Mother's going away," said Lucy in a solemn voice, and a hush fell on the three of them.

"And grandma's coming here to live," added Harry after the silence had grown so depressing that Virginia had started to cry.

"Not to live, precious," corrected Mrs. Pendleton quickly. "Just to spend two days with you. Mother will be home in two days."

"Mother will be home in two days," repeated Lucy. "May I stay away from school while you're away, mamma ?"

"And may I stop learning my letters ?" asked Harry.

"No, darlings, you must do just as if I were here. Grandma will take care of you. Now promise me that you will be good."

They promised obediently, awed to submission by the stupendous importance of the change. It is probable that they would have observed with less surprise any miraculous upheaval in the orderly phenomena of nature.

"I don't see how I can possibly leave them—they are so good. and they behave exactly as if they realized how anxious I am," wept Virginia, breaking down when Marthy came to announce that the rector had come and the carriage was at the door.

"Suppose you give it up, Jinny. I—I'll send your father," pleaded Mrs. Pendleton in desperation, as she watched the tragedy of the parting.

But that strange force which the situation had developed in Virginia yielded neither to her mother's prayers nor to the last despairing wails of the children, who realized, at the sight of the black bag in Marthy's hands, that their providence was actually deserting them. The deepest of her instincts—the instinct that was at the root of all her mother love—was threatened, and she rose to battle. The thing she loved best, she had learned, was neither husband nor child, but the one that needed her.

CHAPTER V

FAILURE

She had lain down in her clothes, impelled by the feeling that if there were to be a wreck she should prefer to appear completely dressed; so when the chill dawn came at last and the train pulled into Jersey City, she had nothing to do except to adjust her veil and wait patiently until the porter came for her bag. His colour, which was black, inspired her with confidence, and she followed him trustfully to the platform, where he delivered her to another smiling member of his race. The cold was so penetrating that her teeth began to chatter as she turned to obey the orders of the dusky official who had assumed command of her. Never had she felt anything so bleak as the atmosphere of the station. Never in her life had she been so lonely as she was while she hurried down the long, dim platform in the direction of a gate which looked as if it led into a prison. She was chilled through; her skin felt as if it had turned to india-rubber; there was a sickening terror in her soul ; and she longed above all things to sit down on one of the inhospitable tracks and burst into tears; but something stronger than impulse urged her shivering body onward and controlled the twitching muscles about her mouth. "In a few minutes I shall see Oliver. Oliver is ill and I am going to him," she repeated over and over to herself as if she were reciting a prayer.

Inside the station she declined the offer of breakfast, and was conducted to the ferry, where she was obliged to run in order to catch the boat that was just leaving. Seated on one of the long benches in the saloon, with her bag at her feet and her umbrella grasped tightly in her hand, she gazed helplessly at the other passengers and wondered if any one of them would tell her what to do when she reached the opposite side. The women, she thought, looked hard and harassed, and the men she could not see because of the rows of newspapers behind which they were hidden. Once her wandering gaze caught the eyes of a middle-aged woman in rusty black, who smiled at her above the head of a sleeping child.

"That's a pretty woman," said a man carelessly as he put down his paper, and she realized that he was talking about her to his companion. Then, as the terrible outlines of the city grew more distinct on the horizon, he got up and strolled as carelessly past her to the deck. He had spoken of her as indifferently as he might have spoken of the weather.

As the tremendous battlements (which were not tremendous to any of the other passengers) emerged slowly from the mist and cleft the sombre low-hanging clouds, from which a few flakes of snow fell, her terror vanished suddenly before the excitement which ran through her body. She forgot her hunger, her loneliness, her shivering flesh, her benumbed and aching feet. A sensation not unlike the one with which the rector had marched into his first battle, fortified and exhilarated her. The fighting blood of her ancestors grew warm in her veins. New York developed suddenly from a mere spot on a map into a romance made into brick; and when a ray of sunlight pierced the heavy fog, and lay like a white wing aslant the few falling snow-flakes, it seemed to her that the shadowy buildings lost their sinister aspect and softened into a haunting and mysterious beauty. Somewhere in that place of mystery and adventure Oliver was waiting for her! He was a part of that vast movement of life into which she was going. Then, youth, from which hope is never long absent, flamed up in her, and she was glad that she was still beautiful enough to cause strangers to turn and look at her.

But this mood, also, passed quickly, and a little later, while she rolled through the grey streets, into which the slant sunbeams could bring no colour, she surrendered again to that terror of the unknown which had seized her when she stood in the station. The beauty had departed from the buildings; the pavements were dirty; the little discoloured piles of snow made the crossings slippery and dangerous;

and she held her breath as they passed through the crowded streets on the west side, overcome by the fear of "catching" some malign malady from the smells and the filth. The negro quarters in Dinwiddie were dirty enough, but not, she thought with a kind of triumph, quite so dirty as New York. When the cab turned into Fifth Avenue, she took her handkerchief from her nostrils; but this imposing street, which had not yet emerged from its evil dream of Victorian brownstone, impressed her chiefly as a place of a thousand prisons. It was impossible to believe that those frowning walls, undecorated by a creeper or the shadow of a tree, could really be homes where people lived and children were born.

At first she had gazed with a childish interest and curiosity on the houses she was passing; then the sense of strangeness gave place presently to the exigent necessity of reaching Oliver as soon as possible. But the driver appeared indifferent to her timid taps on the glass at his back, while the horse progressed with the feeble activity of one who had spent a quarter of a century ineffectually making an effort. Her impatience, which she had at first kept under control, began to run in quivers of nervousness through her limbs. The very richness of her personal life, which had condensed all experience into a single emotional centre, and restricted her vision of the universe to that solitary window of the soul through which she looked, prevented her now from seeing in the city anything except the dreary background of Oliver's illness and failure. The naïve wonder with which she had watched the gigantic outlines shape themselves out of the white fog, had faded utterly from her mind. She ached with longing to reach Oliver and to find him well enough to take the first train back to Dinwiddie.

At the hotel her bag and umbrella were wrested from her by an imperious uniformed attendant, and in what seemed to her an incredibly short space of time, she was following him along a velvet-lined corridor on the tenth floor. The swift ascent in the elevator had made her dizzy, and the physical sensation reminded her that she was weak for food. Then the attendant rapped imperatively at a door just beyond a shining staircase, and she forgot herself as completely as it had been her habit to do since her marriage.

"Come in !" responded a muffled voice on the inside, and as the door swung open, she saw Oliver, in his dressing-gown, and with an unshaved face, reading a newspaper beside a table on which stood an untasted cup of coffee.

"I didn't ring," he began impatiently, and then starting to his feet, he uttered her name in a voice which held her standing as if she were suddenly paralyzed on the threshold. "Virginia !"

A sob rose in her throat, and her faltering gaze passed from him to the hotel attendant, who responded to her unspoken appeal as readily as if it were a part of his regular business. Pushing her gently inside, he placed her bag and umbrella on an empty chair, took up the breakfast tray from the table, and inquired, with a kindness which strangely humbled her, if she wished to give an order. When she had helplessly shaken her head, he bowed and went out, closing the door softly upon their meeting.

"What in thunder, Virginia ?" began Oliver, and she realized that he was angry.

"I heard you were sick—that the play had failed. I was so sorry I hadn't come with you," she explained; and then, understanding for the first time the utter foolishness of what she had done, she put her hands up to her face and burst into tears.

He had risen from his chair, but he made no movement to come nearer to her, and when she took down her hands in order to wipe her eyes, she saw an expression in his face which frightened her by its strangeness. She had caught him when that guard which every human being — even a husband—wears, had fallen away, though in her ignorance it seemed to her that he had become suddenly another person. That she had entered into one of those awful hours of self-realization, when the soul must face its limitations alone and make its readjustments in silence, did not occur to her, because she, who had lived every minute of her life under the eyes of her parents or her children, could have no comprehension of the hunger for solitude which was devouring Oliver's heart. She saw merely that he did not want her —that she had not only startled, but angered him by coming; and the bitterness of that instant seemed to her more than she was able to bear. Something had changed him; he was older, he was harder, he was embittered.

"I—I am so sorry," she stammered; and because even in the agony of this moment she could not think long of herself, she added almost humbly: "Would you rather that I should go back again?" Then, by the haggard look of his face as he turned away from her towards the window, she saw that he, also, was suffering, and her soul yearned over him as it had yearned over Harry when he had had the toothache. "Oh, Oliver!" she cried, and again: "Oh, Oliver, won't you let me help you?"

But he was in the mood of despairing humiliation when one may support abuse better than pity. His failure, he knew, had been undeserved, and he was still smarting from the injustice of it as from the blows of a whip. For twenty-four hours his nerves had been on the rack, and his one desire had been to hide himself in the spiritual nakedness to which he was stripped. Had he been obliged to choose a witness to his suffering, it is probable that he would have selected a stranger from the street rather than his wife. The one thing that could have helped him, an intelligent justification of his work, she was powerless to give. In his need she had nothing except love to offer; and love, she felt instinctively, was not the balm for his wound.

Afraid and yet passionately longing to meet his eyes, she let her gaze fall away from him and wander timidly, as if uncertain where to rest, about the disordered room, with its dull red walls, its cheap Nottingham lace curtains tied back with cords, its elaborately carved walnut furniture, and its litter of days old newspapers upon the bed. She saw his neckties hanging in an uneven row over the oblong mirror, and she controlled a nervous impulse to straighten them out and put them away.

"Why didn't you telegraph me?" he asked, after a pause in which she had struggled vainly to look as if it were the most natural thing in the world that he should receive her in this way. "If I had known you were coming, I should have met you."

"Father wanted to, but I wouldn't let him," she answered. "I—I thought you were sick."

In spite of his despair, it is probable that at the moment she was suffering more than he was—since a wound to love strikes deeper, after all, than a wound to ambition. Where she had expected to find her husband, she felt vaguely that she had encountered a stranger, and she was overwhelmed by that sense of irremediable loss which follows the discovery of terrible and unfamiliar qualities in those whom we have known and loved intimately for years. The fact that he was plainly struggling to disguise his annoyance, that he was trying as hard as she to assume a manner he did not feel, only added a sardonic humour to poignant tragedy.

"Have you had anything to eat?" he asked abruptly, and remembering that he had not kissed her when she entered, he put his arm about her and brushed her cheek with his lips.

"No; I waited to breakfast with you. I was in such a hurry to get here."

"By Jove!" he exclaimed, and going over to the bell, he touched it with the manner of a man who is delighted that anything so perfectly practical as food exists in the world.

While he was speaking to the waiter, she took off her hat, and washed the stains of smoke and tears from her face. Her hair was a sight, she thought; but while she gazed back at her stricken eyes in the little mirror over the washstand, she recalled with a throb of gratitude that the stranger on the boat had said she was pretty. She felt so humble that she clung almost with desperation to the thought that Oliver always liked to have people admire her.

When she turned from the washstand, he was reading the newspaper again, and he put it aside with a forced cheerfulness to arrange the table for breakfast.

"Aren't you going to have something too?" she asked, looking disconsolately at the tray, for all her hunger had departed. If he would only be natural she felt that she could bear anything! If he would only stop trying to pretend that he was not miserable and that nothing had happened! After all, it couldn't be so very bad, could it? It wasn't in the least as if one of the children were ill.

She poured out a cup of coffee for him before drinking her own, and putting it down on the table at his side, waited patiently until he should look up again from his paper. A lump as hard as lead had risen in her throat and was choking her.

"Are the children well?" he asked presently, and she answered with an affected brightness more harrowing than tears: "Yes; mother is taking care of them. Lucy still has the little cough, but I'm giving her cod-liver oil. And, what do you think? I have a surprise for you. Harry can read the first lesson in his reader."

He smiled kindly back at her, but from the vacancy in his face, she realized that he had not taken in a word that she had said. His trouble, whatever it was, could absorb him so utterly that he had ceased even to be interested in his children. He, who had borne so calmly the loss of that day-old baby for whom she had grieved herself to a shadow, was plunged into this condition of abject hopelessness merely because his play was a failure! It was not only impossible for her to share his suffering; she realized, while she watched him, that she could not so much as comprehend it. Her limitations, of which she had never been acutely conscious until to-day, appeared suddenly insurmountable. Love, which had seemed to her to solve all problems and to smooth all difficulties, was helpless to enlighten her. It was not love—it was something else that she needed now, and of this something else she knew not even so much as the name.

She drank her coffee quickly, fearing that if she did not take food she should lose control of herself and anger him by a display of hysterics.

"I don't wonder you couldn't drink your coffee," she said with a quivering little laugh. "It must have been made yesterday." Then, unable to bear the strain any longer, she cried out sharply: "Oh, Oliver, won't you tell me what is the matter?"

His look grew hard, while a spasm of irritation contracted his mouth.

"There's nothing you need worry about—except that I've borrowed money, and I'm afraid we'll have to cut down things a bit until I manage to pay it back."

"Why, of course, we'll cut down things," she almost laughed in her relief. "We can live on a great deal less, and I'll market so carefully that you will hardly know the difference. I'll put Marthy in the kitchen and take care of the children myself. It won't be the least bit of trouble."

She knew by his face that he was grateful to her, though he said merely: " I'm a little knocked up, I suppose, so you mustn't mind. I've got a beast of a headache. Martin is going to take 'The Beaten Road' off at the end of the week, you know, and he doesn't think now that he will produce the other. There wasn't a good word for me from the critics, and yet, damn them, I know that the play is the best one that's ever come out of America. But it's real—that's why they fell foul of it—it isn't stuffed with sugar-plums."

" Why, what in the world possessed them ?" she returned indignantly. " It is a beautiful play."

She saw him flinch at the word, and the sombre irritation which his outburst had relieved for a minute, settled again on his features. Her praise, she understood, only exasperated him, though she did not realize that it was the lack of discrimination in it which aroused his irritation. At the moment, intelligent appreciation of his work would have been bread and meat to him, but her pitiful attempts at flattery were like bungling touches on raw flesh. Had he written the veriest rags of sentimental rubbish, he knew she would as passionately have defended their " beauty."

" I'll get dressed quickly and look after some business," he said, " and we'll go home to-night."

Her eyes shone, and she began to eat her eggs with a resolution born of the consoling memory of Dinwiddie. If only they could be at home again with the children, she felt that all this trouble and misunderstanding would vanish. With a strange confusion of ideas, it seemed to her that Oliver's suffering had been in some mysterious way produced by New York, and that it existed merely within the circumscribed limits of this dreadful city.

" Oh, Oliver, that will be lovely !" she exclaimed, and tried to subdue the note of joy in her voice.

" I shan't be able to get back to lunch, I'm afraid. What will you do about it ?"

" Don't bother about me, dearest. I'll dress and take a little walk just to see what Fifth Avenue is like. I can't get lost if I go perfectly straight up the street, can I ?"

"Fifth Avenue is only a block away. You can't miss it. Now I'll hurry and be off."

She knew that he was anxious to be alone, and so firmly was she convinced that this mood of detachment would leave him as soon as he was in the midst of his family again, that she was able to smile tolerantly when he kissed her hastily, and seizing his hat, rushed from the room. For a time, after he had gone she amused herself putting his things in order and packing the little tin trunk he had brought with him; but the red walls and the steam heat in the room sickened her at last, and when she had bathed and dressed and there seemed nothing left for her to do except get out her work-bag and begin darning his socks, she decided that she would put on her hat and go out for a walk. It did not occur to her to feel hurt by the casual manner in which Oliver had shifted the responsibility of her presence—partly owing to a personal inability to take a selfish point of view about anything, and partly because of that racial habit of making allowances for the male in which she had been sedulously trained from her infancy.

At the door the porter directed her to Fifth Avenue, and she ventured cautiously as far as the flowing rivulet at the corner, where she would probably have stood until Oliver's return, if a friendly policeman had not observed her stranded helplessness and assisted her over. "How on earth am I to get back again ?" she thought, smiling up at him; and this anxiety engrossed her so completely that for a minute she forgot to look at the amazing buildings and the curious crowds that hurried frantically in their shadows. Then a pale finger of sunlight pointed suddenly across the high roofs in front of her, and awed, in spite of her preoccupation, by the strangeness of the scene, she stopped and watched the moving carriages in the middle of the street and the never-ending stream of people that passed on the wet pavements. Occasionally, while she stood there, some of the passers-by would turn and look at her with friendly, admiring eyes, as though they found something pleasant in her lovely wistful face and her old-fashioned clothes; and this pleased her so much that she lost her feeling of loneliness. It was a kindly crowd, and because she was young and pretty and worth looking at, a part of the exhilaration of this unknown life passed into her, and she felt for a little while as though she belonged to it. The youth in her responded to the passing call of the streets, to this call which fluted like the sound of pipes in her blood, and lifted her for a moment out of the narrow track of individual experience. It was charming to feel that all these strangers looked kindly upon her, and she tried to show that she returned their interest by letting a a little cordial light shine in her eyes. For the first time in her life the personal boundaries of sympathy fell away from her, and she realized, in a fleeting sensation, something of the vast underlying solidarity of human existence. A humble baby in a go-cart waited at one of the crossings for the traffic to pass, and bending over, she hugged him ecstatically, not because he reminded her of Harry, but simply because he was a baby.

"He is so sweet I just had to squeeze him," she said to his mother, a working woman in a black shawl, who stood behind him.

Then the two women smiled at each other in that free-masonry of motherhood of which no man is aware, and Virginia wondered why people had ever foolishly written of the "indifference of a crowd." The chill which had lain over her heart since her meeting with Oliver. melted utterly in the glow with which she had embraced the baby at the crossing. With the feeling of his warm little body in her arms, everything had become suddenly right again. New York was no longer a dreadful city, and Oliver's failure appeared as brief as the passing pang of a toothache. Her natural optimism had returned like a rosy mist to embellish and obscure the prosaic details of the situation. Like the cheerful winter sunshine, which transfigured the harsh outlines of the houses, her vision adorned the reality in the mere act of beholding it.

Midway of the next block there was a jellewer's window full of gems set in intricate patterns, and stopping before it, she studied the trinkets carefully in the hope of being able to describe them to Lucy. Then a man selling little automatic pigs at the corner attracted her attention, and she bought two for Harry and Jenny, and carried them triumphantly away in boxes under her arm. She knew that she looked countrified and old-fashioned, and that nobody she met was wearing either a hat or a dress which in the least resembled the style of hers; but the knowledge of this did not trouble her, because in her heart she preferred the kind of clothes which were worn in Dinwiddie. The women in New York seemed to her artificial and affected in appearance, and they walked, she thought, as if they were trying to make people look at them. The bold way they laced in their figures she regarded as almost indecent, and she noticed that they looked straight into the eyes of men instead of lowering their lashes when they passed them. Her provincialism, like everything else which belonged to her and had become endeared by habit and association, seemed to her so truly beautiful and desirable that she would not have parted with it for worlds.

Turning presently, she walked down Fifth Avenue as far as Twenty-third Street, and then, confused by the crossing, she passed into Broadway, without knowing that it was Broadway, until she was enlightened by a stranger to whom she appealed. When she began to retrace her steps, she discovered that she was hungry, and she longed to go into one of the places where she saw people eating at little tables; but her terror of what she had heard of the high prices of food in New York restaurants restrained her. General Goode still told of paying six dollars and a half for a dinner he had ordered in an hotel in Fifth Avenue, and her temperamental frugality, reinforced by anxiety as to Oliver's debts, preferred to take no unnecessary risks with the small amount in her pocket-book. Oliver, of course, would have laughed at her petty economies, and have ordered recklessly whatever attracted his appetite; but, as she gently reminded herself again, men were different. On the whole, this lordly prodigality pleased her rather than otherwise. She felt that it was in keeping with the bigness and the virility of the masculine ideal; and if there were pinching and scraping to be done, she immeasurably preferred that it should fall to her lot to do it and not to Oliver's.

At the hotel she found that Oliver had not come in, and after a belated luncheon of tea and toast in the dining-room,

she went upstairs and sat down to watch for his return
between the Nottingham lace curtains at the window. From
the terrific height, on which she felt like a sparrow, she could
see a row of miniature puppets passing back and forth at the
corner of Fifth Avenue. For hours she tried in vain to distinguish the figure of Oliver in the swiftly moving throng,
and in spite of herself she could not repress a feeling of pleasant
excitement. She knew that Oliver would think that she
ought to be depressed by his failure, yet she could not prevent
the return of a childlike confidence in the profound goodness
of life. Everything would be right, everything was eternally
bound to be right from the beginning. That inherited
casuistry of temperament, which had confused the pleasant
with the true for generations, had became in her less a moral
conviction than a fixed quality of soul. To dwell even for
a minute on " the dark side of things " awoke in her the same
instinct of mortal sin that she had felt at the discovery that
Oliver was accustomed to " break " the Sabbath by reading
profane literature.

When, at last, as the dusk fell in the room, she heard his
hasty step in the corridor, a wave of joyful expectancy rose
in her heart and trembled for utterance on her lips. Then
the door opened; he came from the gloom into the pale gleam
of light that shone in from the window, and with her first
look into his face her rising joy ebbed quickly away. A new
element, something for which neither her training nor her
experience had prepared her, entered at that instant into
her life. Not the external world, but the sacred inner circle
in which they had loved and known each other was suddenly
clouded. Everything outside of this was the same, but the
fact confronted her there as grimly as a physical sore. The
evil struck at the very heart of her love, since it was not life,
but Oliver that had changed.

CHAPTER VI

THE SHADOW

OLIVER had changed; for months this thought had lain like a stone on her heart. She went about her life just as usual, yet never for an instant during that long winter and spring did she lose consciousness of its dreadful presence. It was the first thing to face her in the morning, the last thing from which she turned when, worn out with perplexity, she fell asleep at night. During the day the children took her thoughts away from it for hours; but never once, not even while she heard Harry's lessons or tied the pink or the blue bows in Lucy's and Jenny's curls, did she ever really forget it. Since the failure of Oliver's play, which had seemed to her such a little thing in itself, something had gone out of their marriage, and this something was the perfect understanding which had existed between them. There were times when her sympathy appeared to her almost to infuriate him. Even her efforts towards economy—for since their return from New York she had put Marthy into the kitchen and had taken entire charge of the children—irritated rather than pleased him. And the more she irritated him, the more she sought zealously, by innumerable small attentions, to please and to pacify him. Instead of leaving him in the solitude which he sought, and which might have restored him to his normal balance of mind, she became possessed, whenever he shut himself in his study or went alone for a walk, with a frenzied dread lest he should permit himself to " brood " over the financial difficulties in which the wreck of his ambition had placed them. She, who feared loneliness as if it were the smallpox, devised a thousand innocent deceptions by which she might break in upon him when he sat in his study and discover whether he was actually reading the papers or merely pretending to do so. In her natural simplicity, it never occurred to her to penetrate beneath the surface disturbances of his mood. These engrossed her so completely that the cause of them was almost forgotten. Dimly she realized that this strange, almost physical soreness, which made him shrink from her presence as a man with weak eyes shrinks from the light, was the outward sign of a secret violence in his soul, yet she ministered helplessly to each passing explosion of temper as if it were the cause instead of the result of his suffering. Introspection, which had lain under a moral ban in a society that assumed the existence of an unholy alliance between the secret and the evil, could not help her because she had never indulged in it. Partly because of the ingenuous candour of the Pendleton nature, and partly owing to the mildness of a climate which made it more comfortable for Dinwiddians to live for six months of the year on their front porches and with their windows open, she shared the ingrained Southern distrust of any state of mind which could not cheerfully support the observation of the neighbours. She knew that he had turned from his work with disgust, and if he wasn't working and wasn't reading, what on earth could he be doing alone unless he had, as she imagined in desperation, begun wilfully to " nurse his despondency ?" Even the rector couldn't help her here— for his knowledge of character was strictly limited to the types of the soldier and the churchman, and his son-in-law did not belong, he admitted, in either of these familiar classifications. At the bottom of his soul the good man had always entertained for Oliver something of the kindly contempt with which his generation regarded a healthy male, who, it suspected, would decline either to preach a sermon or to kill a man in the cause of morality. But on one line of treatment father and daughter were passionately agreed—whatever happened, it was not good that Oliver should be left by himself for a minute. When he was in the bank, of course, where Cyrus had found him a place as a clerk on an insignificant salary, it might be safely assumed that he was cheered by the unfailing company of his fellow-workers ; but when he came home, the responsibility of his distraction and his cure rested upon Virginia and the children. And since her opinion of her own power to entertain was modest, she fell back with a sublime confidence

on the unrivalled brilliancy and the infinite variety of the
children's prattle. During the spring, as he grew more and
more indifferent and depressed, she arranged that the children
should be with him every instant while he was in the house.
She brought Jenny's high chair to the table in order that the
adorable infant might breakfast with her father ; she kept
Harry up an hour later at night so that he might add the
gaiety of his innocent mirth to their otherwise long and silent
evenings. Though she would have given anything to drop
into bed as soon as the babies were undressed, she forced
herself to sit up without yawning until Oliver turned out the
lights, bolted the door, and remarked irritably that she ought
to have been asleep hours ago.

"You aren't used to sitting up so late, Virginia; it makes
you dark under the eyes," he said one June night as he came
in from the porch where he had been to look up at the stars.

"But I can't go to bed until you do, darling. I get so
worried about you," she answered.

"Why in heaven's name should you worry about me ? I
am all right," he responded crossly.

She saw her mistake, and with her unvarying sweetness,
set out to rectify it.

"Of course, I know you are ; but we have so little time
together that I don't want to miss the evenings."

"So little !" he echoed, not unkindly, but in simple astonishment.

"I mean the children sit up late now, and of course we can't
talk while they are playing in the room."

"Don't you think you might get them to bed earlier ? They
are becoming rather a nuisance, aren't they ?"

He said it kindly enough, yet tears rushed to her eyes as she
looked at him. It was impossible for her to conceive of any
mood in which the children would become " rather a nuisance "
to her, and the words hurt her more than he was ever to know.
It seemed the last straw that she could not bear, said her heart
as she turned away from him. She had borne the extra work
without a complaint; she had pinched and scraped, if not
happily, at least with a smile; she had sat up while her limbs
ached with fatigue and the longing to be in bed—and all
these things were as nothing to the tragic confession that the

15

children had become "rather a nuisance." Of the many
trials she had had to endure, this, she told herself, was the
bitterest.

Though her feet burned and her muscles throbbed with
fatigue, she lay awake for hours, with her eyes wide open in
the moonlight. All the small harassing duties of the morrow,
which usually swarmed like startled bees through her brain
at night, were scattered now by this vague terror which
assumed no definite shape. The delicacy of Lucy's chest,
Harry's stubborn refusal to learn to spell, and even the harrowing certainty that the children's appetites were fast outstrip-
ping the frugal fare she provided—these stinging worries had
flown before a new anxiety which was the more poignant, she
felt, because she could not give it a name. The Pendleton
idealism was powerless to dispel this malign shadow which
corresponded so closely to that substance of evil whose
very existence the Pendleton idealism eternally denied. To
battle with a delusion was virtually to admit one's belief in
its actuality, and this, she reflected passionately, lying awake
there in the darkness, was the last thing she was prepared at
the moment to do. Oliver was changed, and yet her duty
was plainly to fortify herself with the consoling assurance
that, whatever happened, Oliver could never really change.
Deep down in her that essential fibre of her being which was
her soul, which drew its vitality from the racial structure of
which it was a part, and yet which distinguished and separated
her from every other person and object in the universe—this
essential fibre was compacted of innumerable Pendleton
refusals to face the reality. Even with Lucy's chest and
Harry's lessons and the cost of food, she had always felt a
soothing conviction that by thinking hard enough about them
she could make them every one come out right in the morning.
As a normal human being in a world which was not planned
on altruistic principles, it was out of the question that she
should entirely escape an occasional hour of despondency; but
with the narrow outlook of women who lead intense personal
lives, it would have been impossible for her to see anything
really wrong in the universe while Oliver and all the children
were well. God was in His heaven as long as the affairs of
her household worked together for good. "It can't be that

he is different—I must have imagined it," she thought now, breathing softly lest she should disturb the sleeping Oliver. "It is natural that he should be worried about his debts, and the failure of the play went very hard with him, of course— but if he appears at times to have grown bitter, it must be only that I have come to exact too much of him. I oughtn't to expect him to take the same interest in the children that I do——"

Then, rising softly on her elbow, she smoothed the sheet over Jenny's dimpled little body, and bent her ear downward to make sure that the child was breathing naturally in her sleep. In spite of her depression that rosy face framed in hair like spun yellow silk, aroused in her a feeling of ecstasy. Whenever she looked at one of her children—at her youngest child especially—her maternal passion seemed to turn to flame in her blood. Even first love had not been so exquisitely satisfying, so interwoven of all imaginable secret meanings of bliss. Jenny's thumb was in her mouth, and removing it gently, Virginia bent lower and laid her hot cheek on the soft shining curls. Some vital power, an emanation from that single principle of Love which ruled her life, passed from the breath of the sleeping child into her body. Peace descended upon her, swift and merciful like sleep, and turning on her side, she lay with her hand on Jenny's crib, as though in clinging to her child she clung to all that was most worth while in the universe.

The next night Oliver telephoned from the Treadwells that he would not be home to supper, and when he came in at eleven o'clock, he appeared annoyed to find her sitting up for him.

"You ought to have gone to bed, Virginia. You look positively haggard," he said.

"I wasn't sleepy. Mother came in for a few minutes, and we put the children to bed. Jenny wanted to say good-night to you, and she cried when I told her you had gone out. I believe she loves you better than she does anybody in the world, Oliver."

He smiled with something of the casual brilliancy which had first captivated her imagination. In spite of the melancholy which had clouded his charm of late, he had lost neither his glow of physical well-being nor the look of abounding intellectual energy which distinguished him from all other men whom she knew. It was this intellectual energy, she sometimes thought, which purified his character of that vein of earthiness which she had looked upon as the natural, and therefore the pardonable, attribute of masculine human nature.

"If she keeps her looks, she'll leave her mother behind some day," he answered. "You need a new dress, Jinny. I hate that old waist and skirt. Why don't you wear the swishy blue silk I always liked on you?"

"I made it over for Lucy, dear. She had to have a dress to wear to Lily Carrington's birthday party, and I didn't want to buy one. It looks ever so nice on her."

"Doubtless, but I like it better on you."

"It doesn't matter what I wear, but Lucy is so fond of pretty things, and children dress more now than they used to do. What did Susan have to say?"

He had turned to bolt the front door, and while his back was towards her, she raised her hand to smother a yawn. All day she had been on her feet, except for the two hours when she had worked at her sewing-machine, while Harry and Jenny were taking their morning nap. She had not had time to change her dress until after supper, and she had felt so tired then that it had not seemed worth while to do so. There was, in fact, nothing to change to, since she had made over the blue silk, except an old black organdie, cut square in the neck, which she had worn in the months before Jenny's birth. As a girl she had loved pretty clothes; but there were so many other things to think about now, and from the day that her first child had come to her it had seemed to matter less and less what she wore or how she appeared. Nothing had really counted in life except the supreme privilege of giving herself body and soul, in the service of love. All that she was—all that she had—belonged to Oliver and to his children, so what difference could it make to them, since she gave herself so completely, whether she wore new clothes or old?

When he turned to her, she had smothered the yawn, and was smiling. "Is Aunt Belinda just the same?" she asked, for he had not answered her question about Susan.

"To tell the truth, I forgot to ask," he replied, with a laugh. "Susan seemed very cheerful, and John Henry was there, of course. It wouldn't surprise me to hear any day that they are to be married. By the way, Virginia, why did you never tell me what a good rider you are ? Abby Goode says you would have been a better horsewoman than she is if you hadn't given up riding."

"Why, I haven't been in the saddle for years. I stopped when we had to sell my horse Bess, and that was before you came back to Dinwiddie. How did Abby happen to be there ?"

"She stopped to see Susan about something, and then we got to talking—the bunch of us. John Henry asked me to exercise his horse for him when he doesn't go. I rather hope I'll get a chance to go fox-hunting in the autumn. Abby was talking about it."

"Has she changed much ? I haven't seen her for years. She is hardly ever in Dinwiddie."

"Well, she's fatter, but it's becoming to her. It makes her look softer. She's a bit coarse, but she tells a capital story. I always liked Abby."

"Yes, I always liked Abby, too," answered Virginia, and it was on the tip of her tongue to add that Abby had always liked Oliver. "If he hadn't seen me, perhaps he might have married her," she thought, and the remote possibility of such bliss for poor defrauded Abby filled her with an incredible tenderness. She would never have believed that bouncing, boisterous Abby Goode could have aroused in her so poignant a sympathy.

He appeared so much more cheerful than she had seen him since his disastrous trip to New York, that, moved by an unselfish impulse of gratitude towards the cause of it, she put out her hand to him, while he raised his arm to extinguish the light.

"I am so glad about the horse, dear," she said. "It will be nice for you to go sometimes with Abby."

"Why couldn't you come, too, Jinny ?"

"Oh, I shouldn't have time—and, besides, I gave it up long ago. I don't think a mother has any business on horseback."

"All the same, I wish you wouldn't let yourself go to pieces. What have you done to your hands ? They used to be so pretty."

She drew them hastily away, while the tears rose in a mist to her eyes. It was like a man—it was especially like Oliver —to imagine that she could clean up half a house and take charge of three children, yet keep her hands as white and soft as they had been when she was a girl and did nothing except wait for a lover. In a flash of memory, she saw the reddened and knotted hands of her mother, and then a procession of hands belonging to all the mothers of her race that had gone before her. Were her own but a single pair in that chain of pathetic hands that had worked in the exacting service of Love ?

"It is so hard to keep them nice," she said; but her heart cried: " What do my hands matter when it is for your sake that I have spoiled them ?" With her natural tendency to undervalue the physical pleasures of life, she had looked upon her beauty as a passing bloom which would attract her lover to the veiled wonders of her spirit. Fleshly beauty as an end in itself would have appeared to her as immoral a cult as the wilful pursuit of a wandering desire in the male.

" I never noticed until to-night what pretty hands Abby has," he said, innocently enough, as he turned off the gas.

A strange sensation—something which was so different from anything she had ever felt before that she could not give it a name—pierced her heart like an arrow. Then it fled as suddenly as it had come, and left her at ease with the thought: " Abby has had nothing to hurt her hands. Why shouldn't they be pretty ?" But not for Abby's hands would she have given up a single hour when she had washed Jenny's little flannels or dug enchanted garden beds with Harry's miniature trowel.

" She used to have a beautiful figure," she said with perfect sincerity.

" Well, she's got it still, though she's a trifle too large for my taste. You can't help liking her, she's such jolly good company; but, somehow, she doesn't seem womanly. She's too fond of sport and all that sort of thing."

His ideal woman still corresponded to the type which he had chosen for his mate; for true womanliness was inseparably associated in his mind with those qualities which had awakened for generations the impulse of sexual selection in the men of his race. Though he enjoyed Abby, he refused stubbornly to admire her, since evolution, which moves rapidly in the development of the social activities, had left his imagination still sacredly cherishing the convention of the jungle in the matter of sex. He saw woman as dependent upon man for the very integrity of her being, and beyond the divine fact of this dependency, he did not see her at all. But there was nothing sardonic in his point of view, which had become considerably strengthened by his marriage to Virginia, who shared it. It was one of those mental attitudes, indeed, which, in the days of loose thinking and of hazy generalizations, might have proved its divine descent by its universality. Oliver, his Uncle Cyrus, the rector, and honest John Henry, however they may have differed in their views of the universe or of each other, were one at least in accepting the historical dogma of the supplementary being of woman.

And yet, so strange is life, so inexplicable are its contradictions, there were times when Oliver's ideal appeared almost to betray him, and the intellectual limitations of Virginia bored rather than delighted him. Habit, which is a sedative to a phlegmatic nature, acts not infrequently as a positive irritant upon the temperament of the artist; and since he had turned from his work in a passion of disgust at the dramatic obtuseness of his generation, he had felt more than ever the need of some intellectual outlet for the torrent of his imagination. As a wife, Virginia was perfect; as a mental companion, she barely existed at all. She was, he had come to recognize, profoundly indifferent to the actual world. Her universe was a fiction except the part of it that concerned him or the children. He had never forgotten that he had read his play to her one night shortly after Jenny's birth, and she had leaned forward with her chin on her palm and a look in her face as if she were listening for a cry which never came from the nursery. Her praise had had the sound of being recited by rote, and had aroused in him a sense of exasperation which returned even now whenever she mentioned his work. In the days of his courtship the memory of her simplicities clung like an exquisite bouquet to the intoxicating image of her; but in eight years of daily intimacy the flavour and the perfume of mere innocence had evaporated. The quality which had first charmed him was, perhaps, the first of which he had grown weary. He still loved Virginia, but he had ceased to talk to her. "If you go into the refrigerator, Oliver, don't upset Jenny's bottle of milk," she said, looking after him as he turned towards the dining-room.

Her foot was already on the bottom step of the staircase, for she had heard, or imagined that she had heard, a sound from the nursery, and she was impatient to see if one of the children had awakened and got out of bed. All the evening, while she had changed the skin-tight sleeves of the eighties to the balloon ones of the nineties in an old waist which she had had before her marriage and had never worn because it was unbecoming, her thoughts had been of Harry, whom she had punished for some act of flagrant rebellion during the after-noon. Now she was eager to comfort him if he was awake and unhappy, or merely to cuddle and kiss him if he was fast asleep in his bed.

At the top of the staircase she saw the lowered lamp in the nursery, and beside it stood Harry in his little nightgown, with a toy ship in his arms.

"Mamma, I'm tired of bed and I want to play !"

"S—sush, darling, you will wake Jenny. It isn't day yet. You must go back to bed."

"But I'm tired of bed."

"You won't be after I tuck you in."

"Will you sit by me and tell me a story ?"

"Yes, darling, I'll tell you a story if you'll promise not to talk."

Her eyes were heavy with sleep, and her limbs trembled from the exhaustion of the long June day ; but she remembered the punishment of the afternoon, and as she looked at him her heart seemed melting with tenderness.

"And you'll promise not to go away until I'm fast alseep ? —you'll promise, mamma ?"

"I'll promise, precious. No, you mustn't take your ship to bed with you. That's a darling."

Then, as Oliver was heard coming softly up the stairs for fear of arousing the children, she caught Harry's moist hand in hers and stole with him into the nursery.

To Virginia in the long, torrid days of that summer there

seemed time for neither anxiety nor disappointment. Every minute of her eighteen waking hours was spent in keeping the children washed, dressed, and good-humoured. She thought of herself so little that it never occurred to her to reflect whether she was happy or unhappy—hardly, even, whether she was awake or asleep. Twice a week John Henry's horse carried Oliver for a ride with Abby and Susan, and on these evenings he stayed so late that Virginia ceased presently even to make a pretence of waiting supper. Several times, on September afternoons, when the country burned with an illusive radiance as if it were seen through a mirage, she put on her old riding-habit, which she had hunted up in the attic at the rectory, and mounting one of Abby's horses, started to accompany them; but her conscience reproached her so bitterly at the thought that she was seeking pleasure away from the children, that she hurried homeward across the fields before the others were ready to turn. As with most women who are born for motherhood, that supreme fact had not only absorbed the emotional energy of her girlhood, but had consumed in its ecstatic flame even her ordinary capacities for enjoyment. While fatherhood left Oliver still a prey to dreams and disappointments, the more exclusive maternal passion rendered Virginia profoundly indifferent to every aspect of life except the intimate personal aspect of her marriage. She couldn't be happy—she couldn't even be at ease —while she remembered that the children were left to the honest, yet hardly tender, mercies of Marthy.

"I shall never go again," she thought, as she slipped from her saddle at the gate, and, catching up her long riding-skirt, ran up the short walk to the steps. "I must be getting old. Something has gone out of me."

And there was no regret in her heart for this *something* which had fled out of her life, for the flashing desires and the old breathless pleasures of youth which she had lost. For a month this passive joy lasted—the joy of one whose days are full and whose every activity is in useful service. Then there came an October afternoon which she never forgot because it burned across her life like a prairie fire and left a scarred track of memory behind it. It had been a windless day, filled with glittering blue lights that darted like birds down the long ash-coloured roads, and spun with a golden web of air which made the fields and trees appear as thin and as unsubstantial as dreams. The children were with Marthy in the park, and Virginia, attired in the old waist with the new sleeves, was leaning on the front gate watching the slow fall of the leaves from the gnarled mulberry-tree at the corner, when Mrs. Pendleton appeared on the opposite side of the street and crossed the cobblestones of the road with her black alpaca skirt trailing behind her.

"I wonder why in the world mother doesn't hold up her skirt?" thought Virginia, swinging back the little wooden gate while she waited. "Mother, you are letting your train get all covered with dust!" she called, as soon as Mrs. Pendleton came near enough to catch her half-whispered warning.

Reaching down indifferently, the older woman caught up a handful of her skirt and left the rest to follow ignominiously in the dust. From the carelessness of the gesture, Virginia saw at once that her mother's mind was occupied by one of those rare states of excitement or of distress when even the preservation of her clothes had sunk to a matter of secondary importance. When the small economies were banished from Mrs. Pendleton's consciousness, matters had assumed indeed a serious aspect.

"Why, mother, what on earth has happened?" asked Virginia, hurrying toward her.

"Let me come in and speak to you, Jinny. I mean inside the house. One can never be sure that some of the neighbours aren't listening," she said in a whisper.

Hurrying past her daughter, she went into the hall, and, then turning, faced her with her hand on the door-knob. In the dim light of the hall her face showed white and drawn, like the face of a person who has been suddenly stricken with illness. "Jinny, I've just had a visit from Mrs. Carrington—you know what a gossip she is—but I think I ought to tell you that she says people are talking about Oliver's riding so much with Abby."

A pain as sharp as if the teeth of a beast had fastened in her heart, pierced Virginia while she stood there, barring the door with her hands. Her peace, which had seemed indestructible a moment ago, was shattered by a sensation of violent anger

—not against Abby, not against Oliver, not even against the gossiping old women of Dinwiddie—but against her own blindness, her own inconceivable folly! At the moment the civilization of centuries was stripped from her, and she was as simple and as primitive as a female of the jungle. On the surface she was still calm, but to her own soul she felt that she presented the appalling spectacle of a normal woman turned fury. It was one of those instants that are so unexpected, so entirely unnatural and out of harmony with the rest of life, that they obliterate the boundaries of character which separate the life of the individual from the ancient root of the race. Not Virginia, but the primeval woman in her blood, shrieked out in protest as she saw her hold on her mate threatened. The destruction of the universe, as long as it left her house standing in its bit of ground, would have overwhelmed her less utterly.

"But what on earth can they say, mother? It was all my fault. I made him go. He never lifted his finger for Abby."

"I know, darling, I know. Of course. Oliver is not to blame, but people will talk, and I think Abby ought to have known better."

For an instant only Virginia hesitated. Then something stronger than the primitive female in her blood—the spirit of a lady—spoke through her lips.

"I don't believe Abby was to blame, either," she said.

"But women ought to know better, Jinny, and Abby is nearly thirty."

"She always wanted me to go, mother. I don't believe she thought for a minute that she was doing anything wrong. Abby is a little coarse, but she's perfectly good. Nobody will make me think otherwise."

"Well, it can't go on, dear. You must stop Oliver's riding with her. And Mrs. Carrington says she hears that he is going to Atlantic City with them in General Goode's private car on Thursday."

"Abby asked me, too, but, of course, I couldn't leave the children."

"Of course not. Oliver must give it up, too. Oh, Jinny, a scandal, even where one is innocent, is so terrible. A woman—a true woman—would endure death rather than be

talked about. I remember your cousin Jane Pendleton
made an unhappy marriage, and her husband used to get
drunk and beat her and even carry on dreadfully with the
coloured servants—but she said that was better than the
disgrace of a separation."

"But all that has nothing to do with me, mother. Oliver
is an angel, and this is every bit my fault, not Abby's."
The violence in her soul had passed, and she felt suddenly
calm.

"Of course, darling, of course. Now that you see what
it has led to, you can stop it immediately."

They were so alike as they stood there facing each other,
mother and daughter, that they might have represented
different periods of the same life—youth and age meeting
together. Both were perfect products of that social order
whose crowning grace and glory they were. Both were
creatures trained to feel rather than think, whose very goodness was the result not of reason, but of emotion. And,
above all, both were gentlewomen to the innermost cores
of their natures. Passion could not banish for long that
exquisite forbearance which generations had developed from
a necessity into an art.

"I can't stop his going with her, because that would
make people think I believed the things they say—but
I can go, too, mother, and I will. I'll borrow Susan's horse
and go fox-hunting with them to-morrow."

Once again, as on the afternoon when she had heard of
Oliver's illness in New York, Mrs. Pendleton realized that
her daughter's strength was more than a match for hers
when the question related to Oliver.

"But the children, dear—and then, oh, Jinny, you might
get hurt."

To her surprise Jinny laughed.

"I shan't get hurt, mother—and if I did——"

She left her sentence unfinished but in the break there
was the first note of bitterness that her mother had ever
heard from her lips. Was it possible, after all, that there
was "more in it" than she had let appear in her words?
Was it possible that her passionate defence of Abby had been
but a beautiful pretence?

"I'll go straight down to the Treadwells' to ask Susan for her horse," she added cheerfully, "and you'll come over very early, won't you, to stay with the children? Oliver always starts before daybreak."

"Yes, darling, I'll get up at dawn and come over—but, Jinny, promise me to be careful."

"Oh, I'll be careful," responded Virginia lightly, as she went out on the porch.

CHAPTER VII

THE WILL TO LIVE

"It's all horrid talk. There's not a word of truth in it," she thought, true to the Pendleton point of view, as she turned into Old Street on her way to the Treadwells'. Then the sound of horses' hoofs rang on the cobblestones, and, looking past the corner, she saw Oliver and Abby galloping under the wine-coloured leaves of the oak-tree at the crossing. His face was turned back, as if he were looking over his shoulder at the red sunset, and he was laughing as she had not heard him laugh since that dreadful morning in the bedroom of the New York hotel. What a boy he was still! As she watched him it seemed to her that she was old enough to be his mother, and the soreness in her heart changed into an exquisite impulse of tenderness. Then he looked from the sunset to Abby, and at the glance of innocent pleasure that passed between them a stab of jealousy entered her heart like a blade. Before it faded, they had passed the corner, and were cantering wildly up Old Street in the direction of Abby's home.

"It is my fault. I am too settled. I am letting my youth go," she said, with a passionate determination to catch her girlhood and hold it fast before it eluded her for ever. "I am only twenty-eight, and I dress like a woman of forty." And it seemed to her that the one desirable thing in life was this fleet-winged spirit of youth, which passed like a breath, leaving existence robbed of all romance and beauty. An hour before she had not cared, and she would not care now if only Oliver could grow middle-aged and old at the moment when she did. Ah, there was the tragedy! All life was for men, and only a few radiant years of it were given to women. Men were never too old to love, to pursue and capture what-

238

ever joy the fugitive instant might hold for them. But women, though they were allowed only one experience out of the whole of life, were asked to resign even that one at the very minute when they needed it most. " I wonder what will become of me when the children grow big enough to be away all the time as Oliver is," she thought wistfully. " I wish one never grew too old to have babies."

The front door of the Treadwells' house stood open, and in the hall Susan was arranging golden-rod and life-everlasting in a blue china bowl.

" Of course, you may have Belle to-morrow," she said in answer to Virginia's faltering request. " Even if I intended going, I'd be only too glad to lend her to you—but I can't leave mother anyway. She always gets restless if I stay out over an hour."

Mrs. Treadwell's illness had become one of those painful facts which people accept as naturally as they accept the theological dogma of damnation. It was terrible, when they thought of it, but they seldom thought of it, thereby securing tranquillity of mind in the face of both facts and dogmas. Even Virginia had ceased to make her first question when she met Susan: " How is your mother ?"

" But, Susan, you need the exercise. I thought that was why the doctor made Uncle Cyrus get you a horse."

" It was; but I only go for an hour in the afternoon. I begrudge every minute I spend away from mother. Oh, Jinny, she is so pathetic ! It almost breaks my heart to watch her."

" I know, dearest," said Virginia; but at the back of her brain she was thinking: " They looked so happy together, yet he could never really admire Abby. She isn't at all the kind of woman he likes."

So preoccupied was she by this problem of her own creation, that her voice had a strangely far-off sound, as though it came from a distance. " I wish I could help you, dear Susan. If you ever want me, day or night, you know you have only to send for me. I'd let nothing except desperate illness stand in the way of my coming."

It was true, and because she knew that it was true Susan stooped suddenly and kissed her.

"You are looking tired, Jinny. What is the matter?"

"Nothing, except that I'm a sight in this old waist. I made it over to save buying one, but I wish now I hadn't. It makes me look so settled."

"You need some clothes, and you used to be so fond of them."

"That was before the children came. I've never cared much since. It's just as if life were a completed circle, somehow. There's nothing more to expect or to wait for—you'll understand what I mean some day, Susan."

"I think I do now. But only women are like that? Men are different——"

It was the classic phrase again, but on Susan's lips it sounded with a new significance.

"And some women are different, too," replied Virginia. "Now there's Abby Goode, Susan, what do you honestly think of Abby?"

There was a wistful note in the question, and around her gentle blue eyes appeared a group of little lines, brought out by the nervous contraction of her forehead. Was it the wan, smoky light of the dusk, Susan wondered, or was Virginia really beginning to break so soon?

"Why, I like Abby. I always did," she answered, trying to look as if she did not understand what Virginia had meant. "She's a little bit what John Henry calls 'loud,' but she has a good heart and would do anybody a kindness."

She had evaded answering, just as Virginia had evaded asking, the question which both knew had passed unuttered between them—was Abby to be trusted to keep inviolate the ancient unwritten pledge of honourable womanhood? Her character was being tested by the single decisive virtue exacted of her sex.

"I am glad you feel that way," said Virginia in a relieved manner after a minute, "because I should hate not to believe in Abby, and some people don't understand her manner—mother among them."

"Oh, she's all right. I'm sure of it," answered Susan with heartiness.

The wistful sound had passed out of Virginia's voice, while the little lines faded as suddenly from the corners of her eyes.

She looked better already—only she really ought not to wear such dowdy clothes, even though she was happily married, reflected Susan, as she watched her, a few minutes later, pass over the mulberry leaves, which lay, thick and still, on the sidewalk.

At the corner of Sycamore Street a shopkeeper was putting away his goods for the night, and in the window Virginia saw a length of hyacinth-blue silk, matching her eyes, which she had remotely coveted for weeks—never expecting to possess it, yet never quite reconciling herself to the thought that it might be worn by some other woman. That length of silk had grown gradually to symbolize the last glimmer of girlish vanity which motherhood had not extinguished in her heart; and while she looked at it now, in her new recklessness of mood, a temptation, born of the perversity which rules human fate, came to her to go in and buy it while she was still desperate enough to act foolishly and not be afraid. For the first time in her life that immemorial spirit of adventure which lies buried under the dead leaves of civilization at the bottom of every human heart—with whose rearisen ghost men have moved mountains and ploughed jungles and charted illimitable seas—this imperishable spirit stirred restlessly in its grave and prompted her for once to be uncalculating and to risk the future. In the flickering motive which guided her as she entered the shop, one would hardly have recognized the lusty impulse which had sent her ancestors on splendid rambles of knight-errantry, yet its hidden source was the same. The simple purchase of twelve yards of blue silk which she had wanted for weeks ! To an outsider it would have appeared a small matter, yet in the act there was the intrepid struggle of a personal will to enforce its desire upon destiny. She would win back the romance and the beauty of living at the cost of prudence, at the cost of practical comforts, at the cost, if need be, of those ideals of womanly duty to which the centuries had trained her ! For eight years she had hardly thought of herself, for eight years she had worked and saved and planned and worried, for eight years she had given her life utterly and entirely to Oliver and the children—and the result was that he was happier with Abby—with Abby whom he didn't even admire

16

—than he was with the wife whom he both respected and loved ! The riddle not only puzzled, it enraged her. Though she was too simple to seek a psychological answer, the very fact that it existed became an immediate power in her life. She forgot the lateness of the evening, she forgot the children who were anxiously watching for her return. The forces of character, which she had always regarded as divinely fixed and established, melted and became suddenly fluid. She wasn't what she had been the minute before—she wasn't even, she began dimly to realize, what she would probably be the minute afterwards. Yet the impulse which governed her now was as despotic as if it had reigned in undisputed authority since the day of her birth. She knew that it was a rebel against the disciplined and moderate rule of her conscience, but this knowledge, which would have horrified her, had she been in a normal mood aroused in her now merely a breathless satisfaction at the spectacle of her own audacity. The natural Virginia had triumphed for an instant over the Virginia whom the ages had bred.

At home she found Oliver waiting for supper, and the three children in tears for fear she should decide to stay out for ever.

"Oh, mother, we thought you'd gone away never to come back," sobbed Lucy, throwing herself into her arms, "and what would little Jenny have done ?"

"Where in the world have you been, Virginia ?" asked Oliver, a trifle impatiently, for he was not used to having her absent from the house at meal-hours. "I was afraid somebody had been taken ill at the rectory, so I went around to inquire."

"No, nobody was ill," answered Virginia quietly. Though her resolution made her tremble all over, it did not occur to her for an instant that even now she might recede from it. As the rector had gone to the war, so she was going now to battle with Abby. She was afraid, but that quality which had made the Pendletons despise fear since the beginning of Dinwiddie's history, which they had helped to make, enabled her to control her quivering muscles and to laugh at the reproachful protests with which the children surrounded her. Through her mind there shot the thought: "I have a secret from Oliver," and she felt suddenly guilty because for the first time since her marriage she was keeping something back from him. Then, following this, there came the knowledge, piercing her heart, that she must keep her secret because even if she told him, he would not understand. With the casualness of a man's point of view towards an emotion, he would judge its importance, she felt, chiefly by the power it possessed of disturbing the course of his life. Unobservant, and ever ready to twist and decorate facts as she was, it had still been impossible for her to escape the truth that men are by nature incapable of a woman's characteristic passion for nursing sentiment. To struggle to keep a feeling alive for no better reason than that it was a feeling, would appear as wastefully extravagant to Oliver as to the unimaginative majority of his sex. Such pure, sublime, uncalculating folly belonged to woman alone !

When, at last, supper was over and the children were safely in bed, she came downstairs to Oliver, who was smoking a cigar over a newspaper, and asked carelessly:

" At what time do you start in the morning ?"

" I'd like to be up by five," he replied, without lowering his paper. " We're to meet the hounds at Croswell's store at a quarter to six, so I'll have to get off by five at the latest. I wanted my horse fresh for to-morrow, that's why I only went a mile or two this afternoon," he added.

" Susan's to lend me Belle. I'm going with you," she said, after a pause in which he had begun to read his paper again. This habit of treating her as if she were not present when he wanted to read or to work, was, she remembered, one of the things she had insisted upon in the beginning of her marriage.

" By Jove !" he exclaimed, and the paper dropped from his hands. " I'm jolly glad, but what will you do about the children ?"

" Mother is coming to look after them. I'll be back in time to hear Harry's lessons, I suppose ?"

" Why, of course; but, look here, you'll be awfully sore. You haven't ridden after the hounds since I knew you. You might even get a fall."

" I used to go, though, a great deal—and it won't hurt me

to be stiff for a few days. Besides, I want to take up hunting again."

Her motive was beyond him—perhaps because of her nearness, which prevented his getting the proper perspective of vision. For all his keenness of insight, he failed utterly to see into the mysterious mind of his wife. He could not penetrate that subtle interplay of traditional virtues and discover that she was in the clutch of one of the oldest and most savage of the passions.

"Then you'd better go to bed early and get some sleep," he said. "I suppose we'll have a cup of coffee before starting."

"I'll make it on the oil-stove while I am dressing. Marthy won't be up then."

"Well, I'll come upstairs in ten minutes," he replied, taking up his paper again. "I only want to finish this article."

In the morning when she opened the old green shutters and looked out of the window, the horses, having been saddled by candlelight, were standing under the mulberry-tree at the gate. Eight years ago, in her girlhood, she would have awakened in a delicious excitement on the morning of a fox-hunt, and have dressed as eagerly as if she were going to a ball; but to-day, while she lit the oil-stove in the hall-room and put on the kettle of water, she was supported not by the hope of pleasure, but by a dull, an almost indefinable sensation of dread. The instinct of woman to adjust her personality to the changing ideals of the man she loves—this instinct older than civilization, rooted in tragedy, and existing by right of an unconquerable necessity—rose superior at the moment to that more stable maternal passion with which it has conflicted since the beginning of motherhood. While she put on her riding-habit and tied up the plait of her hair, the one thought in Virginia's mind was that she must be, at all costs, the kind of woman that Oliver wanted.

A little later, when they set out under the mulberry-trees, she glanced at him wistfully, as though she wanted him to praise the way she looked in the saddle. But his eyes were on the end of the street, where a little company of riders awaited them, and before she could ask a question, Abby's high voice was heard exclaiming pleasantly upon her presence. Not a particularly imposing figure, because of her rather short legs, when she was on the ground, it was impossible for Virginia to deny that Abby was amazingly handsome on horseback. Plump, dark, with a superb bosom, and a colour in her cheeks like autumnal berries, she had never appeared to better advantage than she did, sitting on her spirited bay mare under an arch of scarlet leaves which curved over her head. Turning at their approach, she started at a brisk canter up the road, and as Virginia followed her, the sound of the horn floated, now loud, now faint, out of the pale mist that spun fanciful silken webs over the trees and bushes.

"Remember to look out for the creeks. That's where the danger comes," said Oliver, riding close to her. And he added nervously: "Don't try to keep up with Abby."

Ahead of them stretched a deserted Virginia road, with its look of brooding loneliness, as if it had waited patiently through the centuries for a civilization which had never come; and on the right of it, beyond a waste of scarlet sumach and sassafras and a winding creek screened in elder bushes, the dawn was breaking slowly under a single golden-edged cloud. Somebody on Virginia's left—a large, raw-boned, passionate huntsman, in an old plum-coloured overcoat with a velvet collar—was complaining loudly that they had started too late and the fox would have gone to his lair before they reached the main party. Except for an oath, which he rapped out by way of an emphasis not intended for the ladies, he might have been conducting a religious revival, so solemnly energetic, so deeply moved, was his manner. The hunt, which observed naturally the characteristics of a society that was ardently individualistic even in its sports, was one of those informal, "go-as-you-please" affairs in which the supreme joy of killing is not hampered by tedious regulations or unnecessary restrictions. The chief thing was to get a run—to start a rare red fox, if luck was good, because he was supposed to run straight by nature and not to move in circles after the inconsiderate manner for the commoner grey sort. But Providence, being inattentive to the needs of hunters in the neighbourhood of Dinwiddie, had decreed that the red fox should live there mainly in the vivid annals of old sportsmen.

"A grey fox with red ears. The best run I ever had. Tried to get in the crotch of a hickory-tree at the end. Was so exhausted he couldn't stir a foot when the hounds got him." While they waited at the cross-roads before a little country store, where the pack of hounds, lean, cringing, habitually hungry creatures, started from beneath an old field pine on the right, Virginia heard the broken phrases blown on the wind, which carried the joyous notes of the horn over the meadows. The casual cruelty of the words awoke no protest in her mind, because it was a cruelty to which she was accustomed. If the sport had been unknown in Dinwiddie, and she had read of it as the peculiar activity of the inhabitants of the British Islands, she would probably have condemned it as needlessly brutal and degrading. But with that universal faculty of the human mind to adjust its morality to fit its inherited physical habits, she regarded "the rights of the fox" to-day with something of the humorous scorn of sentimental rubbish with which her gentler grandmother had once regarded "the rights of the slave." For centuries the hunt had been one of the cherished customs of Dinwiddians; and though she could not bear to see a fly caught in a web, it would never have occurred to her to question the humanity of any sport in which her ancestors had delighted. In her girlhood the sound of the horn had called to her blood with all the intoxicating associations it awoke in the raw-boned, energetic rider in the plum-coloured coat—but to-day both the horn and the familiar landscape around her had grown strange and unhomelike. For the first time since her birth she and the country were out of harmony.

In the midst of the hounds, in the centre of the old field on the right, the huntsman, who was at the same time master and owner of the dogs, brandished a long raw-hide whip, flexible from the handle, which was pleasantly known in Dinwiddie as a "mule-skinner." His face, burned to the colour of ripe wheat, wore a rapt and exalted look, as though the chasing of a small animal to its death had called forth his latent spiritual ardours. Beyond him, like a low, smouldering fire, ran the red and gold of the abandoned field.

"Please be careful, Virginia," said Oliver again, as they left the road and cantered in the direction of a clump of pine woods in a hollow beyond a rotting "snake" fence.

But she had seen his eyes on Abby a minute before, and had heard his laugh as he answered her. A wave of recklessness broke over her, and she felt that she despised fear with all her Pendleton blood, which loved a fight only less passionately than it loved a sermon. Whatever happened—if she broke her neck—she resolved that she would keep up with Abby! With the drumming of the blood in her ears, an almost savage joy awoke in her. Deep down in her, so deep that it was buried beneath the Virginia Pendleton whom she and her world knew, there stirred faintly the seeds of that ancient lust of cruelty from which have sprung the brutal pleasures of men. The part of her—that small secret part —which was primitive answered to the impulse of jealousy as it did to the rapturous baying of the hounds out of the red and gold distance. A branch grazed her cheek; her hat went as she raced down the high banks of a stream; the thicket of elder tore the ribbon from her head, and loosened her dark flying hair from its braid. In that desolate country, in the midst of the October meadows, with the cries of the hounds rising, like the voice of mortal tragedy, out of the tinted mist on the marshes, the drama of human passions— which is the only drama for the world's stage—was played out to an ending: love, jealousy, envy, desire, desperation, regret. . . .

But when the hunt was over, and she rode home, with a bedraggled brush, which had once been grey, tied to her bridle, all the gorgeous pageantry of the autumnal landscape seemed suddenly asking her: "What is the use?" Her mood had altered, and she felt that her victory was as worthless as the mudstained fox's brush that swung mockingly back and forth from her bridle. The excitement of the chase had ebbed away, leaving only the lifeless satisfaction of the reward. She had neglected her children, she had risked her life—and all for the sake of wresting a bit of dead fur out of Abby's grasp. A spirit which was not her spirit, which was so old that she no longer recognized that it had any part in her, which was yet so young that it burned in her heart with the unquenchable flame of youth—this spirit, which was at the same time herself and not herself, had driven her, as helpless as a fallen leaf, in a chase that she despised, towards a triumph that was worthless.

"By Jove, you rode superbly, Virginia! I had no idea you could do it," said Oliver, as they trotted into Dinwiddie.

She smiled back at him, and her smile was tired, dust-stained, enigmatical.

"No, you did not know that I could do it," she answered.

"You'll keep it up now, won't you?" he asked pleadingly.

For an instant, looking away from him over the radiant fields, she pondered the question. The silence which had settled around her was unbroken by the sound of the horses' hoofs, by the laughter of the hunters, by the far-off soughing of the pine-trees in the forest; and into this silence, which seemed to cover an eternity, the two Virginias—the Virginia who desired and the Virginia who had learned from the ages to stifle her desire—wrestled for the first time together.

"Virginia!" floated Abby's breezy tones from the street behind her, and turning, she rode back to the Goodes' gate, where the others were dismounting. "Virginia, aren't you going to Atlantic City with us to-morrow?"

Again she hesitated. Almost unconsciously her gaze passed from Abby to Oliver, and she saw his pride in her in the smile with which he watched her.

"Yes, I'll go with you," she replied after a minute.

She had, for once in her life, done the thing she wanted to do simply because she wanted to do it. She had won back what she was losing; she had fought a fair fight and she had triumphed; yet as she rode down the street to her gate, there was none of the exultation of victory, none of the fugitive excitement of pleasure even in her heart. Like other mortals in other triumphant instants, she was learning that the fruit of desire may be sweet to the eyes and bitter on the lips. She had sacrificed duty to pleasure, and suddenly she had discovered that to one with her heritage of good and evil the two are inseparable.

CHAPTER VIII

THE PANG OF MOTHERHOOD

In the night Harry awoke crying. He had dreamed, he said between his sobs, when Virginia, slipperless and in her nightdress, bent over him, that his mother was going away from him for ever.

"Only for two nights, darling. Here, lean close against mother. Don't you know that she wouldn't stay away from her precious boy?"

"But two nights are so long. Aren't two nights almost for ever?"

"Why, my lamb, it was just two nights ago that grandma came over and told you the Bible story about Joseph and his brothers. That was only a teeny-weeny time ago, wasn't it?"

"But you were here then, mamma. And this morning was almost for ever. You stayed out so long that Lucy said you weren't coming back any more."

"That was naughty of Lucy because she is old enough to know better. Why do you choke that way? Does your throat hurt you?"

"It hurts because you are going away, mamma."

"But I'm going only to be with papa, precious. Don't you want poor papa to have somebody with him?"

"He's so big he can go by himself. But suppose the black man should come in the night while you are away, and I'd get scared and nobody would hear me."

"Grandma would hear you, Harry, and there isn't any black man that comes in the night. You must put that idea out of your head, dear. You're getting too big a boy to be afraid of the dark."

"Four isn't big, is it?"

"You're nearer five than four now, honey. Let me button your nightgown, and lie down and try to go to sleep while mamma sings to you. Does your throat really hurt you?"

"It feels as if it had teensy-weensy marbles in it. They came there when I woke up in the dark and thought that you were going away to-morrow."

"Well, if your throat hurts you, of course mamma won't leave you. Open your mouth wide now so I can look at it."

She lighted a candle while Harry, kneeling in the middle of his little bed, followed her with his blue eyes, which looked three times their usual size because of his flushed cheeks and his mounting excitement. His throat appeared slightly inflamed when she held the candle close to it, and after tucking him beneath the bedclothes, she poured a little camphorated oil into a cup and heated it on the small alcohol lamp she kept in the nursery.

"Mamma is going to put a nice bandage on your throat, and then she is going to lie down beside you and sing you to sleep," she said cheerfully, as she cut off a strip of flannel from an old petticoat and prepared to saturate it with the heated oil.

"Will you stay here all night?"

"All night, precious, if you'll be good and go fast asleep while I am singing."

Holding tightly to her nightdress, Harry cuddled down between the pillows with a contented sigh. "Then I don't mind about the marbles in my throat," he said.

"But mamma minds, and she wants to cure them before morning. Now lie very still while she wraps this good flannel bandage over the sore places."

"I'll lie very still if you'll hold me, mamma."

Blowing out the candle, she crept into the little bed beside him, and lay singing softly until his hands released their desperate grasp of her nightdress, and he slipped quietly off to sleep. Even then, remembering her promise, she did not go back to her bedroom until daylight.

"I wonder what makes Harry so afraid of the dark?" she asked, when Oliver awoke and turned questioningly towards her. "He worked himself really sick last night just from pure nervousness. I had to put camphorated oil on his throat and chest, and lie beside him until morning. He is sleeping quietly now, but it simply frightens me to death when one of them complains of sore throat."

"You've spoiled him, that's what's the matter," replied Oliver, yawning. "As long as you humour him, he'll never outgrow these night terrors."

"But how can you tell whether the fright makes him sick or sickness brings on the fright? His throat was really red, there's no doubt about that, but I couldn't see last night that it was at all ulcerated."

"He gives you more trouble than both the other children put together."

"Well, he's a boy, and boys do give one more trouble. But, then, you have less patience with him, Oliver."

"That's because he's a boy, and I like boys to show some pluck even when they are babies. Lucy and Jenny never raise these midnight rows whenever they awake in the dark."

"They are not nearly so sensitive. You don't understand Harry."

"Perhaps I don't, but I can see that you are ruining him."

"Oh, Oliver ! How can you say such a cruel thing to me ?"

"I didn't mean to be cruel, Jinny, and you know it, but all the same, it makes me positively sick to see you make a slave of yourself over the children. Why, you look as if you hadn't slept for a week. You are positively haggard."

"But I have to be up with Harry when he is ill. How in the world could I help it ?"

"You know he kicks up these rows almost every night, and you humour everyone of his whims as if it were the first one. Don't you ever get tired ?"

"Of course I do ; but I can't let my child suffer even if it is only from fear. You haven't any patience, Oliver. Don't you remember the time when you used to be afraid of things ?"

"I was never afraid of the dark in my life. No sensible child is, if he is brought up properly."

"Do you mean I am not bringing up my children——" Her tears choked her and she could not finish the sentence.

"I don't mean anything except that you are making an old woman of yourself before your time. You've let yourself go until you look ten years older than——"

He checked himself in time, but she understood without his words that he had started to say, "ten years older than Abby." Yes, Abby did look young — amazingly young; but, then, what else had she to think of ?

She lay down, but she was trembling so violently that she sat up quickly again in order to recover her self-possession more easily. It seemed to her that the furious beating of her heart must make him understand how he had wounded her. It was the first discussion approaching a quarrel they had had since their marriage, for she, who was so pliable in all other matters, had discovered that she could become as hard as iron where the difference related to Harry.

"You are unjust, Oliver. I think you ought to see it," she said in a voice which she kept by an effort from breaking.

"I'll never see it, Jinny." And some dogged impulse to hurt her more made him add : "It's for Harry's sake as well as yours that I'm speaking."

"For Harry's sake ? Oh, you don't mean—you can't really mean that you think I'm not doing the best for my child, Oliver ?"

A year ago Oliver would have surrendered at once before the terror in her eyes; but in those twelve long months of effort, of hope, of balked ambition, of bitter questioning, and of tragic disillusionment, a new quality had developed in his character, and the generous sympathy of youth had hardened at thirty-four to the cautious cynicism of middle-age. It is doubtful if even he himself realized how transient such a state must be to a nature whose hidden springs were moved so easily by the mere action of change—by the effect of any alteration in the objects that surrounded him. Because the enthusiasm of youth was exhausted at the minute, it seemed to him that he had lost it for ever. And to Virginia, who saw but one thing at a time, and to whom that one thing was always the present instant, it seemed that the firm ground upon which she trod had crumbled beneath her.

"Well, if you want the truth," he said quietly (as if any mother ever wanted the truth about such a matter), "I think you make a mistake to spoil Harry as you do."

"But," she brought out the words with a pathetic quiver,

"I treat him just as I do the others, and you never say anything about my spoiling them."

"Oh, the others are girls. Girls aren't so easily ruined somehow. They don't get such hard knocks later on, so it makes less difference about them."

As she sat there in bed, propped up on her elbow, which trembled violently against the pillows, with her cambric nightdress, trimmed only with a narrow band of crocheted lace, opened at her slender throat, and her hair, which was getting thin at the temples, drawn unbecomingly back from her forehead, she looked, indeed, as Oliver had thought, "at least ten years older than Abby." Though she was not yet thirty, the delicate, flower-like bloom of her beauty was already beginning to fade. The spirit which had animated her yesterday appeared to have gone out of her now. He thought how lovely she had been at twenty when he saw her for the first time after his return to Dinwiddie; and a sudden anger seized him because she was letting herself break, because she was so needlessly sacrificing her youth and her beauty.

An hour later she got up and dressed herself, with the feeling that she had not rested a minute during the night. Harry was listless and fretful when he awoke, and while she put on his clothes, she debated with herself whether or not she should summon old Doctor Fraser from around the corner. When his lesson hour came, he climbed into her lap and went to sleep with his hot little head on her shoulder, and though he seemed better by evening, she was still so anxious about him that she forgot that she had promised Abby to go with them to Atlantic City until Oliver came in at dusk and reminded her.

"Aren't you going, Virginia?" he inquired, as he hunted in the closet for his bag which she had not had time to pack.

"I can't, Oliver. Harry isn't well. He has been unlike himself all day, and I am afraid to leave him."

"He looks all right," he remarked, bending over the child in Virginia's lap. "Does anything hurt you, Harry?"

"He doesn't seem to know exactly what it is," answered Virginia, "but if he isn't well by morning, I'll send for Doctor Fraser."

"He's got a good colour, and I believe he's as well as he ever was," replied Oliver, while a curious note of hostility sounded in his voice. "There's nothing the matter with the boy," he added more positively after a minute. "Aren't you coming, Virginia?"

She looked up at him from the big rocking-chair in which she sat with Harry in her arms, and as she did so, both became conscious that the issue had broadened from a question of her going to Atlantic City into a direct conflict of wills. The only thing that could make her oppose him had happened for the first time since her marriage. The feminine impulse to yield was overmatched by the maternal impulse to protect. She would have surrendered her soul to him for the asking; but she could not surrender, even had she desired to do so, the mother lover which had passed into her from out the ages before she had been, and which would pass through her into the ages to come after her.

"Of course, if the little chap were really suffering, I'd be as anxious about staying as you are," said Oliver impatiently; "but there's nothing the matter. You're all right, aren't you, Harry?"

"Yes, I'm all right," repeated Harry, yawning, and snuggling closer to Virginia, "but I'm sleepy."

"He isn't all right," insisted Virginia obstinately. "There's something wrong with him. I don't know what it is, but he isn't in the least like himself."

"It's just your imagination. You've got the children on the brain, Virginia. Don't you remember the time you woke me in the night and sent me after Doctor Fraser because Jenny had a bad attack of the hiccoughs?"

"I know," acknowledged Virginia humbly. She could be humble enough, but what good did that do when she was, as he told himself irritably, "as stubborn as a mule"? Her softness—she had seemed as soft as flowers when he married her—had been her greatest charm for him after her beauty; and now, at the end of eight years, in which she had appeared as delightfully invertebrate as he could have desired, she revealed to his astonished eyes a backbone that was evidently made of iron. She was immovable, he admitted, and because she was immovable he was conscious of a sharp, unreasonable impulse to reduce her to the pliant curves of her girlhood. After eight years of an absolute supremacy, which had been far from good for him, his will had been tripped up at last by so small a thing as a mere whim of Virginia's.

"You told Abby you would go," he urged, exasperated rather than soothed by her humility. "And it's too late now for her to ask anyone else."

"I'm so sorry, dear, but I never once thought about it. I've been so worried all day."

He looked at the child, lying flushed and drowsy in Virginia's arms, and his face hardened until a latent brutality crept out around his handsome, but loosely moulded, lips. The truth was that Harry had never looked healthier than he did at that instant in the firelight, and the whole affair appeared to Oliver only another instance of what he called Virginia's "sensational motherhood."

"Can't you see for yourself that he's perfectly well?" he asked.

"I know he looks so, dear, but he isn't."

"Well, here's your mother. Leave it to her. She will agree with me."

"Why, what is it, Jinny?" asked Mrs. Pendleton, laying her bundle on the couch (for she had come prepared to spend the night), and regarding Oliver with the indulgent eyes of an older generation.

"Virginia says at the last minute that she won't go with us," said Oliver, angry, yet caressing as he always was in his manner to his mother-in-law, to whom he was sincerely devoted. "She's got into her head that there's something wrong with Harry, but you can tell by looking at the child that he is perfectly well."

"But I was up with him last night, mother. His throat hurts him," broke in Virginia in a voice that was full of emotion.

"He certainly looks all right," remarked Mrs. Pendleton, "and I can take care of him if anything should be wrong." Then she added very gravely, "If you can't go, of course Oliver must stay at home, too, Virginia."

"I can't," said Oliver; "not just for a whim, anyway. It would break up the party. Besides, I didn't get a holiday all summer, and I'll blow up that confounded bank unless I take a change."

In the last quarter of an hour the trip had become of tremendous importance to him. From a trivial incident which he might have relinquished a week ago without regret, the excursion with Abby had attained suddenly the dignity and the power of an event in his life. Opposition had magnified inclination into desire.

"I don't think it will do for Oliver to go without you, Jinny," said Mrs. Pendleton, and the gravity of her face showed how carefully she was weighing her words.

"But I can't go, mother. You don't understand," replied Virginia, while her lips worked convulsively. No one could understand—not even her mother. Of the three of them, it is probable that she alone realized the complete significance of her decision.

"Well, it's too late now, anyway," remarked Oliver shortly. "You wouldn't have time to dress and catch the train even if you wanted to."

Taking up his bag, he kissed her carelessly, shook hands with Mrs. Pendleton, and throwing a " Good-bye, General !" to Harry, went out of the door.

As he vanished, Virginia started up quickly, called " Oliver !" under her breath, and then sat down again, drawing her child closer in her arms. Her face had grown grey and stricken like the face of an old woman. Every atom of her quivered with the longing to run after him, to yield to his wish, to promise anything he asked of her. Yet she knew that if he came back, they would only pass again through the old wearing struggle of wills. She had chosen not as she desired to, but as she must, and already she was learning that life forces one in the end to abide by one's choices.

"Oh, Virginia, I am afraid it was a mistake," said Mrs. Pendleton in an agonized tone. The horror of a scandal, which was stronger in the women of her generation than even the horror of illness, still darkened her mind.

A shiver passed through Virginia and left her stiller and graver than before.

"No, it was not a mistake, mother," she answered quietly.

" I did what I was obliged to do. Oliver could not understand."

As she uttered the words, she saw Oliver's face turned to Abby with the gay and laughing expression she had seen on it when the two rode down Old Street together, and a wave of passionate jealousy swept over her. She had let him go alone; he was angry with her; and for three days he would be with Abby almost every minute. And suddenly, she heard spoken by a mocking voice at the back of her brain: " You look at least ten years older than Abby."

" It does seem as if he might have stayed at home," remarked Mrs. Pendleton; " but he is so used to having his own way that it is harder for him to give it up than for the rest of us. Your father says you have spoiled him."

She had spoiled him—this she saw clearly now, she who had never seen anything clearly until it was too late for sentimentality to work its harm. From the day of her marriage she had spoiled him because spoiling him had been for her own happiness as well as for his. She had yielded to him since her chief desire had been simply to yield and to satisfy. Her unselfishness had been merely selfishness cloaked in the familiar aspect of duty. Another vision of him, not as he looked when he was riding with Abby, but as he had appeared to her in the early days of their marriage, floated before her. He had been hers utterly then—hers with his generous impulses, his high ideals, his undisciplined emotions. And what had she done with him ? What were her good intentions—what was her love, even, worth—when her intentions and her love alike had been so lacking in wisdom ? It was as if she condemned herself with a judgment which was not her own, as if her lifelong habit of seeing only the present instant had suddenly deserted her.

" He has been so nervous and unlike himself ever since the failure of his play, mother," she said. " It's hard to understand, but it meant more to him than a woman can realize."

" I suppose so," returned Mrs. Pendleton sympathetically. " Your father says that he spoke to him bitterly the other day about being a failure. Of course, he isn't one in the least, darling," she added reassuringly.

"I sometimes think that Oliver's ambition was the greatest thing in his life," said Virginia musingly. "It meant to him, I believe, a great deal of what the children mean to me. He felt that it was himself, and yet in a way closer than himself. Until that dreadful time in New York I never understood what his work may mean to a man."

"I wish you could have gone with him, Jinny."

"I couldn't," replied Virginia, as she had replied so often before. "I know Harry doesn't look sick," she went on with that soft obstinacy which never attacked and yet never yielded a point, "but something tells me that he isn't well."

An hour later, when she put him to bed, he looked so gay and rosy that she almost allowed herself the weakness of a regret. Suppose nothing was wrong, after all? Suppose, as Oliver had said, she was merely "sensational"? While she undressed in the dark for fear of awaking Jenny, who was sleeping soundly in her crib on Virginia's side of the bed, her mind went back over the two harrowing days through which she had just lived, and she asked herself, not if she had triumphed for good over Abby, but if she had really done what was right both for Oliver and the children. After all, the whole of life came back simply to doing the thing that was right. So unused was she to the kind of introspection which weighs emotions as if they were facts, that she thought slowly, from sheer lack of practice in the subtler processes of reasoning. Worry, the plain, ordinary sort of worry with which she was unhappily familiar, had not prepared her for the piercing anguish which follows the probing of the open wounds in one's soul. To lie sleepless over butchers' bills was different, somehow, from lying sleepless over the possible loss of Oliver's love. It was different, and yet, just as she asked herself over and over again on those other nights if she had done right to run up so large an account at Mr. Dewlap's, so she questioned her conscience now in the hope of finding justification for Oliver. "Ought I to have gone on the hunt yesterday?" she asked kneeling, with sore and aching limbs, by the bedside. "Had I a right to risk my life when the children are so young that they need me every minute? It is true nothing happened. Providence watched over me; but, then, something might have happened, and

I could have blamed only myself. I was jealous—for the first time in my life, I was jealous—and because I was jealous, I did wrong and neglected my duty. Yesterday I sacrificed the children to Oliver, and to-day I sacrificed Oliver to the children. I love Oliver as much, but I have made the children. They came only because I brought them into the world. I am responsible for them—I am responsible for them," she repeated passionately; and a moment later, she prayed softly: "O Lord, help me to want to do what is right!"

Through the night, tired and sore as she was, she hardly closed her eyes, and she was lying wide awake, with her hand on the railing of Jenny's crib, and her gaze on the half-bared bough of the old mulberry-tree in the street, when a cry, or less than a cry, a small, choking whimper, from the nursery, caused her to spring out of bed with a start, and slip into her wrapper which lay across the edge of the quilt.

"I'm coming, darling," she called softly. And the answer came back in Harry's voice: "Mamma, I'm afraid!"

Without waiting to put on her slippers, for one of them had slid under the bed, she ran across the carpet and through the doorway into the adjoining room.

"What is it, my lamb? Does anything hurt you?" she asked auxiously.

"Im afraid, mamma."

"What are you afraid of? Mamma is here, precious."

His little hands were hot when she clasped them, and the pathetic wonder in his blue eyes made her heart stand still with a fear greater than Harry's. Ever since the children had come she had lived in terror of a serious illness attacking them.

"Where does it hurt you, darling? Can't you tell me?"

"It feels so funny when I swallow, mamma. It's all full of flannel."

"Will you open your mouth wide, then, and let mamma mop your throat with turpentine?"

But Harry hated turpentine even more than he hated the sore throat, and he protested with tears while she found the bottle in the bathroom and swathed the end of the wire mop in cotton. When she brought it to his bedside, he fought so strenuously that she was obliged at last to give up. His fever had excited him, and he sobbed violently while she applied the bandages to his throat and chest.

"Is it any better, dear?" she asked desperately at the end of an hour in which he had lain, weeping and angry, in her arms.

"It feels funny. I don't like it," he sobbed, pushing her from him.

"Then I'll send for Doctor Fraser. He'll make you well."

But he didn't want Doctor Fraser, who gave the meanest medicines. He didn't want anybody. He hated everybody. He hated Lucy. He hated Jenny. When at last day came, and Marthy appeared to know what Virginia wanted for breakfast, he was still vowing passionately that he hated them all.

"Marthy, run at once for Doctor Fraser. Harry is quite sick," said Virginia, pale to the lips.

"But I won't see him, mamma, and I won't take his medicines. They are the meanest medicines."

"Perhaps he won't give you any, precious, and if he does, mamma will taste every single one for you."

Then Jenny began to beg to get up, and Lucy, who had been watching with dispassionate curiosity from the edge of her little bed, was sent to amuse her until Marthy's return.

"Suppose I had gone!" thought Virginia, while an overwhelming thankfulness swept the anxiety out of her mind. Not until the servant reappeared, dragging the fat old doctor after her, did Virginia remember that she was still barefooted, and go into her bedroom to search for her slippers.

"You don't think he is seriously sick, do you, doctor? Is there any need to be alarmed?" she asked, and her voice entreated him to allay her anxiety.

The doctor, a benevolent soul in a body which had run to fat from lack of exercise, was engaged in holding Harry's tongue down with a silver spoon, while, in spite of the child's furious protests, he leisurely examined his throat. When the operation was over, and Harry, crying, choking, and kicking, rolled into Virginia's arms, she put the question again, vaguely rebelling against the gravity in the kind old face which was turned half away from her :

"There's nothing really the matter, is there, doctor ?"

He turned to her, and laid a caressing, if heavy, hand on her shoulder, which shook suddenly under the thin folds of her dressing-gown. After forty years in which he had watched suffering and death, he preserved still his native repugnance to contact with any side of life that did not have a comfortable feeling to it.

"Oh, we'll get him all right soon, with some good nursing," he said gently, "but I think we're going to have a bit of an illness on our hands."

"But not serious, doctor ?   It isn't anything serious ?"

She felt suddenly so weak that she could hardly stand, and instinctively she reached out to grasp the large, protecting arm of the physician.   Even then his bland professional smile, which had in it something of the serene detachment of the everlasting purpose of which it was a part, did not fade, hardly changed even, on his features.

"Well, I think we'd better get the other children away.   It might be serious if they all had it on our hands."

"Had it ?   Had what ?   Oh, doctor—not—diphtheria ?"

She brought out the word with a face of such unutterable horror that he turned his eyes away, lest the memory of her look should interfere with his treatment of the next case he visited.   There was something infernal in the sound of the thing which always knocked over the mothers of his generation.   He had never seen one of them who could hear it without going to pieces on his hands; and for that reason he never mentioned the disease by name unless they drove him to it. They feared it as they might have feared the plague—and even more !   If the medical profession would begin calling it something else, he wondered if the unmitigated terror of it wouldn't partially subside.

"Well, it looks like that now, Jinny," he said soothingly; "but we'll come out all right, never fear.   It isn't a bad case, you know, and the chief thing is to get the other children out of danger."

At this she went over like a log on the bed, and it was only after he had found the bottle of camphor on the mantelpiece and held it to her nostrils, that she revived sufficiently to sit up again.   But as soon as her strength came back, her courage surprised and rejoiced him. After that one sign of weakness she became suddenly strong, and he knew by the expression of her face, for he had had great experience with mothers, that he could count on her not to break down again while he needed her.

"I'd like to get a tent made of some sheets and keep a kettle boiling under it," he said, for he was an old man and belonged to the dark ages of medicine. "But first of all I'll get the children over to your mother's. They'd better not come in here again. I'll ask the servant to attend to them."

"You'll find her in the dining-room," replied Virginia, while she straightened Harry's bed and made him more comfortable. The weakness had passed, leaving a numbed and hardened feeling as though she had turned to wood; and when, a little later, she looked out of the door to wave good-bye to Lucy and Jenny, she was amazed to find that she felt almost indifferent. Every emotion, even her capacity for physical sensation, seemed to respond to the immediate need of her, to the exhaustless demands on her bodily strength and her courage. As long as there was anything to be done, she was sure now that she should be able to keep up and not lose control of herself.

"May we come back soon, mamma?" asked Lucy, standing on tiptoe to wave at her.

"Just as soon as Harry is well, darling. Ask grandpa to pray that he will be well soon, won't you?"

"Jenny'll pay," lisped the baby, from Doctor Fraser's arms, where, with her cap on one side and her little feet kicking delightedly, she was beguiled by the promise of a birthday cake over at grandma's.

"I'll look in again in an hour or two," said the doctor in his jovial tones as he swung down the stairs. Then Lucy pattered after him, and in a few minutes the front door closed loudly behind them, and Virginia went back to the nursery, where Harry was coughing the strangling cough that tore at her heart.

By nightfall he had grown very ill, and when the next dawn came, it found her, wan, haggard, and sleepless, fighting beside the old doctor under the improvised tent of sheets which covered the little bed. The thought of self went from her so utterly that she only remembered she was alive when Marthy brought food and tried to force it between her lips.

"But you must swallow it, ma'am. You need to keep up your strength."

"How do you think he looks, Marthy? Does he feel quite so hot to you? He seems to breathe a little better, doesn't he?"

And during the long day, while the patch of sunlight grew larger, lay for an hour like yellow silk on the window-sill, and then slowly dwindled into the shadow, she sat, without moving, between the bed and the table on which stood the bottles of medicine, a glass, and a pitcher of water. When the child slept, overcome by the stupor of fever, she watched him, with drawn breath, lest he should fade away from her if she were to withdraw her passionate gaze for an instant. When he awoke and lay moaning, while his little body shook with the long, stifling gasps that struggled between his lips, she held him tightly clasped in her arms, with a woman's pathetic faith in the power of a physical pressure to withstand the immaterial forces of death. A hundred times during the day he aroused himself, stirred faintly in his feverish sleep, and called her name in the voice of terror with which he used to summon her in the night.

"It isn't the black man now, darling, is it? Remember there is no black man, and mamma is close here beside you."

No, it wasn't the black man; he wasn't afraid of the darkness now, but he would like to have his ship. When she brought it, he played for a few minutes, and dozed off still grasping the toy in his hands. At twelve the doctor came, and again at four, when the patch of sunlight, by which she told the hours, had begun to grow fainter on the window-sill.

"He is better, doctor, isn't he? Don't you notice that he struggles less when he breathes?"

He looked at her with an expression of contemplative pity in his old watery eyes, and she gave a little cry and stretched out her hands, blindly groping.

"Doctor, I'll do anything—anything, if you'll only save him." An impulse to reach beyond him to some impersonal, cosmic Power greater than he was, made her add desperately:

" I'll never ask for anything else in my life. I'll give up everything, if you'll only promise me that you will save him."

She stood up, drawing her thin figure, as tense as a cord,
to its full height, and beneath the flowered blue dressing-gown
her shoulder blades showed sharply under their fragile covering of flesh. Her hair, which she had not undone since the
first shock of Harry's illness, hung in straight folds on either
side of her pallid and haggard face. Even the colour of her
eyes seemed to have changed, for their flower-like blue had
faded to a dull grey.

" If we can pull through the night, Jinny," he said huskily ;
and added almost sternly, " you must bear up, so much
depends on you. Remember, it is your first serious illness,
but it may not be your last. You've got to take the pang of
motherhood along with the pleasure, my dear——"

The pang of motherhood ! Long after he had left her, and
she had heard the street gate click behind him, she sat motionless, repeating the words, by Harry's little bed. The pang
of motherhood—this was that she was suffering—the poignant suspense, the quivering waiting, the abject terror of
loss, the unutterable anguish of the nerves, as if one's heart
were being slowly torn out of one's body. She had had the
joy, and now she was enduring the inevitable pang which is
bound up, like a hidden pulse, in every mortal delight. Never
pleasure without pain, never growth without decay, never
life without death. The Law ruled even in love, and all the
pitiful little sacrifices which one offered to Omnipotence,
which one offered blindly to the Power that might separate,
with a flaming sword, the cause from the effect, the substance
from the shadow—what of them ? While Harry lay there,
wrapped in that burning stupor, she prayed, not as she had
been taught to pray in her childhood, not with the humble
and resigned worship of civilization, but in the wild and
threatening lament of a savage who seeks to reach the ears of
an implacable deity. In the last twenty-four hours the
Unknown Power she entreated had changed, in her imagination, to an idol who responded only to the shedding of blood.

" Only spare my child and I will give up everything else !"
she cried from the extremity of her anguish. The sharp edge
of the bed hurt her bosom and she pressed frantically against

it. Had it been possible to lacerate her body, to cut her flesh
with knives, she might have found some pitiable comfort in
the mere physical pain. Beside the agony in her mind, a
pang of the flesh would have been almost a joy.

When at last she rose from her knees, Harry lay, breathing
quietly, with his eyes closed and the toy ship on the blanket
beside him. His childish features had shrunken in a day
until they appeared only half their natural size, and a faint
bluish tinge had crept over his face, wiping out all the sweet
rosy colour. But he had swallowed a few spoonfuls of his
last cup of broth, and the painful choking sound had ceased
for a minute. The change, slight as it was, had followed so
closely upon her prayers, that, while it lasted, she passed
through one of those spiritual crises which alter the whole
aspect of life. An emotion, which was a curious mixture of
superstitious terror and religious faith, swept over her,
reviving and invigorating her heart. She had abased herself
in the dust before God—she had offered all her life to Him if
He would spare her child—and had He not answered ? Might
not Harry's illness, indeed, have been sent to punish her for
her neglect ? A shudder of abhorrence passed through her
as she remembered the fox-hunt, and her passion of jealousy.
The roll of blue silk, lying upstairs in a closet in the third
storey, appeared to her now not as a temptation to vanity,
but as a reminder of the mortal sin which had almost cost her
the life of her child. And suppose God had not stopped her
in time—suppose she had gone to Atlantic City as Oliver had
begged her to do ?

In the room the light faded softly, melting first like frost
from the mirror in the corner beyond the Japanese screen,
creeping slowly across the marble surface of the washstand,
lingering, in little ripples, on the green sash of the window-sill.
Out of doors it was still day, and from where she sat by
Harry's bed, she could see, under the raised tent, every detail
of the street standing out distinctly in the grey twilight.
Across the way the houses were beginning to show lights at
the windows, and the old lamplighter was balancing himself
unsteadily on his ladder at the corner. On the mulberry-tree
near the crossing the broad bronze leaves swung back and
forth in the wind, which sighed restlessly around the house

and drove the naked tendrils of a summer vine against the green shutters at the window. The fire had gone down, and after she had made it up very softly, she bent over Harry again, as if she feared that he might have slipped out of her grasp while she had crossed the room.

"If he only lives, I will let everything else go. I will think of nothing except my children. It will make no difference to me if I do look ten years older than Abby does. Nothing on earth will make any difference to me, if only God will let him get well."

And with the vow, it seemed to her that she laid her youth down on the altar of that unseen Power whose mercy she invoked. Let her prayer only be heard and she would demand nothing more of life—she would spend all her future years in the willing service of love. Was it possible that she had imagined herself unhappy thirty-six hours ago—thirty-six hours ago when her child was not threatened? As she looked back on her past life, it seemed to her that every minute had been crowned with happiness. Even the loss of her newborn baby appeared such a little thing—such a little thing beside the loss of Harry, her only son. Mere freedom from anxiety showed to her now as a condition of positive bliss.

Six o'clock struck, and Marthy knocked at the door with a cup of milk.

"Do you think he'll be able to swallow any of it?" she asked, and there were tears in her eyes.

"He is better, Marthy, I am sure he is better. Has mother been here this afternoon?"

"She stopped at the door, but she didn't like to come in on account of the children. They are both well, she says, and send you their love. Do you want any more water in the kettle, ma'am?"

The kettle, which was simmering away beside Harry's bed, under the tent of sheets, was passed to Marthy through the crack in the door; and when in a few minutes the girl returned with fresh water, Virginia whispered to her that he had taken three spoonfuls of milk.

"And he let me mop his throat with turpentine," she said in quivering tones. "I am sure—oh, I am sure he is better."

"I am praying every minute," replied Marthy, weeping;

and it seemed suddenly to Virginia that a wave of under-standing passed between her and the ignorant mulatto girl, whom she had always regarded as of different clay from herself. With that miraculous power of grief to level all things, she felt that the barriers of knowledge, of race, of all the pitiful superiorities with which human beings have obscured and decorated the underlying spirit of life, had melted back into the nothingness from which they had emerged in the beginning. This feeling of oneness, which would have surprised and startled her yesterday, appeared no natural to her now, that, after the first instant of recogni-tion, she hardly thought of it again.

"Thank you, Marthy," she answered gently, and closing the door, went back to her chair under the raised corner of the sheet. When the doctor came at nine o'clock she was sitting there, in the same position, so still and tense that she seemed hardly to be breathing, so ashen grey that the sheet hanging above her head showed deadly white by contrast with her face. In those three hours she knew that the clinging tendrils of personal desire had relaxed their hold for ever on life and youth.

"If he doesn't get worse, we'll pull him through," said the doctor, turning from his examination of Harry to lay his hand, which felt as heavy as lead, on her shoulder. "We've an even chance—if his heart doesn't go back on us." And he added, "Most mothers are good nurses, Jinny, but I never saw a better one than you are—unless it was your own mother. You get it from her, I reckon. I remember when you went through diphtheria how she sent your father to stay with one of the neighbours, and shut herself up with old Ailsey to nurse you. I don't believe she undressed or closed her eyes for a week."

Her own mother! So she was not the only one who had suffered this anguish—other women, many women, had been through it before she was born. It was a part of that imme-morial pang of motherhood of which the old doctor had spoken. "But, was I ever in danger? Was I as ill as Harry?" she asked.

"For twenty-four hours we thought you'd slip through our fingers every minute. 'Twas only your mother's nursing

that kept you alive—I've told her that twenty times. She
never spared herself an instant, and, it may have been my
imagination, but she never seemed to me to be the same
woman afterwards. Something had gone out of her."

Now she understood, now she knew, something had gone
out of her, also, and this something was youth. No woman
who had fought with death for a child could ever be the same
afterwards—could ever value again the small personal joys,
when she carried the memory of supreme joy or supreme
anguish buried within her heart. She remembered that her
mother had never seemed young to her, not even in her
earliest childhood; and she understood now why this had been
so, why the deeper experiences of life rob the smaller ones of
all vividness, of all poignancy. It had been so easy for her
mother to give up little things, to deny herself, to do without,
to make no further demands on life after the great demands
had been granted her. How often had she said unthinkingly
in her girlhood, "Mother, you never want anything for yourself." Ah, she knew now what it meant, and with the knowledge a longing seized her to throw herself into her mother's
arms, to sob out her understanding and her sympathy, to let
her feel before it was too late that she comprehended every
step of the way, every throb of the agony!

"I'd spend the night with you, Jinny, if I didn't have to
be with Milly Carrington, who has two children down with
it," said the doctor; "but if there's any change, get Marthy
to come for me. If not, I'll be sure to look in again before
daybreak."

When he had gone, she moved the night lamp to the corner
of the washstand, and after swallowing hastily a cup of
coffee which Marthy had brought to her before the doctor's
visit, and which had grown quite tepid and unpalatable, she
resumed her patient watch under the raised end of the sheet.
The whole of life, the whole of the universe even, had narrowed
down for her into that faint circle of light which the lamp
drew around Harry's little bed. It was as if this narrow
circle beat with a separate pulse, divided from the rest of
existence by its intense, its throbbing vitality. Here was
concentrated for her all that the world had to offer of hope,
fear, rapture, or anguish. The littleness and the terrible

significance of the individual destiny were gathered into that faintly quivering centre of space—so small a part of the universe, and yet containing the whole universe within itself !

Outside, in the street, she could see a half-bared bough of the mulberry-tree, arching against a square of window, from which the white curtains were drawn back; and in order to quiet her broken and disjointed thoughts, she began to count the leaves as they fell, one by one, turning softly at the stem, and then floating out into the darkness beyond. "One. Two. How long that leaf takes to loosen. He is better. The doctor certainly thought that he was better. If he only gets well. O God, let him get well, and I will serve you all my life ! Three—four—five. For twenty-four hours we thought you would slip through our fingers. Somebody said that—somebody—it must have been the doctor. And he was talking of me, not of Harry. That was twenty-six years ago, and my mother was enduring then all this agony that I am feeling to-night. Twenty-six years ago—perhaps at this very hour, she sat beside me alone as I am sitting now by Harry. And before that other women went through it. All the world over, wherever there are mothers—north, south, east, west—from the first baby that was born on the earth—they have every one suffered what I am suffering now—for it is the pang of motherhood ! To escape it one must escape birth and escape the love that is greater than one's self." And she understood suddenly that suffering and love are inseparable, that when one loves another more than one's self, one has opened the gate by which anguish will enter. She had forgotten to count the leaves, and when she remembered and looked again, the last one had fallen. Against the parted white curtains, the naked bough arched black and solitary. Even the small silent birds that had swayed dejectedly to and fro on the branches all day had flown off into the darkness. Presently, the light in the window went out, and as the hours wore on, a fine drizzling rain began to fall, as soft as tears, from the starless sky over the mulberry-tree. A sense of isolation greater than any she had ever known attacked her like a physical chill, and rising, she went over to the fire and stirred the pile of coal into a flame. She was alone in her despair, and she realized, with a feeling of terror, that one is always alone when one despairs, that there is a secret chamber in every soul where neither love nor sympathy can follow one. If Oliver were here beside her—if he were standing close to her in that throbbing circle around the bed— she would still be separated from him by the immensity of that inner space which is not measured by physical distances. "No, even if he were here, he could not reach me," she said, and an instant later, with one of those piercing illuminations which visit even perfectly normal women in moments of great intensity, she thought quickly, "If every woman told the truth to herself, would she say that there is something in her which love had never reached?" Then, reproaching herself because she had left the bed for a minute, she went back again and bent over the unconscious child, her whole slender body curving itself passionately into an embrace. His face was ashen white, except where the skin around his mouth was discoloured with a faint bluish tinge. His flesh, even his bones, appeared to have shrunk almost away in twenty-four hours. It was impossible to imagine that he was the rosy, laughing boy, who had crawled into her arms only two nights ago. The disease held him like some unseen spiritual enemy, against which all physical weapons were as useless as the little toys of a child. How could one fight that sinister power which had removed him to an illimitable distance while he was still in her arms? The troubled stupor, which had in it none of the quiet and the restfulness of sleep, terrorized her as utterly as if it had been the personal spirit of evil. The invisible forces of Life and Death seemed battling in the quivering air within that small circle of light.

While she bent over him, he stirred, raised himself, and then fell back in a paroxysm of coughing. The violence of the spasm shook his fragile little body as a rough wind shakes a flower on a stalk. Over his face the bluish tinge spread like a shadow, and into his eyes there came the expression of wondering terror which she had seen before only in the eyes of young startled animals. For an instant it seemed almost as is the devil of disease were wrestling inside of him, as if the small vital force she called life would be beaten out in the struggle. Then the agony passed; the strangling sound ceased, and he grew quiet, while she wiped the poison from his mouth and nostrils, and made him swallow a few drops of milk out of a teaspoon.

At the moment, while she fell on her knees by his bedside, it seemed to her that she had reached that deep place beyond which there is nothing.

*   *   *   *   *

"You've pulled him through. We'll have him out of bed before many days now," said the old doctor at daybreak. And he added cheerfully: "By the way, your husband came in the front door with me. He wanted to rush up here at once, but I'm keeping him away because he is obliged to go back to the bank."

"Poor Oliver!" said Virginia gently. "It is terrible on him. He must be so anxious." But even while she uttered the words, she was conscious of a curious sensation of unreality, as though she were speaking of a person whom she had known in another life. It was three days since she had seen Oliver, and in those three days she had lived and died many times.

CHAPTER IX

THE PROBLEM OF THE SOUTH

"FATHER, I want to marry John Henry," said Susan, just as she had said almost ten years ago, "Father, I want to go to college."

It was a March afternoon, ashen and windy, with flocks of small fleecy clouds hurrying across the changeable blue sky, and the vague, roving scents of early spring in the air. After his dinner, which he had taken for more than fifty years precisely at two o'clock, Cyrus had sat down for a peaceful pipe on the back porch before returning to the office. Between the sunken bricks in the little walled-in yard, blades of vivid green grass had shot up, seeking light out of darkness, and along the grey wooden ledge of the area the dauntless sunflowers were unfolding their small stunted leaves. On the railing of the porch a moth-eaten cat—the only animal for whom Cyrus entertained the remotest respect—was contentedly licking the shabby fur on her side.

"Father, I want to marry John Henry," repeated Susan, raising her voice to a higher key and towering like a flesh and blood image of Victory over the sagging cane chair in which he sat.

Taking his pipe from his mouth, he looked up at her; and so little had he altered in ten years, that the thought flashed through her mind that he had actually suffered no change of expression since the afternoon on which she had asked him to send her to college. As a man he may not have been impressive, but as a defeating force who could say that he had not attained his fulfilment ? It was as if the instinct of patriarchal tyranny had entrenched itself in his person as in a last stronghold of the disappearing order. When he died many things would pass away out of Dinwiddie—not only the soul and body of Cyrus Treadwell, but the vanishing myth of the "strong man," the rule of the individual despot, the belief in the inalienable right of the father to demand blood sacrifices. For in common with other men of his type, he stood equally for industrial advancement and for domestic immobility. The body social might move, but the units that formed the body social must remain stationary.

"Well, I don't think I'd worry about marrying, if I were you," he replied, not unkindly, for Susan inspired him with a respect against which he had struggled in vain. "You are very comfortable now, ain't you? And I'll see that you are well provided for after my death. John Henry hasn't anything except his salary, I reckon."

Marriage as an economic necessity was perfectly comprehensible to him, but it was difficult for him to conceive of anybody indulging in it simply as a matter of sentiment. That April afternoon was so far away now that it had ceased to exist even as an historical precedent.

"Yes, but I want to marry him, and I am going to," replied Susan decisively.

"What arrangements would you make about your mother? It seems to me that your mother needs your attention."

"Of course, I couldn't leave mother. If you agree to it, John Henry is willing to come here to live as long as I have to look after her. If not, I shall take her away with me; I have spoken to her, and she is perfectly willing to go."

The ten years which had left Cyrus at a standstill had developed his daughter from a girl into a woman. She spoke with the manner of one who realizes that she holds the situation in her hands, and he yielded to this assumption of strength as he would have yielded ten years ago had she been clever enough to use it against him. It was his own manner in a more attractive guise, if he had only known it; and the Treadwell determination to get the thing it wanted most was asserting itself in Susan's desire to win John Henry quite as effectively as it had asserted itself in Cyrus's passion to possess the Dinwiddie and Central Railroad. Though the ends were different, the quality which moved father and daughter towards these different ends was precisely the same. In Cyrus, it was force degraded; in Susan, it was force refined;

but the peculiar attribute which distinguished and united them was the possession of the power to command events.

"Take your mother away?" he repeated. "Why, where on earth would you take her?"

"Then you'll have to agree to John Henry's coming here. It won't make any difference to you, of course. You needn't see him except at the table."

"But what would James say about it?" he returned, with the cowardice natural to the habitual bully. The girl had character, certainly, and though he disliked character in a woman, he was obliged to admit that she had not failed to make an impression.

"James won't care, and besides," she added magnificently, "it is none of his business."

"And it's none of mine, either, I reckon," said Cyrus with a chuckle.

"Well, of course, it's more of mine," agreed Susan, and her delicious laugh drowned his chuckle.

She had won her point, and, strange to say, she had pleased him rather than otherwise. He had suddenly a comfortable feeling in his digestive organs as well as a sense of virtue in his soul. It was impossible not to feel proud of her as she towered there above him with her superb body, as fine and as supple as the body of a race-horse, and her splendid courage that made him wish while he looked at her that she, instead of James, had been born a male. She was not pretty—she had never been pretty—but he realized for the first time that there might be something better even for a woman than beauty.

"Thank you, father," she said as she turned away, and he was glad again to feel that she had conquered him. To be conquered by one's own blood was different from being conquered by a business acquaintance.

"You mustn't disturb the household, you know," he said; but his voice did not sound as dry as he had endeavoured to make it.

"I shan't disturb anybody," responded Susan with the amiability of a woman who, having gained her point, can afford to be pleasant. Then, wheeling about suddenly on the threshold, she added: "By the way, I forgot to tell you that

Mandy was here three times this morning asking to see you. She is in trouble about her son. He was arrested for shooting a policeman over at Cross's Corner, you know, and the people down there are so enraged, she's afraid of lynching. You read about it in the paper, didn't you ?"

Yes, he had read about the shooting—Cross's Corner was only three miles away; but, if he had ever known the name of Mandy's son, he had forgotten it so completely that seeing it in print had suggested nothing to his mind.

"Well, she doesn't expect me to interfere, does she ?" he asked shortly.

"I believe she thought you might go over and do something—I don't know what; help her engage a lawyer probably. She was very pitiable ; but, after all, what can one do for a negro that shoots a policeman ? There's Miss Willy calling me !"

She ran indoors; and taking his pipe, which was still smoking, from his mouth, Cyrus leaned back in his chair and stared intently at the small fleecy clouds in the west. The cat, having cleaned herself to her satisfaction, jumped down from the railing, and after rubbing against his thin legs, leaped gently into his lap.

"Tut-tut !" he remarked grimly; but he did not attempt to dislodge the animal, and it may be that some secret part of him was gratified by the attention. He was still sitting there some minutes later, when he heard the warning click of the back gate, and the figure of Mandy appeared at the corner of the kitchen wall. Rising from his chair, he shook the cat from his knees, and descending the steps, met the woman in the centre of the walk, where a few hardy dandelions were flattened like buttons between the bricks.

"Howdy, Mandy ? I'm sorry to hear that you're having trouble with that boy of yours." He saw at once that she was racked by a powerful emotion, and any emotion affected him unpleasantly as something extravagant and indecent. Sweat had broken out in glistening clusters over her face and neck, and her eyes, under the stray wisps of hair, had in them an expression of dumb and uncomprehending submission.

"Ain't you gwineter git 'im away, Marster ?" she began,

and stronger even than her terror was the awe of Cyrus which
subdued her voice to a tone of servile entreaty.

"Why did he shoot a policeman ? He knew he'd hang
for it," returned Cyrus sharply. And he added, "Of course I
can't get him away. He'll have to take his deserts. Your
race has got to learn that when you break the law you must
pay for it."

At first he had made as if to push by her, but when she did
not move, he thought better of it and waited for her to speak.
The sound of her heavy breathing, like the breathing of some
crouching beast, awoke in him a curious repulsion. If only
one could get rid of such creatures after their first youth was
over ! If only every careless act could perish with the impulse
that led to it ! If only the dried husks of pleasure did not
turn to weapons against one ! These thoughts—or disjointed
snatches of thoughts like these—passed in a confused whirl
through his brain as he stood there. For an instant it was
almost as if his accustomed lucidity of purpose had deserted
him; then the disturbance ceased, and with the renewal of
order in his mind, his lifelong habit of prompt decision returned to him.

"Your race has got to learn that when you break the law
you must pay for it," he repeated—for on that sound principle of justice he felt that he must unalterably take his stand.

"He's all de boy I'se got, Marster," rejoined the negress,
with an indifference to the matter of justice which had led
others of her colour into those subterranean ways where
abstract principles are not. "You ain' done furgot 'im,
Marster," she added piteously. "He 'uz born jes two mont's
atter Miss Lindy turnt me outer hyer—en he's jes ez w'ite ez
ef'n he b'longed ter w'ite folks."

But she had gone too far—she had outraged that curious
Anglo-Saxon instinct in Cyrus which permitted him to sin
against his race's integrity, yet forbade him to acknowledge,
even to himself, that he bore any part in the consequences of
that sin. Illogical, he might have admitted, but there are
some truths so poisonous that no honest man could breathe
the same air with them.

Taking out his pocket-book, he slowly drew a fifty dollar
bill from its innermost recesses, and as slowly unfolded it.

He always handled money in that careful fashion—a habit which he had inherited from his father and his grandfather before him, and of which he was entirely unconscious. Filtering down through so many generations, the mannerism had ceased at last to be merely a physical peculiarity, and had become strangely spiritual in its suggestion. The craving for possession, the singleness of desire, the tenacity of grasp, the dread of relinquishment, the cold-blooded determination to keep intact the thing which it had cost so much to acquire —all that was bound up in the spirit of Cyrus Treadwell, and all that would pass at last with that spirit from off the earth, was expressed in the gesture with which he held out the bit of paper to the woman who had asked for his help. "Take this —it is all I can do for you," he said, "and don't come whining around me any more. Black or white, the man that commits a murder has got to hang for it."

A sound broke from the negress that resembled a human cry of grief less than it did the inarticulate moan of an animal in mortal pain. Then it stopped suddenly, strangled by that dull weight of usage beneath which the primal impulse in her was crushed back into silence. Instinctively, as if in obedience to some reflex action, she reached out and took the money from his hand, and still instinctively, with the dazed look of one who performs in delirium the customary movements of every day, she fell back, holding her apron deprecatingly aside while he brushed past her. And in her eyes as she gazed after him there dawned the simple wonder of the brute that asks of Life why it suffers.

Beyond the alley into which the gate opened, Cyrus caught sight of Gabriel's erect figure hurrying down the side street in the direction of the Old Ladies' Home, and calling out to him, he scrambled over the ash-heaps and tomato cans, and emerged, irritated but smiling, into the sunlight.

"I'm on my way to the bank. We'll walk down together," he remarked almost gently, for, though he disapproved of Gabriel's religious opinions and distrusted his financial judgment, the warlike little rector represented the single romance of his life.

"I had intended stopping at the Old Ladies' Home, but I'll go on with you instead," responded Gabriel. "I've just

had a message from one of our old servants calling me down
to Cross's Corner," he pursued, " so I'm in a bit of a hurry.
That's a bad thing, that murder down there yesterday, and
I'm afraid it will mean trouble for the negroes. Mr. Blylie,
who came to market this morinng, told me a crowd had tried
to lynch the fellow last night."

"Well, they've got to hang when they commit hanging
crimes," replied Cyrus stubbornly. "There's no way out of
that. It's just, ain't it ?"

"Yes, I suppose so," admitted Gabriel ; "though, for my
part, I've a feeling against capital punishment—except, of
course, in cases of rape, where, I confess, my blood turns
against me."

"An eye for an eye and a tooth for a tooth—that's the law
of God, ain't it ?"

"The old law, yes—but why not quote the law of Christ
instead ?"

"It wouldn't do—not with the negroes," returned Cyrus,
who entertained for the Founder of Christianity something
of the sentimental respect mingled with an innate distrust of
His common sense with which he regarded His disciple.

"We can't condemn it until we've tried it," said Gabriel
thoughtfully, and he went on after a moment: "The terrible
thing for us about the negroes is that they are so grave a
responsibility—so grave a responsibility. Of course, we
aren't to blame—we didn't bring them here; and yet I sometimes feel as if we had really done so."

This was a point of view which Cyrus had never considered,
and he felt an immediate suspicion of it. It looked, somehow, as if it were insidiously leading the way to an appeal
for money.

"It's the best thing that could have happened to them,"
he replied shortly. "If they'd remained in Africa, they'd
never have been civilized or—or Christianized."

"Ah, that is just where the responsibility rests on us. We
stand for civilization to them; we stand even—or at least
we used to stand—for Christianity. They haven't learned
yet to look above or beyond us, and the example we set them
is one that they are condemned, for sheer lack of any finer
vision, to follow. The majority of them are still hardly more

than uneducated children, and that very fact makes an appeal to one's compassion which becomes at times almost unbearable."

But this was more than Cyrus could stand even from the rector, whose conversation he usually tolerated because of the perverse, inexplicable liking he felt for the man. The charm that Gabriel exercised over him was almost feminine in its subtlety and in its utter defiance of any rational sanction. It may have been that his nature, incapable though it was of love, was not entirely devoid of the rarer capacity for friendship—or it may have been that, with the inscrutable irony which appears to control all human attractions, the caged brutality in his heart was soothed by the unconscious flattery of the other's belief in him. Now, however, he felt that Gabriel's highfalutin nonsense was carrying him away. It was well enough to go on like that in the pulpit; but on weekdays, when there was business to think of and every minute might mean the loss of a dollar, there was no use dragging in either religion or sentiment. Had he put his thoughts plainly, he would probably have said : "That's not business, Gabriel. The trouble with you—and with most of you old-fashioned Virginians—is that you don't understand the first principles of business." These words, indeed, were almost on his lips, when, catching the rector's innocent glance wandering round to him, he contented himself with remarking satirically :

"Well, you were always up in the clouds. It doesn't hurt you, I reckon, though I doubt if it does much toward keeping your pot boiling."

"I must turn off here," said Gabriel gently. "It's the shortest way to Cross's Corner."

"Do you think any good will come of your going ?"

"Probably not ; but I couldn't refuse."

Much as he respected Cyrus, he was not sorry to part from him, for their walk together had left him feeling suddenly old and incompetent to battle with the problems of life. He knew that Cyrus, even though he liked him, considered him a bit of a fool, and with a humility which was unusual in him (for in his heart he was absolutely sure that his own convictions were right and that Cyrus's were wrong) he began to ask himself if, by any chance, the other's verdict could be secretly justified. Was he in reality the failure that Cyrus believed him to be ? Or was it merely that he had drifted into that "depressing view" of existence against which he so earnestly warned his parishioners ? Perhaps it wasn't Cyrus after all who had produced this effect. Perhaps the touch of indigestion he had felt after dinner had not entirely disappeared. Perhaps it meant that he was "getting on" —sixty-five his last birthday. Perhaps—but already the March wind, fresh and bud-scented, was blowing away his despondency. Already he was beginning to feel again that fortifying conviction that whatever was unpleasant could not possibly be natural.

Ahead of him the straight ashen road flushed to pale red where it climbed a steep hill-side, and when he gained the top, the country lay before him in all the magic loveliness of early spring. Out of the rosy earth innumerable points of tender green were visible in the sunlight and invisible again beneath the faintly rippling shadows that filled the hollows. From every bough, from every bush, from every creeper which clung trembling to the rail fences, this wave of green, bursting through the sombre covering of winter, quivered, as delicate as foam, in the brilliant sunshine. On either side labourers were working, and where the ploughs pierced the soil they left narrow channels of darkness.

In the soul of Gabriel, that essence of the spring, which is immortally young and restless, awakened and gave him back his youth, as it gave the new grass to the fields and the longing for joy to the hearts of the ploughmen. He forgot that he was "getting on." He forgot the unnatural depression which had made him imagine for a moment that the world was a more difficult place than he had permitted himself to believe —so difficult a place, indeed, that for some people there could be no solution of its injustice, its brutality, its dissonance, its inequalities. The rapture in the song of the bluebirds was sweeter than the voice of Cyrus to which he had listened. And in a meadow on the right, an old grey horse, scarred, dim-eyed, spavined, stood resting one crooked leg, while he gazed wistfully over the topmost rail of the fence into the vivid green of the distance—for into his aching old bones, also, there had passed a little of that longing for joy which was born of the miraculous softness and freshness of the spring.   To him as well as to Gabriel and to the ploughmen and to the blue-birds flitting, like bits of fallen sky, along the " snake fences," Nature, the great healer, had brought her annual gift of the resurrection of hope.

" Cyrus means well," thought Gabriel, with a return of that natural self-confidence without which no man can exist happily and make a living.   " He means well, but he takes a false view of life."   And he added after a minute: " It's odd how the commercial spirit seems to suck a man dry when it once gets a hold on him."

He walked on rapidly, leaving the old horse and the plough-men behind him, and around his energetic little figure the grey dust, as fine as powder, spun in swirls and eddies before the driving wind, which had grown boisterous.   As he moved there alone in the deserted road, with his long black coat flapping against his legs, he appeared so insignificant and so unheroic that an observer would hardly have suspected that the greatest belief on the earth—the belief in Life—in its universality in spite of its littleness, in its justification in spite of its cruelties—that this belief shone through his shrunken little body as a flame shines through a vase.

At the end of the next mile, midway between Dinwiddie and Cross's Corner, stood the small log cabin of the former slave who had sent for him, and as he approached the narrow path that led, between oyster shells, from the main road to the single flat brown rock before the doorstep, he noticed with pleasure how tranquil and happy the little rustic home appeared under the windy brightness of the March sky.

" People may say what they please, but there never were happier or more contented creatures than the darkeys," he thought.   " I doubt if there's another peasantry in the world that is half so well off or half so picturesque."

A large yellow rooster, pecking crumbs from the threshold, began to scold shrilly, and at the sound the old servant, a decrepit negress in a blue gingham dress, hobbled out into the path and stood peering at him under her hollowed palm. Her forehead was ridged and furrowed beneath her white turban, and her bleared old eyes looked up at him with a blind and groping effort at recognition.

"1 got your message, Aunt Mehitable. Don't you know me?"

"Is dat you, Marse Gabriel? I made sho' you wan' gwineter let nuttin' stop you f'om comin'."

"Don't I always come when you send for me?"

"You sutney do, suh. Dat's de gospel trufe—you sutney do."

As he looked at her standing there in the strong sunlight, with her palsied hand, which was gnarled and roughened until it resembled the shell of a walnut, curving over her eyes, he felt that a quality at once alien and enigmatical separated her not only from himself, but from every other man or woman who was born white instead of black. He had lived beside her all his life—and yet he could never understand her, could never reach her, could never even discern the hidden stuff of which she was made. He could make laws for her, but no child of a white mother could tell whether those laws ever penetrated that surface imitation of the superior race and reached the innate differences of thought, feeling, and memory which constituted her being. Was it development or mimicry that had brought her up out of savagery and clothed her in her blue gingham dress and her white turban, as in the outward covering of civilization?

Her look of crumbling age and the witch-like groping of her glance had cast a momentary spell over him. When it was gone, he said cheerfully:

"You mustn't be having troubles at your time of life, Aunt Mehitable," and in his voice there was the subtle recognition of all that she had meant to his family in the past, of all that his family had meant to her. Her claim upon him was the more authentic because it existed only in his imagination, and in hers. The tie that knit them together was woven of impalpable strands, but it was unbreakable while he and his generation were above the earth.

"Dar ain' no end er trouble, Marse Gabriel, ez long ez dar's yo' chillen en de chillen er yo' chillen ter come atter you. De ole ain' so techy—dey lets de hornet's nes' hang in peace whar de Lawd put hit—but de young dey's diff'rent."

"I suppose the neighbourhood is stirred up about the murder. What in God's name was that boy thinking of?"

The old blood crimes that never ceased where the white and the black races came together ! The old savage folly and the new freedom ! The old ignorance, the old lack of understanding, and the new restlessness, the new enmity !

" He wan' thinkin' er nuttin', Marse Gabriel. We ole uns kin set down en steddy, but de young dey up en does wid dere brains ez addled ez de inside uv er bad aig. 'T wan' dat ar way in de old days w'en we all hed de say so ez ter w'at wuz en w'at wan't de way ter behave."

Like an institution left from the ruins of the feudal system, which had crumbled as all ancient and decrepit things must crumble when the wheels of progress roll over them, she stood there wrapped in the beliefs and customs of that other century to which she belonged. Her sentiments had clustered about the past, as his had done, until the border-line between the romance and the actuality had vanished. She could not help him because she, also, possessed the retrospective, not the constructive, vision. He was not conscious of these thoughts, and yet, although he was unconscious of them, they coloured his reflections while he stood there in the sunlight, which had begun to fall aslant the blasted pine by the roadside. The wind had lowered until it came like the breath of spring, bud-scented, caressing, provocative. Even Gabriel, whose optimism lay in his blood and bone rather than in his intellect, yielded for a moment to this call of the spring as one might yield to the delicious melancholy of a vagrant mood. The long straight road, without bend or fork, had warmed in the paling sunlight to the colour of old ivory; in a neighbouring field a young maple-tree rose in a flame of buds from the ridged earth where the ploughing was over; and against the azure sky in the south a flock of birds drifted up, like brown smoke, from the marshes.

" Tell me your trouble, then," he said, dropping into the cane-seated chair she had brought out of the cabin and placed between the flat stone at the doorstep and the well-brink, on which the yellow rooster stood spreading his wings. But Aunt Mehitable had returned to the cabin, and when she reappeared she was holding out to him a cracked saucer on which there was a piece of preserved watermelon rind and a pewter spoon.

"Dish yer is de ve'y same sort er preserves yo' mouf use'n ter water fur w'en you wuz a chile," she remarked as she handed the sweet to him. Whatever her anxiety or affliction could have been, the importance of his visit had evidently banished it from her mind. She hovered over him as his mother may have done when he was in his cradle, while the cheerful self-effacement in which slavery had trained her lent a pathetic charm to her manner.

"How peaceful it looks," he thought, sitting there, with the saucer in his hand, and his eyes on the purple shadows that slanted over the ploughed fields. "You have a good view of the low-grounds, Aunt Mehitable," he said aloud; and added immediately, "what's that noise in the road? Do you hear it?"

The old woman shook her head.

"I'se got sorter hard er heahin', Marse Gabriel, but dar's al'ays a tur'able lot er fuss gwine on w'en de chillen begin ter come up f'om de fields. 'T wuz becase uv oner dem ar boys dat I sont fur you," she pursued. "He went plum outer his haid yestiddy en fout wid a w'ite man down yonder at Cross's Co'nder, en dar's gwineter be trouble about'n hit des ez sho'ez you live."

Seated on the flat stone, with her hands hanging over her knees, and her turbaned head swaying gently back and forth as she talked, she waited as tranquilly as the rock waited for the inevitable processes of nature. The patience in her look was the dumb patience of inanimate things; and her half-bared feet, protruding from the broken soles of her shoes, were encrusted with the earth of the fields until one could hardly distinguish them from the ground on which they rested.

"It looks as if there was something like a fight down yonder by the blasted pine," said the rector, rising from his chair. "I reckon I'd better go and see what they're quarrelling about."

The negress rose also, and her dim eyes followed him while he went down the little path between the borders of oyster shells. As he turned into the open stretch of the road, he glanced back at her, and stopping for a moment, waved his hand with a gesture that was careless and reassuring. The fight, or whatever it was that made the noise, was still some distance ahead in the shadow of the pine-tree, and as he walked towards it he was thinking casually of other matters—of the wretched condition of the road after the winter rains ; of the need of greater thrift among the farmers, both white and black ; of the touch of indigestion which still troubled him. There was nothing to warn him that he was approaching the supreme event in his life, nothing to prepare him for a change beside which all the changes of the past would appear as unsubstantial as shadows.   His soul might have been the soul in the grass, so little did its coming or its going affect the forces around him.

"If this shooting pain keeps up, I'll have to get a prescription from Doctor Fraser," he thought, and the next minute he cried out suddenly, "God help us !" and began to run down the road in the direction of the blasted pine. There was hardly a breath between the instant when he had thought of his indigestion and the instant when he had called out sharply on the name of God, yet that flash of time had been long enough to change the ordinary man into the hero. The spark of greatness in his nature flamed up and irradiated all that had been merely dull and common clay a moment before. As he ran on, with his coat-tails flapping around him, and his thin legs wobbling from the unaccustomed speed at which he moved, he was so unimposing a figure that only the Diety who judges the motives, not the actions, of men would have been impressed by the spectacle. Even the three hearty brutes—and it took him but a glance to see that two of them were drunk, and that the third, being a sober rascal, was the more dangerous—hardly ceased their merry torment of the young negro in their midst when he came up with them.

"I know that boy," he said. "He is the grandson of Aunt Mehitable.   What are you doing with him ?"

A drunken laugh answered him, while the sober scoundrel—a lank, hairy ne'er-do-well, with a tendency to epilepsy, whose name he remembered to have heard—pushed him roughly to the roadside.

"You git out of this here mess, parson. We're goin' to teach this damn nigger a lesson, and I reckon when he's learned it in hell, he won't turn his grin on a white woman again in a jiffy."

"Fo' de Lawd, I didn't mean nuttin', Marster!" screamed the boy, livid with terror. "I didn't know de lady was dar— fo' de Lawd Jesus, I didn't! My foot jes slipped on de plank w'en I wuz crossin', en I knocked up agin her."

"He jostled her," observed one of the drunken men judicially, "an' we'll be roasted befo' we'll let a damn nigger jostle a white lady—ever if she ain't a lady—in these here parts."

In the rector's bone and fibre, drilled there by the ages that had shaped his character before he began to be, there was all the white man's horror of an insult to his womankind. But deeper even than this lay his personal feeling of responsibility for any creature whose fathers had belonged to him and had toiled in his service.

"I believe the boy is telling the truth," he said; and he added with one of his characteristic bursts of impulsiveness, "but whether he is or not, you are too drunk to judge."

There was going to be a battle, he saw, and in the swiftness with which he discerned this, he made his eternal choice between the preacher and the fighter. Stripping off his coat, he reached down for a stick from the roadside; then spinning round on the three of them he struck out with all his strength, while there floated before him the face of a man he had killed in his first charge at Manassas. The old fury, the old triumph, the old blood-stained splendour returned to him. He smelt the smoke again, he heard the boom of the cannon, the long sobbing rattle of musketry, and the thought stabbed through him, "God forgive me for loving a fight!"

Then the fight stopped. There was a patter of feet in the dust as the young negro fled like a hare up the road in the direction of Dinwiddie. One of the men leaped the fence and disappeared into the tangled thicket beyond; while the other two, sobered suddenly, began walking slowly over the ploughed ground on the right. Ten minutes later Gabriel was lying alone, with the blood oozing from his mouth, on the trodden weeds by the roadside. The shadow of the pine had not moved since he watched it; on the flat rock in front of the cabin the old negress stood, straining her eyes in the faint sunshine; and up the long road the March wind still blew, as soft, as provocative, as bud-scented.

BOOK THIRD

THE ADJUSTMENT

CHAPTER I

THE CHANGING ORDER

" So this is life," thought Virginia, while she folded her mourning veil, and laid it away in the top drawer of her bureau. Like all who are suddenly brought face to face with tragedy, she felt at the moment that there was nothing else in existence. All the sweetness of the past had vanished so utterly that she remembered it only as one remembers a dream from which one has abruptly awakened. Nothing remained except this horrible sense of the pitiful insufficiency of life, of the inexorable finality of death. It was a week since the rector's death, and in that week she had passed out of her girlhood for ever. Of all the things that she had lived through, this alone had had the power to crush the hope in her, and the odour of crape which floated through the crack of the drawer sickened her with its reminder of that agonized sense of loss which had settled over her at the funeral. She was only thirty—the best of her life should still be in the future—yet as she looked back at her white face in the mirror it seemed to her that she should never emerge from the leaden hopelessness which had descended like a weight on her body. Above the harsh black of her dress, which added ten years to her appearance, she saw the darkened circles rimming her eyes, the faded pallor of her skin, the lustreless wave of her hair, which had once had a satiny sheen on its ripples.

" Grief makes a person look like this," she thought. " I shall never be a girl again—Oliver was right: I am the kind to break early." Then, because to think of herself in the midst of such sorrow seemed to her almost wicked, she turned away from the mirror, and laid her crape-trimmed hat on the shelf in the wardrobe. She was wearing a dress of black Henrietta cloth, which had been borrowed from one of her neighbours who had worn mourning, and the blouse and sleeves hung with an exaggerated fulness over her thin arms and bosom. All that had distinguished her beauty—the radiance, the colour, the flower-like delicacy of bloom and sweetness—these were blotted out by her grief and by the voluminous mourning dress of the nineties. A week had changed her, as even Harry's illness had not changed her, from a girl into a woman; and horrible beyond belief, with the exception of her mother, it had changed nothing else in the universe! The tragedy that had ruined her life had left the rest of the world—even the little world of Dinwiddie—moving as serenely, as indifferently, on its way towards eternity. On the morning of the funeral she had heard the same market waggons rumble over the cobblestones, the same droning songs of the hucksters, the same casual procession of feet on the pavement. A passionate indignation had seized her because life could be so brutal to death, because the terror and the pity that flamed in her soul shed no burning light on the town where her father had worked and loved and fought and suffered and died. A little later the ceaseless tread of visitors to the rectory door had driven this thought from her mind; but through every minute, while he lay in the closed room downstairs, while she sat beside her mother in the slow, crawling carriage that went to the old churchyard, while she stood with bowed head listening to the words of the service—through it all there had been the feeling that something must happen to alter a world in which such a thing had been possible, that life must stop, that the heavens must fall, that God must put forth His hand and work a miracle in order to show His compassion and His horror.

But nothing had changed. After the funeral her mother had come home with her, and the others, many with tear-stained faces, had drifted in separate ways back to eat their separate dinners. For a few hours Dinwiddie had been shaken out of its phlegmatic pursuit of happiness; for a few hours it had attained an emotional solidarity which swept it up from the innumerable bypaths of the personal to a height where the personal rises at last into the universal. Then the ebb had come; the sense of tragedy had lessened slowly with the prolongation of feeling; and the universal vision had dissolved and crystallized into the pitiless physical needs of the individual. After the funeral a wave almost of relief had swept over the town at the thought that the suspension and the strain were at an end. The business of keeping alive, and the moral compulsion of keeping abreast of one's neighbours, reasserted their supremacy even while the carriages, quickening their pace a trifle on the return drive, rolled out of the churchyard. Now at the end of a week only Virginia and her mother would take the time from living to sit down and remember.

In the adjoining room, which was the nursery, Mrs. Pendleton was sitting beside the window, with her Bible open on her knees, and her head bent a little in the direction of Miss Priscilla, who was mending a black dress by the table.

"It is so sweet of you, dear Miss Priscilla," she murmured in her vague and gentle voice as Virginia entered. So old, so pallid, so fragile she looked, that she might have been mistaken by a stranger for a woman of eighty, yet the impossibility of breaking the habit of a lifetime kept the lines of her face still fixed in an expression of anxious cheerfulness. For more than forty years she had not thought of herself, and now that the opportunity had come for her to do so, she found that she had almost forgotten the way that one went about it. Even grief could not make her selfish any more than it could make her untidy. Her manner, like her dress, was so little a matter of impulse, and so largely a matter of discipline and of conscience, that it expressed her broken heart hardly more than did the widow's cap on her head or the mourning brooch that fastened the crape folds of her collar.

"Do you want anything, mother darling? What can I do for you?" asked Virginia, stooping to kiss her.

"Nothing, dear. I was just telling Miss Priscilla that I had had a visit from Mr. Treadwell, and that—her voice quivered a little—"he showed more feeling than I should have believed possible. He even wanted to make me an allowance."

Miss Priscilla drew out her large linen handkerchief, which was like a man's, and loudly blew her nose. "I always said there was more in Cyrus than people thought," she observed.

"Here, I've shortened this dress, Jinny, until it's just about your mother's length."

She tried to speak carelessly, for though she did not concur in the popular belief that to ignore sorrow is to assuage it, her social instinct, which was as strongly developed as Mrs. Pendleton's, encouraged her to throw a pleasant veil over affliction.

"You're looking pale for want of air, Jinny," she added after a minute, in which she had thought, "The child has broken so in the last few days that she looks years older than Oliver."

"I'm trying to make her go driving," said Mrs. Pendleton, leaning forward over the open page of her Bible.

"But I can't go, mother ; I haven't the heart for it," replied Virginia, choking down a sob.

"I don't like to see you looking so badly, dear. You must keep up your strength for the children's sake, you know."

"Yes, I know," answered Virginia, but her voice had a weary sound.

A little later, when Miss Priscilla had gone, and Oliver came in to urge her to go with him, she shook her head again still palely resolute, still softly obstinate.

"But, Jinny, it isn't right for you to let your health go," he urged. "You haven't had a breath of air for days and you're getting sallow."

His own colour was as fine as ever; he grew handsomer, if a trifle stouter, as he grew older ; and at thirty-five there was all the vigour and the charm of twenty in his face and manner. In one way only he had altered, and of this alteration, he, as well as Virginia, was beginning faintly to be aware. Comfort was almost imperceptibly taking the place of conviction, and the passionate altruism of youth would yield before many years to the prudential philosophy of middle age. Life had defeated him. His best had been thrown back at him, and his nature, embittered by failure, was adjusting itself gradually to a different and a lower standard of values. Though he could not be successful, it was still possible, even within the narrow limits of his income and his opportunities, to be comfortable. And, like other men who have lived day by day with heroically unselfish women, he had fallen at last into the habit of thinking that his being comfortable was, after all, a question of supreme importance to the universe. Deeply as he had felt the rector's death, he, in common with the rest of Dinwiddie, was conscious of breathing more easily after the funeral was over. To his impressionable nature, alternations of mood were almost an essential of being, and there was something intolerable to him in any slowly harrowing grief. To watch Virginia nursing every memory of her father because she shrank from the subtle disloyalty of forgetfulness, aroused in him a curious mingling of sympathy and resentment.

"I wish you'd go, even if you don't feel like it—just to please me, Virginia," he urged; and after a short struggle she yielded to his altered tone, and got down her hat from the shelf of the wardrobe.

A little later, as the dogcart rolled out of Dinwiddie into the country road, she looked through her black grenadine veil on a world which appeared to have lost its brightness. The road was the one along which she had ridden on the morning of the fox-hunt; ahead of them lay the same fields, sown now with the tender green of the spring; the same creeks ran there, screened by the same thickets of elder; the same pines wafted their tang on the March wind that blew, singing, out of the forest. It was all just as it had been on that morning—and yet what a difference!

"Put up your veil, Virginia—it's enough to smother you."

But she only shook her head, shrinking farther down into the shapeless borrowed dress as though she felt that it protected her. Following the habit of people whose choice has been instinctive rather than deliberate, a choice of the blood, not of the brain, they had long ago exhausted the fund of conversation with which they had started. There was nothing to talk about—since Virginia had never learned to talk of herself, and Oliver had grown reticent recently about the subjects that interested him. When the daily anecdotes of the children had been aired between them with an effort at breeziness, nothing remained except the endless discussion of Harry's education. Even this had worn threadbare of late, and with the best intentions in the world, Virginia had failed to supply anything else of sufficient importance to take its place. An inherited habit, the same habit which had made it possible for Mrs. Pendleton to efface her broken heart, prompted her to avoid any allusion to her grief in which she sat shrouded as in her mourning veil.

"The spring is so early this year," she remarked once, with her gaze on the rosy billows of an orchard. "The peach-trees have almost finished blooming."

Then, as he made no answer except to flick at John Henry's bay mare with his whip, she asked daringly: "Are you writing again, Oliver?"

A frown darkened his forehead, and she saw the muscles about his mouth twitch as though he were irritated. For all his failure and his bitterness, he did not look a day older, she thought, than when she had first seen him driving down High Street in that unforgettable May. He was still as ardent, still as capable of inspiring first love in the imagination of a girl. The light and the perfume of that enchanted spring seemed suddenly to envelop her, and moved by a yearning to recapture them for an instant, she drew closer to him, and slipped her hand through his arm.

"Oh, I'm trying my luck with some trash. Nothing but trash has any chance of going in this damned business."

"You mean it's different from your others? It's less serious?"

"Less serious? Well, I should say so. It's the sort of ice-cream soda-water the public wants. But if I can get it put on, it ought to run, and a play that runs is obliged to make money. I doubt if there's anything much better than money, when it comes to that."

"You used to say it didn't matter."

"Did I? Well, I was a fool, and I've learned better. These last few years have taught me that nothing else on earth matters much."

This was so different from what that other Oliver—the Oliver of her first love—might have said, that involuntarily her clasp on his arm tightened. The change in him, so gradual at first that her mind, unused to subtleties, had hardly grasped it, was beginning to frighten her.

"You have such burdens, dear," she said, and he noticed that her voice had acquired the toneless sweetness of her mother's. "I've tried to be as saving as I could, but the children have been sick so much that it seems sometimes as if we should never get out of debt. I am trying now to pay off the bills I was obliged to make while Harry was ill in October. If I could only get perfectly strong, we might let Marthy go, now that Jenny is getting so big."

"You work hard enough as it is, Virginia. You've been awfully good about it," he answered, but his manner was almost casual, for he had grown to take for granted her un-selfishness with something of the unconcern with which he took for granted the comfortable feeling of the spring weather. In the early days of their marriage, when her fresh beauty had been a power to rule him, she had taught him to assume his right to her self-immolation on the altar of his comfort; and with the taste of bitterness which sometimes follows the sweets of memory, she recalled that their first quarrel had arisen because she had insisted on getting out of bed to make the fires in the morning. Then, partly because the recollection appeared to reproach him, and partly because, not possessing the critical faculty, she had never learned to acknowledge the existence of a flaw in a person she loved, she edged closer to him, and replied cheerfully:

"I don't mind the work a bit, if only the children will keep well so we shan't have to spend any more money. I shan't need any black clothes," she added, with a trembling lip. "Mrs. Carrington has given me this dress, as she has gone out of mourning, and I've got a piece of blue silk put away that I am going to have dyed."

He glanced at the shapeless dress, not indignantly as he would once have done, but with a tinge of quiet amusement.

"It makes you look every day of forty."

"I know it isn't becoming, but at least it will save having to buy one."

In spite of the fact that her small economies had made it possible for them to live wholesomely, and with at least an appearance of decency, on his meagre salary, they had always aroused in him a sense of bitter exasperation. He respected her, of course, for her saving, yet in his heart he knew that she would probably have charmed him more had she been a spendthrift—since the little virtues are sometimes more

deadly to the passion of love than are the large vices. While
he nodded, without disputing the sound common sense in
her words, she thought a little wistfully how nice it would
be to have pretty things if only one could afford them. Some
day, when the children's schooling was over and Oliver had
got a larger salary, she would begin to buy clothes that were
becoming rather than durable. But that was in the future,
and, meanwhile, how much better it was to grudge every
penny she spent on herself as long as there were unpaid bills
at the doctor's and the grocer's. All of which was, of course,
perfectly reasonable, and like other women who have had
a narrow experience of life, she cherished the delusion that a
man's love, as well as his philosophy, is necessarily rooted in
reason.

When they turned homeward, the bay mare, pricked by
desire for her stable, began to travel more rapidly, and the
fall of her hoofs, accompanied by the light roll of the wheels,
broke the silence which had almost imperceptibly settled
upon them. Not until the cart drew up at the gate did
Virginia realize that they had hardly spoken a dozen words
on the drive back.

" I feel better already, Oliver," she said gratefully, as he
helped her to alight. Then hastening ahead of him, she ran
up the walk and into the hall, where her mother, looking wan
and unnatural in her widow's cap, greeted her with the
question :

" Did you have a pleasant drive, dear ?"

*   *   *   *   *

For six months Mrs. Pendleton hid her broken heart under
a smile, and went softly about the small daily duties of the
household, facing death, as she had faced life, with a sublime
unselfishness and the manner of a lady. Her hopes, her joys,
her fears even, lay in the past; there was nothing for her to look
forward to, nothing for her to dread in the future. Life had
given her all that it had to offer of bliss or sorrow, and for
the rest of her few years she would be like one who, having
finished her work before the end of the day, sits waiting
patiently for the words of release to be spoken. As the months
went on, she moved like a gentle shadow about her daughter's
little home. So wasted and pallid was her body that at times

Virginia feared to touch her lest she should melt like a phantom out of her arms. Yet to the last she never faltered, never cried out for mercy, never sought to hasten by a breath that end which was to her as the longing of her eyes, as the brightness of the sunlight, as the sweetness of the springtime. Once, looking up from Lucy's lesson which she was hearing, she said a little wistfully, "I don't think, Jinny, it will be long now," and then, checking herself reproachfully, she added, "But God knows best. I can trust Him."

It was the only time that she had ever spoken of the thought which was in her mind day and night, for when she could no longer welcome her destiny, she had accepted it. Her faith, like her opinions, was childlike and uncritical—the artless product of a simple and incurious age. The strength in her had gone, not into the building of knowledge, but into the making of character, and she had judged all thought as innocently as she had judged all literature, by its contribution to the external sweetness of living. A child of ten might have demolished her theories, and yet because of them, or in spite of them, she had translated into action the end of all reasoning, the profoundest meaning in all philosophy. But she was born to decorate instead of to reason. Though her mind had never winnowed illusions from realities, her hands had patiently woven both illusions and realities into the embroidered fabric of Life.

For six months she went about the house and helped Virginia with the sewing, which had become burdensome since the children, and especially Harry, were big enough to wear daily holes in their stockings. Then, when the half year was over, she took to her bed one evening after she had carefully undressed, folded her clothes out of sight, and read a chapter in her Bible. In the morning she did not get up, and at the end of a fortnight, in which she apologized for making extra work whenever food was brought to her, she clasped her hands on her thin breast, smiled once into Virginia's face, and died so quietly that there was hardly a perceptible change in her breathing. She had gone through life without giving trouble, and she gave none at the end. As she lay there in her little bed in Virginia's spare room, to which she had moved after Gabriel's death in order that the rectory

might be got ready for the new rector, she appeared so shadowy
and unearthly that it was impossible to believe that she had
ever been a part of the restless strivings and the sombre
violences of life. On the candle-stand by her bed lay her
spectacles, with steel rims because she had never felt that she
could afford gold ones; and a single October rose, from which
a golden petal had dropped, stood in a vase beside the Bible.
On the foot of the bed hung her grey flannelette wrapper, with
a patch in one sleeve over which Harry had spilled a bottle
of shoe polish, while through the half-shuttered window the
autumn sunshine fell in long yellow bars over the hemp rugs
on the floor. And she was dead ! Her mother was dead—
no matter how much she needed her, she would never come
back. Out of the vacancy around her, some words of her
own, spoken in her girlhood, returned to her. "There is only
one thing I couldn't bear, and that is losing my mother."
Only one thing ! And now that one thing had happened,
and she was not only bearing it, she was looking ahead to a
future in which that one thing would be always beside her,
always in her memory. Whatever the years brought to her,
they could never bring her mother again—they could never
bring her a love like her mother's.

Out of that same vacancy, which seemed to swallow and
to hold everything, which seemed to exist both within and
outside of herself, a multitude of forgotten images and impressions flashed into being. She saw the nursery fireside
in the rectory, and her mother, with hair that still shone like
satin, rocking back and forth in the black wicker chair with
the sagging bottom. She saw her kneeling on the old frayed
red and blue drugget, her skirt pinned up at the back of her
waist, while she bathed her daughter's scratched and aching
feet in the oblong tin foot-tub. She saw her, as beautiful
as an angel, in church on Sunday mornings, her worshipful
eyes lifted to the pulpit, an edge of tinted light falling on
the open prayer-book in her hand. She saw her, thin and
stooping, a shadow of all that she had once been—waiting—
waiting—— She had always been there. It was impossible
to realize that a time could ever come when she would not be
there—and now she was gone !

And behind all the images, all the impressions, the stubborn thought persisted that this was life—that one could never escape it—that whatever happened, one must come back to it at the last. " I have my children still left—but for my children I could not live !" she thought, dropping on her knees by the bedside, and hiding her face in the grey wrapper.

*　　　　*　　　　*　　　　*　　　　*

After this it seemed to her that she ceased to live except in the lives of her children, and her days passed so evenly, so monotonously, that she only noticed their flight when one of the old people in Dinwiddie remarked to her with a certain surprise: " You've almost a grown daughter now, Jinny," or " Harry will soon be getting as big as his father. Have you decided where you will send him to college ?" She was not unhappy—had she ever stopped to ask herself the question, she would probably have answered : " If only mother and father were living, I should be perfectly satisfied "; yet in spite of her assurances, there existed deep down in her—so deep that her consciousness had never fully grasped the fact of its presence—a dumb feeling that something was missing out of life, that the actuality was a little less bright, a little less perfect than it had appeared through the rosy glamour of her virgin dreams. Was this " something missing " merely one of the necessary conditions of mortal existence ? Or was there somewhere on the earth that stainless happiness which she had once believed her marriage would bring to her ? " I should be perfectly satisfied if only——" she would some-times say in the night, and then check herself before she had ended the sentence. The lack, real as it was, was still too formless to lend itself to the precision of words; it belonged less to circumstances than to the essential structure of life. And yet, as she put it to herself in her rare moments of de-pression, she had so much to be thankful for ! The children grew stronger as they grew older—since Harry's attack of diphtheria, indeed, there had been no serious illness in the family, and as she approached middle age her terror of ill-ness increased rather than diminished. The children made up for much; they ought to have made up for everything— and yet did they ? There was no visible fault that she could attribute to them. With her temperamental inability to see flaws, she was accustomed to think of them as perfect children, as children whom she would not change, had she the power, by so much as a hair or an outline. They grew up, straight, fine, and fearless, full of the new spirit, eager to test life, to examine facts, possessed by that awakening feeling for truth which had always frightened her a little in Susan. Vaguely, without defining the sensation, she felt that they were growing beyond her, that she could no longer keep up with them, that every year they were leaving her a little farther behind them. They were fond of her, but she understood from something Jenny said one day that they had ceased to be proud of her. It was while they were looking over an old photograph album of Susan's that, coming to a picture of Virginia, taken the week before her wedding, Jenny cried out: "Why, there's mother!" and slipped it out of the page.

"I never saw that before," Lucy said, leaning over with a laugh. "You were so young when you married, mother, and you wore such tight sleeves, and a bustle!"

"Would you ever have believed she was as pretty as that?" asked Jenny, with the unconscious brutality of childhood.

"If you are ever as beautiful as your mother was, you may thank your stars," said Susan dryly. And by the expression in her face Virginia knew that she was thinking, "If that was my child, I'd slap her!"

Harry, who had been stuffing fruit-cake on the sofa—sweets were his weakness—rose suddenly and came over to the group.

"If you are ever as beautiful as she is now, you may thank your stars, Miss Yellow Frisk!" he remarked crushingly.

It was a little thing—so little that it seemed ridiculous to think of it as among the momentous happenings in a life—but with that extraordinary proneness of the little to usurp the significant places of memory, it had become at last one of the important milestones in her experience. At the end, when she forgot everything else, she would not forget Harry's foolish words, nor the look in his indignant boyish face when he uttered them. Until then she had not admitted to herself that there was a difference in her feeling for her children, but with the touch of his sympathetic, not over clean, hand on her shoulder, she knew that she should never again think of the three of them as if they were one in her interest and her love. The girls were good children, dear children—she would have let herself be cut in pieces for either of them had it been necessary—but between Harry and herself there was a different bond, a closer and a deeper dependency, which strengthened almost insensibly as he grew older. Her daughters she loved, but her son, as is the inexplicable way of women, she adored blindly and without wisdom. If it had been possible to ruin him, she would have done so, but, unlike many other sons, he seemed, by virtue of that invincible strength with which he had been born, to be proof against both spoiling and flattery. He was a nice boy even to strangers; even to Susan, with her serene judgment of persons, he appeared a thoroughly nice boy! He was not only a tall, lean, habitually towselled-headed youngster, with a handsome sunburned face and a pair of charming, slightly quizzical blue eyes, but he was, as his teachers and his school reports bore witness, possessed of an intellectual brilliancy which made study as easy, and quite as interesting to him, as play. Unlike his father, he had entered life endowed with a cheerful outlook upon the world, and with that temperament of success which usually but by no means inevitably, accompanies it. Whatever happened, he would make the best of it, he would "get on," and it was impossible to imagine him in any hole so deep that he could not, sooner or later, find the way out of it. The Pendleton and the Treadwell spirits had contributed their best to him. If he derived from Cyrus, or from some obscure strain in Cyrus's ancestry, a wholesome regard for material success, a robust determination to achieve results combined with that hard, clear vision of affairs which makes such achievement easy, he had inherited from Gabriel his genial temper, his charm of manner, and his faith in life, which, though it failed to move mountains, had sweetened and enriched the mere act of living. Though he was less demonstrative than Lucy, who had outgrown the plainness and the reticence of her childhood and was developing into a coquettish, shallow-minded girl, with what Miss Priscilla called " a glib tongue," Virginia learned gradually, in the secret way mothers learn things, that his love for her was, after his ambition, the strongest force in his character. Between him and his father there had existed ever since his babyhood a curious, silent, yet ineradicable hostility. Whether the fault was Oliver's or Harry's—whether the father resented the energy and the initiative of his son, or the son resented the indifference and the self-absorption of his father—Virginia had never discovered. For years she fought against admitting the discord between them. Then, at last, on the occasion of a quarrel, when it was no longer possible to dissemble, she followed Oliver into his study, which had once been the "back parlour," and pleaded with him to show a little patience, a little sympathy, with his son. "He's a boy any father would be proud of——" she finished, almost in tears.

"I know he is," he answered irritably; "but the truth is, he rubs me the wrong way. I suppose the trouble is that you have spoiled him."

"But he isn't spoiled. Everybody says——"

"Oh, everybody!" he murmured disdainfully, with a shrug of his fine shoulders.

He looked back at her with the sombre fire of anger still in his eyes, and she saw, without trying to see, without even knowing that she did see, all the changes that years had wrought in his appearance. Physically, he was a finer animal than he had been when she married him, for time, which had sapped her youth and faded her too delicate bloom, had but added a deeper colour to the warm brown of his skin, a steadier glow to his eyes, a more silvery gloss to his hair. At forty he was a handsomer man than he had been at twenty-five; yet, in spite of this, some virtue had gone out of him—here, too, as in life, "something was missing." The generous impulses, the high heart for adventure, the enthusiasm of youth, and youth's white rage for perfection—where were these? It was as if a rough hand had passed over him, coarsening here, blotting out there, accentuating elsewhere. The slow, insidious devil of compromise had done its work. Once he had made one of the small band of fighters who fight not for advantage, but for the truth; now he stood in that middle place with the safe majority who are "neither for God nor for His enemies." Life had done this to him—life and Virginia. It was not only that he had "grown soft," as he

would have expressed it, nor was it even wholly that he had
grown selfish, for the canker which ate at the roots of his
personality had affected not his character merely, but the very
force of his will.   Though the imperative he obeyed had always
been not " I must," but " I want," his natural loftiness of
purpose might have saved him from the results of his weakness
had he not lost gradually the capacity for successful resistance
with which he had started.   If only in the beginning she had
upheld, not his inclinations, but his convictions; if only she
had sought, not to soothe his weakness, but to stimulate his
strength; if only she had seen for once the thing as it was,
not as it ought to have been——

He was buried in his work now, and there were months
during this year when she appeared hardly to see him, so
engrossed, so self-absorbed had he become.   Sometimes she
would remember, stifling the pang it caused, the nights when
he had written his first plays in Matoaca City, and that he
had made her sit beside him with her sewing because he could
not think if she were out of the room.   Now, he could write
only when he was alone; he hated an interruption so much
that she often let the fire go out rather than open his closed
door to see if it was burning.   If she went in to speak to him,
he laid his pen down and did not take it up again while she
was there.   Yet this change had come so stealthily that it
had hardly affected her happiness.   She had grown accustomed to the difference before she had realized it sufficiently
to suffer.   Sometimes she would say to herself a little wonder-
ingly, " Oliver used to be so romantic;" for with the majority
of women whose marriages have surrendered to an invasion
of the commonplace, she accepted the comfortable theory
that the alteration was due less to circumstances than to the
natural drying of the springs of sentiment in her husband's
character.   Occasionally she would remember with a smile
her three days' jealousy of Abby; but the brevity and the
folly of this had established her the more securely in her
impregnable position of unquestioning belief in him.   She
had started life believing, as the women of her race had
believed for ages before her, that love was a Divine gift which
came but once in a lifetime, and which, coming once, remained
for ever indestructible.   People, of course, grew more prac-

tical and less intense as they left youth farther behind them; and though this misty principle would have dissolved at once had she applied it to herself (for she became more sentimental as she approached middle age), behind any suspicious haziness of generalization there remained always the sacred formula: "Men are different." Once, when a sharp outbreak of the primal force had precipitated a scandal in the home of one of her neighbours, she had remarked to Susan that she was "devoutly thankful that Oliver did not have that side to his nature."

"It must be a disagreeable side to live with," Susan, happily married to John Henry, and blissfully expectant of motherhood, had replied; "but as far as I know, Oliver never had a light fancy for a woman in his life—not even before he was married. I used to tell him that it was because he expected too much. Physical beauty by itself never seemed to attract him—it was the angel in you that he first fell in love with."

A glow of pleasure flushed Virginia's sharpened features, mounting to the thin little curls on her forehead. These little curls, to which she sentimentally clung in spite of the changes in the fashions, were a cause of ceaseless worry to Lucy, who had developed into a "stylish" girl, and would have died sooner than she would have rejected the universal pompadour of the period. It was the single vanity that Virginia had ever permitted herself, this adhering at middle age to the quaint and rather coquettish hairdressing of her girlhood: and Fate had punished her by threading the little curls with grey, while Susan's stiff roll (she had adopted the newer mode) remained bravely flaxen. But Susan was one of those women who, lacking a fine fair skin and defying tradition, are physically at their best between forty and fifty.

"Oliver used to be so romantic," said Virginia, as she had said so often to herself, while the glow paled slowly from her cheeks, leaving them the colour of faded rose-leaves.

"Not so romantic as you were, Jinny."

"Oh, I am still," she laughed softly. "Lucy says I take more interest in her lovers now than she does." And she added after a minute: "Girls are so different to-day from what they used to be—they are so much less sentimental."

"But I thought Lucy was. She has enough flirtations for her age, hasn't she ?"

"She has enough attention, of course—for the funny part is that, though she's only sixteen and not nearly so pretty as Jenny, the men are all crazy, as Miss Willy says, about her. But, somehow, it's different. Lucy enjoys it, but it isn't her life. As for Jenny, she's still too young to have taken shape, I suppose, but she has only one idea in her head, and that is going to college. She never gives a boy a thought."

"That's queer, because she promises already to be the most beautiful girl in Dinwiddie."

"She is beautiful. I am quite sure that it isn't because she is my daughter that I think so. But, all the same, I'm afraid she'll never be as popular as Lucy is. She is so distant and overbearing to men that they are shy of her."

"And you'll let her go to college ?"

"If we can afford it—and now that Oliver hopes to get one of his plays put on, we may have a little more money. But it does seem such a waste to me. I never saw that it could possibly do a woman any good to go to college—though, of course, I always sympathized with your disappointment, dear Susan. Jenny is bent on it now ; but I feel so strongly that it would be better for her to come out in Dinwiddie and go to parties and have attention."

"And does Oliver feel that, too ?"

"Oh, he doesn't care. Jenny is his favourite, and he will let her do anything he thinks she has set her heart on. But he has never put his whole life into the children's as I have done."

"But if she goes, will you be able to send Harry ?"

"Of course, Harry's education must come before everything else—even Oliver realizes that. Do you know, I've hardly bought a match for ten years that I haven't stopped to ask myself if it would take anything from Harry's education. That's why I've gone as shabby as this almost ever since he was born—that and my longing to give the girls a few pretty things."

"You haven't bought a dress for yourself since I can remember. I should think you would wear your clothes out making them over."

The look in Virginia's face showed that the recollection Susan had invoked was not entirely a pleasant one.

" I've done with as little as I could," she answered. " Only once was I really extravagant, and that was when I bought a light blue silk which I didn't have made up until years afterwards when it was dyed black. Dyed things never hold their own," she concluded pensively.

" You are too unselfish—that is your only fault," said Susan impulsively. " I hope they appreciate all you have been to them."

" Oh, they appreciate me," returned Virginia with a laugh. " Harry does, anyhow."

" I believe Harry is your darling, Jinny."

" I try not to make any difference in my feeling—they are all the best children that ever lived—but—Susan, I wouldn't breathe this to anybody on earth but you—I can't help thinking that Harry loves me more than the others do. He— he has so much more patience with me. The girls sometimes laugh at me because I am old-fashioned and behind the times, and I can see that it annoys them because I am ignorant of things which they seem to have been born knowing."

" But it was for their sake that you let yourself go ; you gave up everything else for them from the minute that they were born."

A tear shone in Virginia's eye, and Susan knew, without having it put into words, that a wound somewhere in that gentle heart was still hurting. " I'd like to slap them !" she thought fiercely, and then she said aloud with a manner of cheerful conviction:

" You are a great deal too good for them, Jinny, and some day they will know it."

A longing came over her to take the thin little figure in her arms and shake back into her something of the sparkle and the radiance of her girlhood. Why did beauty fade ? Why did youth grow middle aged ? Above all, why did love and sacrifice so often work their own punishment ?

CHAPTER II

THE PRICE OF COMFORT

VIRGINIA knelt on the cushioned seat in the bay-window of her bedroom, gazing expectantly down on the pavement below. It was her forty-fifth birthday, and she was impatiently waiting for Harry, who was coming home for a few days before going abroad to finish his studies at Oxford. The house was a new, impeccably modern dwelling, produced by a triumph of the utilitarian genius of the first decade of the twentieth century, and Oliver had bought it at a prodigious price a few years after his dramatic success had lifted him from poverty into comfort. The girls, charmed to have made the momentous passage into Sycamore Street, were delighted with the space and elegance of their new home, but Virginia had always felt somehow as if she were visiting. The drawing-room, and especially the butler's pantry, awed her. She had not dared to wash those august shelves with soda, nor to fasten her favourite strips of white oilcloth along their shining surfaces. The old joy of " fixing-up " her storeroom had been wrested from her by the supercilious mulatto butler, who wore immaculate shirt fronts, but whom she suspected of being untidy beneath his magnificent exterior. Once when she had discovered a bucket of apple-parings tucked away under the sink, where it had stood for days, he had given " notice " so unexpectedly and so haughtily that she had been afraid ever since to look under dish-towels or into hidden places while he was absent. Out of the problem of the South " the servant question " had arisen to torment and intimidate the housekeepers of Dinwiddie; and inferior service at high wages was regarded of late as a thing for which one had come to be thankful. Had they still lived in the little house, Virginia would gladly have done her work for the sake of the peace and the cleanliness which it would have ensured; but since the change in their circumstances, Oliver and the girls had grown so dependent upon the small luxuries of living that she put up with anything—even with the appalling suspicion that every mouthful she ate was not clean—rather than take the risk of having her three servants desert in a body. When she had unwisely complained to Oliver, he had remarked impatiently that he couldn't be bothered about the house-keeping, and Lucy had openly accused her of being "fussy."

After this she had said nothing more, but, gathering sud-denly all her energies, she had precipitated a scene with the servants (which ended, to her relief, in the departure of the magnificent butler), and had reorganized at a stroke the affairs of her household. For all her gentleness, she was not incapable of decisive action, and though it had always been easier for her to work herself than to direct others, her native talent for domesticity had enabled her to emerge triumphantly out of this crisis. Now, on her forty-fifth birthday, she could reflect with pride (the pride of a woman who has mastered her traditional *métier de femme*) that there was not a house in Dinwiddie which had better food or smoother service than she provided in hers. For more and more, as Oliver absorbed himself in his work, which kept him in New York many months of the year, and the children grew so big that they no longer needed her, did her life centre around the small monotonous details of cooking and cleaning. Only when, as occasionally happened, the rest of the family were absent together—Oliver about his plays, Lucy on a visit to Richmond, and Harry and Jenny at college—an awful sense of futility descended upon her, and she felt that both the purpose and the initiative were sapped from her character. Sometimes, during such days or weeks of loneliness, she would think of her mother's words, uttered so often in the old years at the rectory: "There isn't any pleasure in making things unless there's somebody to make them for."

Beyond the window, the November day, which had been one of placid contentment for her, was slowly drawing to its close. The pale red line of an autumn sunset lingered in the west above the huddled roofs of the town, while the mournful dusk of evening was creeping up from the earth. A few chilled and silent sparrows hopped dejectedly along the bared boughs of the young maple-tree in front of the house, and every now and then a brisk pedestrian would pass on the concrete pavement below. Inside, a cheerful fire burned in the grate, and near it, on one end of the chintz-covered couch, lay Oliver's present to her—a set of black bear furs, which he had brought down with him from New York. Turning away from the window, she slipped the neck-piece over her shoulders, and as she did so she tried to stifle the wonder whether he would have bought them—whether even he would have remembered the date—if Harry had not been with him. Last year he had forgotten her birthday—and never before had he given her so costly a present as this. They were beautiful furs, but even she, with her ignorance of the subtler arts of dress, saw that they were too heavy for her, that they made her look shrunken and small, and accentuated the pallor of her skin, which had the colour and the texture of withered rose-leaves. "They are just what Jenny has always wanted, and they would be so becoming to her. I wonder if Oliver would mind my letting her take them back to Bryn Mawr after the holidays?"

If Oliver would mind! The phrase still remained after the spirit which sanctified it had long departed. In her heart she knew—though her happiness rested upon her passionate evasion of the knowledge—that Oliver had not only ceased to mind, that he had even ceased to notice whether she wore his gifts or gave them to Jenny.

A light step flitted along the hall; her door opened without shutting again, and Lucy, in a street gown made in the princess style, hurried across the room and turned a slender back appealingly towards her.

"Oh, mother, please unhook me as fast as you can. The Peytons are going to take me in their car over to Richmond, and I've only a half-hour in which to get ready."

Then, as Virginia's hands fumbled a little at an obstinate hook, Lucy gave an impatient pull of her shoulders, and reached back, straining her arms, until she tore the offending fastenings from her dress. She was a small, graceful girl, not particularly pretty, not particularly clever, but possessing some indefinable quality which served her as successfully as either beauty or cleverness could have done. Though she was the most selfish and the least considerate of the three children, Virginia was like wax in her hands, and regarded her dashing, rather cynical, worldliness with naïve and uncomprehending respect. She secretly disapproved of Lucy, but it was a disapproval which was tempered by admiration. It seemed miraculous to her that any girl of twenty-two should possess so clearly formulated and critical a philosophy of life, or should be so utterly emancipated from the last shackles of reverence. As far as her mother could discern, Lucy respected but a single thing, and that single thing was her own opinion. For authority she had as little reverence as a savage; yet she was not a savage, for she represented instead the perfect product of over-civilization. The world was bounded for her by her own presonality. She was supremely interested in what she thought, felt, or imagined, and beyond the limits of her individuality, she was frankly bored by existence. The joys, sorrows, or experiences of others failed even to arrest her attention. Yet the very simplicity and sincerity of her egoism robbed it of offensiveness, and raised it from a trait of character to the dignity of a point of view. The established law of self-sacrifice which had guided her mother's life was not only personally distasteful to her—it was morally indefensible. She was engaged not in illustrating precepts of conduct, but in realizing her independence; and this realization of herself appeared to her as the supreme and peculiar obligation of her being. Though she was less fine than Jenny, who in her studious way was a girl of much character, she was by no means as superficial as she appeared, and might in time, aided by fortuitous circumstances, make a strong and capable woman. Her faults, after all, were due in a large measure to a training which had consistently magnified in her mind the space which she would ultimately occupy in the universe.

And she had charm. Without beauty, without intellect, without culture, she was still able to dominate her surroundings by her inexplicable but undeniable charm. She was one of those women of whom people say, " It is impossible to tell what attracts men in a woman." She was indifferent, she was casual, she was even cruel; yet every male creature she met

fell a victim before her. Her slightest gesture had a fascination for the masculine mind; her silliest words a significance.
"I declare men are the biggest fools where women are concerned," Miss Priscilla had remarked, watching her; and the
words had adequately expressed the opinion of the feminine
half of Dinwiddie's population.

From sixteen to twenty-two she had remained as indifferent
as a star to the impassioned moths flitting around her. Then,
a month after her twenty-second birthday, she had coolly
announced her engagement to a man whom she had seen
but six times—a widower at that, twelve years older than
herself, and the father of two children. The blow had fallen,
without warning, upon Virginia, who had never seen the man,
and did not like what she had heard of him. Unwisely, she
had attempted to remonstrate, and had been met by the
reply, " Mother, dear, you must allow me to decide what is
for my happiness," And a manner which said, " After all, you
know so much less of life than I do, how can you advise me ?"

It was intolerable, of course, and the worst of it was that,
rebel as she might against the admission, Virginia could not
plausibly deny the truth of either the remark or the manner.
On the face of it, Lucy must know best what she wanted, and
as for knowledge of life, she was certainly justified in considering her mother a child beside her. Oliver, when the case
was put before him, showed a sympathy with Virginia's point
of view and a moral inability to coerce his daughter into
accepting it. " She knows I never liked Craven," he said ;
" but, after all, what are we going to do about it ? She's old
enough to decide for herself, and you can't in this century
put a girl on bread and water because she marries as she
chooses."

Nothing about duty ! nothing about consideration for her
family ! nothing about the awful responsibility of entering
lightly into such sacred relations ! Lucy was evidently in
love—if she hadn't been, why on earth should she have precipitated herself into an affair whose only object was a lack
of reason that was conclusive ?—but she might have been
engaging a chauffeur for all the solemnity she put into the
arrangements. She had selected her clothes and planned her
wedding with a practical wisdom which had awed and sad-

dened her mother. All the wistful sentiments, the tender
evasions, the consecrated dreams that had gone into the
preparations for Virginia's marriage, were buried somewhere
under the fragrant past of the eighties; and the memory of
them made her feel not forty-five, but a hundred. Yet the
thing that troubled her most was a feeling that she was in
the power of forces which she did not understand—a sense
that there were profound disturbances beneath the familiar
surface of life.

When Lucy had gone out, with her dress open down the
back and a glimpse of her smooth girlish shoulders showing
between the fastenings, Virginia went over to the window
again, and was rewarded by the sight of Harry's athletic figure
crossing the street.

In a minute he came in, kissing her with the careless tenderness which was one of her secret joys.

"Halloo! little mother! All alone? Where are the
others?" He was the only one of her children who appeared
to enjoy her, and sometimes when they were alone together,
he would turn and put his arms about her, or stroke her hands
with an impulsive, protecting sympathy. There were moments when it seemed to her that he pitied her because the
world had moved on without her; and others when he came
to her for counsel about things of which she was not only
ignorant, but even a little afraid. Once he had consulted her
as to whether he should go in the football team at his college,
and had listened respectfully enough to her timid objections.
Respect, indeed, was the quality in which he had never failed
her, and this, even more than his affection, had become a
balm to her in recent years, when Lucy and Jenny occasionally
lost patience and showed themselves openly amused by her
old-fashioned opinions. She had never forgotten that he
had once taken her part when the girls had tried to persuade
her to brush back the little curls from her temples and wear
her hair in a pompadour.

"It would look so much more suitable for a woman of your
age, mother dear," Lucy had remarked sweetly with a condescending deference which had made Virginia feel as if she
were a thousand.

"And it would be more becoming, too, now that your hair

is turning grey," Jenny had added, with an intention to be kind and helpful which had gone wrong somehow and turned into officiousness.

"Shut up, and don't be silly geese," Harry had growled at them, and his rudeness in her behalf had given Virginia a delicious thrill, which was increased by the knowledge that his manners were usually excellent even to his sisters. "You let them fuss all they want to, mother," he concluded, "but your hair is a long sight better than theirs, and don't you let them nag you into making a mess of it."

All of which had been sweet beyond words to Virginia, though she was obliged to admit that his judgment was founded upon a deplorable lack of discrimination in the matter of hairdressing—since Lucy and Jenny both had magnificent hair, while her own had long since lost its gloss and grown thin from neglect. But if it had been really the truth, it could not have been half so sweet to her.

"Lucy is dressing to motor over to Richmond with the Peytons, and your father went out to ride. Harry, why won't you let me go on to New York to see you off?"

He was sailing the following week for England, and he had forbidden her to come to his boat, or even to New York, for a last glimpse of him.

"Oh, I hate having a scene at the boat, mother. It always makes me feel creepy to say good-bye. I never do it if I can help."

"I know you don't, darling—you sneaked off after the holidays without telling me what train you were going by. But this is for such a long time. Two years, Harry!"

Her voice broke, and turning away, she gazed through the window at the young maple-tree as though her very soul were concentrated upon the leafless boughs.

He stirred uneasily, for, like most men of twenty-one, he had a horror of sentiment.

"Oh, well, you may come over next summer, you know. I'll speak to father about it. If his play goes over to London, he'll have to be there, won't he?"

"I suppose so," she replied, choking down her tears, and becoming suddenly cheerful. "And you'll write to me once a week, Harry?"

"You bet! By the way, I've had nothing to eat since ten o'clock, and I feel rather gone. Have you some cake around anywhere?"

"But we'll have supper in half an hour, and I've ordered waffles and fried chicken for you. Hadn't you better wait?"

Her cheerfulness was not assumed now, for with the turn to practical matters, she felt suddenly that the universe had righted itself. Even Harry's departure was forgotten in the immediate necessity of providing for his appetite.

"Well, I'll wait, but I hope you've prepared for an army. I could eat a hundred waffles."

He snapped his jaws, and she laughed delightedly. For all his twenty-one years, and the scholarship which he had won so easily and which was taking him abroad, he was as boyish and as natural as he had been at ten. Even his love of sweets had not lessened with the increase of his dignity. To think of his demanding cake the minute after he had entered the house!

"Father's play made a great hit," he said presently, still steering carefully away from the reefs of emotion. "I suppose you read all about it in the papers?"

She shook her head, smiling. Though she tried her best to be as natural and as unemotional as he was, she could not keep her adoration out of her eyes, which feasted on him like the eyes of one who had starved for months. How handsome he was, with his broad shoulders, his fine, sunburned face, and his frank, boyish smile! It was a pity he had to wear glasses —yet even his glasses seemed to her individual and charming. She couldn't imagine a single way in which he could be improved, and all the while she was perfectly sure that it wasn't in the least because she was his mother—that she wasn't a bit prejudiced in her judgment. It appeared out of the question that anybody—even a stranger—could have found fault with him. "No, I haven't had time to read the papers; I've been so busy getting ready for Lucy's wedding," she answered. "But your father told me about it. It must be splendid—only I wish he wouldn't speak so contemptuously of it," she added regretfully. "He says it's trash, and yet I'm sure everybody spoke well of it, and they say it is obliged to

make a great deal of money. I can't understand why his
success seems to irritate rather than please him."

"Well, he thinks, you know, that it is only since he's
cheapened himself that he has had any hearing."

"Cheapened himself?" she repeated wistfully. "But his
first plays failed entirely, so these last ones must be a great
deal better if they are such splendid successes."

"Well, I suppose it's hard for us to understand his point
of view. We talked about it one night in New York when we
were dining with Margaret Oldcastle—she takes the leading
part in 'Pretty Fanny,' you know."

"Yes, I know. What is she like?"

A strange, still look come into her face, as though she
waited with suspended breath for his answer.

"She's a charmer on the stage. I heard father tell her
that she made the play, and I'm not sure that he wasn't
right."

"But you saw her off the stage, didn't you?"

"Oh yes, she asked me to dinner. She didn't look nearly
so young, then, and she's not exactly pretty; but, somehow,
it didn't seem to matter. She's got genius—you couldn't
be with her ten minutes without finding out that. I never
saw anyone in my life so much alive. When she's in a room,
even if she doesn't speak, you can't keep your eyes off her.
She's like a bright flame that you can't stop looking at—not
even if there are a lot of prettier women there, too."

"Is she dark or fair?"

He stopped to think for a moment.

"To save my life I can't remember, but I think she's
dark—at least, her eyes are, though her hair may be light.
But you never think of her appearance when she's talking. I
believe she's the best talker I ever heard—better even than
father."

His enthusiasm had got the better of him, and it was evident
that Oliver's success had banished for a time at least the
secret hostility which had existed between father and son.
That passion for material results, which could not be separated
from the Treadwell spirit without robbing that spirit of its
vitality, had gradually altered the family attitude towards
Oliver's profession. Art, like business, must justify itself by

its results, and to a commercial age there could be no justifiable results that could not bear translation into figures. Success was the chief end of man, and success could be measured only in terms of money.

"There's your father's step," said Virginia, whose face looked drawn and pallid in the dusk. "Let me light the lamp, darling. He hates to read his paper by anything but lamplight."

But he had jumped up before she had finished and was hunting for matches in the old place under the clock on the mantel-piece. She was such a little, thin, frail creature that he laughed as she tried to help him.

"So Lucy is going to marry that old rotter, is she?" he asked pleasantly as his father entered. "Well, father! I was just asking mother why she let Lucy marry that old rotter?"

"But the dear child has set her heart on him, and he is really very nice to us," replied Virginia hurriedly. Though she was disappointed in Lucy's choice, it seemed dreadful to her to speak of a man who was about to enter the family as a "rotter."

"You stop it, Harry, if you have the authority. I haven't," answered Oliver carelessly. "Is your neuralgia better, Virginia?"

"It's quite gone, dear. Doctor Powell gave me some aspirin, and it cured it." She smiled gratefully at him, with a touching pleasure in the fact that he had remembered to ask. As she glanced quickly from father to son, eager to see them reconciled, utterly forgetful of herself, something of the anxious cheerfulness of Mrs. Pendleton's spirit appeared to live again in her look. Though her freshness had withered, she was still what is called "a sweet-looking woman," and her expression of simple goodness lent an appealing charm to her features.

"Are you going back to New York soon, father?" asked Harry, turning politely in Oliver's direction. From his manner, which had lost its boyishness, Virginia knew that he was trying with all his energy to be agreeable, yet that he could not overcome the old feeling of constraint and lack of sympathy.

"Next week. 'The Home' is to be put on in February, and I'm obliged to be there for the rehearsals."

"Does Miss Oldcastle take the leading part ?"

"Yes."

Crossing the room, Oliver held out his hands to the fire, and then turning, stretched his arms, with a stifled yawn, above his head. The only fault that could be urged against his appearance was that his figure was becoming a trifle square, that he was beginning to look a little too well-fed, a little too comfortable. For the rest, his hair, which had gone quite grey, brought out the glow and richness of his colour and lent a striking emphasis to his dark, shining eyes.

"Do you think that the new play is as good as 'Pretty Fanny' ?" asked Virginia.

"Well, they're both rot, you know," he answered with a laugh.

"Oh, Oliver, how can you, when all the papers spoke so admiringly of it ?"

"Why shouldn't they ? It is perfectly innocuous. The kind of thing any father might take his daughter to see. We shan't dispute that, anyhow."

His flippancy not only hurt, it confused her. It was painful enough to have him speak so slightingly of his success, but worse than this was the feeling it aroused in her that he was defying authority. Even if her innate respect for the printed word had not made her accept as final the judgment of the newspapers, there was still the incontestable fact that so many people had paid to see "Pretty Fanny" that both Oliver and Miss Oldcastle had reaped a small fortune. She glanced in a helpless way at Harry, and he said suddenly :

"Don't you think Jenny ought to come home to be with mother after Lucy marries ? You are obliged to go to New York so often that she will get lonely."

"It's a good idea," agreed Oliver amiably, " but there's another case where you'll have to use greater authority than mine. When I stopped reforming people," he added gaily, " I began with my own family."

"The dear child would come in a minute if I suggested it," said Virginia; " but she enjoys her life at college so much that I wouldn't have her give it up for anything in the world.

It would make me miserable to think that any of my children made a sacrifice for me."

"You needn't worry. We've trained them differently," said Oliver, and though his tone was slightly satirical, the satire was directed at himself, not at his wife.

"I am sure it is what I should never want," insisted Virginia, almost passionately, while she rose in response to the announcement of supper, and met Lucy, in trailing pink chiffon, on the threshold.

"Are you sure your coat is warm enough, dear?" she asked. "Wouldn't you like to wear my furs? They are heavier than yours."

"Oh, I'd love to, if you wouldn't mind, mother."

Raising herself on tiptoe, Lucy kissed Harry, and then ran to the mirror, eager to see if the black fur looked well on her.

"They're just lovely on me, mother! I feel gorgeous!" she exclaimed triumphantly, and indeed her charming girlish face rose like a white flower out of the rich dark furs.

In Virginia's eyes, as she turned back in the doorway to watch her, there was a radiant self-forgetfulness which illumined her features. For a moment she lived so completely in her daughter's youth that her body seemed to take warmth and colour from the emotion which transfigured her.

"I am so glad, darling," she said. "It gives me more pleasure to see you in them than it does to wear them myself." And though she did not know it, she embodied her gentle philosophy of life in that single sentence.

CHAPTER III

MIDDLE AGE

JENNY had promised to come home a week before Lucy's wedding, but at the last moment, while they waited supper for her, a telegram announced with serious brevity that she was "detained." Twenty-four hours later a second telegram informed them that she would not arrive until the evening before the marriage, and at six o'clock on that day, Virginia, who had been packing Lucy's trunks ever since breakfast, looked out of the window at the sound of the door-bell, and saw the cab which had contained her second daughter standing beside the curbstone.

"Mother, have you the change to pay the driver?" asked a vision of stern loveliness floating into the room. With the winter's glow in her cheeks and eyes and the bronze sheen on her splendid hair, which was brushed in rippling waves from her forehead and coiled in a severely simple knot on her neck, she might have been a wandering goddess, who had descended, with immortal calm, to direct the affairs of the household. Her white shirtwaist, with its starched severity, suited her austere beauty and her look of almost superhuman composure.

"Take off your hat, darling, and lie down on the couch while I finish Lucy's packing," said Virginia, when she had sent the servant downstairs to pay the cabman. Her soul was in her eyes while she watched Jenny remove her plain felt hat, with its bit of blue scarf around the crown—a piece of millinery which presented a deceptive appearance of inexpensiveness—and pass the comb through the shining arch of her hair.

"I am so sorry, mother dear, I couldn't come before, but there were some important lectures I really couldn't afford to miss. I am specializing in biology, you know."

319

Her manner, calm, sweet, and gently condescending, was such as she might have used to a child whom she loved and with whom she possessed an infinite patience. One felt that while talking, she groped almost unconsciously for the simplest and shortest words in which her meaning might be conveyed. She did not lie down as Virginia had suggested, but straightening her short skirt, seated herself in an upright chair by the table and crossed her slender feet in their sensible, square-toed shoes. While she gazed at her, Virginia remembered, with a smile, that Harry had once said his sister was as flawless as a geometrical figure, and he couldn't look at her without wanting to twist her nose out of shape. In spite of her beauty, she was not attractive to men, whom she awed and intimidated by a candid assumption of superiority. For Lucy's conscienceless treatment of the male she had unmitigated contempt. Her sister, indeed, had she not been her sister, would have appeared to her as an object for frank condemnation—" one of those women who waste themselves in foolish flirtations." As it was, loving Lucy, and being a loyal soul, with very scientific ideas of her own responsibility for her sister as well as for that abstract creature whom she classified as " the working woman," she thought of Lucy tenderly as a " dear girl, but simple." Her mother, of course, was also " simple "; but, then, what could one expect of a woman whose only education had been at the Dinwiddie Academy for Young Ladies ? To Jenny, education had usurped the place which the Church had always occupied in the benighted mind of her mother. All the evils of our civilization—and these evils shared with the working woman the first right to her attention—she attributed to the fact that the former generations of women had had either no education at all, or worse even than that, had had the meretricious brand of education which was supplied by an army of Miss Priscillas. For Miss Priscilla herself, entirely apart from the Academy, which she described frankly, to Virginia's horror, as " a menace," she entertained a sincere devotion, and this ability to detach her judgments from her affections made her appear almost miraculously wise to her mother, who had been born a Pendleton.

" No, I'm not tired. Is there anything I can help you

about, mother ?" she asked, for she was a good child and very helpful—the only drawback to her assistance being that when she helped she invariably commanded.

"Oh no, darling, I'll be through presently—just as soon as I get this trunk packed. Lucy's things are lovely! I wish you had come in time to see them. Miss Willy and I spent all yesterday running blue ribbons in her underclothes, and though we began before breakfast, we had to sit up until twelve o'clock so as to get through in time to begin on the trunks this morning."

Her eyes shone as she spoke, and she would have enjoyed describing all Lucy's clothes, for she loved pretty things, though she never bought them for herself, finding it impossible to break the habit of more than twenty years of economy; but Jenny, who was proud of her sincerity, looked so plainly bored that she checked her flowing descriptions.

"I hope you brought something beautiful to wear to-morrow, Jenny ?" she ventured timidly, after a silence.

"Of course I had to get a new dress, as I'm to be maid of honour, but it seemed so extravagant, for I had two perfectly good white chiffons already."

"But it would have hurt Lucy, dear, if you hadn't worn something new. She even wanted me to order my dress from New York, but I was so afraid of wounding poor little Miss Willy—she has made my clothes ever since I could remember—that I persuaded the child to let her make it. Of course, it won't be stylish, but nobody will look at me, anyway."

"I hope it is coloured, mother. You wear black too much. The psychological effect is not good for you."

With her knees on the floor and her back bent over the trunk into which she was packing a dozen pairs of slippers wrapped in tissue paper, Virginia turned her head and stared in bewilderment at her daughter, whose classic profile showed like marble flushed with rose in the lamplight.

"But at my time of life, dear ? Why, I'm in my forty-sixth year."

"But forty-six is still young, mother. That was one of the greatest mistakes women used to make—to imagine that they must be old as soon as men ceased to make love to them.

21

It was all due to the idea that men admired only schoolgirls and that as soon as a woman stopped being admired she had stopped living."

" But they didn't stop living really. They merely stopped fixing up."

" Oh, of course. They spent the rest of their lives in the storeroom or the kitchen slaving for the comfort of the men they could no longer amuse."

This so aptly described Virginia's own situation that her interest in Lucy's trousseau faded abruptly, while a wave of heartsickness swept over her. It was as if the sharp and searching light of truth had fallen suddenly upon all the frail and lovely pretences by which she had helped herself to live and to be happy. A terror of the preternatural insight of youth made her turn her face away from Jenny's too critical eyes.

" But what else could they do, Jenny ? They believed that it was right to step back and make room for the young," she said. with a pitiful attempt at justification of her exploded virtues.

" Oh, mother !" exclaimed Jenny still sweetly, " who ever heard of a man of that generation stepping back to make room for anybody ?"

" But men are different, darling. One doesn't expect them to give up like women."

" Oh, *mother !*"—this time the sweetness had borrowed an edge of irony. It was Science annihilating tradition, and the tougher the tradition the keener the blade which Science must apply.

" I can't help it, dear, it is the way I was taught. My darling mother felt like that "—a tear glistened in her eye— " and I am too old to change my way of thinking."

" Mother, mother, you silly pet !" Rising from her chair, Jenny put her arms about her and kissed her tenderly. " You can't help being old-fashioned, I know. You are not to blame for your ideas; it is Miss Priscilla." Her voice grew stern with condemnation as she uttered the name. " But don't you think you might try to see things a little more rationally ? It is for your own sake I am speaking. Why should you make yourself old by dressing as if you were eighty simply because your grandmother did so ?"

She was right, of course, for the trouble with Science is

not its blindness, but its serene infallibility. As useless to reject her conclusions as to deny the laws and the principles of mathematics ! After all manner of denials, the laws and the principles would still remain. Virginia, who had never argued in her life, did not attempt to do so with her own daughter. She merely accepted the truth of Jenny's inflexible logic; and with that obstinate softness which is an inalienable quality of tradition, went on believing precisely what she had believed before. To have made them think alike, it would have been necessary to melt up the two generations and pour them into one—a task as hopeless as an endeavour to blend the Dinwiddie Young Ladies' Academy with a modern college. Jenny's clearly formulated and rather loud morality was unintelligible to her mother, whose conception of duty was that she should efface herself and make things comfortable for those around her. The obligation to think independently was as incomprehensible to Virginia as was that wider altruism which had swept Jenny's sympathies beyond the home into the factory, and beyond the factory into the world where there were " evils." Her own instinct had always been the true instinct of the lady to avoid " evil," not to seek it ; to avoid it honestly, if possible, and, if not honestly—well, to avoid it any at cost. The love of truth for truth's sake was one of the last of the virtues to descend from philosophy into a working theory of life, and it had been practically unknown to Virginia until Jenny had returned, at the end of her first year, from college. To be sure, Oliver used to talk like that long ago, but it was so long ago that she had almost forgotten it.

" You are very clever, dear—much too clever for me," she said, rising from her knees. " I wonder if Lucy has anything else she wants to go into this trunk ? It might be packed a little tighter."

In response to her call, the door opened and Lucy entered breathlessly, with her hair, which she had washed and not entirely dried, hanging over her shoulders.

" What is it, mother ? Oh, Jenny, you have come ! I'm so glad !"

The sisters kissed delightedly. In spite of their lack of sympathy, they were very fond of each other.

"Do you want to put anything else in this trunk before I lock it, Lucy?"

"Could you find room for my blue flannel bath robe? I'll want it on top where I can get it out without unpacking, and oh, mother, won't you please put my alcohol stove and curling-irons in my travelling bag?"

She was prettily excited, and during the last few days she had shown an almost childlike confidence in her mother's opinions about the trivial matters of packing.

"Mother, I don't want to come down yet—my hair isn't dry. Will you send supper up to me? I'll dress about nine o'clock when Bertie and the girls are coming."

"Of course I will, darling. I'll go straight downstairs and fix your tray. Is there anything you can think of that you would like?"

At this Jenny broke into a laugh. "Why, anybody would think she was dying instead of being married!"

"Just a cup of coffee. I really couldn't swallow a morsel," replied Lucy, whose single manifestation of sentiment had been a complete loss of appetite. "You needn't laugh, Jenny. Wait until you are going to be married, and see if you are able to eat anything."

Putting the tray back into the trunk, Virginia closed it almost caressingly. For twenty-four hours, as Lucy's wedding began to draw nearer, she had been haunted by the feeling that she was losing her favourite child, and though her reason told her that this was not true—that Lucy was, in fact, less fond of her than either of the others, and far less dear to her heart than Harry—still she was unable wholly to banish the impression. It seemed only yesterday that she had sat waiting, month after month, week after week, day after day, for her to be born. Only yesterday that she had held her, a baby, in her arms, and now she was packing the clothes which that baby would carry away when she went off with her husband! Something of the hushed expectancy of those long months of approaching motherhood enveloped her again with the thought of Lucy's wedding to-morrow. After all, Lucy was her first child—neither of the others had been awaited with quite the same brooding ecstasy, with quite the same radiant dreams. To neither of the others had she given herself at the hour of birth with such an abandonment of her soul and body. And she had been a good child—all day with a lump in her throat Virginia had assured herself again and again that no child could have been better. A hundred little charming ways, a hundred bright, delicious tricks of expression and of voice, followed her from room to room, as though Lucy had indeed, as Jenny said, been dying upstairs instead of waiting to be married. And all the time, while she arranged the supper tray and attended to the making of the coffee so that it might be perfect, she was thinking, "Mother must have felt like this when I was married, and I never knew it, I never suspected." She saw her little bedroom at the rectory, with her own figure, in the floating tulle veil, reflected in the mirror, and her mother's face, that face from which all remembrance of self seemed to have vanished, looking at her over the bride's bouquet of white roses. If only she had told her then that she understood! If only she had ever really understood until to-night! If only it was not too late to turn back now and gather that plaintive figure, waiting with the white roses, into her arms!

The next morning she was up at daybreak, finishing the packing, preparing the house before leaving for church, making the final arrangements for the wedding breakfast. When at last Lucy, with reddened eyes and tightly curled hair, appeared in the pantry while her mother was helping to wash a belated supply of glass and china which had arrived from the caterer's, Virginia felt that the parting was worse even than Harry's going to college.

"Mother, I've the greatest mind on earth not to do it."

"My pet, what is the matter?"

"I can't imagine why I ever thought I wanted to marry! I don't want to do it a bit. I don't want to go away and leave you and father. And, mother, I really don't believe that I love him!"

It was so like Lucy after months of cool determination, of perfect assurance, of stubborn resistance to opposition—it was so exactly like her to break down when it was too late and to begin to question whether she really wanted her own way after she had won it. And it was so like Virginia that at the first sign of weakness in her child she should grow suddenly strong and efficient.

"My darling, it is only nervousness. You will be better as soon as you begin to dress. Come upstairs, and I will fix you a dose of aromatic ammonia."

"Do you really think it's too late to stop it ?"

"Not if you feel you are going to regret it; but you must be very sure that it isn't merely a mood, Lucy."

At the first sign that the step was not yet irrevocable the girl's courage returned.

"Well, I suppose I'll have to get married now," she said; "but if I don't like it, I'm not going to live with him."

"Not live with your husband ! Why, Lucy !"

"It's perfectly absurd to think I'll have to live with a man if I find I don't love him. Ask Jenny if it isn't."

Ask Jenny ! This was her incredible suggestion ! This was her reverence for authority, for duty, for the thundering admonitions of Saint Paul ! As far as Saint Paul was concerned, he might as well have been the ponderous anecdotal minister in the brick Presbyterian church around the corner.

"But Jenny is so—so——" murmured Virginia, and stopped because words failed her. Had Jenny been born in any family except her own, she would probably have described her as "dangerous," but it was impossible to brand her daughter with so opprobrious an epithet. The word, owing to the metaphorical yet specific definition of it which she had derived from the rector's sermons in her childhood, invariably suggested fire and brimstone to her imagination.

"Well, I'm not going to do it unless I want to," returned Lucy positively. "And you may look as shocked as you please, mother, but you needn't pretend that you wouldn't be glad to see me."

The difference between the two girls, as far as Virginia could see, was that Jenny really believed her awful ideas were right, and Lucy merely believed that they might help her the more effectively to follow her wishes.

"Of course I'd be glad to see you; but, Lucy, it pains me so to hear you speak flippantly of your marriage. It is the most sacred day in your life, and you treat it as lightly as if it were a picnic."

"Do I ? Poor little day, have I hurt its feelings ?"

They were on the way upstairs, following a procession of wedding presents which had just arrived by express, and glancing round over the heads of the servants, she made a laughing face at her mother. Clearly, she was incorrigible, and her passing fear, which had evidently been entirely due, as Virginia had suspected, to one of her rare attacks of nervousness, had entirely disappeared. In her normal mood she was perfectly capable of taking care of herself not only within the estate of matrimony, but in an African jungle. She would in either situation inevitably get what she wanted, and in order to get it she would shrink as little from sacrificing a husband as from enslaving a savage.

And yet a few hours later, when she stood beneath her bridal veil and gazed at her image in the cheval-glass in her bedroom, she presented so enchanting a picture of virgin innocence that Virginia could hardly believe that she harboured in her breast, under the sacred white satin of her bride's gown, the heretical opinions which she had uttered downstairs in the pantry. Her charming face had attuned its expression so perfectly to the dramatic values of the moment that she appeared, in the words of that sentimental soul, Miss Priscilla, to be listening already to "The Voice that Breathed o'er Eden."

"Doesn't mother look sweet ?" she asked, catching sight of Virginia's face in the mirror. "I love her in pale grey, only she ought to have some flowers."

"I told father to order her a bunch of violets," answered Jenny. "I wonder if he remembered to do it."

A look of pleasure, the first she had worn for days, flitted over Virginia's face. She had all her mother's touching appreciation of insignificant favours, and, perhaps because her pleasure was so excessive, people shrank a little from arousing it. Like most persons who thought perpetually of others, she was not accustomed to being thought of very often in return.

But Oliver had remembered, and when the purple box was brought up to her, and Jenny pinned the violets on her dress, a blush mantled her thin cheeks, and she looked for a moment almost as young and lovely as her daughters. Then

Oliver came after Lucy, and gathering up her train, the girl smiled at her mother and hurried out of the room. At the last minute her qualms appeared suddenly to depart. Whatever happened in the months and years that came afterwards, she had determined to get all she could out of the excitement of the wedding. She had cast no loving glance about the little room, where she was leaving her girlhood behind her; but Virginia, lingering for an instant after the others had gone out, looked with tear-dimmed eyes at the small white bed and the white furniture decorated in roses. She suffered in that minute with an intensity and a depth of feeling that Lucy had never known in the past—that she would never know in the future—for it is given to mothers to live not once, but twice or thrice or as many times as they have children to live for. And the sunlight, entering through the high window, fell very gently on the anxious love in her eyes, on the fading white rose-leaves of her cheeks, and on the silvery mist of curls framing her forehead.

* * * * *

That afternoon, when Lucy had motored off with her husband, and Oliver and Jenny had gone riding together, Virginia went back again into the room and put away the scattered clothes the girl had left. On the bed was the little pillow, with the embroidered slip over a cover of pink satin Virginia had made, and taking it from the bed she put it into one of the boxes which had been left open until the last minute. As she did so, it was as if a miraculous wand was waved over her memory, softening Lucy's image until she appeared to her in all the angelic sweetness and charm of her childhood. Her egoism, her selfishness, her lack of consideration and of reverence, all those faults of an excessive individualism embodied in the girl, vanished so completely that she even forgot they had ever existed. Once again she felt in her breast the burning rapture of young motherhood; once again she gathered her first-born child—hers alone, hers out of the whole world of children !—into her arms. A choking sensation rose in her throat, and, dropping a handful of photographs which she had started to put away, she hurried from the room, as though she were leaving something dead there that she loved.

Downstairs the caterers and the florists were in possession, carting away glass and china, dismantling decorations, and ejecting palms as summarily as though they had come uninvited. The servants were busy sweeping floors and moving chairs and sofas back into place, and in the kitchen the negro cook was placidly beginning preparations for supper. For a time Virginia occupied herself returning the ornaments to the drawing-room mantelpiece, and the illustrated gift-books to the centre table. When this was over she looked about her with the nervous expectancy of a person who has been overwhelmed for months by a multitude of exigent cares, and realized, with a start, that there was nothing for her to do. To-morrow Oliver and Jenny were both going away— he to New York to attend the rehearsals of his play, and she back to finish her year at college—and Virginia would be left in an empty house with all her pressing practical duties suddenly ended.

"You will have such a nice long rest now, mother dear," Lucy had said, as she clung to her before stepping into the car, and Virginia had agreed unthinkingly that a rest for a little while would, perhaps, do her good. Now, turning away from the centre table, where she had laid the last useless volume in place, she walked slowly through the library to the dining-room, and then from the dining-room into the pantry. Here the dishes were all washed, the cup-towels were drying in an orderly row beside the sink, and the two maids and the butler were "drawing a breath" in wooden chairs by the stove.

"There was enough chicken, salad, and ice-cream left for supper, wasn't there, Wotan?"

On being assured that there was enough for a week, she gave a few directions about the distribution of the other food left from the wedding breakfast, and then went out again and into Oliver's study. A feeling of restlessness more acute than any she had ever known kept her walking back and forth between the door and the window, which looked out into a square of garden, where a few lonely sticks protruded out of the discoloured snow on the grass. She had lived for others so long that she had at last lost the power of living for herself.

There was nothing to do to-day; there would be nothing to

do to-morrow; and, unless Jenny came home to be married, there would be nothing to do next year or the years after that. While Oliver was in Dinwiddie, she had, of course, the pleasure of supplying his food and of watching him eat it; but beyond that, even when he sat in the room with her, there was little conversation between them. She herself loved to talk, for she had inherited her mother's ability to keep up a honeyed flow of sound about little things; but she had learned long ago that there were times when her voice, rippling on about nothing, only irritated him, and with her feminine genius for adaptability, she had made a habit of silence. He never spoke to her of his work except in terms of flippant ridicule which pained her, and the supreme topic of the children's school reports had been absent now for many years. Companionship of a mental sort had always been lacking between them, yet so reverently did she still accept the traditional fictions of marriage, that she would have been astonished at the suggestion that a love which could survive the shocks of tragedy might at last fade away from a gradual decline of interest. Nothing had happened. There had been no scenes, no quarrels, no jealousies, no recriminations— merely a gentle, yet deliberate, withdrawal of personalities. He had worshipped her at twenty-two, and now, at forty-seven, there were moments when she realized with a stab of pain that she bored him; but beyond this she had felt no cause for unhappiness, and until the last year no cause even for apprehension. The libertine had always been absent from his nature; and during all the years of their marriage he had, as Susan put it, hardly so much as looked at another woman. Whatever came between them, it would not be physical passion, but a far subtler thing.

Going to his desk, she took up a photograph of Margaret Oldcastle and studied it for a moment—not harshly, not critically, but with a pensive questioning. It was hardly a beautiful face, but in its glowing intellectuality it was the face of a woman of power. So different was the look of noble reticence it wore from that of the conventional type of American actress that, while she gazed at it, Virginia found herself asking vaguely, "I wonder why she went on the stage?" The woman was not a pretty doll—she was not a voluptuous enchantress—the coquetry of the one and the flesh of the other were missing. If the stories Virginia had heard of her were to be trusted, she had come out of poverty not by the easy steps of managers' favours, but by hard work, self-denial, and discipline. Though Virginia had never seen her, she felt instinctively that she was an " honest woman."

And yet why did this face, which had in it none of the charms of the seductress, disturb her so profoundly ? She was too little given to introspection, too accustomed to think always in concrete images, to answer the question; but her intuition, rather than her thought, made her understand dimly that the things she feared in Margaret Oldcastle were the qualities in which she herself was lacking. Whatever power the woman possessed drew its strength and its completeness from a source which Virginia had never recognized as being necessary or even beneficent to love. After all, was it not petty and unjust in her to be hurt by Oliver's friendship for a woman who had been of such tremendous assistance to him in his work ? Had he not said a hundred times that she had succeeded in making his plays popular without making them at the same time ridiculous ?

Putting the photograph back in its place on the desk, she turned away and began walking again over the strip of carpet which led from the door to the window. In the yard the dried stalks of last year's flowers looked so lonely in the midst of the dirty snow, that she felt a sudden impulse of sympathy. Poor things, they had outlived their usefulness. The phrase occurred to her again, and she remembered how often her father had applied it to women whose children had all married and left them.

" Poor Matilda ! She is restless and dissatisfied, and she doesn't understand that it is because she has outlived her usefulness." At that time " poor Matilda " had seemed to her an old woman—but, perhaps, she wasn't in reality much over forty. How soon women grew old a generation ago ! Why, she felt as young to-day as she did the morning on which she was married. She felt as young, and yet her hair was greying, her face was wrinkled, and, like poor Matilda, she had outlived her usefulness. While she stood there that peculiar sensation which comes to women when their youth is over—

the sensation of a changed world—took possession of her. She felt that life was slipping, slipping past her, and that she was left behind like a bit of the sentiment or the law of the last century. Though she still felt young, it was not with the youth of to-day. She had no part in the present; her ideals were the ideals of another period; even her children had outgrown her. She saw now with a piercing flash of insight, so penetrating, so impersonal, that it seemed the result of some outside vision rather than of her own uncritical judgment, that life had treated her as it treats those who give, but never demand. She had made the way too easy for others; she had never exacted of them; she had never held them to the austerity of their ideals. Then the illumination faded as if it had been the malicious act of a demon, and she reproached herself for allowing such thoughts to enter her mind for an instant.

"I don't know what can be the matter with me. I never used to brood. I wonder if it can be my time of life that makes me so nervous and apprehensive?"

For so long she had waited for some definite point of time, for the children to begin school, for them to finish school, for Harry to go off to college, for Lucy to be married, that now, when she realized that there was nothing to expect, nothing to prepare for, her whole nature, with all the multitudinous fibres which had held her being together, seemed suddenly to relax from its tension. To be sure, Oliver would come home for a time at least after his rehearsals were over, Jenny would return for as much of the holidays as her philanthropic duties permitted, and, if she waited long enough, Harry would occasionally pay her a visit. They all loved her; not one of them, she told herself, would intentionally neglect her—but not one of them needed her! She had outlived her usefulness!

The next afternoon, when Oliver and Jenny had driven off to the station, she put on her street clothes, and went out to call on Susan, who lived in a new house in High Street. Mrs. Treadwell, having worn out everybody's patience except Susan's, had died some five years before, and the incorrigible sentimentalists of Dinwiddie—there were many of them—expressed publicly the belief that Cyrus had never been "the same man since his wife's death." As a matter of fact, Cyrus, who had retired from active finance in the same year that he lost Belinda, had missed his business considerably more than he had missed his wife, whose loss, if he had ever analyzed it, would have resolved itself into the absence of somebody to bully. But on the very day that he had retired from work he had begun to age rapidly, and, now standing on Susan's porch, he suggested to Virginia an orange from which every drop of juice had been squeezed. Of late he had taken to giving rather lavishly to churches, with a vague, superstitious hope, perhaps, that he might buy the salvation he had been too busy to work out in other ways. And so acute had become his terror of death, Virginia had heard, that after every attack of dyspepsia he despatched a cheque to the missionary society of the church he attended.

Upstairs, in her bedroom, Susan, who had just come in, was "taking off her things," and she greeted Virginia with a delight which seemed, in some strange way, to be both a balm and a stimulant. One thing, at least, in her life had not altered with middle age, and that was Susan's devotion. She was a large, young, superbly vigorous woman of forty-five, with an abundant energy which overflowed outside of her household in a dozen different directions. She loved John Henry, but she did not love him to the exclusion of other people; she loved her children, but they did not absorb her. There was hardly a charity or a public movement in Dinwiddie in which she did not take a practical interest. She had kept her mind as alert as her body, and the number of books she read had always shocked Virginia a little, who felt that time for reading was obliged to be time subtracted from more important duties.

"I've thought of you so much, Jinny darling. You mustn't let yourself begin to feel lonely."

Virginia shook her head with a smile; but in spite of her effort not to appear depressed, there was a touching wistfulness in her eyes.

"Of course, I miss the dear children; but I'm so thankful that they are happy."

"I wish Jenny would come back home to stay with you."

"She would if I asked her, Susan"—her face showed her pleasure at the thought of Jenny's willingness for the sacrifice

—" but I wouldn't have her do it for the world. She's so different from Lucy, who was quite happy as long as she could have attention and go to parties. Of course, it seems to me more natural for a girl to be like that, especially a Southern girl; but Jenny says that she is obliged to have something to think about besides men. I wonder what my dear father would have thought of her ?"

" She'll take you by surprise some day, and marry as suddenly as Lucy did."

" That's what Oliver says, but Miss Priscilla is sure she'll be an old maid, because she's so fastidious. It's funny how much more women exact of men now than they used to. Don't you remember what a heroine the women of Miss Priscilla's generation thought Mrs. Tom Peachey was because she supported Major Peachey by taking boarders while he just drank himself into his grave ? Well, somebody mentioned that to Jenny the other day, and she said it was ' disgusting.' "

" I always thought so," said Susan, " but, Jinny, I'm more interested in you than I am in Mrs. Peachey. What are you going to do with yourself ?" Almost unconsciously both had eliminated Oliver as the dominant figure in Virginia's future.

" I don't know, dear. I wish my children were as young as yours. Bessie is just six, isn't she ?"

" You ought to have had a dozen children. Didn't you realize that Nature intended you to do it ?"

" I know "—a pensive look came into her face—" but we were very poor, and after the three came so quickly, and the little one that I lost, Oliver felt that we could not afford to have any others. I've so often thought that I was never really happy except when I had a baby in my arms."

" It's a devilish trick of Nature's that she makes them stop coming at the very time that you want them most. Forty-five is not much more than half a lifetime, Jinny."

" And when one has lived in their children as I have done, of course, one feels a little bit lost without them. Then, if Oliver were not obliged to be away so much——"

Her voice broke, and Susan, leaning forward impulsively, put her arms about her.

" Jinny darling, I never saw you depressed before."

" I was never like this until to-day. It must be the weather —or my age. I suppose I shall get over it."

" Of course you will get over it; but you mustn't let it grow on you. You mustn't be too much alone."

"How can I help it ? Oliver will be away almost all winter, and when he is at home, he is so absorbed in his work that he sometimes doesn't speak for days. Of course, it isn't his fault," she added hastily; "it is the only way he can write."

" And you're alone now for the first time for twenty-five years. That's why you feel it so keenly."

The look of unselfish goodness which made Virginia's face almost beautiful at times passed like an edge of light across her eyes and mouth. "Don't worry about me, Susan. I'll get used to it."

" You will, dear, but it isn't right. I wish Harry could have stayed in Dinwiddie. He would have been such a comfort to you."

"But I wouldn't have had him do it! The boy is so brilliant. He has a future before him. Already he has had several articles accepted by the magazines "—her face shone— " and I hope that he will some day be as successful as Oliver has been without going through the long struggle."

" Can't you go to England to see him in the summer ?"

" That's what I want to do." It was touching to see how her animation and interest revived when she began talking of Harry. " And when Oliver's play is put on in February, he has promised to take me to New York for the first night."

"I am glad of that. But, meanwhile, you mustn't sit at home and think too much, Jinny. It isn't good for you. Can't you find an interest ? If you would only take up reading again. You used to be fond of it."

" I know, but one gets out of the habit. I gave it up after the children came, when there was so much that was really important for me to do, and now, to save my life, I can't get interested in a book except for an hour or two at a time. I'm always stopping to ask myself if I'm not neglecting something, just as I used to do while the children were little. You see, I'm not a clever woman like you. I was made just to be a wife and mother, and nothing else."

"But you're obliged to be something else now. You are only forty-five. There may be forty more years ahead of you, and you can't go on being a mother every minute of your time. Even if you have grandchildren, they won't be like your own. You can't slave over them in the way you used to do over yours. The girls' husbands and Harry's wife would have something to say about it."

"Do you know, Susan, I try not to be little and jealous, but when you said 'Harry's wife' so carelessly just now it brought a lump to my throat."

"He will marry some day, darling, and you might as well accustom yourself to the thought."

"I know, and I want him to do it. I shall love his wife as if she were my daughter; but—but it seems to me at this minute as if I could not bear it!"

The grey twilight, entering through the high window above her head, enveloped her as tenderly as if it were the atmosphere of those romantic early eighties to which she belonged. The small, aristocratic head, with its quaint, old-fashioned clusters of curls on the temples, the delicate stooping figure, a little bent in the chest, the whole pensive, exquisite personality which expressed itself in that manner of gentle self-effacement—these things spoke to Susan's heart, through the softness of the dusk, with all the touching appeal of the past. It was as if the inscrutable enigma of time waited there, shrouded in mystery, for a solution which would make clear the meaning of the blighted promises of life. She saw herself and Virginia on that May afternoon twenty-five years ago, standing with eager hearts on the edge of the future; she saw them waiting, with breathless, expectant lips, for the miracle that must happen! Well, the miracle had happened, and like the majority of miracles, it had descended in the act of occurrence from the zone of the miraculous into the region of the ordinary. This was life, and looking back from middle age, she felt no impulse to regret the rapturous certainties of youth. Experience, though it contained an inevitable pang, was better than ignorance. It was good to have been young; it was good to be middle-aged; and it would be good to be old. For she was one of those who loved life, not because it was beautiful, but because it was life.

" I must go," said Virginia, rising in the aimless way of a person who is not moving toward a definite object.

" Stay and have supper with us, Jinny. John Henry will take you home afterward."

" I can't, dear. The—the servants are expecting me."

She kissed Susan on the cheek, and taking up her little black silk bag, turned to the door.

" Jinny, if I come by for you to-morrow, will you go with me to a board meeting or two ? Couldn't you possibly take an interest in some charity ?" It was a desperate move, but at the moment she could think of no other to make.

" Oh, I am interested, Susan ; but I have no executive ability, you know. And—and, then, poor dear father used to have such a horror of women who were always running about to meetings. He would never even let mother do church work—except, of course, when there was a cake sale or a fair of the missionary society."

Susan's last effort had failed, and as she followed Virginia downstairs and to the front door, a look almost of gloom settled on her large cheerful face.

" Try to pay some calls every afternoon, won't you, dear ?" she said at the door. " I'll come in to see you in the morning when we get back from marketing."

Then she added softly : " If you are ever lonesome and want me, telephone for me day or night. There's nothing on earth I wouldn't do for you, Jinny."

Virginia's eyes were wonderful with love and gratitude as they shone on her through the twilight. " We've been friends since we were two years old, Susan, and, do you know, there is nobody in the world that I would ask anything of as soon as I would of you."

A look of unutterable understanding and fidelity passed between them; then, turning silently away, Virginia descended the steps and walked quickly along the path to the pavement, while Susan, after watching her through the gate, shut the door and went upstairs to the nursery.

The town lay under a thin crust of snow, which was beginning to melt in the chill rain that was falling. Raising her umbrella, Virginia picked her way carefully over the icy streets, and Miss Priscilla, who was looking in search of diversion out of her front window, had a sudden palpitation of the heart because it seemed to her for a minute that " Lucy Pendleton had returned to life." So one generation of gentle shades after another had moved in the winter's dusk under the frosted lamps of High Street.

Through the windows of her house a cheerful light streamed out upon the piles of melting snow in the yard, and at the door one of her coloured servants met her with the news that a telegram was on the hall table. Before opening it she knew what it was, for Oliver's correspondence with her had taken this form for more than a year.

" Arrived safely. Very busy. Call on John Henry if you need anything."

She put it down and turned hastily to letters from Harry and Jenny. The first was only a scrawl in pencil, written with that boyish reticence which always overcame Harry when he wrote to one of his family; but beneath the stilted phrases she could read his homesickness and his longing for her in every line.

" Poor boy, I am afraid he is lonely," she thought, and caressed the paper as tenderly as if it had been the letter of a lover. He had written to her every Sunday since he had first gone off to college, and several times she knew that he had denied himself a pleasure in order to send her her weekly letter. Already she had begun to trust to his " sense of responsibility " as she had never, even in the early days of her marriage, trusted to Oliver's.

Opening the large square envelope which was addressed in Jenny's impressive handwriting, she found four closely written pages entertainingly descriptive of the girl's journey back to college and of the urgent interests she found awaiting her there. In this letter there was none of the weakness of implied sentiment, there was none of the plaintive homesickness she had read in Harry's. Jenny wrote regularly and affectionately because she felt that it was her duty to do so, for, unlike Lucy, who was heard from only when she wanted something, she was a girl who obeyed sedulously the promptings of her conscience. But if she loved her mother, she was plainly not interested in her. Her attitude towards life was masculine rather than feminine; and Virginia had long since learned that in the case of a man it is easier to inspire love than it is to hold his attention. Harry was different, of course—there was a feminine, or at least a poetic, streak in him which endowed him with that natural talent for the affections which is supposed to be womanly; but Jenny resembled Oliver in her preference for the active rather than for the passive side of experience.

Going upstairs, Virginia took off her hat and coat, and, without changing her dress, came down again with a piece of fancy-work in her hands. Placing herself under the lamp in Oliver's study, she took a few careful stitches in the centre-piece she was embroidering for Lucy, and then letting her needle fall, sat gazing into the wood-fire which crackled softly on the brass andirons. From the lamp on the desk an amber glow fell on the dull red of the leather-covered furniture, on the pale brown of the walls, on the rich blending of Oriental colours in the rug at her feet. It was the most comfortable room in the house, and for that reason she had fallen into the habit of using it when Oliver was away. Then, too, his personality had impressed itself so ineffaceably upon the surroundings which he had chosen and amid which he had worked, that she felt nearer to him while she sat in his favourite chair, breathing the scent of the wood-fire he loved.

She thought of the "dear children," of how pleased she was that they were all well and happy, of how "sweet" Harry and Jenny were about writing to her; and so unaccustomed was she to thinking in the first person, that not until she took up her embroidery again and applied her needle to the centre of a flower, did she find herself saying aloud: "I must send for Miss Willy to-morrow and engage her for next week. That will be something to do."

And looking ahead she saw days of endless stitching and basting, of endless gossip accompanied by the cheerful whirring of the little dressmaker's machine. "I used to pity Miss Willy because she was obliged to work," she thought with surprise, "but now I almost envy her. I wonder if it is work that keeps her so young and brisk? She's never had anything in her life, and yet she is so much happier than some people who have had everything."

The maid came to announce supper, and, gathering up her

fancy-work, Virginia laid it beside the lamp on the end of Oliver's writing-table. As she did so, she saw that her photograph, taken the year of her marriage, which he usually carried on his journeys, had been laid aside and overlooked when he was packing his papers. It was the first time he had forgotten it, and a little chill struck her heart as she put it back in its place beside the bronze letter rack. Then the chill sharpened suddenly until it became an icy blade in her breast, for she saw that the picture of Margaret Oldcastle was gone from its frame.

CHAPTER IV

LIFE'S CRUELTIES

THERE was a hard snowstorm on the day Oliver returned to Dinwiddie, and Virginia, who had watched from the window all the afternoon, saw him crossing the street through a whirl of feathery flakes. The wind drove violently against him, but he appeared almost unconscious of it, so buoyant, so full of physical energy was his walk. Never had he looked more desirable to her, never more lovable, than he did at that instant. Something, either a trick of imagination or an illusion produced by the flying whiteness of the storm, gave him back for a moment the glowing eyes and the eager lips of his youth. Then, as she turned towards the door, awaiting his step on the stairs, the mirror over the mantel showed her her own face, with its fallen lines, its soft pallor, its look of fading sweetness. She had laid her youth down on the altar of her love, while he had used love, as he had used life, merely to feed the flame of the unconquerable egoism which burned like genius within him.

He came in, brushing a few flakes of snow from his sleeve, and it seemed to her that the casual kindness of his kiss fell like ice on her cheek as he greeted her. It was almost three months since he had seen her, for he had been unable to come home for Christmas, but from his manner he might have parted from her only yesterday. He was kind—he had never been kinder—but she would have preferred that he should strike her.

"Are you all right?" he asked gently, turning to warm his hands at the fire. "Beastly cold, isn't it?"

"Oh yes, I am all right, dear. The play is a great success, isn't it?"

His face clouded. "As such things go. It's awful rot, but it's made a hit—there's no doubt of that."

"And the other one, 'The Home'—when is the first night of that?"

"Next week. On Thursday. I must get back for it."

"And I am to go with you, am I not? I have looked forward to it all winter."

At the sound of her anxious question, a contraction of pain, the look of one who has been touched on the raw, crossed his face. Though she was not penetrating enough to discern it, there were times when his pity for her amounted almost to a passion, and at such moments he was conscious of a blind anger against Life, as against some implacable personal force, because it had robbed him of the hard and narrow morality on which his ancestors leaned. The scourge of a creed which had kept even Cyrus walking humbly in the straight and flinty road of Calvinism, appeared to him in such rare instants as one of the spiritual luxuries which a rationalistic age had destroyed; for it is not granted to man to look into the heart of another, and so he was ignorant alike of the sanctities and the passions of Cyrus's soul. What he felt was merely that the breaking of the iron bonds of the old faith had weakened his powers of resistance as inevitably as it had liberated his thought. The sound of his own rebellion was in his ears, and, filled with the noise of it, he had not stopped to reflect that the rebellion of his ancestors had seemed less loud only because it was inarticulate. Was it really that his generation had lost the capacity for endurance, the spiritual grace of self-denial, or was it simply that it had lost its reticence and its secrecy with the passing of its inflexible dogmas?

"Why, certainly you must go if you would care to," he answered.

"Perhaps Jenny will come over from Bryn Mawr to join us. The dear child was so disappointed that she couldn't come home for Christmas."

"If I'd known in time that she wasn't coming, I'd have found a way of getting down just for dinner with you. I hope you weren't alone, Virginia."

"Oh no; Miss Priscilla came to spend the day with me.

You know she used to take dinner with us every Christmas at the rectory."

A troubled look clouded his face. " Jenny ought to have been here," he said ; and asked suddenly, as if it were a relief to him to change the subject : " Have you had news of Harry ?"

The-light which the name of Harry always brought to her eyes shone there now, enriching their faded beauty. " He writes to me every week. You know he hasn't missed a single Sunday letter since he first went off to school. He is wild about Oxford, but I think he gets a little homesick sometimes, though of course he'd never say so."

" He'll do well, that boy. The stuff is in him."

" I'm sure he's a genius if there ever was one, Oliver. Only yesterday Professor Trimble was telling me that Harry was far and away the most brilliant pupil he had ever had."

" Well, he's something to be proud of. And now what about Lucy ? Is she still satisfied with Craven ?"

" She never writes about anything else except about her house. Her marriage seems to have turned out beautifully. You remember I wrote you that she was perfectly delighted with her stepchildren, and she really appears to be as happy as the day is long."

" You never can tell. I thought she'd be back again before two months were up."

" I know. We all prophesied dreadful things—even Susan."

" That reminds me, I came down on the train with John Henry, and he said that Uncle Cyrus was breaking rapidly."

" He has never been the same since his wife's death," replied Virginia, who was a victim of this sentimental fallacy. " It's strange, isn't it ?—because we used to think they got on so badly."

" I wonder if it is really that ? Well, is there any other news ? Has anything else happened ?"

With his back to the fire, he stood looking down on her with kindly, questioning eyes. He had done his best; from the moment when he had entered the room and met the touching brightness in her face, he had struggled to be as natural, to be as affectionate even, as she desired. At the moment, so softened, so self-reproachful was his mood, he would willingly have cut off his arm for her could the sacrifice in any manner have secured her happiness. But there were times when it seemed easier to give his life for her than to live it with her; when to shed his blood would have cost less than to make conversation. He yearned over Virginia, but he could not talk to her. Some impregnable barrier of personality separated them as if it were a wall. Already they belonged to different generations; they spoke in the language of different periods. At forty-seven, that second youth, the Indian summer of the emotions, which lingers like autumnal sunshine in the lives of most men and of a few women, was again enkindling his heart. And with this return of youth, he felt the awakening of infinite possibilities of feeling, of the ancient ineradicable belief that happiness lies in possession. Love, which had used up her spirit and body in its service, had left him untouched by its exactions. While she, having fulfilled her nature, was content to live anew not in herself, but in her children, the force of personal desire was sweeping over him again, with all the flame and splendour of adolescence. The "something missing" waited there, just a little beyond, as he had seen it waiting in that enchanted May when he fell in love with Virginia. And between him and his vision of happiness there interposed merely his undisciplined conscience, his variable, though honest, desire to do the thing that was right. Duty, which had controlled Virginia's every step, was as remote and aloof from his life as was the creed of his fathers. Like his age, he was adrift among disestablished beliefs, among floating wrecks of what had once been rules of conduct by which men had lived. And the widening responsibilities, the deepening consciousness of a force for good greater than creed or rules, all the awakening moral strength which would lend balance and power to his age, these things had been weakened in his character by the indomitable egoism which had ordered his life. There was nothing for him to fall back upon, nothing that he could place above the restless surge of his will.

Sitting there in the firelight, with her loving eyes following his movements, she told him, bit by bit, all the latest gossip of Dinwiddie. Sudan's eldest girl had developed a beautiful

voice and was beginning to take lessons ; poor Miss Priscilla
had had a bad fall in Old Street while she was on the way
to market, and at first they feared she had broken her hip,
but it turned out that she was only dreadfully bruised; Major
Peachey had died very suddenly and she had felt obliged to
go to his funeral; Abby Goode had been home on a visit and
everybody said she didn't look a day over twenty-five, though
she was every bit of forty-four. Then, taking a little pile of
samples from her work-basket which stood on the table, she
showed him a piece of black brocaded satin. " Miss Willy
is making me a dress out of this to wear in New York with
you. I don't suppose you noticed whether or not they were
wearing brocade."

No, he hadn't noticed, but the sample was very pretty, he
thought. " Why don't you buy a dress there, Virginia ?
It would save you so much trouble."

" Poor little Miss Willy has set her heart on making it,
Oliver. And, besides, I shan't have time if we go only the
day before."

A flush had come to her face; at the corners of her mouth
a tender little smile rippled; and her look of faded sweetness
gave place for an instant to the warmth and the animation
of girlhood. But the excitement of girlhood could not restore
to her the freshness of youth. Her pleasure was the pleasure
of middle age; the wistful expectancy in her face was the
expectancy of one whose interests are centred on little things.
That inviolable quality of self-sacrifice, the quality which
knit her soul to the enduring soul of her race, had enabled
her to find happiness in the simple act of renouncement.
The quiet years had kept undiminished the inordinate
capacity for enjoyment, the exaggerated appreciation of
trivial favours, which had filled Mrs. Pendleton's life with a
flutter of thankfulness; and while Virginia smoothed the
piece of black brocade on her knee, she might have been the
rearisen pensive spirit of her mother. Of the two, perhaps
because she had ceased to wish for anything for herself, she
was happier than Oliver.

All through dinner, while her soft, anxious eyes dwelt on
him over the bowl of pink roses in the centre of the table,
he tried hard to throw himself into her narrow life, to talk

only of things in which he felt that she was interested. Slight as the effort was, he could see her gratitude in her face, could hear it in the gentle, silvery sound of her voice. When he praised the dinner, she blushed like a girl; when he made her describe the dress which Miss Willy was making, she grew as excited as if she had been speaking of the sacred white satin she had worn as a bride. So little was needed to make her happy—that was the pathos ! She was satisfied with the crumbs of life, and yet they were denied her. Though she had been alone ever since Lucy's wedding, she accepted his belated visit as thankfully as if it were a gratuitous gift. " It is so good of you to come down, dear, when you are needed every minute in New York," she murmured, with a caressing touch on his arm, and, looking at her, he was reminded of Mrs. Pendleton's tremulous pleasure in the sweets that came to her on little trays from her neighbours. Once she had said eagerly: " It will be so nice to see Miss Oldcastle, Oliver," and he had answered in a constrained tone, which he tried to make light and casual, " I am not sure that the part is going to suit her."

Then he had changed the subject abruptly by rising from the table and asking her to let him see her latest letter from Harry.

The next morning he went out after breakfast to consult Cyrus about some investments, while Virginia laid out the lengths of brocade on the bed in the spare room, and sat down to wait for the arrival of the dressmaker. Outside, the trees were still white from the storm, and the wind, blowing through them, made a dry, crackling sound as if it were rattling thorns in a forest. Though it was intensely cold, the sunshine fell in golden bars over the pavement and filled the town with a dazzling brilliancy through which the little seamstress was seen presently making her way. Alert, bird-like, consumed with her insatiable interest in other people, she entered, after she had removed her bonnet and wraps, and began to spread out her patterns. It was twenty-odd years since she had made the white satin dress in which Virginia was married, yet she looked hardly a day older than she had done when she knelt at the girl's feet and envied her happiness while she pinned up the shining train. Failing love, she had filled her life with an inextinguishable curiosity; and this passion, being independent of the desires of others, was proof alike against disillusionment and the destructive processes of time.

"So Mr. Treadwell has come home," she remarked, with a tentative flourish of the scissors. "I declare he gets handsomer every day that he lives. It suits him somehow to fill out, or it may be that I'm partial to fat like my poor mother before me."

"He does look well, but I'd hardly call him fat, would you?"

"Well, he's stouter than he used to be, anyway. Did he say when he was going to take you back with him?"

"Next Wednesday. We'll have to hurry to get this dress ready in time."

"I'll start right in at it. Have you made up your mind whether you'll have it princess or a separate waist and skirt?"

"I'm a little too thin for a princess gown, don't you think? Hadn't I better have it made like that black poplin which everybody thought looked so well on me?"

"But it ain't half so stylish as the princess. You just let me put a few cambric ruffles inside the bust and you'll stand out a plenty. I was reading in a fashion sheet only yesterday that they are trying to look as flat as they can manage in Paris."

"Well, I'll try it," murmured Virginia uncertainly, for her standards of dress were so vague that she was thankful to be able to rely on Miss Willy's self-constituted authority.

"You just leave it to me," was the dressmaker's reply, while she thrust the point of the scissors into the gleaming brocade on the bed.

The morning passed so quickly amid cutting, basting, and gossip, that it came as a surprise to Virginia when she heard the front door open and shut and Oliver's rapid step mounting the stairs. Meeting him in the hall, she led the way into her bedroom, and asked with the caressing, slightly conciliatory manner which expressed so perfectly her attitude toward life:

"Did you see Uncle Cyrus?"

"Yes, and he was nicer than I have ever known him to be. By the way, Virginia, I've transferred enough property to you to bring you in a separate income. This was really what I went down about."

"But what is the matter, dear? Don't you feel well? Have you had any worries that you haven't told me?"

"Oh, I'm all right; but it's better so in case something should happen."

"But what could possibly happen? I never saw you look better. Miss Willy was just saying so."

He turned away, not impatiently, but as one who is seeking to hide an emotion which has become too strong. Then, without replying to her question, he muttered something about "a number of letters to write before dinner," and hurried out of the room and downstairs to his study.

"I wonder if he has lost money," she thought, vaguely troubled, as she instinctively straightened the brushes he had disarranged on the bureau. "Poor Oliver! He seems to think about nothing but money now, and he used to be so romantic."

He used to be so romantic! She repeated this to Susan that evening when, after Miss Willy's departure for the night, she took her friend into the spare room to show her the first shapings of the princess gown.

"Do you remember that we used to call him an incurable Don Quixote?" she asked. "And now he has become so different that at times it makes me smile to think of him as he was when I first knew him. I suppose it's better so, it's more normal. He used to be what Uncle Cyrus called 'flighty,' bent on reforming the world and on improving people, you know, and now he doesn't seem to care whether outside things are good or bad, just as long as his plays go well and he can give us all the money we want."

"It's natural, isn't it?" asked Susan. "One can't stay young for ever, you see."

"And yet in some ways he doesn't appear to be a bit older. I like his hair being grey, don't you? It makes his colour look even richer than before."

"Yes," said Susan, "I like his hair and I like him. Only I wish he didn't have to leave you by yourself so much of the time."

"He is going to take me back with him on Wednesday.

Miss Willy is making this dress for me to wear. I want to look nice because, of course, everybody will be noticing Oliver."

"It's lovely, and I'm sure you'll look as sweet as the angel that you are, Jinny," answered Susan, stooping to kiss her.

By Tuesday night the dress was finished, and Virginia was stuffing the sleeves with tissue paper before packing it into her trunk, when Oliver came into the room and stood watching her in silence.

"I do hope it won't get crumpled," she said anxiously as she spread a towel over the tray. "Miss Willy is so proud of it, and I don't believe I could have got anything prettier in New York."

"Virginia," he said suddenly, "you've set your heart on going to-morrow, haven't you?"

Turning from the trunk, she looked up at him with a tender, inquiring smile. Above her head the electric light, with which Oliver and the girls had insisted on replacing the gas-jets that she preferred, cast a hard glitter over the hollowed lines of her face and over the thinning curls which she had striven to brush back from her temples. Her figure, unassisted as yet by Miss Willy's ruffles, looked so fragile in the pitiless glare that his heart melted in one of those waves of sentimentality which, because they were impotent to affect his conduct, cost him so little. As she stood there, he realized more acutely than he had ever done before how utterly stationary she had remained since he married her. With her sweetness, her humility, her old-fashioned courtesy and consideration for others, she belonged still in the honey-scented twilight of the eighties. While he had moved with the world, she, who was confirmed in the traditions of another age, had never altered in spirit since that ecstatic moment when he had first loved her. The charm, the grace, the virtues, even the look of gentle goodness which had won his heart, were all there just as they had been when she was twenty. Except for the fading flesh, the woman had not changed; only the needs and the desires of the man were different. Only the resurgent youth in him was again demanding youth for its mate.

"Why, my trunk is all packed," she replied. "Has anything happened?"

"Oh no ; I was only wondering how you would manage to amuse yourself. You know I shall be at the theatre most of the time."

"But you mustn't have me on your mind a minute, Oliver. I won't go a step unless you promise me not to worry about me a bit. It's all so new to me that I shall enjoy just sitting in the hotel and watching the people."

"Then we'd better go to the Waldorf. That might interest you more."

His eagerness to provide entertainment for her, touched her as deeply as if it had been a proof of his love instead of his anxiety, and she determined in her heart that if she were lonesome a minute he must never suspect it. Ennui, having its roots in an egoism she did not possess, was unknown to her.

"That will be lovely, dear. Lucy wrote me when she was there on her wedding trip that she used to sit for hours in the corridor looking at the people that went by, and that it was as good as a play."

"That settles it. I'll telegraph for rooms," he said cheerfully, relieved to find that she fell in so readily with his suggestion.

She was giving a last caressing pat to the tray before closing the trunk, and the look of her thin hands, with their slightly swollen knuckles, caused him to lean forward suddenly and wrest the keys away from her.

"Let me do that. I hate to see you stooping," he said.

The telegram was sent, and late the next evening, as they rolled through the brilliant streets towards the hotel, Virginia's interest was as effervescent as if she were indeed the girl that she almost felt herself to have become. The sound of the streets excited her like martial music, and little gasps of surprise and pleasure broke from her lips as the taxicab turned into Broadway. It was all so different from her other visit when she had come alone to find Oliver, sick with failure, in the dismal bedroom of that hotel. Now it seemed to her that the city had grown younger, that it was more awake, that it was brighter, gayer, and that she herself had a part in its brightness and its gaiety. The crowds on Broadway seemed keeping step to some happy tune, and she felt that her heart was dancing with them, so elated, so girlishly irresponsible was her mood.

"Why, Oliver, there is a sign of your play with a picture of Miss Oldcastle on it!" she exclaimed delightedly, pointing to an advertisement before a theatre they were passing. Then, suddenly, it appeared to her that the whole city was waving this advertisement. Wherever she turned "The Home" stared back at her, an orgy of red and blue surrounding the smiling effigy of the actress. And this proof of Oliver's fame thrilled her as she had not been thrilled since the telegram had come announcing that Harry had won the scholarship which would take him to Oxford. The woman's power of sinking her ambition and even her identity into the activities of the man was deeply interwoven with all that was essential and permanent in her soul. Her keenest joys, as well as her sharpest sorrows, had never belonged to herself, but to others. It was doubtful, indeed, if, since the day of her marriage, she had been profoundly moved by any feeling which was centred merely in a personal desire. She had wanted things for Oliver and for the children, but for herself there had been no separate existence apart from them.

"Oliver, I never dreamed that it would be like this. The play will be a great success—even a greater one than the last, won't it, dear?" Her face, with its exquisite look of exaltation, of self-forgetfulness, was turned eagerly towards the crowd of feverish pleasure-seekers that passed on, pursuing its little joys, under the garish signs of the street.

"Well, it ought to be," he returned; "it's bad enough anyway."

His eyes, like hers, were fixed on the thronging streets, but, unlike hers, they reflected the restless animation, the pathetic hunger, which made each of those passing faces appear to be the plastic medium of an insatiable craving for life. Handsome, well preserved, a little over coloured, a little square of figure, with his look of worldly importance, of assured material success, he stood to-day, as Cyrus had stood a quarter of a century ago, as an imposing example of that Treadwell spirit from which his youth had revolted.

That night, when they had finished dinner, and Oliver, in response to a telephone message, had hurried down to the theatre, Virginia went upstairs to her room, and, after putting on the lavender silk dressing-gown which Miss Willy had made for the occasion, sat down to write her weekly letter to Harry.

"MY DARLING BOY,

"I know you will be surprised to see from this letter that I am really in New York at last—and at the Waldorf! It seems almost like a dream to me, and whenever I shut my eyes, I find myself forgetting that I am not in Dinwiddie; but, you remember, your father had always promised me that I should come for the first night of his new play, which will be acted to-morrow. You simply can't imagine till you get here how famous he is and how interested people are in everything about him, even the smallest trifles. Wherever you look you see advertisements of his plays (he has three running now), and coming up Broadway for only a block or two last night, I am sure that I saw Miss Oldcastle's picture a dozen times. I should think she would hate dreadfully to have to make herself so conspicuous, for she has a nice, refined face; but Oliver says all actresses have to do it if they want to get on. He takes all the fuss they make over him just as if he despised it, though I am sure that in his heart he can't help being pleased. While we were having dinner, everybody in the dining-room was turning to look at him, and if I hadn't known, of course, that not a soul was thinking of me, I should have felt badly because I hadn't time to change my dress after I got here. All the other women were beautifully dressed (I never dreamed that there were so many diamonds in the world. Miss Willy would simply go crazy over them), but I didn't mind a bit, and if anybody thought of me at all, of course, they knew that I had just stepped off the train. After dinner your father went to the theatre, and I sat downstairs alone in the corridor for a while and watched the people coming and going. It was perfectly fascinating at first. I never saw so many beautiful women, and their hair was arranged in such a lovely way, all just alike, that it must have taken hours to do each head. The fashions that are worn here are not in the least like those of Dinwiddie, though Miss Willy made my black brocade exactly like one in a fashion plate that came directly from Paris, but I know that you aren't as much interested in this as Lucy and Jenny would be. The dear girls are both well, and Lucy is carried away with her stepchildren. She says she doesn't see why every woman doesn't marry a widower. Isn't that exactly like Lucy ? She is always so funny. If only one of you were here with me, I should enjoy every minute, but after I'd sat there for a while in the midst of all those strangers, I began to feel a little lonely, so I came upstairs to write you this letter. New York is a fascinating place to visit, but I am glad I live in Dinwiddie where everybody knows me.

"And now, my dearest boy, I must tell you how perfectly overjoyed I was to get your last letter, and to know that you are so delighted with Oxford. I think of you every minute, and I pray for you the last thing at night before I get into bed. Try to keep well and strong, and if you get a cold, be sure not to let it run on till it turns to a hacking cough. Remember that Doctor Fraser always used to say that every cough, no matter how slight, is dangerous. I hope you aren't studying too hard or overdoing athletics. It is so easy to tax one's strength too much when one gets excited. I am sure I don't know what to think of the English students being " standoffish " with Americans. It seems very foolish of them not to be nice and friendly, especially to Virginians, who were really English in the beginning. But I am glad that you don't mind, and that you would rather be a countryman of George Washington than a countryman of George the Third. Of course England is the greatest country in the world—you remember your grandfather always said that—and we owe it everything that we have, but I think it very silly of English people to be stiff and ill-mannered.

"I hope you still read your Bible, darling, and that you find time to go to church once every Sunday. Even if it seems a waste of time to you, it would have pleased your grandfather, and for his sake I hope you will go whenever you can possibly do so. It was so sweet of you to write in Addison's Walk because you did not want to miss my Sunday letter and yet the day was too beautiful not to be out of doors. God only knows, my boy, what a comfort you are to me. There was never a better son nor one who was loved more devotedly."

"Your Mother."

23

In the morning, with the breakfast tray, there arrived a bunch of orchids from one of Oliver's theatrical friends, who had heard that his wife was in town; and while Virginia laid the box carefully in the bath-tub, her eyes shone with the grateful light which came into them whenever someone did her a small kindness or courtesy.

"They will be lovely for me to wear to-night, Oliver. It was so nice of him to send them, wasn't it ?"

"Yes, it was rather nice," Oliver replied, looking up from his paper at the pleased sound of her voice. Ever since his return at a late hour last night, she had noticed the nervousness in his manner and had sympathetically attributed it to his anxiety about the fate of his play. It was so like Oliver to be silent and self-absorbed when he was anxious.

Through the day he was absent, and when he returned in the evening to dress for the theatre, she was standing before the mirror fastening the bunch of orchids on the front of her gown. As he entered, she turned toward him with a look of eager interest, of pleasant yet anxious excitement. She had never in her life, except on the morning of her wedding day, taken so long to dress; but it seemed to her important that as Oliver's wife she should look as nice as she could.

"Am I all right ?" she asked timidly, while she cast a doubtful glance in the mirror at the skirt of the black brocade.

"Yes, you're all right," he responded, without looking at her, and the suppressed pain in his voice caused her to move suddenly toward him with the question : "Aren't you well, Oliver ?"

"Oh, I'm well, but I'm tired. I had a headache on the way up and I haven't been able to shake it off."

"Shall I get you something for it ?"

"No, it will pass. I'd like a nap, but I suppose it's time for me to dress."

"Yes, it's half-past six, and we've ordered dinner for seven."

He went into the dressing-room, and turning again to the mirror, she changed the position of the bunch of orchids, and gave a little dissatisfied pat to the hair on her forehead. If only she could bring back some of the bloom and the freshness of youth ! The glow had gone out of her eyes; the winged happiness, which had given her face the look as of one flying towards life, had passed, leaving her features a little wan and drawn, and fading her delicate skin to the colour of withered flowers. Yet the little smile, which lingered like autumn sunshine around her lips, was full of that sweetness which time could not destroy, because it belonged not to her flesh, but to an unalterable quality of her soul; and this sweetness, which she exhaled like a fragrance, would cause perhaps one of a hundred strangers to glance after her with the thought: " How lovely that woman must once have been !"

" Are you ready ?" asked Oliver, coming out of his dressing-room, and again she started and turned quickly towards him, because it seemed to her that she was hearing his voice for the first time. So nervous, so irritable, so quivering with suppressed feeling, was the sound of it, that she hesitated between the longing to offer sympathy and the fear that her words might only add to his suffering.

" Yes, I am quite ready," she answered, without adding that she had been ready for more than an hour; and picking up her wrap from the bed, she passed ahead of him through the door which he had opened. As he stopped to draw the key from the lock, her eyes rested with pride on the gloss of his hair, which had gone grey in the last year, and on his figure, with its square shoulders and its look of obvious distinction, as of a man who had achieved results so emphatically that it was impossible either to overlook or to belittle them. How splendid he looked ! And what a pity that, after all his triumphs, he should still be so nervous on the first night of a play !

In the elevator there was a woman in an ermine wrap, with Titian hair under a jewelled net; and Virginia's eyes were suffused with pleasure as she gazed at her. " I never saw anyone so beautiful !" she exclaimed to Oliver, as they stepped out into the hall; but he merely replied indifferently: " Was she ? I didn't notice." Then his tone lost its deadness. " If you'll wait here a minute, I'd like to speak to Cranston about something," he said, almost eagerly. " I shan't keep you a second."

" Don't worry about me," she answered cheerfully, pleased at the sudden change in his manner. " Stay as long as you like. I never get tired watching the people."

He hurried off, while, dazzled by the lights, she drew back behind a sheltering palm, and stood a little screened from the brilliant crowd in which she took such innocent pleasure. "How I wish Miss Willy could be here," she thought, for it was impossible for her to feel perfect enjoyment while there existed the knowledge that another person would have found even greater delight in the scene than she was finding herself. "How gay they all look—and there are not any old people. Everybody, even the white-haired women, dress as if they were girls. I wonder what it is that gives them all this gloss as if they had been polished, the same gloss that has come on Oliver since he has been so successful? What a short time he stayed. He is coming back already, and every single person is turning to look at him."

Then a voice beyond the palm spoke as distinctly as if the words were uttered into her ear. "That's Treadwell over there—a good-looking man, isn't he?—but have you seen the dowdy, middle-aged woman he is married to? It's a pity that all great men marry young; and now they say, you know, that he is madly in love with Margaret Oldcastle——"

CHAPTER V

BITTERNESS

In the night, after a restless sleep, she awoke in terror. A hundred incidents, a hundred phrases, looks, gestures, which she had thought meaningless until last evening, flashed out of the darkness and hung there, blazing, against the background of the night. Yesterday these things had appeared purposeless; and now it seemed to her that only her incredible blindness, only her childish inability to face any painful fact until it struck her between the eyes, had kept her from discovering the truth before it was thrust on her by the idle chatter of strangers. A curious rigidity, as if she had been suddenly paralyzed, passed from her heart, which seemed to have ceased beating, and crept through her limbs to her motionless hands and feet. Though she longed to call out and awaken Oliver, who, complaining of insomnia, spent the night in the adjoining room, this immobility, which was like the graven immobility of death, held her imprisoned there as speechless and still as if she lay in her coffin. Only her brain seemed on fire, so pitilessly, so horribly alive had it become.

From the street beyond the dim square of the window, across which the curtains were drawn, she could hear the ceaseless passing of carriages and motor-cars; but her thoughts had grown so confused that for a long while, as she lay there, chill and rigid under the bedclothes, she could not separate the outside sounds from the tumult within her brain. "Now that I know the truth I must decide what is best to do," she thought quite calmly. "As soon as this noise stops I must think it all over and decide what is best to do." But around this one lucid idea the discordant roar of the streets seemed to gather force until it raged with the violence of a storm. It was impossible to think clearly until this noise, which, in some strange

357

way, was both in the street outside and within the secret
chambers of her soul, had subsided and given place to
the quiet of night again. Then gradually the tempest of
sound died away, and in the midst of the stillness which followed it she lived over every hour, every minute, of that last
evening when it had seemed to her that she was crucified by
Oliver's triumph. She saw him as he came towards her down
the shining corridor, easy, brilliant, impressive, a little bored
by his celebrity, yet with the look of vital well-being, of
second youth, which separated and distinguished him from
the curious gazers among whom he moved. She saw him
opposite to her during the long dinner, which she could not
eat; she saw him beside her in the car which carried them
to the theatre; and clearer than ever, as if a burning iron had
seared the memory into her brain, she saw him lean on the
railing of the box, with his eyes on the stage where Margaret
Oldcastle, against the lowered curtain, smiled her charming
smile at the house. It had been a wonderful night, and
through it all she had felt the iron nails of her crucifixion
driven into her soul.

Breaking away from that chill of terror with which she had
awakened, she left the bed and went over to the window,
where she drew the heavy curtains aside. In Fifth Avenue
the electric lights sparkled like frost on the pavement, while
beyond the roofs of the houses the first melancholy glow of a
winter's sunrise was suffusing the sky with red. While she
watched it, a wave of unutterable loneliness swept over her—
of that profound spiritual loneliness which comes to one at
dawn in a great city, when knowledge of the sleeping millions
within reach seems only to intensify the fact of individual
littleness and isolation. She felt that she stood alone, not
merely in the world, but in the universe; and the thought that
Oliver slept there in the next room made more poignant this
feeling, as though she were solitary and detached in the midst
of limitless space. Even if she called him and he came to her,
she could not reach him. Even if he stood at her side, the
immeasurable distance between them would not lessen.

When the morning came, she dressed herself in her prettiest
gown, a violet cloth, with ruffles of old lace at the throat and
wrists; but this dress, of which she had been so proud in

Dinwiddie that she had saved it for months in order to have it fresh for New York, appeared somehow to have lost its charm and distinction, and she knew that last evening had not only destroyed her happiness, but had robbed her of her confidence in the taste and the workmanship of Miss Willy. Knowledge, she saw now, had shattered the little beliefs of life as well as the large ones.

Oliver liked to breakfast in his dressing-gown, fresh from his bath and eager for the papers, so when he came hurriedly into the sitting-room, the shining tray was already awaiting him, and she sat pouring his coffee in a band of sunlight beside the table. This sunlight, so merciful to the violet gown, shone pitilessly on the darkened hollows which the night had left under her eyes, and on the little lines which had gathered around her bravely smiling mouth.

" It was a wonderful success; all the papers say so, Oliver," she said, when he had seated himself at the other end of the table and taken the coffee from her hand, which shook in spite of her effort.

" Yes, it went off well, there's no doubt of it," he answered cheerfully, so cheerfully that for a minute a blind hope shot trembling through her mind.   Could it all have been a dream ? Was there some dreadful mistake ?   Would she presently discover that she had imagined that night of useless agony through which she had passed ?

" The audience was so sympathetic.   I saw a number of women crying in the last act when the heroine comes back to her old home."

" It caught them.   I thought it would.   It's the kind of thing they like."

He opened a paper as he spoke, and seeing that he wanted to read the criticisms, she broke his eggs for him, and then, turning to her own breakfast, tried in vain to swallow the piece of toast which she had buttered.   But it was useless. She could not eat; she could not even drink her coffee, which had stood so long that it had grown tepid.   A feeling of spiritual nausea, beside which all physical sensations were as trivial and meaningless as the stinging of wasps, pervaded her soul and body, and choked her, like unshed tears, whenever she tried to force a bit of food between her trembling lips.

All the casual interests with which she filled her days, those seemingly small, yet actually tremendous interests without which daily life becomes almost unlivable, flagged suddenly and died while she sat there. Nothing mattered any longer, neither the universe nor that little circle of it which she inhabited, neither life nor death, neither Oliver's success nor the food which she was trying to eat. This strange sickness which had fallen upon her affected not only her soul and body, but everything that surrounded her, every person or object at which she looked, every stranger in the street below, every roof which she could see sharply outlined against the glittering blue of the sky. Something had passed out of them all, some essential quality which united them to reality, some inner secret of being without which the animate and the inanimate alike became no better than phantoms. The spirit which made life vital had gone out of the world. And she felt that this would always be so, that the next minute and the next year and all the years that came afterwards would bring to her merely the effort of living—since Life, having used her for its dominant purpose, had no further need of her. Once only the thought occurred to her that there were women who might keep their own even now by fighting against the loss of it, by passionately refusing to surrender what they could no longer hold as a gift. But with the idea there came also that self-knowledge which told her that she was not one of these. The strength in her was the strength of passiveness; she could endure, but she could not battle. Long ago, as long ago as the night on which she had watched in the shadow of death beside Harry's bed, she had lost that energy of soul which had once flamed up in her with her three days' jealousy of Abby. It was her youth and beauty then which had inspirited her, and she was wise enough to know that the passions which become youth appear ridiculous in middle age.

Having drunk his coffee, Oliver passed his cup to her, and laid down his paper.

"You look tired, Virginia. I hope it hasn't been too much for you ?"

"Oh no. Have you quite got over your headache ?"

"Pretty much, but those lights last night were rather trying. Don't put any cream in this time. I want the stimulant."

" Perhaps it has got cold. Shall I ring for fresh ?"

" It doesn't matter. This will do quite as well. Have you any shopping that you would like to do this morning ?"

Shopping ! When her whole world had crumbled around her ! For an instant the lump in her throat made speech impossible; then, summoning that mild yet indestructible spirit, which was as the spirit of all those generations of women who lived in her blood, she answered gently:

" Yes, I had intended to buy some presents for the girls."

"Then you'd better take a taxi-cab for the morning. I suppose you know the names of the shops you want to go to ?"

" Oh yes; I know the names. Are you going to the theatre ?"

" I've got to change a few lines in the play, and the sooner I go about it the better."

" Then don't bother about me, dear. I'll just put on my long coat over this dress and go out right after breakfast."

" But you haven't eaten anything," he remarked, glancing at her plate.

" I wasn't hungry. The fresh air will do me good. It has turned so much warmer, and the snow is all melting."

As she spoke, she rose from the table and began to prepare herself for the street, putting on the black hat with the ostrich tip and the bunch of violets on one side, which didn't seem just right since she had come to New York, and carefully wrapping the ends of her fur neck-piece around her throat. It was already ten o'clock, for Oliver had slept late, and she must be hurrying if she hoped to get through her shopping before luncheon. While she dressed, a wan spirit of humour entered into her, and she saw how absurd it was that she should rush about from shop to shop, buying things that did not matter in order to fill a life that mattered as little as they did. To her, whose mental outlook had had in it so little humour, it seemed suddenly that the whole of life was ridiculous. Why should she have sat there, pouring Oliver's coffee and talking to him about insignificant things, when her heart was bursting with this sense of something gone out of existence, with this torturing realization of the irretrievable failure of love ?

Taking up her muff and her little black bag from the

bureau, she looked back at him with a smile as she turned
towards the door.

"Good-bye. Will you be here for luncheon?"

"I'm afraid I can't. I've an appointment down town, but
I'll come back as early as I can."

Then she went out and along the hall to the elevator, in
which there was a little girl, who reminded her of Jenny, in
charge of a governess in spectacles. She smiled at her
almost unconsciously, so spontaneous, so interwoven with her
every mood was her love for children; but the little girl,
being very proper for her years, did not smile back, and a stab
of pain went through Virginia's heart.

"Even children have ceased to care for me," she thought.

At the door, where she waited a few minutes for her taxi-
cab, a young bride, with her eyes shining with joy, stood
watching her husband while he talked with an acquaintance,
and it seemed to Virginia that it was a vision of her own
youth which had risen to torment her. "That was the way I
looked at Oliver twenty-five years ago," she said to herself;
"twenty-five years ago, when I was young and he loved me."
Then, even while the intolerable pain was still in her heart,
she felt that something of the buoyant hopefulness of that
other bride entered into her and restored her courage. A
resolution, so new that it was born of the joyous glance of a
stranger, and yet so old that it seemed a part of that lost
spirit of youth which had once carried her in a wild race over
the Virginian meadows, a resolution which belonged at the
same time to this other woman and to herself, awoke in her
and mingled like a draught of wine with her blood. "I will
not give up," she thought. "I will go to her. Perhaps she
does not know—perhaps she does not understand. I will go to
her, and everything may be different." Then her taxi-cab was
called, and stepping into it, she gave the name, not of a shop,
but of the apartment house in which Margaret Oldcastle lived.

It was one of those February days when, because of the
promise of spring in the air, men begin suddenly to think
of April. The sky was of an intense blue, with little clouds,
as soft as feathers, above the western horizon. On the pavement the last patches of snow were rapidly melting, and the
gentle breeze which blew in at the open window of the cab

was like a caressing breath on Virginia's cheek. "It must be that she does not understand," she repeated, and this thought gave her confidence and filled her with that unconquerable hope of the future without which she felt that living would be impossible. Even the faces in the street cheered her, for it seemed to her that, if life were really what she believed it to be last night, these men and women could not walk so buoyantly, could not smile so gaily, could not spend so much thought and time on the way they looked and the things they wore. "No, it must have been a mistake, a ghastly mistake," she insisted almost passionately. "Some day we shall laugh over it together as we laughed over my jealousy of Abby. He never loved Abby, not for a minute, and yet I imagined that he did and suffered agony because of it." And her taxi-cab went on merrily between the cheerful crowds on the pavements, gliding among gorgeous motor-cars and carriages drawn by high-stepping horses, and pedlers' carts drawn by horses that stepped high no longer, among rich people and poor people, among surfeited people and hungry people, among gay people and sad people, among contented people and rebellious people—among all these, who hid their happiness or their sorrow under the mask of their features, her cab spun onward bearing her lightly on the most reckless act of her life.

At the door of the apartment house she was told that Miss Oldcastle could not be seen, but, after sending up her card and waiting a few moments in the hall before a desk which reminded her of a gilded squirrel-cage, she was escorted to the elevator and borne upward to the ninth landing. Here, in response to the tinkle of a little bell outside of a door, she was ushered into a reception-room, which was so bare alike of unnecessary furniture and of the Victorian tradition to which she was accustomed, that for an instant she stood confused by the very strangeness of her surroundings. Then a charming voice, with what sounded to her ears as an affected precision of speech, said: "Mrs. Treadwell, this is so good of you!" and, turning, she found herself face to face with the other woman in Oliver's life.

"I saw you at the play last night," the voice went on, "and I hoped to get a chance to speak to you, but the reporters simply invaded my dressing-room. Won't you sit here in the sunshine? Shall I close the window, or, like myself, are you a worshipper of the sun?"

"Oh no, leave it open. I like it." At any other moment she would have been afraid of an open window in February; but it seemed to her now that if she could not feel the air in her face she should faint. With the first sight of Margaret Oldcastle, as she looked into that smiling face, in which the inextinguishable youth was less a period of life than an attribute of spirit, she realized that she was fighting, not a woman, but the very structure of life. The glamour of the footlights had contributed nothing to the flame-like personality of the actress. In her simple frock of brown woollen, with a wide collar of white lawn turned back from her splendid throat, she embodied not so much the fugitive charm of youth, as that burning vitality over which age has no power. The intellect in her spoke through her noble rather than beautiful features, through her ardent eyes, through her resolute mouth, through every perfect gesture with which she accompanied her words. She stood not only for the elemental forces, but for the free woman; and her freedom, like that of man, had been built upon the strewn bodies of the weaker. The law of sacrifice, which is the basic law of life, ruled here as it ruled in mother-love and in the industrial warfare of men. Her triumph was less the triumph of the individual than of the type. The justice, not of society, but of nature, was on her side, for she was one with evolution and with the resistless principle of change. Vaguely, without knowing that she realized these things, Virginia felt that the struggle was useless; and with the sense of failure there awoke in her that instinct of good breeding, that inherited obligation to keep the surface of life sweet, which was so much older and so much stronger than the revolt in her soul.

"You were wonderful last night. I wanted to tell you how wonderful I thought you," she said gently. "You made the play a success—all the papers say so this morning."

"Well, it was an easy play to make successful," replied the other, while a fleeting curiosity, as though she were trying to explain something which she did not quite understand, appeared in her face, and made it, with its redundant vitality, almost coarse for an instant. "It's the kind the public wants, you couldn't help making it go."

The almost imperceptible conflict which had flashed in their eyes when they met had died suddenly down, and the dignity which had been on the side of the other woman appeared to have passed from her to Virginia. This dignity, which was not that of triumph, but of a defeat which surrenders everything except the inviolable sanctities of the spirit, shielded her like an impenetrable armour against both resentment and pity. She stood there wrapped in a gentleness more unassailable than any passion.

"You did a great deal for it, and a great deal for my husband," she said, while her voice lingered unconsciously over the word. "He has told me often that without your acting he could never have reached the position he holds."

Then, because it was impossible to say the things she had come to say, because even in the supreme crises of life she could not lay down the manner of a lady, she smiled the grave smile with which her mother had walked through a ruined country, and taking up her muff, which she had laid on the table, passed out into the hall. She had let the chance go by, she had failed in her errand, yet she knew that, even though it cost her her life, even though it cost her a thing far dearer than life—her happiness—she could not have done otherwise. In the crucial moment it was principle and not passion which she obeyed; but this principle, filtering down through generations, had become so inseparable from the sources of character, that it had passed at last through the intellect into the blood. She could no more have bared her soul to that other woman than she could have stripped her body naked in the market-place.

At the door her cab was still waiting, and she gave the driver the name of the toy shop at which she intended to buy presents for Lucy's stepchildren. Though her heart was breaking within her, there was no impatience in her manner when she was obliged to wait some time before she could find the particular sort of doll for which Lucy had written; and she smiled at the apologetic shopgirl with the forbearing consideration for others which grief could not destroy. She put her own anguish aside as utterly in the selection of the doll as she would have done had it been the peace of nations, and not a child's pleasure, that depended upon her effacement of self. Then, when the purchase was made, she took out her shopping list from her bag and passed as conscientiously to the choice of Jenny's clothes. Not until the morning had gone, and she rolled again up Fifth Avenue towards the hotel, did she permit her thoughts to return to the stifled agony within her heart.

To her surprise, Oliver was awaiting her in their sitting-room, and with her first look into his face, she understood that he had reached in her absence a decision against which he had struggled for days. For an instant her strength seemed fainting as before an impossible effort. Then the shame in his eyes awoke in her the longing to protect him, to spare him, to make even this terrible moment easier for him than he could make it alone. With the feeling, a crowd of memories thronged through her mind, as though called there by that impulse to shield which was so deeply inter-woven with the primal passion of motherhood. She saw Oliver's face as it had looked on that spring afternoon when she had first seen him; she saw it as he put the ring on her hand at the altar; she saw it bending over her after the birth of her first child; and then suddenly his face changed to the face of Harry, and she saw again the little bed under the hanging sheet, and herself sitting there in the faintly quivering circle of light. She watched again the slow fall of the leaves, one by one, as they turned at the stem and drifted against the white curtains of the window across the street.

"Oliver," she said gently, so gently that she might have been speaking to her sick child, "would you rather that I should go back to Dinwiddie to-night?"

He did not answer, but, turning away from her, laid his head down on his arm, which he had outstretched on the table, and she saw a shiver of pain pass through his body as if it had been struck a physical blow. And just as she had put herself aside when she bought the doll, so now she forgot her own suffering in the longing to respond to his need.

"I can take the night train; now that I have seen the play there is no reason why I should stay. I have got through my shopping.

Raising his head, he looked up into her face. "Whatever happens, Virginia, will you believe that I never wanted to hurt you?" he asked.

For a moment she felt that the strain was intolerable, and a fear entered her mind lest she should faint or weep, and so make things harder than they should be able to bear.

"You mean that something must happen—that there will be a break between us?" she said.

Leaving the table, he walked to the window and back before he answered her.

"I can't go on this way. I'm not that sort. A generation ago, I suppose, we should have done it—but we've lost grip, we've lost endurance." Then he cried out suddenly, as if he were justifying himself: "It is hell. I've been in hell for a year—don't you see it?"

After his violence, her voice sounded almost lifeless, so quiet, so utterly free from passion, was its quality.

"As long as that—for a year?" she asked.

"Oh, longer, but it has got worse. It has got unendurable. I've fought—God knows I've fought—but I can't stand it. I've got to do something. I've got to find a way. You must have seen it coming, Virginia. You must have seen that this thing is stronger than I am."

"Do—do you want her so much?" and she, who had learned from life not to want, looked at him with the pity which he might have seen in her eyes had he stabbed her.

"So much that I'm going mad. There's no other end to it. It's been coming on for two years—all the time I've been away from Dinwiddie I've been fighting it."

She did not answer, and when, after the silence had grown oppressive, he turned back from the window through which he had been gazing, he could not be sure that she had heard him. So still she seemed that she was like a woman of marble.

"You're too good for me, that's the trouble. You've been too good for me from the beginning," he said.

Unfastening her coat, which she had kept on, she laid it on the sofa at her back, and then put up her hands to take out her hatpins.

"I must pack my things," she said suddenly. "Will you engage my berth back to Dinwiddie for to-night?"

He nodded without speaking, and she added hastily: "I shan't go down again before starting. But there is no need that you should go to the train with me."

At this he turned back from the door where he had waited with his hand on the knob. "Won't you let me do even that?" he asked, and his voice sounded so like Harry's that a sob broke from her lips. The point was so small a one—all points seemed to her so small—that her will died down and she yielded without protest. What did it matter—what did anything matter to her now?

"I'll send up your luncheon," he added almost gratefully. "You will be ill if you don't eat something."

"No, please don't. I am not hungry," she answered, and then he went out softly, as though he were leaving a sickroom, and left her alone with her anguish—and her packing.

Without turning in her chair, without taking off her hat, from which she had drawn the pins, she sat there like a woman in whom the spirit has been suddenly stricken. Beyond the window the perfect day, with its haunting reminder of the spring, was lengthening slowly into afternoon, and through the slant sunbeams the same gay crowd passed in streams on the pavements. On the roof of one of the opposite houses a flag was flying, and it seemed to her that the sight of that flag waving under the blue sky was bound up for ever with the intolerable pain in her heart. And with that strange passivity of the nerves which nature mercifully sends to those who have learned submission to suffering, to those whose strength is the strength, not of resistance, but of endurance, she felt that as long as she sat there, relaxed and motionless, she had in a way withdrawn herself from the struggle to live. If she might only stay like this for ever, without moving, without thinking, without feeling, while she died slowly, inch by inch, spirit and body.

A knock came at the door, and as she moved to answer it, she felt that life returned in a slow throbbing agony, as if her blood were forced back again into veins from which it had ebbed. When the tray was placed on the table beside her, she looked up with a mild, impersonal curiosity at the waiter, as the dead might look back from their freedom and detachment on the unreal figures of the living. "I wonder what he thinks about it all ?" she thought vaguely, as she searched in her bag for his tip. " I wonder if he sees how absurd and unnecessary all the things are that he does day after day, year after year, like the rest of us ? I wonder if he ever revolts with this unspeakable weariness from waiting on other people and watching them eat ?" But the waiter, with his long, sallow face, his inscrutable eyes, and his general air of having petrified under the surface, was as enigmatical as life.

After he had gone out, she rose from her untasted luncheon, and going into her bedroom, took the black brocaded gown off the hanger and stuffed the sleeves with tissue paper as carefully as if the world had not crumbled around her. Then she packed away her wrapper and her bedroom slippers and shook out and folded the dresses she had not worn. For a time she worked on mechanically, hardly conscious of what she was doing, hardly conscious even that she was alive. Then slowly, softly, like a gentle rain, her tears fell into the trunk, on each separate garment as she smoothed it and laid it away.

At half-past eight o'clock she was waiting with her hat and coat on when Oliver came in, followed by the porter who was to take down her bags. She knew that he had brought the man in order to avoid all possibility of an emotional scene; and she could have smiled, had her spirit been less wan and stricken, at this sign of a moral cowardice which was so characteristic. It was his way, she understood now, though she did not put the thought into words, to take what he wanted, escaping at the same time the price which nature exacts of those who have not learned to relinquish. Out of the strange colourless stillness which surrounded her, some old words of Susan's floated back to her as if they were spoken aloud: " A Treadwell will always get the thing he wants most in the end." But while he stabbed her, he would look away in order that he might be spared the memory of her face.

Without a word, she followed her bags from the room, without a word she entered the elevator, which was waiting, and without a word she took her place in the taxi-cab standing beside the curbstone. There was no rebellion in her thoughts, merely a dulled consciousness of pain, like the consciousness of one who is partially under an anæsthetic. The fighting courage, the violence of revolt, had no part in her soul, which had been taught to suffer and to renounce with dignity, not with heroics. Her submission was the submission of a flower that bends to a storm.

As she sat there in silence, with her eyes on the brilliant street, where the signs of his play stared back at her under the flaring lights, she began to think with automatic precision, as though her brain were moved by some mechanical power over which she had no control. Little things crowded into her mind—the face of the doll she had bought for Lucy's stepchild that morning, the words on one of the electric signs on the top of a building they were passing, the leopard skin coat worn by a woman on the pavement. And these little things seemed to her at the moment to be more real, more vital, than her broken heart and the knowledge that she was parting from Oliver. The agony of the night and the morning appeared to have passed away like a physical pang, leaving only this deadness of sensation and the strange, almost unearthly clearness of external objects. "It is not new. It has been coming on for years," she thought "He said that, and it is true. It is so old that it has been here for ever, and I seem to have been suffering it all my life—since the day I was born, and before the day I was born. It seems older than I am. Oliver is going from me. He has always been going from me—always since the beginning," she repeated slowly, as if she were trying to learn a lesson by heart. But so remote and shadowy did the words appear, that she found herself thinking the next instant : " I must have forgotten my smelling-salts. The bottle was lying on the bureau, and I can't remember putting it into my bag." The image of this little glass bottle, with the gold top, which she had left behind was distinct in her memory; but when she tried to think of the parting from Oliver and of all that she was suffering, everything became shadowy and unreal again.

At the station she stood beside the porter while he paid the driver, and then, entering the doorway, they walked hurriedly—so hurriedly that she felt as if she were losing her breath—in the direction of the gate and the waiting train. And with each step as they passed down the long platform, which seemed to stretch into eternity, she was thinking: " In a minute it will be over. If I don't say something now, it will be too late. If I don't stop him now, it will be over for ever—everything will be over for ever."

Beside the night coach, in the presence of the conductor and the porter, who stood blandly waiting to help her into the train, she stopped suddenly, as though she could not go any farther, as though the strength which had supported her until now had given way and she were going to fall. Through her mind there flashed the thought that even now she might hold him if she were to make a scene, that if she were to go into hysterics he would not leave her, that if she were to throw away her pride and her self-respect and her dignity, she might recover by violence the outer shell at least of her happiness. How could he break away from her if she were only to weep and to cling to him ? Then, while the idea was still in her mind, she knew that to a nature such as hers violence was impossible. It took passion to war with passion, and in this she was lacking. Though she were wounded to the death, she could not revolt, could not shriek out in her agony, could not break through that gentle yet invincible reticence which she had won from the past.

Down the long platform a child came running with cries of pleasure, followed by a man with a red beard, who carried a suit-case. As they approached the train, Virginia entered the coach, and walked rapidly down the aisle to where the porter was waiting beside her seat.

For the first time since they had reached the station Oliver spoke. " I am sorry I couldn't get the drawing-room for you," he said. " I am afraid you will be crowded; " and this anxiety about her comfort, when he was ruining her life, did not strike either of them, at the moment, as ridiculous.

"It does not matter," she answered; and he put out his hand.

" Good-bye, Virginia," he said, with a catch in his voice.

" Good-bye," she responded quietly, and would have given her soul for the power to shriek aloud, to overcome this indomitable instinct which was stronger than her personal self.

Turning away, he passed between the seats to the door of the coach, and a minute later she saw his figure hurrying back along the platform down which they had come together a few minutes ago.

CHAPTER VI

THE FUTURE

A CHILL rain was falling when Virginia got out of the train the next morning, and the raw-boned nags hitched to the ancient "hacks" in the street appeared even more dejected and forlorn than she had remembered them. Then one of the noisy negro drivers seized her bag, and a little later she was rolling up the long hill in the direction of her home. Dinwiddie was the same; nothing had altered there since she had left it—and yet what a difference! The same shops were unclosing their shutters; the same crippled negro beggar was taking his place at the corner of the market; the same maids were sweeping the sidewalks with the same brooms; the same clerk bowed to her from the drug-store where she bought her medicines; and yet something—the only thing which had ever interested her in these people and this place—had passed out of them. Just as in New York yesterday, when she had watched the sunrise, so it seemed to her now that the spirit of reality had faded out of the world. What remained was merely a mirage in which phantoms in the guise of persons made a pretence of being alive.

The front door of her house stood open, and on the porch one of the coloured maids was beating the dust out of the straw mat. "As if dust makes any difference when one is dead," Virginia thought wearily; and an unutterable loathing passed over her for all the little acts by which one rendered tribute to the tyranny of appearances. Then, as she entered the house, she felt that the sight of the familiar objects she had once loved oppressed her, as though the spirit of melancholy resided in the pieces of furniture, not in her soul. This weariness, so much worse than positive pain, filled her with disgust for all the associations and the sentiments she had known in the past. Not only the house and the furniture

372

and the small details of housekeeping, but the street and the town and every friendly face of a neighbour had become an intolerable reminder that she was still alive.

In her room, where a bright fire was burning, and letters from the girls lay on the table, she sat down in her wraps and gazed with unseeing eyes at the flames. "The children must not know. I must keep it from the children as long as possible," she thought dully, and it was so natural to her to plan sparing them, that for a minute the idea took her mind away from her own anguish. "If I could only die like this, then they need never know," she found herself reflecting coldly a little later, so coldly that she seemed to have no personal interest, no will to choose in the matter. "If I could only die like this, nobody need be hurt—except Harry," she added.

For the first time, with the thought of Harry, her restraint suddenly failed her. "Yes, it would hurt Harry. I must live because Harry would want me to," she said aloud; and as though her strength were reinforced by the words, she rose and prepared herself to go downstairs to breakfast—prepared herself, too, for the innumerable little agonies which would come with the day, for the sight of Susan, for the visits from the neighbours, for the eager questions about the fashions in New York which Miss Willy would ask. And all the time she was thinking clearly: "It can't last for ever. It must end some time. Who knows but it may stop the next minute, and one can stand a minute of anything."

The day passed, the week, the month, and gradually the spring came and went, awakening life in the trees, in the grass, in the fields, but not in her heart. Even the dried sticks in the yard put out shoots of living green and presently bore blossoms, and in the borders by the front gate, the crocuses, which she had planted with her own hands a year ago, were ablaze with gold. All nature seemed joining in the resurrection of life, all nature, except herself, seemed to flower again to fulfilment. She alone was dead, and she alone among the dead must keep up this pretence of living which was so much harder than death.

Once every week she wrote to the children, restrained yet gently flowing letters, in which there was no mention of Oliver. It had been so long, indeed, since either Harry or the girls had associated their parents together, that the omission called forth no question—hardly, she gathered, any surprise. Their lives were so full, their interests were so varied, that, except at the regular intervals when they sat down to write to her, it is doubtful if they ever seriously wondered about her. In July, Jenny came home for a month, and Lucy wrote regretfully that she was "so disappointed that she couldn't join mother somewhere in the mountains"; but beyond this, the girls' lives hardly appeared to touch hers even on the surface. In the month that Jenny spent in Dinwiddie, she organized a number of societies and clubs for the improvement of conditions among working girls, and in spite of the intense heat (the hottest spell of the summer came while she was there), she barely allowed herself a minute for rest or for conversation with her mother.

"If you would only go to the mountains, mother," she remarked the evening before she left. "I am sure it isn't good for you to stay in Dinwiddie during the summer."

"I am used to it," replied Virginia a little stubbornly, for it seemed to her at the moment that she would rather die than move.

"But you ought to think of your health. What does father say about it?"

A contraction of pain crossed Virginia's face, but Jenny, whose vision was so wide that it had a way of overlooking things which were close at hand, did not observe it.

"He hasn't said anything," she answered, with a strange stillness of voice.

"I thought he meant to take you to England, but I suppose his plays are keeping him in New York."

Rising from her chair at the table—they had just finished supper—Virginia reached for a saucer and filled it with ice-cream from a bowl in front of her.

"I think I'll send Miss Priscilla a little of this cream," she remarked. "She is so fond of strawberry."

The next day Jenny went, and again the silence and the loneliness settled upon the house, to which Virginia clung with a morbid terror of change. Had her spirit been less broken, she might have made the effort of going North as Jenny had urged her to do, but when her life was over, one place seemed as desirable as another, and it was a matter of profound indifference to her whether it was heat or cold which afflicted her body. She was probably the only person in Dinwiddie who did not hang out of her window during the long nights in search of a passing breeze. But with that physical insensibility which accompanies prolonged torture of soul, she had ceased to feel the heat, had ceased even to feel the old neuralgic pain in her temples. There were times when it seemed to her that if a pin were stuck into her body she should not know it. The one thing she asked—and this Life granted her, except during the four weeks of Jenny's visit—was freedom from the need of exertion, freedom from the obligation to make decisions. Her housekeeping she left now to the servants, so she was spared the daily harassing choices of the market and the table. There remained nothing for her to do, nothing even for her to worry about, except her broken heart. Her friends she had avoided ever since her return from New York, partly from an unbearable shrinking from the questions which she knew they would ask whenever they met her, partly because her mind was so engrossed with the supreme fact that her universe lay in ruins, that she found it impossible to lend a casual interest to other matters. She, who had effaced herself for a lifetime, found suddenly that she could not see beyond the immediate presence of her own suffering.

Usually she stayed closely indoors through the summer days, but several times, at the hour of dusk, she went out alone and wandered for hours about the streets which were associated with her girlhood. In High Street, at the corner where she had first seen Oliver, she stood one evening until Miss Priscilla, who had caught sight of her from the porch of the Academy (which, owing to the changing fashions in education and the infirmities of the teacher, was the Academy no longer), sent out her negro maid to beg her to come in and sit with her. "No, I'm only looking for something," Virginia had answered, while she hurried back past the church and down the slanting street to the twelve stone steps which led up the terraced hill-side at the rectory. Here, in the purple summer twilight, spangled with fireflies, she felt for a minute that her youth was awaiting her; and opening the gate, she passed as softly as a ghost along the crooked path to the two great paulownias, which were beginning to decay, and to the honeysuckle arbour, where the tendrils of the creeper brushed her hair like a caress. Under the light of a young moon, it seemed to her that nothing had changed since that spring evening when she had stood there and felt the wonder of first love awake in her heart. Nothing had changed, except that love and herself. The paulownias still shed their mysterious shadows about her, the red and white roses still bloomed by the west wing of the house, the bed of mint still grew, rank and fragrant, beneath the dining-room window. When she put her hand on the bole of the tree beside which she stood, she could still feel the initials V. O., which Oliver had cut there in the days before their marriage. A light burned in the window of the room which had been the parlour in the days when she lived there, and as she gazed at it, she almost expected to see the face of her mother, with its look of pathetic cheerfulness, smiling at her through the small greenish panes. And then the past, in which Oliver had no part, the past which belonged to her and to her parents, that hallowed, unforgettable past of her childhood, which seemed bathed in love as in a flood of light; this past enveloped her as the magic of the moonbeams enveloped the house in which she had lived. While she stood there, it was more living than the present, more real than the aching misery in her heart.

The door of the house opened and shut; she heard a step on the gravelled path; and bending forward out of the shadow, she waited breathlessly for the sound of her father's voice. But it was a young rector, who had recently accepted the call to Saint James's Church, and his boyish face, rising out of the sacred past, awoke her with a shock from the dream into which she had fallen.

"Good-evening, Mrs. Treadwell. Were you coming to see me?" he asked eagerly, pleased, she could see, by the idea that she was seeking his services.

"No, I was passing, and the garden reminded me so of my girlhood that I came in for a minute."

"It hasn't changed much, I suppose?" His alert, business-like gaze swept the hill-side.

"Hardly at all. One might imagine that those were the same roses I left here."

"An improvement or two wouldn't hurt it," he remarked

with animation. "These old trees make such a litter in the spring that my wife is anxious to get them down. Women like tidiness, you know, and she says, while they are blooming, it is impossible to keep the yard clean."

"I remember. Their flowers cover everything when they fall, but I always loved them."

"Well, one does get attached to things. I hope you have had a pleasant summer in spite of the heat. It must have been a delight to have your daughter at home again. What a splendid worker she is. If we had her in Dinwiddie for good it wouldn't be long before the old town would awaken. Why, I'd been trying to get those girls' clubs started for a year, and she took the job out of my hands and managed it in two weeks."

"The dear child is very clever. Is your wife still in the mountains?"

"She's coming back next week. We didn't feel that it was safe to bring the baby home until that long spell of heat had broken." Then, as she turned towards the step, he added hastily: "Won't you let me walk home with you?"

But this, she felt, was more than she could bear, and making the excuse of an errand on the next block, she parted from him at the gate, and hurried like a shadow back along High Street.

Until October there was no word from Oliver, and then at last there came a letter, which she threw, half read, into the fire. The impulsive act, so unlike the normal Virginia, soothed her for an instant, and she said over and over to herself, while she moved hurriedly about the room, as though she were seeking an escape from the moment before her: "I'm glad I didn't finish it. I'm glad I let it burn." Though she did not realize it, this passionate refusal to look at or to touch the thing that she hated was the last stand of the Pendleton idealism against the triumph of the actuality. It is possible that until that moment she had felt far down in her soul that by declining to acknowledge in words the fact of Oliver's desertion, by hiding it from the children, by ignoring the processes which would lead to his freedom, she had, in some obscure way, deprived that fact of all power over her life. But now, while his letter, blaming himself and yet pleading with her for his liberty, lay there, crumbling slowly to ashes under her eyes, her whole life, with its pathos, its subterfuge, its losing battle against the ruling spirit of change, seemed crumbling there also, like those ashes, or like that vanished past to which she belonged. "I'm glad I let it burn," she repeated bitterly, and yet she knew that the words had never really burned, that the flame which was consuming them would never die until she lay in her coffin. Stopping in front of the fire, she stood looking down on the last shred of the letter, as though it were in reality the ruins of her life which she was watching. A dull wonder stirred in her mind amid her suffering—a vague questioning as to why this thing, of all things should have happened ? "If I could only know why it was—if I could only understand, it might be easier," she thought. "But I tried so hard to do what was right, and, whatever the fault was, at least I never failed in love. I never failed in love," she repeated. Her gaze, leaving the fire, rested for an instant on a little alabaster ash-tray which stood on the end of the table, and a spasm crossed her face, which had remained unmoved while she was reading his letter. Every object in the room seemed suddenly alive with memories. That was his place on the rug; the deep chintz-covered chair by the hearth was the one in which he used to sit, watching the fire at night, before going to bed; the clock on the mantel was the one he had selected; the rug, which was threadbare in places, he had helped her to choose; the pile of English reviews on the table he had subscribed to; the little glass water-bottle on the candlestand by the bed, she had bought years ago because he liked to drink in the night. There was nothing in which he did not have a part. Every trivial incident of her life was bound up with the thought of him. She could no more escape the torment of these associations than she could escape the fact of herself. For so long she had been one with him in her thoughts that their relationship had passed, for her, into that profound union of habit which is the strongest union of all. Even the years in which he had grown gradually away from her, had appeared to her to leave untouched the deeper sanctities of their marriage.

A knock came at the door, and the cook, with a list of groceries in her hand, entered to inquire if her mistress were going to market. With the beginning of the autumn, Virginia had tried to take an interest in her housekeeping again, and the daily trip to the market had relieved, in a measure, the terrible vacancy of her mornings. Now it seemed to her that the remorseless exactions of the material details of living offered the only escape from the tortures of memory. " Yes, I'll go," she said : reaching out her hand for the list, and her heart cried : " I cannot live if I stay in this room any longer. I cannot live if I look at these things." As she turned away to put on her hat, she was seized by a superstitious feeling that she might escape her suffering by fleeing from these inanimate reminders of her marriage. It was as though the chair and the rug and the clock had become possessed with some demoniacal spirit. " If I can only get out of doors I shall feel better," she insisted; and when she had hurriedly pinned on her hat and tied her tulle ruff at her throat, she caught up her gloves and ran quickly down the stairs and out into the street. But as soon as she had reached the sidewalk, the agony, which she had thought she was leaving behind her in the closed room upstairs, rushed over her in a wave of realization, and, turning again, she started back into the yard, and stopped, with a sensation of panic, beside the bed of crimson dahlias at the foot of the steps. Then, while she hesitated, uncertain whether to return to her bedroom or to force herself to go on to the market, those hated familiar objects flashed in a blaze of light through her mind, and, opening the gate, she passed out on the sidewalk, and started at a rapid step down the deserted pavement of Sycamore Street. " At least nobody will speak to me," she thought; but while the words were still on her lips she saw a door in the block open wide, and one of her neighbours come out on his way to his business. Turning hastily, she fled into a cross street, and then, gathering courage, went on, trembling in every limb, towards the old market, which she used because her mother and her grandmother had used it before her.

The fish-carts were still there, just as they had been when she was a girl, but the army of black-robed housekeepers had changed or melted away. Here, also, the physical details of life had survived the beings for whose use or comfort they had come into existence. The meat and the vegetable stalls were standing in orderly rows about the octagonal building; wilted cabbage leaves littered the dusty floor; flies swarmed around the bleeding forms hanging from the hooks in the sunshine; even Mr. Dewlap, hale and red-cheeked, offered her white pullets out of the wooden coop at his feet. So little had the physical scene changed since the morning, more than twenty-five years ago, of her meeting with Oliver, that while she paused there beside Mr. Dewlap's stall, one of the older generation might have mistaken her for her mother.

"My dear Virginia," said a voice at her back, and, turning, she found Mrs. Peachey, a trifle rheumatic, but still plump and pretty. "I'm so glad you come to the old market, my child. I suppose you cling to it because of your mother, and then things are really so much dearer up-town, don't you think so?"

"Yes, I dare say they are. But I've got into the habit of coming here."

"One does get into habits. Now, I've bought chickens from Mr. Dewlap for forty years. I remember your mother and I used to say that there were no chickens to compare with his white pullets."

"I remember. Mother was a wonderful housekeeper."

"And you are too, my dear. Everybody says that you have the best table in Dinwiddie!" Her small rosy face, framed in the shirred brim of her black silk bonnet, was wrinkled with age, but even her wrinkles were cheerful ones, and detracted nothing from the charming archness of her expression. Unconquerable still, she went her sprightly way, on rheumatic limbs, towards the grave.

"Have you seen dear Miss Priscilla?" asked Virginia, striving to turn the conversation away from herself, and shivering with terror lest the other should ask after Oliver, whom she had always adored.

"I stopped to inquire about her on my way down. She had had a bad night, the maid said, and Doctor Fraser is afraid that the cold she got when she went driving the other day has settled upon her lungs."

"Oh, I am so sorry!" exclaimed Virginia, but she was conscious of an immeasurable relief because Miss Priscilla's illness was absorbing Mrs. Peachey's thoughts.

"Well, I must be going on," said the little lady, and though she flinched with pain when she moved, the habitual cheerfulness of her face did not alter. "Come to see me as often as you can, Jinny. I can't get about much now, and it is such a pleasure for me to have somebody to chat with. People don't visit now," she added regretfully, " as much as they used to."

"So many things have changed," said Virginia, and her eyes, as she gazed up at the blue sky over the market, had a yearning look in them. So many things had changed—ah, there was the pang!

On her way home, overcome by the fear that Miss Priscilla might die thinking herself neglected, Virginia stopped at the Academy, and was shown into the chamber behind the parlour, which had once been a classroom. In the middle of her big tester bed, the teacher was lying, propped among pillows, with her cameo brooch fastening the collar of her nightgown and a purple wool shawl, which Virginia had knit for her, thrown over her shoulders.

"Dear Miss Priscilla, I've thought of you so often. Are you better to-day?"

"A little, Jinny, but don't worry about me. I'll be out of bed in a day or two." Though she was well over eighty-five, she still thought of herself as a middle-aged woman, and her constant plans for the future amazed Virginia, whose hold upon life was so much slighter, so much less tenacious. "Have you been to market, dear? I miss so being able to sit by the window and watch people go by. Then I always knew when you and Susan were on your way to Mr. Dewlap."

"Yes, I've begun to go again. It fills in the day."

"I never approved of your letting your servants market for you, Jinny. It would have shocked your mother dreadfully."

"I know," said Virginia, and her voice, in spite of her effort to speak cheerfully, had a weary sound, which made her add with sudden energy: "I've brought you a partridge. Mr. Dewlap had such nice ones. You must try to eat it for supper."

"How like you that was, Jinny. You are your mother all over again. I declare I am reminded of her more and more every time that I see you."

Tears sprang to Virginia's eyes, while her thin, blue-veined hands gently caressed Miss Priscilla's swollen and knotted fingers.

" You couldn't tell me anything that would please me more," she answered.

" I used to think that Lucy would take after her, but she grew up differently."

" Yes, neither of the girls is like her. They are dear, good children, but they are very modern."

" Have you heard from them recently ?"

" A few days ago, and they are both as well as can be."

" And what about Harry ? I've always believed that Harry was your favourite, Jinny."

For an instant, Virginia hesitated, with her eyes on the pot of red geraniums blooming between the white muslin curtains at the window. In his little cage in the sunlight, Miss Priscilla's canary, the last of many generations of Dickys, burst suddenly into song.

" I believe that Harry loves me more than anybody else in the world does," she answered at last. " He'd come to me to-morrow if he thought I needed him."

Lying there in her great white bed, with her enormous body, which she could no longer turn, rising in a mountain of flesh under the linen sheet, the old teacher closed her eyes, lest Virginia should see her soul yearning over her as it had yearned over Lucy Pendleton after the rector's death. She thought of the girl, with the flower-like eyes and the braided wreath of hair, flitting in white organdie and blue ribbons, under the dappled sunlight in High Street, and she said to herself, as she had said twenty-five years ago : " If there was ever a girl who looked as if she were cut out for happiness, it was Jinny Pendleton."

" They say that Abby Goode is going to be married at last," remarked Virginia abruptly, for she knew that such bits of gossip supplied the only pleasant excitement in Miss Priscilla's life.

" Well, it's time. She waited long enough," returned the teacher, and she added : " I always knew that she was crazy about Oliver by the way she flung herself at his head." She had never liked Abby, and her prejudices, which had survived the shocks of life, were not weakened by the approaching presence of Death. It was characteristic of her that she should pass into eternity with both her love and her scorn undiminished.

"She was a little boisterous as a girl, but I never believed any harm of her," answered Virginia mildly; and then, as Miss Priscilla's lunch was brought in on a tray, she kissed her tenderly, with a curious feeling that it was for the last time, and went out of the door and down the gravelled walk into High Street. An exhaustion greater than any she had ever known oppressed her as she dragged her body, which felt dead, through the glorious October weather. Once, when she passed Saint James's Church, she thought wearily : "How sorry mother would be if she knew," while an intolerable pain, which seemed her mother's pain as well as her own, pierced her heart. Then, as she hurried on, with that nervous haste which she could no longer control, the terrible haunted blocks appeared to throng with the faded ghosts of her youth. A grey-haired woman leaning out of the upper window of an old house nodded to her with a smile, and she found herself thinking : "I rolled hoops with her once in the street, and now she is watching her grandchild go out in its carriage." At any other moment she would have bent, enraptured, over the perambulator, which was being wheeled, by a nurse and a maid, down the front steps into the street; but to-day the sight of the soft baby features, lovingly surrounded by lace and blue ribbons, was like the turn of a knife in her wound. "And yet mother always said that she was never so happy as she was with my children," she reflected, while her personal suffering was eased for a minute by the knowledge of what her return to Dinwiddie had meant to her mother. "If she had died while I lived away, I could never have got over it; I could never have forgiven myself," she added, and there was an exquisite relief in turning even for an instant away from the thought of herself.

When she reached home, luncheon was awaiting her; but after sitting down at the table and unfolding her napkin, a sudden nausea seized her, and she felt that it was impossible to sit there facing the mahogany sideboard, with its gleaming rows of silver, and watch the precise, slow-footed movements of the maid, who served her as she might have served a wooden image. "I took such trouble to train her, and now it makes me sick to look at her," she thought, as she pushed back her chair and fled hastily from the room into Oliver's study across the hall. Here her work-bag lay on the table,

and taking it up, she sat down before the fire, and spread out
the centrepiece, which she was embroidering, in an intricate
and elaborate design, for Lucy's Christmas. It was almost
a year now since she had started it, and into the luxuriant
sprays and garlands there had passed something of the restless love and yearning which had overflowed from her heart.
Usually she was able to work on it in spite of her suffering,
for she was one of those whose hands could accomplish
mechanically tasks from which her soul had revolted: but
to-day even her obedient fingers faltered and refused to keep
at their labour. Her eyes, leaving the needle she held,
wandered beyond the window to the branches of the young
maple-tree, which rose, like a pointed flame, toward the
cloudless blue of the sky.

In the evening, when Susan came in, with a newspaper in
her hand, and a passionate sympathy in her face, Virginia
was still sitting there, gazing at the dim outline of the tree
and the strip of sky which had faded from azure to grey.

" Oh, Jinny, my darling, you never told me ! "

Taking up the piece of embroidery from her lap, Virginia
met her friend's tearful caress with a frigid and distant
manner. "There was nothing to tell. What do you mean ?"
she asked.

" Is—is it true that Oliver has left you ? That—that——"
Susan's voice broke, strangled by emotion, but Virginia,
without looking up from the rose on which she was working
in the firelight, answered quietly:

" Yes, it is true. He wants to be free."

" But you will not do it, darling ? The law is on your
side."

With her eyes on the needle, which she held carefully poised
for the next stitch, Virginia hesitated, while the muscles of
her face quivered for an instant and then grew rigid again.

" What good would it do," she asked, " to hold him to
me when he wishes to be free ?" And then, with one of those
flashes of insight which came to her in moments of great
emotional stress, she added quietly: " It is not the law, it
is life."

Putting her arms around her, Susan pressed her to her
bosom, as she might have pressed a suffering child whom she
was powerless to help or even to make understand.

"Jinny, Jinny, let me love you!" she begged.

"How did you know?" asked Virginia, as coldly as though she had not heard her. "Has it got into the papers?"

For an instant Susan's pity struggled against her loyalty. "General Goode told me that there had been a good deal about Oliver and—and Miss Oldcastle in the New York papers for several days," she answered, "and this morning a few lines were copied in the Dinwiddie *Bee*. Oliver is so famous it was impossible to keep things hushed up, I suppose. But you knew all this, Jinny darling."

"Oh yes, I knew that," answered Virginia. Then, rising suddenly from her chair, she said almost irritably: "Susan, I want to be alone. I can't think until I am alone." By her look Susan knew that until that minute some blind hope had kept alive in her, some childish pretence that it might all be a dream, some passionate evasion of the ultimate outcome.

"But you'll let me come back? You'll let me spend the night with you, Jinny?"

"If you want to, you may come. But I don't need you. I don't need anybody. I don't need anybody," she repeated bitterly; and this bitterness appeared to change not only her expression, but her features and her carriage and that essential attribute of her being which had been the real Virginia.

Awed in spite of herself, Susan put on her hat again, and bent over to kiss her. "I'll be back before bedtime, Jinny. Don't shut me away, dear. Let me share your pain with you."

At this something that was like a smile trembled for an instant on Virginia's face.

"You are good, Susan," she responded; but there was no tenderness, no gratitude even, in her voice. She had grown hard with the implacable hardness of grief.

When the door had closed behind her friend, she stood looking through the window until she saw her pass slowly as though she were reluctant to go, down Sycamore Street in the direction of her home. "I am glad she has gone," she thought coldly. "Susan is good, but I am glad she has gone." Then, turning back to the fire, she took up the piece of embroidery and mechanically folded it before she laid it away. While her hands were still on the bag in which she

kept it, a shiver went through her body, and a look of resolution passed over her features, making them appear as if they
were sculptured in marble.

"He will be sorry some day," she thought. "He will be
sorry when it is too late, and if I were there now—if I were
to see him, it might all be prevented. It might all be prevented and we might be happy again." In her distorted mind,
which worked with the quickness and the intensity of delirium,
this idea assumed presently the prominence and the force
of an hallucination. So powerful did it become that it
triumphed over all the qualities which had once constituted
her character—over the patience, the sweetness, the unselfish
goodness—as easily as it obscured the rashness and folly of
the step which she planned. "If I could see him, it might
all be prevented," she repeated obstinately, as though some
one had opposed her; and, going upstairs to her bedroom,
she packed her little handbag and put on the travelling dress
which she had worn in New York. Then, very softly, as
though she feared to be stopped by the servants, she went
down the stairs and out of the front door; and, very softly,
carrying her bag, she passed into the street and walked
hurriedly in the direction of the station. And all the way
she was thinking : "If I can only see him again, this may not
happen and everything may be as it was before when he still
loved me." So just and rational did this idea appear to her,
that she found herself wondering passionately why she had
not thought of it before. It was so easy a way out of her
wretchedness that it seemed absurd of her to have overlooked
it. And this discovery filled her with such tremulous excitement, that when she opened her purse to buy her ticket, her
hands shook as if they were palsied, and the porter, who held
her bag, was obliged to count out the money. The whole
of life, which had looked so dark an hour ago, had become
suddenly illuminated.

Once in the train, her nervousness left her, and when an
acquaintance joined her after they had started, she was able
to talk connectedly of trivial occurrences in Dinwiddie. He
was a fat, apoplectic-looking man, with a bald head which
shone like satin, and a drooping moustache slightly discoloured
by tobacco. His appearance, which she had never objected
to before, seemed to her grotesque; but in spite of this, she

could smile almost naturally at his jokes, which she thought inconceivably stupid.

"I suppose you heard about Cyrus Treadwell's accident," he said at last when she rose to go to her berth. "Got knocked down by an automobile as he was getting off a street car at the Bank. It isn't serious, they say, but he was pretty well stunned for a while."

"No, I hadn't heard," she answered, and thought: "I wonder why Susan didn't tell me." Then she said good-night and disappeared behind the curtains of her berth, where she lay, without undressing, until morning.

"This is the way; there is no other way to stop it," she thought, and all night the rumble of the train and the flashing of the lights in the darkness outside of her window kept up a running accompaniment to the words. "It is a sin—and there is no other way to stop it. He is committing a sin, and when I see him he will understand it, and it will be as it was before." This idea, which was as fixed as an obsession of delirium, seemed to occupy some central space in her brain, leaving room for a crowd of lesser thoughts which came and went fantastically around it like the motley throng of a circus. She thought of Cyrus Treadwell's accident, of the stupid jokes the man from Dinwiddie had told her, of the noises of the train, which would not let one sleep, of the stations which blazed out, here and there, in the darkness. But in the midst of this confusion of images and impressions, a clear voice was repeating somewhere in her brain: "This is the way; there is no other way to stop it before it is too late."

In the morning, when she arrived in New York, and gave the driver the name of the little hotel at which she had stopped on her first visit, this glowing certainty faded like the excitement of fever from her mind, and she relapsed into the stricken hopelessness of the last six months. The bleakness of her spirits fell like a cloud on the brilliant October day, and the sunshine, which lay in golden pools on the pavements, appeared to increase the sense of universal melancholy which had followed so sharply on the brief exaltation of the night. "I must see him; it is the only way," her brain still repeated, but the ring of conviction was gone from the words. Her flight from Dinwiddie showed to her now in all the desperate folly with which it might have appeared to a stranger. The

impulse which had brought her had ebbed away, and with the
impulse had passed also the confidence and the energy of
her resolve.

At the hotel, where the red bedroom into which they
ushered her appeared to have waited unaltered for the second
tragedy of her life, she bathed and dressed herself, and after
a cup of black coffee, taken because a sensation of dizziness
had alarmed her lest she should faint in the street, she put
on her hat again and went out into Fifth Avenue. She remembered the name of the hotel at the head of Oliver's letter,
and she directed her steps towards it now with an automatic
precision of which her mind seemed almost unconscious. All
thought of asking for him had vanished, yet she was drawn
to the place where he was by a force which was more irresistible than any choice of the will. An instinct stronger
than reason was guiding her steps.

In Fifth Avenue the crowd was already beginning to
stream by on the sidewalks, and as she mingled with it, she recalled that other morning when she had moved among these
people and had felt that they looked at her kindly because
she was beautiful and young. Now the kindness had given
way to indifference in their eyes. They no longer looked at
her; and when a shop window, which she was passing, showed
her a reflection of herself, she saw only a commonplace
middle-aged figure, with a look of withered sweetness in the
face, which had grown suddenly wan. And the sight of this
figure fell like a weight on her heart, destroying the last vestige
of courage.

Before the door of the hotel in which Oliver was staying,
she stood so long, with her vacant gaze fixed on the green
velvet carpet within the hall, that an attendant in livery came
up at last and inquired if she wished to see anyone. Arousing herself with a start, she shook her head hurriedly and
turned back into the street; for when the crucial moment
came her decision failed her. Just as she had been unable
to make a scene on the night when they had parted, so now
it was impossible for her to descend to the vulgarity of thrusting her presence into his life. Unless the frenzy of delirium
seized her again, she knew that she should never have the
strength to put the desperation of thought into the desperation of action. What she longed for was not to fight, not to

struggle, but to fall, like a wounded bird, to the earth, and be forgotten.

At the crossing, where there was a crush of motor-cars and carriages, she stopped for a moment and thought how easy it would be to die in the crowded street before returning to Dinwiddie. " All I need do is to slip and fall there, and in a second it would be over." But so many cars went by that she knew she should never be able to do it, that much as she hated life, something bound her to it which she lacked the courage to break. There shot through her mind the memory of a soldier her father used to tell about, who was always first on the field of battle, but had never found the courage to charge. " He was like me; for I might stand here for ever and yet not find the courage to die."

A beggar came up to her and she thought : " He is begging of me, and yet I am more miserable than he is." Then, while she searched in her bag for some change, it seemed to her that the faces gliding past her became suddenly distorted and twisted as though the souls of the women in the rapidly moving cars were crucified under their splendid furs. " That woman in the sable cloak is beautiful, and yet she, also, is in torture," she reflected with an impersonal coldness and detachment. " I was beautiful, too, but how did it help me ?" And she saw herself as she had been in her girlhood with the glow of happiness, as of one flying, in her face, and her heart filled with the joyous expectancy of the miracle which must happen. " I am as old now as Miss Willy was then—and how I pitied her !" Tears rushed to her eyes, which had been so dry a minute before, while the memory of that lost gaiety of youth came over her in a wave that was like the sweetness of the honeysuckle blooming in the rectory garden.

A policeman, observing that she had waited there so long, held up the traffic until she had crossed the street, and after thanking him, she went on again towards the hotel in which she was staying. " He was kind about helping me over," she said to herself with an impulse of gratitude; and this casual kindness seemed to her the one spot of light in the blackness which surrounded her.

As she approached the hotel, her step flagged, and she felt suddenly that even that passive courage which was hers— the courage of endurance—had deserted her. She saw the

dreadful hours that must ensue before she went back to
Dinwiddie, the dreadful days that would follow after she got
there, the dreadful weeks that would run on into the dreadful
years.   Silent, grey, and endless, they stretched ahead of
her, and through them all she saw herself, a little hopeless
figure, moving towards that death which she had not had the
courage to die.   The thoughts of the familiar streets, of the
familiar faces, of the house, of the furniture, of the leaf-
strewn yard in which her bed of dahlias was blooming—all
these aroused in her the sense of spiritual nausea which she
had felt when she went back to them after her parting from
Oliver.   Nothing remained except the long empty years, for
she had outlived her usefulness.

At the door of the hotel the hall porter met her with a
cheerful face, and she turned to him with the instinctive
reliance on masculine protection which had driven her to the
friendly shelter of the policeman at the crossing in Fifth
Avenue.   In reply to her helpless questions, he looked up
the next train to Dinwiddie, which left within the hour, and
after buying her ticket, assisted her smilingly into the taxi-cab.
While she sat there, in the middle of the seat, with her little
black bag rocking back and forth as the cab turned the
corners, all capacity for feeling, all possibility of sensation
even, seemed to have passed out of her body.   The impulse
which was carrying her to Dinwiddie was the physical impulse which drives a wounded animal back to die in its shelter.
Even the flaring advertisements of Oliver's play, which was
still running in a Broadway theatre, aroused no pain, hardly
any thought of him or of the past, in her mind.   She had
ceased to suffer, she had ceased even to think; and when, a
little later, she followed the station porter down the long platform, she was able to brush aside the memory of her parting
from Oliver as lightly as though it were the trivial sting of a
wasp.   When she remembered the agony of the last year,
of yesterday, of the morning through which she had just
lived, it appeared almost ridiculous.   That death which she
had lacked the courage to die seemed creeping over her soul
before it reached the outer shell of her body.

In the train she was attacked by a sensation of faintness,
and remembering that she had eaten nothing all day, she
went into the dining-car and sat down at one of the little

tables. When her luncheon was brought, she ate almost ravenously for a minute. Then her sudden hunger was followed by a disgust for the look of the dishes and the cinders on the tablecloth, and after paying her bill, for which she waited an intolerable time, she went back to her chair in the next coach, and watched, with unseeing eyes, the swiftly moving landscape, which rushed by in all the brilliant pageantry of October. Several seats ahead of her, two men were discussing politics, and one of them, who wore a clerical waistcoat, raised his voice suddenly so high that his words penetrated the wall of blankness which surrounded her thoughts : " I tell you it is the greatest menace to our civilization !" and then, as he controlled his excitement, his speech dropped quickly into indistinctness.

" How absurd of him to get so angry about it," thought Virginia with surprise, " as if a civilization could make any difference to anybody on earth." And she wtached the clergyman for a minute, as if fascinated by the display of his earnestness. " What on earth can it matter to him ?" she wondered mildly, " and yet to look at him one would think that his heart was bound up in the question." But in a little while she turned away from him again, and lying back in her chair, stared across the smooth plains to the pale golden edge of the distant horizon. Through the long day she sat, without moving, without taking her eyes from the landscape, while the sunlight faded slowly away from the fields and the afterglow flushed and waned, and the stars shone out, one by one, through the silver web of the twilight. Once, when the porter had offered her a pillow, she had looked round to thank him; once when a child, toddling along the aisle, had fallen at her feet, she had bent over to lift it, but beyond this, she had stirred only to hand her ticket to the conductor when he aroused her by touching her arm. Where the sunset and the afterglow had been, she saw at last only the lights of the train reflected in the smeared glass of the window, but so unconscious was she of any change in that utter vacancy at which she looked, that she could not have told whether it was an hour or a day after leaving New York that she came back to Dinwiddie. Even then she would still have sat there, speechless, inert, unseeing, had not the porter taken her bag from the rack over her head and accompanied her from

the glare of the train out into the dimness of the town, where
the crumbling "hacks" hitched to the decrepit horses still
waited. Here her bag was passed over to a driver, whom
she vaguely remembered, and a few minutes later she rolled,
in one of the ancient vehicles, under the pale lights of the
street which led to her home. In the drug store at the
corner she saw Miss Priscilla's maid buying medicines, and
she wondered indifferently if the teacher had grown suddenly
worse. Then, as she passed John Henry's house, she recognized his large shadow as it moved across the white shade at
the window of the drawing-room. "Susan was coming to
spend last night with me," she said aloud, and for the first
and last time in her life, an ironic smile quivered upon her lips.

With a last jolt the carriage drew up at the sidewalk
before her home; the driver dismounted, grinning, from his
box; and in the lighted doorway, she saw the figure of her
maid, in trim cap and apron, waiting to welcome her. Not
a petal had fallen from the bed of crimson dahlias beside the
steps; not a leaf had changed on the young maple-tree, which
rose in a spire of flame toward the stars. Inside, she knew,
there would be the bright fire, the cheerful supper table, the
soft bed turned down—and the future.

On the porch she stopped and looked back into the street
as she might have looked back at the door of a prison. The
negro driver, having placed her bag in the hall, stood waiting
expectantly, with his hat in his hand, and his shining black
eyes on her face; and opening her purse, she paid him, before
walking past the maid over the threshold. Ahead of her
stretched the staircase which she would go up and down for
the rest of her life. On the right she could look into the
open door of the dining-room, and opposite to it, she knew
that the lamp was lit and the fire burning in Oliver's study.
Then, while a wave of despair, like a mortal sickness, swept
over her, her eyes fell on an envelope which lay on the little
silver card-tray on the hall table, and as she tore it open,
she saw that it contained but a single line:

"Dearest Mother, I am coming home to you,
　　　　　　　　　　　　　　"HARRY."

FOR THE BEST IN CLASSICS, LOOK FOR THE

☐ **WUTHERING HEIGHTS**

Emily Brontë

An intensely original work, this story of the passionate love between Cathy and Heathcliff is recorded with such truth, imagination, and emotional intensity that it acquires the depth and simplicity of ancient tragedy.

372 pages ISBN: 0-14-043001-6 **$2.95**

☐ **UTOPIA**

Thomas More

Utopia revolutionized Plato's classical blueprint of the perfect republic, and can be seen as the source of Anabaptism, Mormonism, and even Communism. Witty, immediate, vital, prescient, it is the work of a man who drank deep of the finest spirit of his age.

154 pages ISBN: 0-14-044165-4 **$2.95**

☐ **THE SCARLET LETTER**

Nathaniel Hawthorne

Publicly disgraced and ostracized by the harsh Puritan community of seventeenth-century Boston, Hester Prynne draws on her inner strength to emerge as the first true heroine of American fiction.

284 pages ISBN: 0-14-039019-7 **$2.25**

☐ **WINESBURG, OHIO**

Sherwood Anderson

Introduced as "The Tales and the Persons," this timeless cycle of short stories lays bare the lives of the friendly but solitary people of small town America at the turn of the century.

248 pages ISBN: 0-14-039059-6 **$4.95**

☐ **CANDIDE**

Voltaire

One of the glories of eighteenth-century satire, *Candide* was the most brilliant challenge to the prevailing thought that held "all is for the best in the best of all possible worlds."

144 pages ISBN: 0-14-044004-6 **$2.25**

☐ **PRIDE AND PREJUDICE**

Jane Austen

While Napoleon transformed Europe, Jane Austen wrote a novel in which a man changes his manners and a young lady her mind. In Austen's world of delicious social comedy, the truly civilized being maintains a proper balance between reason and energy.

400 pages ISBN: 0-14-043072-5 **$2.25**

FOR THE BEST IN CLASSICS, LOOK FOR THE

FOR THE BEST IN CLASSICS, LOOK FOR THE

☐ THE OCTOPUS

Frank Norris

Based on an actual bloody dispute between wheat farmers and the Southern Pacific Railroad, *The Octopus* is a stunning novel of the waning days of the frontier West, extraordinarily abundant in characters and details and magnificent in sweep and scale.

656 pages   *ISBN: 0-14-039040-5*   **$5.95**

☐ BILLY BUDD, SAILOR AND OTHER STORIES

Herman Melville

The centerpiece of these compelling and mysteriously powerful tales is a classic confrontation between good and evil, the story of the innocent young Budd unable to defend himself against a wrongful accusation.

386 pages   *ISBN: 0-14-039053-7*   **$3.95**

☐ ETHAN FROME

Edith Wharton

Working his unproductive farm in austere New England and struggling to maintain a bearable existence with his suspicious and hypochondriac wife, Ethan Frome is an enduring figure of despair and forbidden emotion.

202 pages   *ISBN: 0-14-039058-8*   **$3.95**

☐ THE LAST OF THE MOHICANS

James Fenimore Cooper

Angered by his materialistic society, Hawkeye (Natty Bumppo) shares the solitude and sublimity of the wilderness with his Indian friend Chingachgook. This portrait of fierce individualism and courage is an integral part of the American frontier mythos.

352 pages   *ISBN: 0-14-039024-3*   **$4.95**

You can find all these books at your local bookstore, or use this handy coupon for ordering:

Penguin Books By Mail
Dept. BA Box 999
Bergenfield, NJ 07621-0999

Please send me the above title(s). I am enclosing _____
(please add sales tax if appropriate and $1.50 to cover postage and handling). Send check or money order—no CODs. Please allow four weeks for shipping. We cannot ship to post office boxes or addresses outside the USA. *Prices subject to change without notice.*

Ms./Mrs./Mr. _____

Address _____

City/State _____ Zip _____

Sales tax: CA: 6.5%   NY: 8.25%   NJ: 6%   PA: 6%   TN: 5.5%

FOR THE BEST IN PAPERBACKS, LOOK FOR THE

In every corner of the world, on every subject under the sun, Penguin represents quality and variety—the very best in publishing today.

For complete information about books available from Penguin—including Pelicans, Puffins, Peregrines, and Penguin Classics—and how to order them, write to us at the appropriate address below. Please note that for copyright reasons the selection of books varies from country to country.

In the United Kingdom: For a complete list of books available from Penguin in the U.K., please write to *Dept E.P., Penguin Books Ltd, Harmondsworth, Middlesex, UB7 0DA.*

In the United States: For a complete list of books available from Penguin in the U.S., please write to *Dept BA, Penguin, Box 120, Bergenfield, New Jersey 07621-0120.*

In Canada: For a complete list of books available from Penguin in Canada, please write to *Penguin Books Ltd, 2801 John Street, Markham, Ontario L3R 1B4.*

In Australia: For a complete list of books available from Penguin in Australia, please write to the *Marketing Department, Penguin Books Ltd, P.O. Box 257, Ringwood, Victoria 3134.*

In New Zealand: For a complete list of books available from Penguin in New Zealand, please write to the *Marketing Department, Penguin Books (NZ) Ltd, Private Bag, Takapuna, Auckland 9.*

In India: For a complete list of books available from Penguin, please write to *Penguin Overseas Ltd, 706 Eros Apartments, 56 Nehru Place, New Delhi, 110019.*

In Holland: For a complete list of books available from Penguin in Holland, please write to *Penguin Books Nederland B.V., Postbus 195, NL-1380AD Weesp, Netherlands.*

In Germany: For a complete list of books available from Penguin, please write to *Penguin Books Ltd, Friedrichstrasse 10-12, D-6000 Frankfurt Main I, Federal Republic of Germany.*

In Spain: For a complete list of books available from Penguin in Spain, please write to *Longman, Penguin España, Calle San Nicolas 15, E-28013 Madrid, Spain.*

In Japan: For a complete list of books available from Penguin in Japan, please write to *Longman Penguin Japan Co Ltd, Yamaguchi Building, 2-12-9 Kanda Jimbocho, Chiyoda-Ku, Tokyo 101, Japan.*